"*DANCE*! DUST COMING YOUR WAY!"

Pov hit his comm-link. "Helm! Change course."

"I see it," Athena responded. "Forty degrees starboard, people, on the mark, do it *now*. Get *Dance* out of our draft. All skyriders under our lee."

Net swung quickly, turning outward toward open space. As *Net* turned, Pov trimmed the sails to a protective mode, then spun the sky-sail far to port to shield the aftward core as *Net* escaped the dust storm in its path.

"Advise *Dance* we have minimal damage," Captain Andreos ordered as soon as they were clear. "That was close. Any acknowledgment from *Dance,* Comm?"

"Not yet. Helm reports *Dance* is not behind us, sir. We do not have a fix on her in this soup." Moments later, Comm called out, "Sir!" Contact with *Dance*. They are reporting . . ." Comm turned, her eyes wide. "Major hull damage, Captain. Both skysails have collapsed. . . ."

If you and/or a friend would like to receive the *ROC Advance*, a bimonthly newsletter featuring all the newest and hottest ROC books and authors, on a complimentary basis, please fill out this form and return it to:

ROC Books/Penguin USA
375 Hudson Street
New York, NY 10014

Your Address
Name _____
Street _____ Apt. # _____
City _____ State _____ Zip _____

Friend's Address
Name _____
Street _____ Apt. # _____
City _____ State _____ Zip _____

THE CLOUDSHIPS OF ORION

Siduri's Net

▼

P. K. McAllister

A ROC BOOK

To Richard

ROC
Published by the Penguin Group
Penguin Books USA Inc., 375 Hudson Street,
New York, New York 10014, U.S.A.
Penguin Books Ltd, 27 Wrights Lane,
London W8 5TZ, England
Penguin Books Australia Ltd, Ringwood,
Victoria, Australia
Penguin Books Canada Ltd, 10 Alcorn Avenue,
Toronto, Ontario, Canada M4V 3B2
Penguin Books (N.Z.) Ltd, 182–190 Wairau Road,
Auckland 10, New Zealand

Penguin Books Ltd, Registered Offices:
Harmondsworth, Middlesex, England

First published by Roc,
an imprint of Dutton Signet,
a division of Penguin Books USA Inc.

First Printing, November, 1994
10 9 8 7 6 5 4 3 2 1

 REGISTERED TRADEMARK—MARCA REGISTRADA

Printed in the United States of America

ACKNOWLEDGMENTS

My thanks to my agent, Richard Curtis, for his timely ideas; to Tom for all his help with this book; and especially to my editor, Amy Stout, for her support and encouragement.

Chapter 1

In the old days on Earth, he had read, a sailing ship gave a man the rolling of a wooden deck, the splash of seawater tossed high into the wind, and the joy of a trim and lovely ship plunging deep into each wave and rising as swiftly toward the sky. Sleek dolphins would leap ecstatically in front of the prow, racing the ship in their play, plunging smoothly into the cool salty water, rising swiftly, as madly possessed with the rush of the air and the ship's speed as the humans who drove her.

On Earth his people had never been sailors, preferring the solidity of earth and the open road, the bright color of their wagons, the next turning of the highway, and the bonds of family. But gypsies had always been travelers, and when humankind left Earth for other worlds, a few gypsies traveled with them on the new roads among the stars. Pov Janusz had never sailed Earth's oceans, but he often thought of those earlier ships when he went outboard to inspect *Net*'s sails.

High above Epsilon Tauri's star-system, *Siduri's Net* and her senior cloudship, *Siduri's Dance*, sailed against the luminescent clouds of a comet's tail, their magnetic sails spread wide to gather a rich harvest. For six weeks *Net* and *Dance* had sailed the comet's tail, pacing the comet's blazing descent toward the local sun. With each new course into the tail, they had filled their holds, returned briefly to open space to sort their catch of power isotopes, then plunged again into the glowing tail. Two more courses, another several days, and, their holds filled with rare product, the two cloudships would turn out-system toward Tania's Ring, the Tauri world which held their contract for tritium fuel and unusual ices, atomic treasures that fueled Tania's newborn colony economy.

I should come out here more often, Pov thought wistfully, as he always did when he had the chance to watch *Net* from outboard. In design, his cloudship vaguely resembled the older wind-driven ships, but suggested other analogues in the large triangular prow that housed the control decks, the wide wings of the forward hull that powered the collecting sails, and the jumble of spheres and suspended bridges aft where *Net*'s crew of three hundred lived, worked, and played.

Sometimes Pov saw in *Net* a fierce bird of prey, her wings stretched wide in flight, her head lifted proudly. Other times he saw the young sea goddess after whom *Net* was named, sporting playfully in the sea by her enchanted island, or he saw an alien beast, wise and strong and lovely, sedately feeding through a rich pasture. *Net* was many things to him—even after three years as her sailmaster and most of his life aboard the Tauri cloudships, he never tired of looking at her.

Three hours into this latest course, *Net* had developed a sail fault neither he nor his Second Sail, Tully Haralpos, could track to its origin, and so he had come outship in his sister Kate's skyrider to data-track the collecting sails, not a smart personal move in plasma but necessary despite the risk. If the sails faltered, the dust in the comet gas could punch holes through *Net*'s unprotected hull, a lethal rain of micrometeorites that could kill a ship. Dust was one of the larger risks of sailing plasma, one of the reasons a sail fault had to be tracked down before it phased into an irretrievable disaster. So far he and Kate had tracked the starboard spinnaker, finding nothing in particular, and now were working their way up the topside skysail that projected far above *Net*'s prow, a tedious comparison of magnetic-field realities to the sail computer's ideas of perfection.

He glanced at his sister in her pilot's chair, where she watched her control board intently, determined to pilot a perfect sweep along the rearward curve of the sails. Kate never did a thing by halves, and had taken to driving her skyrider, one of the tiny guide ships that preceded the lead cloudship on every comet run, with all the intensity that had made a baby sister the chief plague of Pov's adolescence.

At nineteen, Ekaterina Janusz was small-boned and slender, with the dusky female beauty of dark eyes and wiry black hair common to their gypsy heritage. In another time on an older world, Kate might have danced the flamenco, jingling her bracelets high and stamping her feet while the nongypsy outsiders, the *gaje*, tossed coins in her guitarist's case. Here Kate wore a close-fitting ship suit worth wolf whistles and flew her skyrider with skilled abandon, brashly skirting the pilotmaster's safety rules and indulged for her brashness.

As Kate turned the skyrider to begin another sweep, a side screen beeped for attention. She glanced at it and clicked her tongue.

"What is it?" he asked.

"*Dance* is signaling a twenty-degree shift to port," Kate said, giving him a dark look.

"*Again?*"

"I told you they would. What the hell is this, anyway?"

As lead ship on this comet run, *Dance* had a responsibility to *Net* in its wake, one she was choosing to ignore on this last course. Sudden changes of course distorted the smooth bow wave of the lead ship's passage through the flowing gas, a disturbance that impacted directly on the ship following her. As *Dance* began to turn, fitfully visible in the roiling gas ahead, Pov could see the whorls of gas behind her tighten into dangerous eddies for *Net*'s unstable sails. He swore softly.

Net changed course to match *Dance*'s new tack, meeting the disturbed plasma as squarely as she could. As the starboard sail swung with the turn, Kate touched her controls and took the skyrider down and portside, allowing the starboard sail to swing unimpeded over their heads. On his sail monitors, Pov saw *Net*'s sails begin to react as the roiled gas spilled into them, maybe multiplying the sail fault to God knew where and complicating the multiple stresses on the sail points, an instability *Net* could not afford. The radio link from *Net*'s Sail Deck pinged for his attention.

"Sorry, sir," said Avi Selenko, the sail comm watch. "I told them you were still inspecting the sails." Her irritation showed in slipped consonants more Russki than ship-Czech; Avi's Czech always suffered when she got mad.

"They said no more turns for four hours," Pov objected.

"To them, I'll guess, that's now a former reality. Sorry, sir. Please let us know when you restart tracking."

"Acknowledged, *Net*. Thank you." The comm clicked off.

Pov scowled at his monitors, not liking what he saw as *Net* turned more sharply against the gas flow, following *Dance*'s tack lead. The port spinnaker sagged badly in response to the sharper turn, twisting the inflowing gas along the inner edges of the opposite sails. The sails'll ruff soon, he thought. A moment later the stressed port sail ruffed, bouncing an irregular field wave across the entire cone of the sails. The ruff rebounded off the bottom edge of the opposite spinnaker, then slowly ricocheted back across the sails. Like interlaced water ripples on a pool, the ruff worked itself out across the sails' standing field wave. Then the sails shivered violently as the port sail unexpectedly ruffed again.

Pov swore quietly and pulled a sail-integrity display onto his own screen, then called Tully on Sail Deck.

"Tully, keep an eye out," he warned. "I haven't found the fault, but I think we're getting a good idea where it is." Even under the stress of a course change, a port sail should not ruff this badly.

"Somewhere on the port spinnaker," Tully agreed. "I'm trying to find the point source on the edge."

Then the port spinnaker ruffed a third time, adding to the complicated wave pattern now dancing its confusion across *Net*'s disturbed sails. A few moments later, a fourth ruff added its lacery as *Net* continued her turn to port. Pov scowled fiercely, his heartbeat accelerating, as *Net*'s sails nearly faltered, then slowly steadied again—not enough, but some. In their weakened state, *Net*'s sails could not tolerate this stress for long.

"Tully . . ."

"Athena's trying to keep our turn as slow as she can," Tully answered tensely, "but *Dance* is still turning too fast. . . ." Then Tully swore abruptly as a sliding gap appeared in the port spinnaker, ripping downward from the edge. "Blast! There's the fault. Helm! Portsail's ripping. Back and down!"

"On the green, Sail," Athena Mikelos replied calmly on Tully's channel. "Kate, we are turning back and down."

"I see you," Kate called. As *Net* turned sharply starboard, Kate soared the skyrider inward and dodged behind the safety of the ship's prow, then drifted downward behind the bottomsail. Over the open channel to Sail Deck, Pov heard Tully give rapid instructions to a repair crew about the port generator, then report briefly to Shipmaster Andreos, *Net*'s senior captain.

"Turning now," Athena said. "Report to me, Pov."

"Stress building on the starboard sails, not badly," Pov said, though the compensating forces of the counterturn had helped slow the portsail rip. "Port rip stabilizing." The gap mended itself up a hundred meters, then slowly crept down again. "Keep it easy."

"That's on."

Net continued her turn downward, seeking smoother plasma and a better safety from *Dance*'s wake. As a random eddy spun hard into the sails, the two starboard sails shuddered badly but held their integrity into the counterturn, slowing the acceleration of the echo pattern that still shook the sails. As Pov watched, the sail rip inched agonizingly down, abruptly zippered up again, then ripped as abruptly downward, opening a wide gap. Pov winced, guessing how much radiation had just squirted through *Net*'s port hull.

"Slow the turn a little, Athena," he suggested.

"Acknowledged."

Now the starboard spinnaker ruffed as the pressures counterstressed the sail, sending ripples across the sails that forced the portside rip upward again, a small benefit of a ruff he could do without. One ruff, yes, maybe even two at a pinch, but not from both sides. He watched the starboard ruff ripple itself into a new set of echoes, bouncing back and forth across the sails and complicating itself with each new pass. The portsail rip bounced up and down like mercury in a tube.

"Christ," he muttered helplessly.

"Completing down and starboard," Athena said at last.

Athena slowed *Net*'s descent as *Net* reached smoother plasma below *Dance*'s wake and turned the ship to face the gas stream hull-on. The sails steadied in the smoother gas flow, its stresses evening out on all her sail points. Pov sighed feelingly as the portsail slowly reformed itself on his monitor, mending itself upward clear to the outer edge. He heard Tully's slow hiss of relief echo his own.

"Yay," Tully muttered. "Good guys win again."

"That's a deal," Pov agreed.

He took a deep breath, then another, trying to counter the adrenaline still surging into his body from the narrowly averted threat to the ship. They had saved the sail, and likely *Net* had taken only minor damage. Even so, Medical would likely be treating some mild radiation sickness over the next few days, a totally unnecessary injury to *Net.*

"Hell," Pov said aloud.

"Damnation' is a better word," Kate said, "especially when yelled at helpless machinery. Mild, to the point, but inoffensive—not even the machine cares."

"Be quiet, you. Take us out a few kilometers and wait until the sails have settled into the new course. Then we'll restart the grid."

Kate tossed her head, though she complained. "Didn't I say that *Dance* couldn't care less about our sails? Didn't I say this wasn't a great time because *Dance* was bound to turn if the particle count dropped, no matter what Sailmaster Ceverny told you? Didn't I say—"

Pov crossed his arms and glared at her. "Yeah, you said all those things. How do you know so much about what *Dance* thinks?"

"Skyriders rise above petty ship loyalties," she informed him loftily, waving her hand. "We tell them things, they tell us things." She turned and gave him a wide crafty smile. In her dotage, Pov thought, Kate would be a formidable old crone, with a gypsy's gift of calculated malice and guile from a lifetime of practice and their mother teaching her every nuance along the way. He eyed Kate warily.

"Andreos will just love to hear that," he grunted. *Net*'s shipmaster generally tolerated the varied antics of *Net*'s young crewpeople, but drew the line at indiscriminate babbling to *Dance.*

"So who's going to tell him? My own brother? Besides, what do skyriders know that's really important? In the economic sense, that is." She keyed the ship

on automatic and swung her chair to face him.
"You're the sailmaster—you go to captain meetings
and learn all the secret stuff. Skyriders just pilot. Our
version of copper tinker and mandolin, right?"

"Bitter, Kate?" he asked, surprised. "I thought you
loved skyriding."

"Of course I love it." Her dark eyes flashed with
irritation. At him? he wondered, a little startled by
her reaction. "I don't want anything else, ever," she
said. "But who do they think they are?" She waved her
hand toward *Dance.* "Wrecking your inspection, as if
you were—"

"Junior sailmaster on junior ship." He shrugged, realizing belatedly that Kate hadn't understood the
near-disaster of the ripped sail—or, more likely, chose
to ignore it. To her it was only another gaje insult,
another irritation on a long list. Kate lived a simpler
life. "Well, that's what I am," he said.

"Oh, yeah? Just watch me stomp over to *Dance* and
jerk a few hairs out of Captain Rybak's beard." She
turned back to her controls and jabbed angrily at
some buttons.

"You would," he said admiringly.

"Just don't dare me, Pov. You know I can't resist
dares." He chuckled as a flush of dark crimson spread
up her slender neck: a few of the dares he had offered
Kate had led his impetuous sister into unexpected em-
barrassments. "Well, I can't, so at least you can respect my weaknesses."

"For a minute there," he said lightly, "I thought
you were mad at me." She turned her head to smile
at him, all the crafty girl-crone disappeared into whatever hold space Kate could put her at will. It was a
wide and loving smile she didn't let him see too often.

"You're such a stupid idiot, Pov."

"Thanks so much."

"Anytime. Just ask me."

Net gracefully steadied on the new course well
below *Dance*'s trajectory, and Kate swept out to the

interior edge of *Net*'s starboard mainsail, waiting for the plasma to restabilize its flow into *Net*'s sails. Pov scowled fiercely at the particle-flow monitor, not liking the complicated swirls and phase changes he saw still impacting his sails. Kate glanced at him.

"Not yet," he said, shaking his head.

The stress release of the torn sail had probably spared the other sail generators from developing faults, but he'd check all the sails, anyway. The port-sail fault now read clearly on his tracking monitor, then abruptly blurred and disappeared as Tully's repair crew switched generators and pulled the defect out of the line. With the fault gone, the sails steadied further as the last of the tiny ripples dissolved on the edges, undisturbed by any new disruptions. He waited a few more moments, then nodded to Kate. Kate turned upward toward the top of the skysail.

"Try the bottom skysail first," he said.

"The faults could have shifted anywhere, Pov."

"So it's intuition."

"Sailmasters don't need intuition," Kate said decisively. "They have *facts*. At least that's what you always tell me."

"So *fact* down to the bottom skysail, please."

"You're the pilot-driver. *Net*, we're restarting our grid."

"Acknowledged," Avi replied from Sail Deck.

Kate reversed in an end-over-end turn and guided their tiny ship gracefully around the ship core and behind the starboard wing, then soared downward to trace a patient grid back and forth along the bottom skysail. Pov frowned at the monitor, waiting for the irregularity that he hoped wasn't there—somewhere—but it happily eluded him.

He adjusted the sweep to finer detail and examined the force lines of the skysail, a tall looping curve projected nearly a thousand meters below the hull. The ship's consoles on Sail Deck constantly monitored the sails during flight, of course, but *Net*'s metal bulk and own movement through plasma generated energy fields that interfered with certain finer measurements. The differences were subtle, but a sailmaster's problems began in subtleties, as cloudships discovered when tiny errors phased all too quickly into disaster. As they almost had, he reminded himself pointedly.

He waited, tapping his fingers on his chair, *willing* a fault into view with mind power. After a few minutes of null result, he leaned forward in his chair to look more closely at the particle-detector screen on Kate's board. "Hmmph. What was *Dance* chasing?"

Kate shrugged and threw him an expressive glance. "Our forward probe's been reading nine ions per cubic for over an hour. This is an okay density, Pov. So why the jigging by *Dance*?"

He shrugged back. "What *Dance* wants, *Dance* gets."

"That could change real fast," Kate said ominously.

"Not for a few years. We've still got our construction loan to pay off."

Kate shrugged. "This application dates back to the first cloudships. Where's the progress?"

She waved negligently at the glowing river of comet gas that streamed past *Net* on every side. On an atmosphered planet, such an ionized storm would shudder with thunder, crackle with lightning, and howl with the high whistling rush of accelerated gases. It was easy to forget, within the safety of *Net*'s metal hull and the distractions of work and *Net*'s small community of people, what truly raged outside the ship's slender defenses. Pov looked at her, bemused.

"Want to go to the Pleiades, Kate?" he asked.

"Name the date, sailmaster," she said firmly. "I'll start packing." She turned and grinned at him.

Twenty years before, *Diana's Arrow*, the first cloudship of many and richly successful ever since, had led her two daughter ships and several other Tauri cloudships to the Pleiades. In the vast drifting Pleiades gas clouds, the lingering remnants of the star nursery that had formed four hundred suns, a cloudship could truly sail a molecular ocean. "I've heard they're beautiful," Kate said softly, and they exchanged a glance. Then she arched an eyebrow. "And I'd just love to be rich."

He snorted. "Kate, you'll never have a soul. Where's your romantic vision?"

"I save my romance for Sergei," she said complacently, "as often and energetically as possible. The vision I'll leave to you."

"Hmph."

They completed the first pass down the skysail, and Kate turned them neatly around to track upward toward the ship, the skyrider monitors scanning the sail forcegrid line by line.

"Dina been around lately?" Kate asked.

"Dina isn't going to be around. She's made that quite clear." It was not a topic he welcomed, but Kate rarely bothered with subtlety.

"After weeks of following you around with glazed eyes, professing all that love and devotion? After balking at the last hour on making it official? Where's the loyalty after all that leading on?"

"Skip it, Kate," he said irritably.

Pov and Dina Kozel had fallen in love during last year's comet run, a dazzling and intense relationship that he lost abruptly after the cloudships redocked at Tania's Ring and Dina visited her Slav relatives on *Dance*. Dina had never really said why, choosing her own way to trash their relationship, but he could guess the likely reason. The anti-bigotry clause written into *Dance*'s maiden contract by a half-crew of wary Greeks had given the Janusz and *Dance*'s three Jewish families a technical protection against an ancient Slav prejudice, but obviously not enough for Dina's aristocratic family to approve her dalliance with a gypsy.

It *was* predictable, he knew. It even had a certain justice, given the Rom's own attitude about outsider alliances with gaje. He should have known better, knew better. Not that it helped to know it now. "I don't want to talk about it." Pov focused pointedly on his sail monitor.

"That I know. How long are you going to grieve, Pov?"

"I said I don't want to talk about it." He raised his head to glare at Kate. "She had a free choice. Leave it alone."

Kate looked at him stubbornly. "So where was *your* choice?"

"Kate, just drop it—like right now. Leave me alone." Kate bit her lip and turned back to her controls.

"Pov," she said a moment later, and he tensed angrily. "Now don't soar off, please—listen to me. I'm not a total idiot and I wouldn't bring it up if I didn't have a reason. Will you listen?" She waited patiently until he shrugged a sour acceptance, then took a deep breath.

"You're a great brother, Pov," she said, "and I love you fanatically. You're decent and smart and good to people, and you deserved somebody better than Dina. But she was the one you wanted. Okay. I'm sorry it didn't work out, whatever I've said before. But Dina's the type who likes to create men and have them beholden to her for the creating, and right now she's creating Benek to replace you."

His head swiveled. "Benek! He's only Fifth Sail!" Benek Zukor was straw-haired and goof-grinned, mediocre on all levels however hard he tried. "Benek?" he exploded. He couldn't believe it.

"He's got great family connections on *Dance*, just like Dina does," Kate pointed out.

"Ship rank isn't hereditary."

"Most of the time and theoretically, but you know better, especially for non-Slavs. The higher rankings still go mainly to the Slav families who started with *Fan*, that and the preferred stock and the swagger and the ship vetos. After all, how did Benek even make sail rank in the first place? You only get that kind of push, especially if you're a goof like Benek, if you've got the family influence. Even if it's not admitted much, a cloudship has its dynasties." She smiled ironically. "It's very Rom, even if most of them haven't the faintest idea of what Rom is, right?"

He shrugged, conceding the point.

"So I'm telling you, Pov. I've been trying to find an opportunity for a couple of weeks, ever since I picked up the news from *Dance*'s skyriders and started skulking after Dina in the corridors. Something is stewing on *Dance*, and it somehow involves Dina—and you. You're so blind on the subject, thinking Dina is this wonderful version of femininity, that you'd never see it until it's too late." She spread her hands. "So I'm warning you. So I'm telling you Dina has her ax out and you're the victim. So wake up."

His jaw tightened. "It'd take more than Dina to disrank me as sailmaster."

"Good. I like that intimidating scowl: it means you've got a few brains left after Dina drained out the rest."

"Ah, come on, Kate!"

"Somebody has to tell you."

"You get appointed?" he asked, suddenly suspecting exactly that.

She flipped her hand negligently. "So Tully suggested. He's your friend, and he doesn't want to *ever* be Second Sail to Benek—he likes you better or some such—but he would have found the telling awkward. After she broke up with you, she sashayed around Tully first, married or not, just to sniff out the possibilities—and had to backpedal fast, believe me, but all you would have heard is Tully and Dina, Dina and Tully, no?"

Pov repressed a groan, knowing she was right, especially back then.

"So Dina finally struck a fast fish at fifth-rank—well, not that fast, considering, and so it's Benek. If you hadn't been so careful to be every place she's *not* lately, you could've seen for yourself." Kate's eyes were full of sympathy. "Ship politics are never fun, especially when somebody's using weapons that aren't right. I'm sorry, Pov."

He thought about it, trying to fit it in with *Dance*'s flirting injury today at *Net*, if it did fit. Dina might think herself mistress of all her schemes, but someone else on *Dance* might be puppeteering, too, with Dina as the oblivious puppet—or maybe not so oblivious. He had thought he knew her, a fatuous assumption that had blown up in his face several weeks before. He thought he knew Sailmaster Ceverny, too, and that possible mistake bothered him even more. Ceverny had trained him as a sail officer, promoted him upward through the sail rankings on *Dance*, then recommended him as *Net*'s sailmaster against weighty objection from the other Powers on *Dance*.

He looked out at the comet's golden river with its charged lightnings, knowing the narrow edge that the cloudships sailed within its tail, and how easily that edge could cut a ship to ribbons if chance turned unlucky. A failure of the sails, a skyrider's inattention ahead at the wrong time, a random dismemberment of the comet hidden by the obscuring gas: *Net* relied on *Dance*, always had, and had returned the support against the hostile environments they faced together.

He struggled with all he knew of *Dance*, his home since boyhood until *Net* was built, trying to imagine *Dance* actively seeking to hurt *Net*. Insults and Slav arrogance, yes, but deliberate damage? Why? Dina's ambition? Her family's?

"Who else knows about this?" he asked.

"It's early. She took up with Benek only a little while ago—but I would like to point out that Dina has a brother on *Dance*'s Sail Deck and *Dance* didn't jig four times on last year's comet runs."

"I doubt if Dina has those kinds of strings," he said judiciously.

Kate shrugged. "All it takes is a suggestion at the right time—it doesn't mean Sailmaster Ceverny is in the plot. But you ought to know. Is it okay that I told you?" She looked at him uncertainly.

He smiled, surprised at the hesitation in her eyes. He wondered how mind-dead he had really been the past weeks, to make Kate hesitate about anything. "Rom forever, Kate. Thanks."

Kate turned the ship again for another pass down the skysail, then glanced back at him cautiously.

"Am I forgiven?" he asked, trying to lighten the mood. "For the time I tied you up and stuffed you in the closet?"

"*Are* you out of your *mind*?" Kate demanded.

Pov chuckled as she started to boil, sputtering impotently, as she always did when he reminded her of his one undeniable and glorious victory. It had taken ten-year-old Kate an hour to get loose, rumpled and red-faced and mad as hell. Pov had never caught her off guard afterward, however sorely she had tempted him, and Kate had promised a "suitable revenge" ever since, merely lacking the right idea.

Kate flipped her hand again as he grinned. "So laugh bravely, sailmaster—while you can." Then she chuckled to herself, enjoying her own joke, and things were all right again, better than they'd been for a while. "Completing sail pattern," Kate said a moment later.

So much for intuition, he thought. "Try the other spinnaker."

"Port?"

"No, starboard. We've already fixed port."

"Sail faults can—"

"Move around, I know. Starboard, Kate."

"Going starboard." Kate glanced at a subsidiary screen. "Dust is up," she warned.

He craned his neck again to look over her shoulder. "Hell," he muttered.

"Damnation," Kate agreed. "This is fairly active

flux. The comet nucleus must be shedding a gas pocket of something besides water ice." She flipped a lever to display more data on the hazard screen. "We've definitely got a dust explosion up ahead."

"What's the dust size?"

"Still in microns, but diameter is rising. The lasers could flash soon."

As she spoke, a brilliant line flashed by outside, pulverizing an invisible meteoroid too heavy for the sails. Two other laser flashes followed immediately after, one splashing on the skyrider's hull as a dust mote pierced the sails and whizzed achingly close. Kate damped the automatic alarm and glanced at him.

"I saw it," he muttered absently. "Damnation."

"True."

Pov studied the dust counter, hesitating as he weighed the risk to *Net* of another sail fault against the risk to the skyrider if the dust conditions worsened. In heavier dust concentrations, the steady flashing of *Net*'s sail lasers resembled a storm of sheet lightning, another of *Net*'s beauties Pov would like to watch someday from outboard, though likely he'd never have much of a chance: skyriding through a swarm of micrometeorites had its own inanity. The lasers flashed again, one bolt again uncomfortably close to their skyrider.

"Pov—" Kate said uneasily.

"I saw it. Take us inboard, Kate. We'll hope there's only the one fault."

The comm chimed. "Sir, the dust count is rising," Avi warned. "The probes say it's getting worse fast and *Dance* is recalling its skyriders. We recommend you come inboard."

"We see it. Thank you, Avi. Coming inboard now."

"Acknowledged, sir. Skyrider coming inboard." The radio clicked off.

Pov sat back to watch the sky change as Kate accelerated into a wide turn outward away from the sails, heading for the skyport behind *Net*'s prow. "Thank you, skyrider," he said formally.

"Thank you, sailmaster," Kate replied. "Hey, when are you going to come out and ride with me just for fun?"

"Fun?"

"Fun, Pov. After 'fairly' and before 'funk' in the dictionary. Fun, you know? All that bed time with Dina and you still don't know what 'fun' is? I'm surprised."

"Soar off," he said mildly.

Kate chuckled to herself, then turned her head to give him another wide smile. "You must be healing. Two weeks ago all I'd gotten myself for that crack is a frozen glare."

"I've been that bad?"

"Yeah, you have—but who's counting?" She shrugged. "Maybe Mother's right—it doesn't work to fall in love with a gaje."

"Sergei isn't Dina. Don't listen to her."

"Not so easy," Kate said absently. "Girls get different rules than sons do."

Kate completed their wide turn under *Net*'s port wing and headed inboard to *Net*. To outsiders, a cloudship seemed a bewildering jumble of different shapes strung together by a dozen bridges and struts, but a spacefaring ship needed little of the sleek styling of an atmosphered craft. With her sails and ship field, *Net* sailed smoothly through the comet's glowing turbulence, a great and lovely alien beast, placid and mild. He smiled, thinking of that image again.

As the skyrider passed under the central companionway, the long corridor linking the prow with holds and stern, a span of lights began rippling on the underside of another bridge ahead, pointing the way toward the landing platform.

"Requesting approach," Kate said into the comm.

Helm Deck acknowledged, directing her downward and warning nearby traffic. Kate concentrated on the flow of data returning to her screens from the sky-dock computer.

"Descending," Kate said into the comm.

"Acknowledged," Helm comm watch replied. "Skyrider descending."

Kate tipped the skyrider sideways and scooted a shortcut through a narrow span between the prow and a downward strut. Pov winced as they cleared the gap with only a few scant meters on either side, a risk he highly doubted the computer had approved: the skyriders liked their fancy piloting over regs and boasted of it. Still . . .

"I could report you for that," he warned.

"But you won't," Kate said complacently. "And the computer will just log it and later Athena will frown and tsk and the other skyriders will admire me fantastically. Approaching dock. Safety cautions, please."

"Rather belated," he grumped and obediently pulled his shoulder straps into place.

"Soar off, sir. I'm driving this boat—spectacularly, you'll notice."

"Just don't crash into *Net* while you're doing it. I've still got work to do today."

"How dull. When are you going to get a life, Pov?"

Pov muttered a useless retort under his breath and suffered Kate's knowing snicker. A gypsy male might have his Rom dignity and rank, but gypsy women usually managed to keep it a draw—and worse when they could arrange it. It kept the wits of both sides alert.

The skyrider steadied on a straight course for the ship platform directly ahead, then lofted up a few meters over the platform edge and set down smoothly on the metal surface. As the wheels touched the deck, *Net*'s artificial-gravity field snatched at them, giving Pov a stomach lurch that he never quite anticipated correctly, for all the skyriding he'd done, and which gave his body a few startled seconds of rechecking its reality. Kate engaged the ground controls and wheeled them briskly toward the irising entry port ahead. However she did it, Kate always landed with wheels down.

As the skyrider stopped inside the skydeck, Pov unbuckled his belts, then stood up and bent over Kate's chair. She looked up.

"Hot jets," he whispered admiringly, probably undoing every useful nag he'd given her today. "Thanks, *chavali*."

"Who's a kid?" she asked in mock indignation, but lost the pose in her smile. "Come to dinner tonight? Sergei's cooking." She rolled her eyes. "Big event. Mother's coming."

"How'd you get her to agree to that?"

Kate shrugged. "Oh, I suspect she wants to present her disdain personally. She's tried ignoring him, tried leaving the room whenever he comes in, tried exclaiming aloud to the ceiling, tried reading the cards with moans and clucks and sighs. I expect we'll see a whole new panoply tonight." Pov grimaced sympathetically. Their mother had her ways of letting her opinions be known, too, not as directly as Kate, but just as surely.

As Rom of a new generation, Pov and Kate had adjusted to patterns far different from the older life his mother still lived in her heart. His mother fretted that her children found too little time to listen to her stories, both too occupied with duties and friends in the larger gaje community aboard *Net* and *Dance*. The Rom had resisted the lure of the outside world for centuries, keeping to their own traditions, surviving the harsh oppressions imposed by a larger society that resented their differences, always remembering their heritage and choosing their own way. Too many Rom in Taurus had chosen the temptations, his mother thought, forgetting who they were, becoming gaje in all but name and complexion and occasional speech. And so she fretted, worrying for her children.

And so Margareta Janusz had *not* approved of Sergei Rublev, a Tania's Ring Russki who had joined

Net's astrophysics group upon *Net*'s commissioning three years before. Practically speaking, Kate had few eligibles among the twenty closely related Rom aboard *Net* and *Dance*, and even their mother admitted that a few of the younger Janusz might have to marry outside the tribe to avoid the birth risks of a couple interrelated too many ways. She did not, however, agree to Kate as one of the few. Never that.

"You just have to outlast her, that's all. Even Mother has to give up eventually."

"You're sure of that?" Kate sighed. "I've warned Sergei, and he's promised to be patient. But I could use you as intermediary, Pov."

"I'll be there." He kissed his sister lightly on the lips, then popped his data carrier from the slot and left for Sail Deck.

Chapter 2

As he stepped onto Sail Deck, Pov stopped a moment to watch the main wallscreen display of the sails, computer-enhanced into shimmering visibility, a delicate rose for the mainsails, the faintest of cobalt blues for skysails above and below, the bright gold of the outwing spinnakers. I'll never tire of the looking, he thought, never.

On either side of the main wallscreen, the sail techs on beta watch sat at the subsidiary monitor stations for infrared, visible-light, UV, and gamma-ray, each intent on smaller screen variants of the main display. On the middle right, between the ultraviolet and visible-light stations, a circular ladder led downward to a computer room used for repair analysis and sail simulations; another door in the far right corner led to conference and training rooms for sail staff, a small lounge and cafeteria for staff on duty, and a data-storage room. On the far left, Avi Selenko sat at the comm station, her head tipped to the side as she listened to her several radio channels.

In midroom at the master's console, Tully Haralpos, *Net*'s Second Sail, lounged casually in a padded chair, his head turning slowly as he shifted attention from his own screens to the main wallscreen and the techs. Pov stepped forward, and Tully heard his footstep, swiveled his chair around. Pov raised an eyebrow, and Tully wiggled his back, trading a silent comment about *Dance* probably unsuitable for the ears of Sail Deck's young staff. Pov sat down beside Tully in the other chair and they scowled together at *Net*'s innocent sails.

Pov and Tully had grown up together on *Ishtar's Fan*, inseparable friends in the larger pack of boys who had coursed *Fan*'s aging corridors. Tully freely joined Pov's family dinners that usually excluded outsider gaje, and Pov learned the freshly spiced tastes of Greek cooking from Tully's mother, however Margareta clicked her tongue about their un-gypsy preparation. A Rom preserved his tradition partly in rituals about food, and the shared meals had stopped abruptly when Pov's mother argued bitterly with Sophia Haralpos, a nasty discussion about comparative purity that had baffled Sophia and had stopped the women from talking for years. It was an old wound that had never completely healed between the families, and one of the several reasons Pov had broken another gypsy tradition and chosen to live alone in his own apartment, away from his *Net* relatives who still shared common quarters near the chemlabs.

Tully had matured into a small wiry man with dark hair curled tightly to his head, somewhat shorter than Pov's own middle height and dressed casually for duty, like Pov, in a simple tunic and trousers, a genial man who liked to scowl but too easily lost the frown in a smile. Right now Tully eyed Pov's data-transfer box with suspicious blue eyes, as if he doubted all now in his fractious mood.

"Well, you took your time," Tully grumped. Tully hated sail faults with all the fervor of a Rom grandmam at a gaje cocktail party, and his infrequent biases, when alerted, included any nearby objects, even animate ones like his sailmaster. Pov clucked at him reprovingly.

"Yes, oh lofty one." He put the carrier on the console, then slid it into the data slot and keyed the transfer. "Any apology from *Dance*, I suppose not?"

"No, but you can expect Captain Andreos to protest again."

"Probably so. Bottom skysail's intact—didn't get to the others."

"Well, good." Tully relaxed a little, enough to look mildly genial. He twisted his black eyebrows, a comment, very Greek, that Pov had seen a thousand times; they traded another glance.

"All the other sails are smooth as a single-molecule curve," Pov said. "I hope."

"I have a repair crew on standby."

"Have them check for other damage to the portsail, I think," Pov said, deciding to worry about it. "Maybe it wasn't all plasma pull that ripped the sail."

"Will do." Tully swiveled back to his console and pushed some buttons, then talked on the comm mike to the repair chief in the computer room below.

Pov glanced casually around Sail Deck as the sail computer digested his data transfer, adding the million or so bits to the other billions in its thoughts. Though he admired computers for their brains, he doubted if he'd enjoy being one. He liked a less cluttered universe that let him admire sail patterns on colored screens. The color enhancement had a technical reason, of course, but the sail tech who'd thought up the good reason had been inspired. He smiled happily at his pretty sails on the main wallscreen, playing the goof.

Speaking of goods, he thought, spotting Benek's empty chair at the UV station.

"Where's Benek?" he asked Tully. "I thought he was on beta watch this month."

"No sign yet. To do what unto?" Tully asked cautiously and squinted at him. "I'm not being an accessory to whatever you're planning."

"Yeah. Nothing unto, just wondering. Dina's history, Tully."

"Oh, *sure* she is," Tully blurted, then flushed uncomfortably and busied himself with the data check as the carrier popped out of the slot. Pov repressed a sigh. Blast Dina, anyway: sails weren't the only thing that ruffed in his life, it seemed. Tully gave him a loyalty rare even on a cloudship, a comrade uninterested in politics and rank dignities and contented in a way Pov probably would never be. Among the Rom, that kind of brotherhood was freely given and expected: Pov valued the connections that arose elsewhere, unbidden and unrequired. In the old days, friendships with gaje were rare, evoking a treasured word, *rai*, for the odd chance of a true friend among gaje outsiders who didn't understand the gypsies and didn't bother to understand even if the Rom bothered to explain, which was seldom. Tully was that kind of true friend, always had been.

Women aren't worth the trouble, he told himself sourly, then toyed with the idea of repeating the thought to Kate just to watch her explode—but decided not. He'd rather reacquire some brains—belatedly, true. He smiled at Tully as the data check chimed itself complete and Tully glanced at him again. "No problem, sail."

"Sure, Pov." But Tully was still cautious. Scorch Dina, anyway: Kate had a point about drained brains.

"Hey, Tully," Pov said impulsively, "come to dinner tonight at Kate's. Mother's got Sergei on the menu." He doubted the invitation could make it worse, considering, and at least Tully had the advantage of familiarity.

"Oh, really?" Tully's eyebrows climbed to his hairline. "Kate thinks that's a step forward?"

"Come anyway. It'll be fun. Park the kids and bring Irisa."

"Easier said than done. As they get older, they're harder to park." Then Tully smiled, losing all traces of his scowl. "I'd like that, Pov."

"Then it's done."

Tully looked past him toward the elevator and abruptly scowled again. Pov turned to look. "Hello, Benek," he drawled. "Watch starts at two bells, not three, or have you forgotten?"

Benek ducked his head and hurried awkwardly to his station. "Sorry, sir," he muttered, and nearly fell over his chair in his haste to sit down. Pov opened his mouth to chew him out some more, then shut it with a snap as Dina Kozel sashayed onto deck a moment later.

"Hi, Pov," she said cheerfully.

"Sailmaster to you, Ms. Kozel. You're off station here."

"So?" Dina waved her hand lazily and strolled over to Benek, then bent to give him an ostentatious kiss, drawn out a little too long to be real. As she straightened, Benek looked up at her and grinned like a pet dog. Pov considered several countertactics—he had security force if he wanted it—then glanced at Tully. Tully made a face, shrugged a shoulder at the two, then pointed at the ceiling to the masters' lounge several levels above.

"Don't you have a captain's meeting?" Tully suggested meaningfully.

"In a while."

Tully got up from his chair and advanced on Dina. "I'm master of the deck right now, sir. I'll handle it. Comm, call security."

Dina whirled and glared at Tully. "What's the matter, Haralpos? Can't Pov handle it anymore?" She struck a pose, all the blond softness and sweet expressions she had used so deftly quite gone. "My uncle has always wondered why *Dance* appointed a gyp to captain's rank." Dina smiled with satisfaction as Pov flushed hotly at the epithet. He got up and took a step toward her, not knowing what he was going to do to her. Tully grabbed his arm, maybe guessing the worst.

"Let it go, Pov. She's not worth it. Let it go."

"Get her off my deck," Pov said, his eyes locked with Dina's, "before I throw her off myself." Benek gulped nervously, his neck cartilage bobbing like flotsam on a wave, looked up at Dina, looked at Pov. "You're a fool, Benek," Pov told him with contempt and turned on his heel to stomp off the deck. As he left, he heard Dina laugh.

The problem with elevators, Pov decided a moment later, was that they left nothing to do but stand around. He could hit the wall hard and regret it badly, or pace two steps left, two steps right, or ... He hit the stop button and exited at the next level to give him some room to walk it off. He glanced at his wristband to check the time, then walked briskly down the wide corridor, his bootheels ringing off the metal floor.

He had walked barely a dozen meters when someone called his name. He slowed and looked back, seeing no one, then saw the open door he had passed at full speed, belatedly realizing which admin level he had exited. He retraced his steps and put his head into the opening. "Yes, sir?"

"What's the rush, Pov?" Captain Andreos looked at him quizzically from behind a broad desk littered with data pages. A tall, big-boned man, Leonidas Andreos fit awkwardly into human-standard chairs but managed to carry it off, as he managed most things, with good style. He was graying now, after nearly twenty years in captain's ranking, first as *Dance*'s holdmaster, then *Net*'s shipmaster, his rugged face lined by too many worries. Pov shifted to his other foot, sorry to have disturbed Andreos unnecessarily.

Like all cloudships, *Net* employed several masters, each supervising a part of *Net* and acting together as a ship's consortium to advise *Net*'s senior captain, the shipmaster. Some decisions Captain Andreos had authority to make himself, but the ship's contract specified in tedious detail the careful limits on that authority, all with an eye to the crew's profits subjected to a single and possibly fallible will. Andreos usually finessed the matter by discussing almost everything with his masters, and the courtesy made *Net*'s leadership collegial and relaxed. On *Dance*, Captain Rybak ran a different kind of ship, but contract language could protect as well as limit: how Andreos chose to consult his masters was *Net*'s affair and not subject to Rybak's ideas of proper command technique.

Andreos was waiting, then alternated his raised eyebrow to the other one as a prompt. "Uh, nothing, sir," Pov mumbled. "Just touring."

"Um." Andreos studied him a moment, then let it go. "Find another sail fault?"

"No, sir. Repair crew's on alert, though."

"I heard the portsail ripped."

"We're checking into that, too."

"Good." Andreos shuffled the papers before him into a neater pile, glanced at his wristband, then snapped off his computer. "I'll walk up with you."

"My pleasure, sir," Pov said sincerely.

Pov stepped backward as Andreos joined him, then walked beside him to the elevator. They rose another two levels to the command level with its conference rooms and suites high in the prow, then walked into the masters' lounge, where Andreos conducted *Net*'s captains' meetings. Pov nodded at Holdmaster Janina Svoboda, an older placid-tempered woman who supervised *Net*'s hold storage and supplies, then he sat down by Milo Cieslak, the ship's lawyer and financial officer, or "chaffer" in ship-speak. A small-bodied fleshy man, Milo was sometimes a cold-blooded and ambivalent man quick to accuse, but he loved to talk, often entranced by his own logic.

Across from Pov, Pilotmaster Athena Mikelos slowly rocked her chair back and forth, her expression closed. A long-legged curvy brunette, closest at twenty-eight to Pov's own age, Athena had dual command of the navigation deck and the skyrider crew, charged with taking *Net* wherever her captains or *Dance* chose to go. Kate idolized Athena and had gone through a phase of copying Athena's walk and speech and gestures, a period Pov had been glad to see end. He preferred the original Athena to the several clones that regularly appeared among the young skyriders. Athena gave him a companionly wink, though her young face still looked severe. Captain Andreos walked around the curve of the table and took another chair, watched by them all.

Five masters, a pattern *Arrow* had set for all the cloudships, as *Arrow*'s traditions had set the custom of the cloudship names: daughter and independent, senior and junior, all named after women who had loved Orion, the celestial hunter repeated from myth to myth across Earth's cultures as Diana's huntsman, India's antlered god, as Babylonia's great Immortal, Gilgamesh. Hidden in that naming was Thaddeus Gray's hope for all the cloudships: the Orion Nebula and its complex of vast interstellar gas clouds, fifteen hundred light-years from Earth and beyond reach until the next breakthrough in ship-drive technology. I'd like to meet Thaddeus Gray, Pov thought. *Arrow*'s great captain had forged a new way of life independent of colony control, preparing for the future when the Orion Nebula might become a possibility. All the cloudships were somehow Gray's: he had led the way, found the means, then given it all to the many masters on the two dozen cloudships who now carried on his tradition.

"Your inspection, Sailmaster?" Andreos asked formally, beginning the meeting.

"We found the fault in the port spinnaker—the hard way, as you know." Pov grimaced. "Tully's crew has replaced the generator and we're monitoring the other sails."

"Good," Andreos repeated for the other captains' benefit.

Milo leaned forward aggressively. "*Are* we going to discuss what's on everybody's mind? How long will we permit Rybak to damage our profits?"

"Speculation." Andreos shrugged. "He'd never admit it, anyway."

"There *was* a richer eddy to chase, wasn't there?" Athena asked quietly.

"Oh, yes. With a dozen course windows to choose, of course: he could have waited. How close to the end of your inspection did *Dance* turn, Pov?"

"I was halfway through it, sir."

"And a sail fault to find while we're sailing in plasma. You did tell Ceverny that?"

"Yes, sir."

Andreos scowled, then turned to Milo. "Can we cite a contract breach?"

Milo pursed his lips. "Maybe a minor clause, but it's subsumed by the general directives in the preamble, as usual. A mere threat doesn't invoke the contract clause I want—and it's not worth the hull damage we'd need to get into that clause. Besides, Tania's Ring would get the repair contract, which we'd have to pay, not *Dance*." He raised his shoulders, dropped them helplessly.

"Bukharin would love to repair *Net*, just to snoop," Athena remarked sourly, referring to Omsk Station's wily Trade Bureau chief. "I've heard that he's thinking about those in-system collectors from Aldebaran: Tania's Ring almost has the extra capital to invest. I *also* heard Aldebaran has already sent out a vendor, waving the specs. Let's face it, captains: cloudship technology is going to get outgrown very fast in the Hyades. We can't compete profitably with a fleet of small in-system collectors, especially if they automate with robots."

"*Arrow* saw it coming," Janina remarked. "Twenty years ago, Gray saw it."

"That was twenty years ago," Athena said and tossed her head, "and we're still stuck here." She pointed accusingly at Milo. "With an unbreakable contract *he* negotiated."

"Soar off, Athena." Milo retorted defensively. "I only signed the damn thing; *Dance* negotiated the main terms. How close were we to injury, Pov?"

"Depends. Ask the star: this close the solar wind's doing most of the shoving. At a medium flow, our sails are nominal—in heavier storm, the risks go up. It was a 'minor irregularity' until we hit the heavier concentration and *Dance* swerved ahead of us."

"Which *Dance* tried to lead us into?" Andreos asked pointedly.

Pov shrugged, wishing he had that answer. He had lived ten years on *Dance*, had considered *Fan* and *Dance* his homeships and Rybak his shipmaster most of his adulthood: he still had friends and family aboard *Dance*, and such bonds weren't easily dislodged with a newer loyalty. This latest incident had disturbing implications, and all of *Net*'s captains knew it.

Ishtar's Fan, the first Slav cloudship built at Aldebaran thirty years before, had lost her first daughter ship, *Ishtar's Jewel*, by accumulating similar irritations until *Jewel* angrily broke contract and followed *Arrow* to the Pleiades. In an effort to recoup her fortunes, *Fan* moved to Perikles at Gamma Tauri and built *Dance*, only to lose her second daughter ship to Russki blandishments and huge bonuses offered by Tania's Ring. Now *Dance* seemed determined to repeat *Fan*'s history, however *Net* complained.

"So what do we do?" Janina asked, spreading her hands. "Nothing?"

"What *can* we do?" Athena said sourly, then tipped her head to the side and shook her dark curls. "On second thought, make that a serious question. Is doing nothing the best tactic? Can incidents compound into a contract violation, Milo?"

"Maybe."

Athena glared at Milo affably. "Milo, Pov has particle probabilities off the scale—you have words on a page. Do they or not? You're the chaffer for the ship and can recite our contract word for word; I've heard you. So?"

Milo scowled, thinking about it. "Probably not," he decided. "*Dance* got a very generous general directive, and it covers a lot of sins like all of God's graces, with you know who as resident God. Captain, can't you meet with Captain Rybak and mesh a little?" Milo liked meshing, especially when he had the lead. "You were his holdmaster for years."

"Hmmph." Andreos pulled at his long nose, then shrugged humorously. "That's a credential?"

Janina twined her fingers in front of her, then sighed, her broad face perplexed. "It's gotten worse this run, sir," she said thoughtfully. "I'm getting resistance from *Dance* on simple hold reports, with my request running up and down their hold echelon before I can even get data-sharing. It's not essential to our hold operations, of course, but we've always traded data back and forth for analysis of a sort. Has their pilotmaster changed procedure, too, Athena?"

"Not that I've noticed. Their chevron reports to us as well as *Dance*." Athena shook her head. "Rybak's always been an autocrat and he's getting older, but not enough to take risks with our profits like this. After all, *Dance* gets half. Does he really want *Net* damaged? Even if we buy out in eight years, *Dance*'s annual profit share from us by then can fund a whole new daughter ship. Or does he want to own us forever?"

"*Arrow*'s daughters still travel with her," Andreos pointed out.

Janina dimpled. "Rybak with delusions of the new Thaddeus Gray? Now that's a combination."

Andreos tapped the table impatiently. "He's still senior captain, Janina. Some respect, please."

"Nuts to that, sir," Athena said, tossing her head. "Respect is earned—and kept, like the profound and everlasting respect we have for you, oh captain sir. At least as long as you're acting instead of talking."

Andreos grunted. "Save the treacle, Athena—and the benign threats." He frowned at her. "Let me think about it and maybe I'll go talk to Rybak when we get in-system. Fair enough?"

Athena pursed her lips, then nodded. "The reason I bring it up, sir, is that Rybak can play other games that can risk my skyriders: *Net* can tolerate a lot more than a skyrider holed by dust. I don't want any of my pilots hurt when my chevron's out in front tomorrow."

"Well, neither do I, of course," Andreos said, still irritated, as if she'd accused him of wishing otherwise. It flicked Athena's own temper, and her cajolery vanished.

"Turning Rybak, captain?" she asked acidly. Andreos glared back.

Pov prudently cleared his throat and intervened. "Athena, send one of your chiefs up to Sail Deck," he suggested. "Then Tully and I can coordinate in protecting the skyriders. And nobody accused you of anything, sir." Pov threw a warning look at Athena, and she shrugged, then let it go.

"Sorry, sir," she said to Andreos, spreading her hands. "It's hard to not call up Rybak myself to bend some ears. Outside the ship field there isn't much between my pilots and blinkout. So I'm a mother type."

"I've noticed," Andreos said tartly. "This isn't the first incident, just the latest in a pattern. There have been other things. . . ." He shrugged again, not elaborating. "I've known Rybak for twenty years, and he's capable of what you suspect, I'm sorry to say. So stay alert, at least until we head in-system." He nodded, dismissing them. "That's all, sirs. Pilotmaster, please remain behind."

Athena rolled her eyes at Pov, knowing Andreos wouldn't let her off so easy. *Grovel*, he mouthed, and Andreos caught it, earning Pov a glare all his own. Pov grinned and waved goodbye, then left with the others.

"When Athena doesn't rile him," Janina said equably, "then I'll worry."

"She apologized," Milo protested, falling in step with Janina and Pov. "How often do we get something as amazing as that?"

Janina made a rude sound and pushed Milo off-stride, hard enough to make Milo stagger. "Go read your contracts, boy." Milo laughed and stomped off toward the elevator. "Wait a minute, Pov, will you?"

"What is it?"

"The sails are all right? You weren't optimizing?"

"So far. It could have gotten worse, but probabilities were low once we got clear. I thought *Dance*'s turn more rude than anything else, even if it caught us badly." He paused and glanced back at the masters' door. "Maybe I was wrong."

"Don't underestimate Rybak, Pov. And keep your gypsy's eye on our sails and Athena's skyriders. I trust the captain's unease—and Athena's intuition that chose to provoke it even more. Those two mesh in a way we tech-minded masters don't."

He nodded, thinking about it. "Surely, Janina." She gave him a wide smile and walked off, heading back to her own station, a sturdy solid woman who managed, like most of the women in his life, to see things he somehow missed. *Men do, women know*, he told himself lightly, repeating one of Kate's favorite barbs.

He lingered in the corridor, watching the view of *Net* through a large hull window that looked backward over the ship. As before, the comet's plasma stream swung in its shimmering bow wave around *Net*, combining in a complicated swirl of glowing smoke far behind the engines. *Net*'s jeweled lights winked in their random patterns, accenting the shadows cast by the glowing gas, great sweeping cloud-shadows that swept steadily over *Net*. Beautiful and dangerous, to sail a comet's tail: he smiled at his dim reflection in the window, a shadowed and dusky Rom face set against the glowing depths that surrounded his ship. Sailing suited him well, he thought, almost enough to undo his Rom soul and make it content ... almost.

"Waiting to stanch the blood?" He startled as Athena's voice sounded just behind him. He turned and pretended to inspect her anxiously.

"Don't see any to tend, pilot."

"It's all inside." Athena thumped her breast dramatically. "Heartblood, the kind that leaches the soul. I may never recover."

"Idiot." He chuckled.

"Thanks for the calloff, Pov. I forget sometimes to notice when he's that worried."

"Bad?"

She shrugged. "I groveled, as you suggested. It helped." She smiled. "Tell Kate she's in trouble for that shortcut under the bridge."

"I already told her. She was nicely contrite."

Athena arched a delicate eyebrow. "And mice fly, I'm sure. Someday Kate'll cut it too close and take out a strut, so I'm putting her in trouble to deter my other hot jets, not that it ever works."

"Being pilotmaster must be tough," Pov retorted, giving her no sympathy. "Getting old, Athena?"

"Not if I can help it." Her grin flashed at him. In her younger days, Athena had take out one of *Dance*'s struts herself, and the incident hadn't slowed her down—nor affected her promotions afterward. Skyriding suited the bold, not that Athena could admit it much now: seniority had its pinches. "I'll send Stefania up to watch your sails with you. Maybe we'll get through the next few days without getting hulled."

"Sure."

Athena nodded to him absently, her quick mind already on something else, and headed off, loping along on her long legs. Pov turned back to the window for a while, watching the roiling luminescent clouds converging behind *Net*, then left reluctantly to sit through Tully's sail watch.

Sergei and Kate shared living quarters near the beta companionway that led to pilot station, though Sergei's own duty took him to the physics labs halfway across the ship. Pov understood the choice as partly Sergei's acknowledgment of his newcomer status on *Net*, with fewer choices over others, but it was typical of Sergei to think of Kate's convenience first. The couple had long passed the first stages of their romance and had settled comfortably into a good relationship. Sergei had made his wishes known about making it official, and only Margareta's hostility had postponed the choosing: Kate still hoped that time—and Sergei's undeniable charm—would soften her mother's open hostility.

As Pov walked down the softly lit residential corridor to Kate's apartment, a brightly wrapped gift under his arm to celebrate the meal, he thought about means to help his sister. Though his mother favored Kate openly, anticipating that Kate would someday succeed her as *puri dai*, the senior female elder of the tribe, an only son still had his weighty influences. Margareta Janusz's formidable will had helped her survive a hard childhood on Earth and had carried her through her widowhood after a chance road accident had killed young Garridan Janusz shortly after Kate's birth. Two decades later, his mother still grieved for her husband, enough to preclude any thought of remarriage, but it was a familiar hurt after so long a time: his mother's usual motives ran strictly to power, as only a Rom matriarch could assert it. It was a gypsy way, the authority of the *puri dai* within the tribe, and a different balancing than the largely patriarchal arrangements that still lingered among the Slavs and Greeks who made up the other crew of *Dance* and *Net*. He liked the different mix, however comfortable the gaje variants might have been: his mother's behavior honed the wits—and weapons could be turned both ways.

He buzzed the door and shifted his package to his other arm. A few moments later, the door opened inward.

"Good evening, Mother," he said firmly.

"So you came," she declared and stomped away from him back to the couch. Pov stepped into the room and heard a murmur of voices in the kitchen beyond, one Kate's light high voice and a rumbling from Sergei in response, then focused on his mother.

She sat with a scowl on her face, dressed gypsy to the hilt with a flowing colored skirt, beaded vest and wide-sleeved blouse, a red patterned kerchief, jewels on her fingers, bangles on her slender bony wrists, gold chains glittering from neck to waist. She looked magnificent and certainly knew it, if only she'd give up her scowl. He crossed the carpeted floor and bent to kiss her, which she accepted graciously enough, then handed her the brightly wrapped package.

"Wine to add to the occasion. You look wonderful, Mother."

"Of course," she snapped, then rolled her black eyes expressively. His mother looked good in a ship suit, too, when she attended her duties as part of Janina's processing crew; she had kept her good figure through the years, and still had much of the dark beauty that had graced her youth. He would always think of her as that younger woman of twenty years ago when he was a boy, though the years had added wrinkles and silvered her dark hair, collapsing her somehow: as he would always be partly a boy to her, she was always the beautiful mother of his youth, one to idolize and adore.

"You're going to lose, too," he told her, then grinned as she reacted. Then she surprised him with a wry smile.

"He does go persistently on." She raised her hand and dangled a silver bracelet. "Bribes, you see." He bent to look at the intricate pattern inscribed into the silver, then raised his eyebrows.

"That must have cost him a month's profit share, Mother. This is a determined man, don't you think?"

"Hmmph. His charm escapes me."

"Really?" He fingered the bracelet a moment longer, knowing Kate had helped Sergei choose the gift. "How long are you going to keep this up? Kate's convinced you're here just to carve him into pieces." She opened her mouth, then shut it again and looked stubborn. He straightened and shrugged, intending the displeasure she would take in that studied indifference. "Your choice, Mother." He turned and started for the kitchen.

"Pov."

"What?"

"Come here and sit down by me." She patted the cushion.

"Why should I? It's been three years, Mother—she's not going to give him up. You wouldn't accept him in our home when she asked, and so she moved out, just as I did—and you know why I moved out. It's the same issue—it's *always* the same issue between us. On this ship, Kate and I don't think the gaje are unpersons put here for the Rom to outwit and fleece. They're friends, part of us. This isn't Europe, and it's not Perikles: it's *Net*. Maybe you don't feel that way, but we do—and so do Karoly and the other younger Rom. Ask him. Ask Tawnie how *she* feels. Or do you even bother to ask now?"

"But he's gaje," she murmured in distress and would not look at him.

"Who else is there for Kate? Lenci is promised to Bavol's Shuri, and Cam's too young. How many kinds of cousin are they, anyway? Two? Or is it three? Karoly? He's twice her age. Everyone else is too young or already married. This isn't exactly a new problem, you know. You scoured Perikles for a bride for me for six years, remember, but none of the tribes would give up a daughter of a rank that would suit you, whatever bride price you offered. And there are no Rom on Tania's Ring."

"In the old days . . ."

"In the old days," he interrupted, "the Rom had other tribes to meet on the road, and didn't understand the connection between dull-eyed children and inbreeding. Add our ship radiation, non-earth environments, and occasional bad luck on nuclear shielding, and you've got more than enough reason for the two miscarriages before you had me and the three after-

ward. Right?" She looked away and twisted her hands
in her lap. "I'm sorry to be blunt, Mother, but you're
hurting Kate. Please stop this."

"And what happens to the Rom?" she asked angrily. "Do we just give up the blood, the knowledge,
everything we are?"

"Kate is Rom, Mother: she'll never be anything else.
And her children will be Rom, because Rom is handed
down through more than blood. You don't have to
wear a kerchief and bangles to be Rom—and you
don't have to shut out the gaje. You have friends on
Hold Deck, you do the gaje work as a tech—are you
any less Rom because of it?"

His mother's eyes shifted to look past him, and he
turned. Kate stood in the doorway, a stack of plates
in her hands. He saw the apprehension in her eyes as
she looked quickly at her mother, then at him.

"Sergei tries silver, I'm lecturing," he told her.
"Mother is going to behave herself."

"Indeed," Margareta said archly, tinkling her bracelets. "Am I?"

"I'll make you a bargain," Pov said, shooting her a
warning look. "You behave and I'll let you spread the
cards for me. Use all that dire prophecy on me for
once instead of wide-eyed gaje. Scare me with what
you know."

His mother snickered and toyed with her bracelets
again, making them clink, then carefully rearranged
the folds of her sleeves. As Sergei appeared in the
doorway behind Kate, her expression clouded again.

"Please, mother," Kate pleaded. "Please."

His mother hesitated, and Pov abruptly lost his patience with his mother's stubborn intolerance. "How
about halfway, Mother?" he asked. "You can have
twelve snippy comments, fourteen dark looks, and six
dismissive waves. Fair enough?" He knew his sarcasm
a mistake the moment after he said it. His mother's
dark eyes hardened, making her look old.

"This is serious, Pov," she said, as if Kate weren't

even there. "I'm not being arbitrary, whatever you think of me. The Rom have preserved their traditions for a millennium with such choices." She lifted her chin, staring him down.

"I agree—but I don't agree Rom tradition is more important than Kate," Pov answered stubbornly. "Now worry about *that* slippage, Mother: maybe the gaje have stolen my soul." He turned to Kate. "What are you cooking? I invited Tully and Irisa."

"I thought you might," Kate said, looking askance at their mother. Margareta promptly scowled at any mention of gaje at a Rom family meal, and Pov returned her glare, daring her to comment. "Goulash and salad suit you?" Kate asked.

"To the brim." She handed him the plates and then disappeared again into the kitchen. He joined her a few minutes later, leaving their mother to fume on the couch. Sergei stood by the counter awkwardly, looking embarrassed. Sergei had patiently adopted all the Rom traditions of keeping a household to please Kate, carefully followed the purity rules as best he could, but he still had a gaje's unbelief that sometimes betrayed him, even after three years of trying to bend himself into a mold not his own. "Sorry, friend," Pov said.

"In some quarters it's called bigotry," Sergei muttered angrily.

"Gaje don't have a corner on it, I agree." Pov kissed Kate's forehead, and she laid her head on his shoulder for a moment, then turned and bustled around again at dinner. "Sorry, Kate."

The outer door buzzed, and Pov stepped back into the living room, then stared at the empty couch where his mother had been sitting. He crossed quickly to the bedroom and glanced in, saw the open bathroom door: she was truly gone. The door buzzed again, and he belatedly answered it, then ushered Tully and his wife into the room, playing the temporary host for Kate and Sergei.

Though Kate joked and smiled throughout dinner, teasing Tully mercilessly about this and that, in repose Pov saw the tightened jaw, the flat looks she gave her plate. Not once did she ask him about their mother's absence, and Pov guessed there would be no more conciliatory gestures from Kate for a while, maybe never again. Tradition of many kinds can be passed on, he thought regretfully, and the Rom were a stubborn breed.

In the limited Rom group aboard *Net*, they lacked enough elders to evoke an impartial *kris*, the ancient Rom tribal council that had resolved internal Rom disputes for centuries. Even adding the two young Rom households aboard *Dance*, the elders who would decide the issue were Rom of his mother's generation and likely to agree with the wrong side. Evoking a *kris* risked Kate's expulsion from the Rom if she disobeyed the likely explicit demand. Mother knows it, too, he realized with an inner chill, seeing a new significance in tonight's pointed snub.

He stared down at his half-filled plate, appalled. Would Mother really risk it? Or was she so confident of Kate's ultimate decision? Pov was not confident, not at all. He knew how Kate adored this man of hers, finding in him a beloved friend and lover, a gentle confidant, fascinating in his differences and a respite from the dark male tempers of her own tribe. His mother had never bothered to find out what truly lay between these two. Margareta Janusz had a clever mind, polished by decades of her gypsy scheming and pride—but even a Rom mother can err with her own child, by assuming too much.

And he had walked right into his mother's ploy, he realized, with tonight's well-intended meddling. He looked up, and Kate caught his glance. She blinked, surprised by the anger that must be in his face, then looked a silent question. He shook his head and got up from the table, taking his wineglass into the kitchen.

He busied himself in the refrigerator, hunting for an excuse if Kate followed him, then stood in front of the open refrigerator door, looking at Kate's neat jars and bottles, a half-eaten pie that sagged stickily on the edges, a cold chicken, a bag of dark meaty synthetic something that was probably a Russki import: Sergei had grown up with meat-vat food, and he'd heard a person could acquire a taste for anything. He sipped his wine and eyed the gelatinous purplish mass, wondering if Sergei's meat glop had graced the goulash he'd just eaten. He liked his meat real, not purple and wiggly. Surely Kate wouldn't go *that* far, he told himself.

He shut the refrigerator door with a bang. Anything you want, Kate, he thought coldly: name it, and I'll move the stars themselves. *Dance* playing dangerous games with his sails, his mother now openly maneuvering against Kate's choice of a beloved: he had thought some loyalties secure.

"Pov?"

He turned and gave Kate an intimidating glare. "Surely you wouldn't, not in goulash."

She dimpled. "You utter idiot." She tipped her head and thought about it, dangling him mercilessly. "But then, I *told* you my revenge would be awful."

"That you did," he said, then menaced her as he walked past her into the other room, earning himself a sharp jab in the ribs as he muscled too close. "But there are always more closets," he promised darkly over his shoulder. "And lots of rope." She chortled all the way back to the table, prancing as she mocked him with gestures centuries older than they were.

"Closets?" Sergei asked, totally confused, and Tully whooped in delight as Kate blushed. Kate obviously hadn't yet told Sergei about that little bit of Janusz history. Sergei looked at Tully's wide grin and then pointedly back at Kate. "Closets?" he asked again.

"Closets," Pov said with intense satisfaction, then shut up as Kate threatened him with her spoon. Tully started a long and involved story about some Greek who went fishing, adding considerably to Sergei's confusion. It was a typical Rom-husbandly state that would no doubt continue on this bit of old news: Kate would see to that, with Tully's obviously obliging help.

Someday, Kate mouthed at Pov as Tully droned onward. Tully's story took another bewildering turn down a wholly random path and poor Sergei shook his head in perplexity. Even Irisa looked dazed.

I can wait, he sent back to Kate, and toasted his sister with his glass.

Chapter 3

The next afternoon on beta watch, Pov sat at his sail command console, watching the shifting colors of his sails on the wallscreen. Duty, Pov, he told himself, and stretched his legs comfortably under the console, then rocked his chair awhile, looking at his sail staff instead of the sails.

Each of the three daily sail watches kept ten sail officers on duty, four in the computer room below and six on Sail Deck, including the Sail Deck chief, himself or Tully or Third Sail Roja Korak. During major sail runs, like today, he usually took Sail himself, handing the following watch to Tully and letting Roja handle the tie-off or an assist. For today's run with *Net* in the lead, he had prudently pulled Roja off night watch to monitor the sail generators. So far the computer hadn't detected another fault slipping around the sails, and Pov counted his Rom luck in that.

"*Dance* signaling," Avi said from her station at the comm. "Ten minutes to slipcourse."

"Acknowledge signal. Inform the skyriders and Helm."

"Yes, sir."

Pov stretched again as Avi sent her messages, then slouched more comfortably in his chair. Today *Net* would give *Dance* the advantage of harvesting off *Net*'s bow wave to finish filling its holds, a final maneuver necessary to *Dance* on the last three comet runs. When *Dance* had built *Net*, the ship engineers had incorporated several of the newer Pleiades sail designs, making *Net* noticeably more efficient than her parent ship, a fact not relished by *Dance*. But ... a day or two to top off *Dance*, a few more to sort the holds, and they'd head outsystem to Tania's Ring, another comet run completed, another progress note in the ship's log, another round of contract payments to settle, another step forward in cloudship destiny. Hooray, he thought sourly, no longer feeling very generous to *Dance*.

Here at Epsilon Tauri, *Siduri's Net* had little opportunity for Gray's pretty sail designs, a restriction that grated at Pov. A coincidence of supernovas in Sol's neighborhood had swept nearby space clear of interstellar gasclouds, creating a largely empty local bubble hundreds of light-years across, with Sol and its principal colonies stranded far from the edges. On those edges, just within reach if a cloudship dared, as *Arrow* had dared, lay the star nursery of the Pleiades, the Ophiuchus Starclouds, and a brilliant crescent of protostars in Taurus-Auriga, with T Tauri as its principal jewel. *Net* deserved more than half a life at Tania's Ring, he thought irritably. His mother might fret about the old ways; Pov found his own reasons to fret about the new.

He glanced again around Sail Deck. Benek Zukor sat at the ultraviolet station, his shoulders hunched as he bent over his monitors: whatever Tully had said when he had thrown Dina off Sail Deck yesterday had apparently reduced Benek to monosyllables and an ostentatious attention to duty. The other sail staff, Pov noted, chose to ignore Benek's acting. Did the staff like Benek? he wondered, eyeing the man. The chance rotation of watch schedules usually put Benek on Roja's nighttime watch, and Pov hadn't had much reason to notice him—until now. Even among the small staff of *Net*'s forty-odd sail techs, Benek had managed to efface himself, Fifth Sail or no.

Should I notice him? Pov wondered, and decided to think about it for a while yet. Tully would probably know best, since Pov's brains were probably disconnected on the subject.

What could Dina possibly see in *him*? he wondered then, but the wondering stung less than he'd expected. Certain choices badly dented a certain credibility. On the other hand, if Dina could see potential in Benek, it didn't say much for what she had seen in Pov Janusz. Pov couldn't decide which idea bothered him most and stored it.

To Benek's right, Sail Tech Celka Matousek sat at infrared, sketching her stylo over her screen to rearrange the computer windows in a configuration she liked better for some reason. When she was done, Celka glanced around the deck abstractedly as she stretched her shoulders and saw Pov watching; she gave him a quick smile. Celka was a pretty blonde in her late teens, mostly Czech in descent and probably smarter than Pov and other distinguished types but content with her current glory, knowing other glory would come in its own time, as it would. Both he and Tully had mental flags on Celka's performance file: she really was very good, quick, alert, mature beyond her years, among the best of *Net*'s young people rising in the ranks.

Two older techs, both First-Ship Slavs like Benek, manned the visible-light and gamma screens; across the room, Avi Selenko, another of *Net*'s Russki additions and already at Sixth Sail rank, sat at the communications station, riding the link to the forward chevron of *Net*'s skyriders and to *Dance* behind. Added to Celka's curvy blondness, Avi's sleek dark hair worn up and smooth, her long legs, and all the length between made pleasant sights to look at, when you're sailmaster and can look and could call it duty. Avi caught him looking nonetheless and wrinkled her nose at him, then self-consciously patted her hair.

Duty, Pov, he thought again, and looked down at his command monitors. A stream of data raced across his screens, reporting on energy flow, charge, and random masses of the ionized particles scooped into the sails. More specialized monitors at the side stations registered specific energy wavelengths: ultraviolet, infrared, some x-ray, and the short span of visible light. Sail data converted easily to light readings, transmuting charge, spin, and mass into detectable radiation lengths: at plasma density and flow, electromagnetism dominated the phenomena and ruled the sails. Computers could do all kinds of things with photon readings, and Sail Deck took as many versions as its staff could track.

Other monitors tracked the extension of the sail webbing, the spiderweb of superconductor filament that supported the sails in full extension. The Pleiades cloudships, Pov had heard, now had sails five kilometers wide, too delicate a fabric for sailing a comet. Athena customarily kept several drones forward to watch for dust concentrations, but the heavy coma, the bright cloud that surrounded the comet nucleus, was often impenetrable to most sensors. To supplement the probes, *Net*'s chevron of six skyriders watched with smaller versions of *Net*'s sails that did not collect, only detected, watching from an exposed position just outside *Net*'s ship field that was usually safe—if they kept alert.

The spiderwebbing gave Pov detailed control over the shape of the sails' magnetic fields: some of the netting stretched a half-kilometer ahead of the ship, creating the looping skysails and widespread spinnakers of full sail. Other netting supported the sails against a sudden influx of particles or dust that made more a rolling charge than discrete missiles punching holes in anything convenient. The sail lasers blasted away at such micrometeroids that might pierce *Net*'s hull or create other havoc inside Janina's collecting holds, but a dust charge of tinier motes merely riffled the sails much as a breeze shook a ship's sails in ocean sailing—pretty to watch but hard on field integrity, itself a standing wave within limited parameters. On the other hand, a riffle didn't bother him, not when *Net* sailed hull-on in smooth plasma flow: the sails were designed to handle it.

"Dust count?" he asked Celka.

"Still high, sir," Celka answered. "Avi and I ran a comparison study last night, and this one is shedding dust high above the average. It may be older than we thought."

"I thought Omsk had it tracked as a short-term comet."

"The low debris density in the orbital trace suggests a younger comet, sir," Celka told him, "but it's not acting that way. We've counted at least a dozen dust storms of Class Eight intensity in the last course, three peaking to Class Two, like the one that nearly caught you yesterday. Either we're uncovering a very large gas pocket across half its face or the nucleus is breaking up." She grimaced. It wasn't a great choice.

"Watch the carbon monoxide." The CO radicals, liberated from the surface grains when heated by Epsilon's solar wind, usually gave advance warning of a bad dust storm—though not always. He thought a moment, considering, then pulled Celka's infrared readings onto his own screen and scowled at them.

"Avi," he said reluctantly, "inform *Dance* we advise against slip course." Captain Rybak would refuse, but he owed the gesture.

"Yes, sir," Avi said. "Not that they'll listen to us peasants," she added, making a wry face.

"That's enough, Avi," he reproved.

"Sir," she said, "one of the nice things about being a peasant is freedom to comment." She grinned at him challengingly.

"Oh, really?" he said, challenging her back.

"Oh, really—at least until you get unreasonable ideas about your worthy self, sailmaster, sir. Then the sun will truly dim." Avi turned back to her comm console, and a ghostly chuckle slipped around the deck from the other staff. Pov scowled, knowing he'd just been neatly pinned flat. "Informing *Dance*," Avi said sedately.

"Thank you, comm."

He caught Roja's open grin and gave him an intimidating stare, then let it go. When Avi stopped saying what she thought, the hell with consequences, then he'd worry.

"*Dance* refuses," Avi said a moment later, as he expected. "Assuming slipcourse in our bow wave."

"Keep alert, people." A ship riding the bow wave of another cloudship could catch a lot of trouble very fast. *Net*'s bow wave concentrated the plasma flow, the reason why *Dance* chose the benefit—but it also concentrated whatever dust and other hell spun back toward them, without much room or time to dodge.

The elevator door swooshed open behind him, and Stefania Bartos, Athena's Second Helm, skipped quickly across the floor and plopped into the chair beside him, gusting an expressive sigh. I have returned, Pov thought, interpreting, but made himself nod congenially. Why did Stefania's trips to the john always involve such a dramatic effort?

"All clear, sailmaster?" Stefania asked in a high nervous voice.

"We're doing fine, Helm. Welcome back."

The mild sarcasm sailed right over Stefania's head. She nodded abstractedly and resumed her watch on the sail operation, her long fingers tapping a steady rhythm on a chair arm. Pov shifted in his chair uneasily, already regretting the end of her brief absence.

Stefania had an uncomfortable gift of worrying herself aloud through every difficulty, a nice counterweight to Athena's own tendency to barge around, Athena said. Nicely blond with a poise that utterly deserted her on Sail Deck, God knew why, Stefania's breathless voice and mannerisms did not mesh well with his patience, however solid Stefania had proved herself in other ways after *Net*'s original Second Helm transferred back to *Dance*. Each time Stefania sat with him on Sail Deck he promised to be more forgiving, but she still drove him crazy every time.

"Sometimes," Stefania said nervously, "I regret being Second Helm. Why do I always get unnerved up here?"

Pov repressed an automatic comment to that and chided himself. Be nice, Pov. Stefania jiggled in her chair, then sighed and patted her hair. Pov shifted again in response and decided to watch Avi. I didn't promise to like *all* women, he told himself silently, just most of them. Avi looks especially nice today. And I don't really *dislike* Stefania; I just wish she . . .

"Why do I keep thinking something's going to happen?" Stefania blurted, commenting to the open air. Pov closed his eyes a moment, repressing another remark he shouldn't make. Stefania waved her hand, then noticed a fingernail to chew and did so, nibbling with tiny bites that Pov somehow felt march up his own person. Be nice, nice, nice. . . . Then Stefania flinched as one of the skysails suddenly brightened into a brilliant actinic blue.

"Report," Pov said quietly, looking over at Celka.

"Rolling dust charge, sir," she replied. "It phased in with the sail frequency and moved on. No damage."

"Dust storm?" Stefania asked breathlessly.

"I doubt it. But if it is," he drawled, "wait until you see the lasers really start blasting. It looks like the sails are exploding." He grinned at her fatuously.

Stefania glared back, finally picking up a little reality about a certain sailmaster and not liking it. Pov wondered suddenly if he irritated Stefania just as much with what he did himself and never noticed, whatever it was. Now that was a thought to comfort.

"You're a big help," Stefania said. "Why don't I sense any sympathy?"

For what? he thought irritably. Flipping all over my Sail Deck? "Sorry, Stef," he said insincerely. "I still think the chevron's too close in. Will you agree to moving the skyriders out another twenty kilometers?"

It was the third time he had asked. Stefania considered the question, her brow creased.

"Too risky," Stefania decided, too quickly and thus probably for the wrong reasons.

"Not as risky as what you're trading for," he grumbled, but *Net*'s Second Helm wasn't clued in to subtle hints. Stefania gasped again as the sails flickered slightly.

He shifted in his chair, then scowled at the main wallscreen as he flipped through a few desperate strategies. When another laser fired, Stefania jumped again, and Pov scowled even more fiercely as his heart rate automatically reacted to her false alarm. Then Stefania began running her fingers at a gallop inches from Pov's own elbow, and he swiveled his chair, choosing the craven.

"Roja, trade chairs with me. I want to watch the generators for a while."

"Yes, sir." As Pov traded chairs with Roja, Celka gave him a wry look, then stifled a giggle behind her hand. Celka thought Stefania a total fool, and had said so aloud in selected company.

"That's enough, sail," he muttered.

"Yes, sir," Celka said demurely.

Ten minutes to relax, he thought, enough to restore me. Then I'll be dutiful.

"Oh!" Stefania exclaimed behind him.

Strategies, he thought desperately. Unluckily for him, sound traveled well in atmosphere, but evacuating Sail Deck to vacuum seemed a little extreme, however the idea tempted. Stefania gasped yet again, then talked loud inanities some more, using Roja as the target. Pov closed his eyes a moment, trying not to wince. He heard Celka laugh at him softly, just loud enough for him to hear.

She drives me crazy, he thought helplessly. I can't help it. Really I can't.

The sails flashed yet again, enough to illuminate even his own monitor, and his attention suddenly diverted from the trivia of a shipmate's behavior. "What's our probe data?" he asked Roja.

"Some minor disturbance ten minutes ago, sir, but the coma haze is still heavy." Roja touched a control switch on the main console. "Some minor radiation levels are up, sir, mostly infrared, but nothing remarkable." Both winced as another flash lighted the sails, enough to flare across the deck.

"Pull in the grid to half-sail," Pov ordered. "Avi, alert *Dance* to a possible duststorm."

"Yes, sir."

He turned and looked at the sail extensions on the main wallscreen. When a pocket of gas exploded off the nucleus, it pulled heavier dust with it, which would fit the elevated infrared reading. Dust emitted infrared, a few degrees of temperature above the usual few degrees of open space, unlike the shorter wavelengths of plasma ions. At this extension, *Net*'s sails could handle some dust, but he preferred a more conservative arrangement.

"What's the hydrogen concentration?" he asked Celka.

"Ions only, sir: no radio-wave ranging at all."

"Carbon monoxide?"

"Slightly elevated. No discernible upswing."

"Damn," he muttered. "Take a sample, Benek."

"Yes, sir."

"Has *Dance* acknowledged?" he asked Avi.

"Not yet, sir. It's hard to punch a signal through our bow wave at their angle." She tipped her head and listened. "All I'm getting is the carrier beam. They *are* back there, aren't they?"

"Ions and ten percent dust, sir," Benek announced. "But that's not enough to flash the sails." On the heel of his words, the spinnaker flashed ruby crimson, a sheeting glare that glanced off every polished trim on the deck. "God!" Benek swore.

"Advise Helm to slow speed!" Pov ordered. "Skyriders break chevron and get back here. Pull in our sails!"

"Carbon monoxide just went up, sir!" Celka called out.

"Warn *Dance*!" The skyrider chevron abruptly dissolved and the skyriders scrambled back to safety behind *Net*'s sails, then swept under *Net*'s hull wings, dashing for home. Pov flinched as the upper skysail flashed again, a ruby crimson glare that swept downward, illuminating both skysails. "Avi, do you have contact with *Dance*?"

"Contact now, sir. Sailmaster Ceverny, we are advising dust storm—"

An instant later, a claxon sounded as several micrometeoroids escaped the sails and punched through *Net*'s upper hold baffles. Other particles still caught in the sails vanished under a nearly continuous sheet lightning of laser fire. Then a glowing reddish arc formed in front of the ship and slipped wide into the bow wave, flowing backward around *Net*, heading for *Dance*.

"*Dance!*" Avi shouted. "Dust coming your way *now*!"

Pov hit his comm-link directly to Athena. "Helm! Change course."

"I see it," Athena responded. "Forty degrees starboard, people, on the mark, do it *now*. Get *Dance* out of our draft. All skyriders still outboard, get under our lee."

Net swung quickly, turning outward toward open space. As *Net* turned, Pov trimmed the sails to a protective mode, then spun the skysail far to port to shield the aftward core as *Net* escaped the dust storm in its path. Five minutes later, *Net* had reached a thinner area of the plasma flow, easily diverted by the ship field and his battened sails, and slowed speed. Pov quietly replaced Roja at the central console, then monitored the steady flow of reports over the all-ship channel. Captain Andreos appeared on Sail Deck moments later.

"Are we clear?" he asked tensely.

"Clear, sir," Pov said. "Some damage to two outer hold doors, but Janina's crew is sealing the holes now." The holds had the advantage of near-vacuum, and apparently none of the dust had holed any habitat sections farther aft, thanks to a convenient initial trajectory and a last push by the edge of the skysail. Pov showed the captain his data screens, and Stefania courteously retreated to a side-station chair.

"Advise *Dance* we have minimal damage," Andreos ordered. He puffed out a breath and scowled at Pov's screens. "That was close. Any acknowledgment from *Dance*, comm?"

"Not yet." Avi glanced at a panel. "Helm reports *Dance* is not behind us, sir. We do not have a fix on her in this soup." She looked guiltily at Andreos. "Uh, in this dense medium, sir."

"Soup will do." Andreos scowled at the wallscreen. "How much warning did we have?" he asked Pov.

"Just minor infrared levels, captain, then a CO flash. I warned *Dance* immediately."

"The sailmaster was not at the central console, sir," Benek blurted in a quavering voice. Pov swiveled to stare at him in surprise. Benek flushed but looked stubborn, then gulped nervously as Andreos also turned to stare. "He was not at his console," he repeated, saying it louder.

"I was at the generator monitor," Pov said angrily. "What does that have to do with anything?"

"He had left his station, sir," Benek repeated again, looking straight at Andreos.

"Pov?" Andreos asked mildly.

"Probe data is displayed on comm monitor, sir, only copied to mine. Whether I was here or over there made little difference." He looked up at Andreos, trying to control his temper at Benek's open ploy.

"Hm. Makes sense to me." Andreos shot Benek an unreadable look, then turned his shoulder to the man.

"Sir!" Avi said, catching the attention of everyone on deck. "Contact with *Dance*. They are reporting ..." She turned, her eyes wide. "Major hull damage, captain, at least a half-dozen holes. Both skysails have collapsed, and ..." She stopped and concentrated, then keyed her console to feed the data directly onto Pov's central screen.

Pov whistled as he and Andreos scanned the data. "The dust storm must have hit them full-strength off our bow wave. They barely made it away."

"Call the holdmaster and assemble some crews to help," Andreos ordered grimly. "Ask *Dance* if they have casualties."

"Captain Rybak is calling now, sir," Avi said. "Transferring from central comm."

"Put him on the screen at Pov's station." In the small viewscreen on Pov's console, an image flicked on of a very angry Captain Rybak, his beard jerking with rage. "How can we help, Captain?" Andreos asked.

"We're handling it," Rybak said harshly, nearly shouting his words. Rybak had a temper that could be awesome, but in all the years Pov had known him he'd never seen the man as angry as he looked now. "I hold you responsible, *Net*."

Pov and Andreos exchanged a surprised glance. "For what, sir?" Pov blurted. "Dust damage?"

"I have eight holes through my hull," Rybak roared and struck his fist hard on his console. "*Three* cargo holds contaminated or vented to space. That's twenty percent of cargo lost, not to mention the cost of repairing the sails and hull. Thank God no one died, or you'd have four times the penalty to pay!"

"Hold that a minute!" Andreos protested. "*Net* isn't responsible for comet instability."

"*Net* had the lead and the duty to warn," Rybak said contemptuously. "Read the operations protocol."

"We did warn," Pov said, reacting hotly to Rybak's tone. "We had ambiguous data and we warned you as soon as we saw a storm coming. In fact, I warned you off from the entire slip course. Read your log." He felt Andreos nudge his shoulder, and Pov struggled to moderate his voice. "I sent a warning as soon as conditions permitted, Captain Rybak, as soon as we had a window on the hazard."

"Not soon enough," Rybak said dismissingly, all his arrogance showing in his patrician face. "I suggest that *Net* review its sailmaster's competence and act accordingly. In the meantime, we will assess our damage and inform you of the bill."

Andreos tightened his fingers on Pov's shoulder. "*Net*'s opinion of its sailmaster is *Net*'s affair, sir. And penalties are set by the intership board, and you know it. You were warned. Pay for your damage yourself."

"We'll see about that," Rybak snapped and abruptly blanked his screen.

"Avi," Andreos said quietly into the silence that followed, "call *Dance*'s holdmaster and ask him directly if he needs assistance—don't go through *Dance*'s central comm. Then call Mr. Haralpos to take over the sail watch. When Tully gets here, Pov, I want to see you in my office."

"Yes, sir." Pov saw Benek turn back to his station and caught the look of satisfaction that crossed the man's sallow face. Andreos had no right to reorder his sail deck watches, excepting emergency or Pov's incapacity: he preferred to test right now if that "incapacity" applied. "I would prefer to finish the watch, captain," he said quietly. It caught Andreos' attention. The man straightened and threw a quick look around the deck at the people who listened and watched, as staff always did.

"I apologize, sailmaster," Andreos said, raising his voice just a little. "Captain Rybak has surprised me again, and I presumed. The end of the watch is quite adequate. By then we'll have more data on the incident to review."

"That's quite all right, sir. Thank you." Andreos laid his hand on Pov's shoulder again and pressed reassuringly, then quickly left Sail Deck.

"I'll be on Helm Deck," Stefania announced, not that anyone objected, and Stefania beat a hasty retreat. As the elevator hissed shut, Avi and Celka both looked back at Pov. He appreciated Avi's thumbs-up, then frowned reprovingly as she turned it into a different gesture for Benek.

"That's enough, Avi," Pov warned.

"Are we on the green?" Avi asked Celka, ignoring him.

"All nominal: shifting to automatics," Celka replied. Her hands moved smoothly over her board. "Roja, take the light watch."

"That's on," Roja called from his station. Both women rose and advanced on Benek. Avi leaned over his chair and whispered something in Benek's ear for several seconds. Pov started to get up to intervene, but then both women parted and strolled back to their stations. Benek had turned a pasty white, too shocked by whatever Avi had said even to swallow. "Taking back the watch," Celka called out.

"That's off," Roja responded.

"Thank *you* sail," Pov announced sardonically and heard Avi snicker softly. The look she then gave Benek was pure venom. She leaned over toward Benek.

"And that's just the first part," she said. "Then you get the second part."

"Avi!"

"Yes, sir?" she asked brightly, turning toward him. She batted her black eyelashes fetchingly.

"Uh . . . never mind."

"That's an off, sir." Avi turned back to her board.

Pov took a deep breath as the sail routine resumed smoothly, as if anything could be routine now. Avi took supplementary reports from *Dance* about her damage, and Pov winced as the other cloudship's damage roster mounted. *Dance* had survived largely intact, true, considering worse possibilities, but her repairs would be expensive. Such crippling could ruin a cloudship, parlaying a repair bill into bankruptcy and seizure by the colony government, dooming the ship to government payroll for the rest of her existence. *Ishtar's Fan*, with her various misfortunes, had skirted that fate for years, and Rybak faced a similar risk now, despite all *Dance*'s years in-system of good runs. And Dina would circulate the news of Benek's claim back to *Dance*, and Rybak would find his scapegoat, with helpers a little closer than Pov found desirable.

A few minutes later, Athena sent him a probe report on his private channel, terse and to the point. Half the comet wasn't there anymore. Young or old, this comet had chosen to disintegrate in their faces without any of the warnings predicted by the cloudship's computer modeling. A younger comet might do that, but rarely—not that true age mattered much now. Had *Dance* been hit by one of the comet's larger fragments, half her crew would have died in that single massive explosion, crippling the ship into a drifting hulk slowly pulverized by other debris. Did Rybak realize that? Pov wondered. Did he even care?

Was I too slow to warn *Dance*? he wondered uneasily. Could Rybak be right? He thought over each of his actions from the time *Dance* assumed slip course to the sudden influx of CO and its sharp warning of disaster at the end. The dust sample was low: the CO reading might vary, but plasma distribution of dust in its charged field always gave some kind of dust warning, something. It didn't make sense. On the other hand, the cloudships had never had a comet disintegrate in their path, as had happened here: did the parameters change that much when a comet broke up? And how could he get the data to run an analysis on a single-event curve?

It didn't make sense. He had warned *Dance* against slip course altogether, and Rybak would not appreciate Pov's foresight in being right. When Pov had been appointed *Net*'s sailmaster, Rybak had grudgingly yielded to Ceverny's recommendation and Pov's other support on *Dance*, but the older man had grumbled afterward in private. Rybak had not wanted a gypsy as *Net*'s sailmaster, for no reason except Pov was gypsy. Pov had accepted the bias with the ranking, determined to prove a Rom sailmaster the measure of any First Ship Slav. He had thought he had succeeded.

Was I too slow? He reviewed everything again, and decided he had not been. *Will the truth be enough?*

Will Net defend me? he wondered then, startled by the abruptness of the doubt. To his dismay, he realized he didn't know the answer, not for certain. He'd had a number of certainties undone in recent weeks: this might be the next.

He smiled as Avi found a weak excuse to walk over to his station, then later walked amiably over to Celka to look at some inconsequential reading she could have easily sent by screen. The others on Sail Deck chimed in, letting him know in subtle ways what they thought of Benek's accusation. Good people, the best. *Gaje,* his mother would say dismissingly of them, caught in her gypsy attitudes that had preserved Rom life for centuries. *Rai,* he amended silently. He would not allow himself to lose them easily, he promised himself, whatever Rybak's machinations against Pov and *Net* herself. He would not easily give up half his world, gaje as it was.

The elder Rom would call that choice foolish—why struggle for something a man didn't need to be himself? To need something the gaje controlled bound a Rom, a restraint the gypsies had always refused, keeping their own way. It was the gypsy choice, one that preserved a way of life for centuries, a way he valued as an essential part of himself. He sensed another choice ahead, one that might strip him of half his life, leaving him half a man.

I need *Net*, he thought sadly. I want her as I have her now, not as some minor sail tech to Sailmaster Zukor, lost in the lower ranks in disgrace. I want her as sailmaster. I want to take her to T Tauri or the Pleiades, where she can be everything she deserves to be. I want that wider horizon that *Dance* chooses to scorn. Why is that wrong?

Easy for you to say "Why want it?" he thought more vigorously, answering that ring of shadowy Rom faces. Easy for you to say "Rom is enough."

Not for me.

Chapter 4

Tully came early at the change of watch, and Pov took the elevator upward to Andreos' office. He checked in the shipmaster's private office and found it empty, then wandered down the corridor, looking through the nearby conference rooms. In one of the smaller rooms he found a glowering Milo Cieslak bent over a report, a disorderly sheaf of papers and data disks spread out in front of him across the polished table.

As Pov sat down in the chair opposite him, Milo looked up and his glower deepened. Pov tried to stifle his answering irritation at the unspoken reproof—at Pov or the problem, whichever beetled Milo's brows. He stretched out his legs, then returned Milo's unfriendly stare. *Net*'s lawyer was not happy, he could see. Well, who was?

"A nice fix, Sailmaster," Milo growled. "What in the hell happened up there? Why did Sail Deck drop the ball? It's the last thing we need."

Pov glared at him. "Why don't you find out the facts before you start shoveling the blame, Milo?" Milo's face smoothed abruptly and he looked at Pov with a different interest, his lean face closed and wary. Pov stared back, not giving an inch.

"Really," he said, then quirked an eyebrow. "No delayed warning? No sailmaster off station and sleeping maybe?"

"Nice of you to assume it was."

"Calm down, Pov. Listen, I'll give you a free downput about me, and you can cash it in whenever you want to make us square." He smiled affably, as if a pretty apology mended everything and put Pov's feelings on adolescent level. Pov twined his fingers together underneath the table and pressed hard, trying to keep his temper.

He and Milo had never meshed well, however much Milo liked to mesh. Milo's Rumanian family had joined *Ishtar's Fan* several years after her commissioning, late enough to deny the Cieslaks First Ship ranking. The difference in status ate at Milo subtly, an ambition he'd never admit and could never attain, despite his marriage into a First Ship family. Poor relations stayed poor relations, a fact of life. Pov remembered how as a boy Milo had carefully avoided him, as if Pov's gypsy taint contaminated with too much contact. Pov had resented it, still did a little.

Milo grimaced. "All I've heard is *Dance*'s side so far—in spades. Their chaffer has been sending me one contract clause after another, and the damage list is already very expensive. They have too much sail damage to continue the run, so you can imagine what their profit just shrank to with their hold losses."

"Any injuries?"

"Some decompression injuries, one very bad, but Medical expects she'll survive: most of the injury is to the hold structures and the loss of product. So tell me."

Pov shrugged. "Andreos can pull the data tapes for you. We had ambiguous readings that justified our not warning at all, but I sent the warning anyway. Avi had some plasma interference, but *Dance* had time to get out of the way—not much time, but that's what happens when you ride a bow wave. It's an excuse." He rocked slowly in his chair and looked distractedly at the door. Where was Captain Andreos?

"I've heard you weren't on station."

Pov's temper abruptly flared again. "I *was* on station, goddammit. I was sitting in a different chair. So what? Since the data came in at Celka's station, it didn't matter where I was sitting." He looked away, fuming.

"Well, I have to ask. Even a gypsy sailmaster has to answer for his . . ."

Pov's eyes snapped back to Milo, and Milo stopped in midword. They eyed each other a long moment, and a slow flush began spreading upward from Milo's collar.

"So that's what made up your mind before I even walked in?" Pov asked bitterly. "Doesn't it matter what really happened? Thanks a lot, Milo." Pov started to get up, and Milo irritably waved at him to sit back down.

"Sit down, Pov. I'm sorry. I was out of line." Milo smiled like a dying man in rictus, obviously jarred out of his usual bigshot-Slav act to be a little human. "Please." Milo gestured at the chair. Pov hesitated and then reseated himself.

I ought to walk out, he thought. I ought to.

Milo jiggled his pen, tapping a quick rhythm on the table, as he looked Pov over. "Somebody's got it in for you good, don't they?" he asked quietly. "And it's not just Rybak. Someone First Ship?"

"Benek Zukor, my Fifth Sail. He's my ex-girlfriend's new protégé. Dina is ambitious."

Milo twisted his mouth. "So drop him right off Sail Deck."

"What kind of waves would that make? Righteous Fifth Sail reports his sailmaster's incompetence and is tossed down the elevator? That'd be fun to explain."

Milo shrugged, then gave Pov a wintry smile. "Well, there's one counterbalance: it's probably in *Net*'s interest to protect you, not that I'm making promises. You're smart enough to realize you're at risk? Good. But if the ship concedes you did anything wrong, we get to pay *Dance* a wish list on penalties."

"You will find, when you review the data tapes, that I *did* do nothing wrong."

"It's always nicest when morality supports the practical. Can I offer you a bit of advice?"

"Sure, Milo."

"Keep your temper under control. You look like you could tear this table apart."

"I could," Pov admitted. And not just the table, he thought.

Milo grimaced. "With cause, I'm conceding that, and I'll try not to add to the mix. Sorry. But I need you calm and assured, doing the righteous sailmaster act. Emotions during contract negotiations are always a weakness unless they're calculated and dropped in at exactly the right point, and I want you to follow my directions on that. Understand?"

"All this took me by surprise, Milo."

"Well, now you're not surprised."

Pov nodded and tried to relax.

"Good," Milo said. "You're a good sailmaster, Pov, but chaffing is a whole different world where straightforward doesn't exist. It's friendly conversation with knives pulled, with the whole ship at risk on a few intemperate words at the wrong time. I've been expecting *Dance* to start something, considering our efficiency and especially our ship history. Captain Rybak isn't stupid: he knows the cloudships have a risky future here in the Hyades, but he doesn't want to start over again in the Pleiades, where *Arrow* is mopping up the profits and won't like us moving in. Here we've got a sure deal. If *Net* buys out early, he loses advantage."

"And so he tries to sabotage us? Hull damage? Radiation injuries?"

"Business is business." Milo shrugged.

"I'm not accepting that. It reeks."

Milo suddenly smiled. "That's because you're a sailmaster: in physics all principles are clear and beautiful. It's not so pretty in what I do. Trust me in this, Pov."

"If you say so," Pov said sourly.

"I am sorry I jumped to conclusions. And that's not

a calculated emotion." Milo's smile deepened. "Sometimes I get to be human."

"It's okay." It really wasn't, but Milo had made the gesture. "Has *Dance* filed its formal protest yet?"

"They may wait until we dock at Tania's Ring, maybe earlier. In the meantime, get a copy of the Sail Deck record and study it: you'll be our key witness at the intership hearing." He looked around at the doorway. "Andreos must be hung up somewhere. Let me find him. We need to coordinate on this."

"Sure." Milo got up and left the room, leaving Pov to stare at his hands.

Keep your temper, Milo had said. Easy for a chaffer who had learned the art, not so easy for Pov. He felt a slow boiling anger at Rybak, at Dina, for risking his post for their own purposes, making him a scapegoat if they could. Benek was only Dina's tool, the idiot, though it was an idiocy he understood too well. He got up and paced along the table and back again, conscious of each footfall, each breath, the steady thudding of his heart, as if they measured out a scale of how much Pov wanted his rank and all it brought him—or the time he had left to possess it.

He wasn't naive, whatever Milo thought in his patronizing way: ship politics had destroyed a master before, choosing convenience over the individual. The Rom solved such disasters by never choosing gaje rank, and by defying society's strictures that accompanied position and owning things. A colored wagon, a cache of jewels beneath a floorboard, a fierce prideful defiance, with a whole gaje society to fleece with fortune-telling and nimble wits: the gypsy life had endured for centuries with such simple gifts. Perhaps compromise undid all the advantage by making a man want something others could control, something beyond the free open air, a rutted narrow road to wend, and the unquestioned bonds of family.

He had considered *Net* a wider circle, as sure a connection as the fierce love of his tribe, a confident trust in the ship and people who encompassed his life. Perhaps it was something to trust safely, but if *Net* chose to protect him, the reasons were alloyed with self-interest. He wished it otherwise: did accepting a compromise defeat the value? Was exclusion, a practice of the Rom for centuries, the only clear truth?

I don't want to be a sacrifice, Pov thought. I don't accept that kind of disposability. Not in a young ship, not even with *Dance*'s predatory attitudes toward *Net*, like an aging mother resenting the youth and strength of her daughter. Just as his mother struggled to keep Kate within an older style of life, *Dance* would now use this incident to restrain *Net*, with himself right in the middle of it. But what does Rybak preserve? Can it even compare to a tradition of centuries?

He clenched a fist and studied the muscles and tendons of his hand, then relaxed it slowly. Not easy.

After a few minutes more, Milo returned with Andreos. "It's a sizable list," Andreos said tiredly as he walked in and handed Pov a paper printout.

Pov scanned the list and sighed. "Can they make it stick, sir?"

Andreos turned to Milo as the chaffer was starting to sit down. "Will you excuse us, Milo?" Milo opened his mouth, then shut it foolishly. Andreos took the chaffer's arm and walked him firmly to the door, then shut it after him. As he turned back to Pov, Andreos answered Pov's look with a shrug and tired smile. "Chaffers think in predictable patterns, and I prefer your full attention, Sailmaster, not reactions to Milo."

"Milo has his point of view," Pov said sourly.

"Indeed he does, leavened by a few additions. I'm sorry I didn't get here sooner before he dropped them on you. His is one viewpoint that needs to be aired, but not the only one."

Andreos sat down heavily across from Pov and took another paper from his tunic pocket. "I also have here a preliminary report from Fifth Sail Zukor. Any reason why he's pushing this? It's hardly consistent with his performance record."

"He's Dina Kozel's new flame. She's, uh, developing him."

"Dina Kozel? Weren't you and she . . ."

"Not anymore." He set his jaw. Andreos grunted noncommittally and handed him Benek's report. Pov frowned as he read it, then looked at Andreos squarely. The captain had supported him in front of his sail crew—he appreciated that: now Pov could see what Andreos, with all his years of experience in the higher captains' politics, really thought of the situation, away from staff morale, away from public appearances, and away from Milo's advice. Pov felt a cold pit in his stomach, an ice that spread upward, as Andreos slowed rubbed his nose and sighed.

"Malice is an interesting emotion," Andreos said and took back Benek's report, then folded it back into his tunic pocket. "It's the small things, the personal things, that always mix in. We bind ourselves in words of iron, our clever clauses in our contracts for our economic benefit—but the human element always shows itself. Zukor and Kozel are both First Ship Slavs, aren't they?"

"And Janusz isn't. Will it come down to that, bloodline?"

Andreos smiled then, the lines in his face easing. "You expect me to say it will, don't you?"

"I don't know what to expect, sir." Pov looked down and studied his hands, and heard Andreos' chair creak as he rocked it.

"I've always liked having the Rom aboard *Dance* and *Net*," Andreos said musingly. "Until the true nomads joined us, some part of the frontier would always escape us." Pov looked up, surprised. "Not all the gaje are blind, my young gypsy friend—or so easily fooled by sleight-of-hand, Rom or otherwise." Andreos got up and poured himself a glass of water from the carafe on the sideboard and took a long swallow. "I don't like it here at Tania's Ring," he said. "Too many Slavs on every side—and I can be enough of a bigot to draw broad categories of Slavic this and Slavic that: there are similar rumors, totally untrue, about us Greeks." He leaned forward, his eyes narrowed. "I won't see *Net* bankrupted nor made less than she was built for. Quite aside from justice, of course."

"Thank you, sir—I think."

"Why did you leave your station, Pov?"

"Well, sir ..." Pov began, then realized nothing but the truth would sound credible. "It's Stefania, sir. It's 'ooh' this and 'ah' that and cute starts and breathless exclamations, and she drives me crazy every time she's on Sail Deck. You said the human always gets mixed in." Pov looked away unhappily. "She's just that way, I know, and means no harm—hell, I bug people, too, but ... So I made Roja trade places with me for a while. It meant maybe twenty seconds I didn't see the infrared readings on my own screens—but it wasn't that kind of data, there it is and so move fast. I moved earlier than some other sailmaster might—and my staff was tops through it all." He fretted, suddenly realizing that Celka and Avi might be in trouble, too. If Rybak wanted to ply a wide brush.

"None of your staff is at risk, Pov," Andreos reassured him. "This all sits on you."

"Great." Pov gave him a rueful grimace, then accepted it with a shrug. "Could Rybak really take something like this and make it into a wish list?"

Andreos calmly reseated himself. "He might—if he gets Russki help."

"From Bukharin?" Pov thought about that, realizing what the Tania's Ring trade chief might do if he got a whiff of contention between the cloudships—as he almost certainly would. "Rybak isn't that stupid."

"No? When Rybak rebuilds his sail assembly, you can bet he'll put in *Arrow*'s sail designs and add it to the repair bill—with suitable padding, he could make a very long list, enough to bankrupt *Net*. What if

Dance's list is so long we can't make the payments? Tania's Ring helpfully steps in and assumes the payments we can't make—at a price of a majority of our shares, of course. *Dance* gets its construction payments, Tania's Ring gets us, and in a few years, *Dance* finds new pastures to graze while we toil on forever for the New Rodina."

"God, sir."

Andreos shrugged. "Even if we skate past outright bankruptcy, Bukharin would love to use his money well, just to help us out. Say a loan for a minority proprietary share in *Net* that he can wheedle into more, or maybe a veto on ship operations, after suitable consultation, of course. The erosion starts small, and there are lots of trajectories to waking up one morning and finding you're owned. Don't scowl, young man. If you're shipmaster material, which I think you are, you have to grow up and stop thinking everything has the beauty of those sails of yours."

Pov stared at him levelly. "I don't like it, sir."

Andreos smiled. "I agree, but there it is, like it or not. I've watched Bukharin negotiate with Milo and *Dance*'s chaffer often enough to know Bukharin plays his own game always, and sometimes the biter can get bit. I think Rybak is a biter who might get surprised."

"Do you really think Captain Rybak planned all this?"

"I doubt it. But who knows what sticky webs our Ms. Kozel has been spinning with her relatives on *Dance*? I don't think Ceverny would cooperate—he's too much a sailmaster in the important ways—but there are lesser types on his staff who think ambition excuses anything. They could have looped in Rybak by pushing the right buttons. Even so, I doubt Captain Rybak expected that long a list, but since it's here, he wants us to pay for it." He smiled grimly. "Maybe we will."

"Absolutely not, sir," Pov said indignantly. "*Net* was not negligent!"

"I told you justice didn't have much to do with it. Could your sails handle a protostar?"

"Sir?"

"T Tauri, to be specific. A protostar isn't something I'd like to toy with—I prefer disintegrating comets— but the Taurus-Auriga starstream is the only coherent nebula complex near the Hyades."

"Nearly three hundred lights away, sir. That's a lot of reaction mass to get there."

"And a hydrogen sea to harvest when we do. Could they handle it?"

Pov blinked. "The design specs come from *Arrow* herself—what they'd share, of course—and they've been harvesting interstellar clouds for a couple of decades. But we haven't lost yet, Captain!"

Andreos shrugged. "First shipmaster's rule, Pov. Always have your next move planned before you need it: improvising is useful in its place, but risky for the long term. I want to tempt Bukharin with a hold of pure tritium for those ambitious dreams of his for Tania's Ring. If we can disturb a few lines of alliance, it might be a move at *Dance*'s expense that I can turn to our profit. Besides, however irritating we find the current relationship, we are still partners with *Dance*, with Bukharin fidgeting in the wings wanting to cut in. Do you understand?"

"No, sir," Pov said firmly.

Andreos chuckled. "Draw up the design parameters and give me a report—confidentially." He motioned Pov to his feet, then stayed him with a flick of his long fingers. "Another shipmaster's rule, Pov, probably the fundamental: all that matters is the ship and the people who are that ship—and when somebody forces a choice between ship and people, it's always the ship that wins. Does that bother you, too?"

Pov smiled. "In a way. You're saying that *Net* is a Rom tribe."

"Exactly. And Captain Rybak may be the ultimate gaje." Andreos relaxed, apparently more worried than he'd let on. About what? Pov's cooperation? Or merely the risk to *Net*? Or did his shipmaster understand Pov's love of Sail Deck more than Pov assumed? I don't understand anything, Pov thought as Andreos dismissed him with a nod. Pov got up and walked to the door, then turned back.

"About that first rule, sir: when did *you* stop believing in beauty? I think you're very disappointed in Captain Rybak."

Andreos smiled sadly. "I was a young man under Rybak—I learned everything I know from him. Yes, I'm disappointed. But that doesn't mean the principle is wrong: it just means I'm fallible and not the shipmaster I could be." He saluted Pov with his water glass. "Go along now, Pov. Let me mourn a little."

Pov touched his heels together softly and nodded deeply, offering his respect. "Yes, sir."

He spent most of beta watch in his quarters, repressing his impulse to wander down to Pilot Deck or Janina's holdmaster's station, knowing it could easily turn into his own mourning. Captain Andreos, with his talk of captain's politics and scheming, had calmed him more than Milo's lectures, but he knew himself poor company. So he inflicted himself only on Pov Janusz, a tolerant fellow for his own feelings.

His small apartment was located on an outward projection just forward of the central holds, chosen for its view window looking sideways across *Net*. In his comfortable chair, he could watch the lights winking on the prow and the shadows moving on the forward bridges that linked the prow to nearby structures; by stepping closer to the window and craning moderately, he could even glimpse the engines far behind the body of the ship. It was a view he liked, another way to watch *Net*. Tonight he turned off the room lights and sat in his watching chair, nursing a glass of Sergei's vodka, a holiday present he usually drank to celebrate a suitable good occasion and usually not alone.

Until recently, Dina had sat in the other chair by the window, chattering in a way he had found fascinating, especially when she found yet a new trajectory to her favorite topic of sex. He turned his glass in his hand as it balanced on the upholstered chair arm, smiling slightly as he remembered several particular nights. It was one way to live wholly in the present, assuming certain things could last forever. How much of how he felt now was sexual ego? How much was love? He still hadn't sorted it out, hoping some magical spell would name it while he wasn't thinking about it. No such luck. He saluted Dina sourly with his glass. He had thought himself an intelligent man, a good judge of people: how had he been so wrong about Dina? That bothered him more than it probably ought to: women had made fools of men before.

Illusions can be shattered in different ways, and Dina had chosen a rather brutal variety. At least he hadn't pleaded too long—he had that much pride left—and hadn't humiliated himself by following her around, letting everyone see the rejection in all its barbed and pointed commentary. He had retreated into silent misery for several weeks, enough to worry Kate out of her mind, and had finally resolved it by resolutely *not* thinking about Dina, ever, and had practiced the skill determinedly. But he would have to think about Dina now. Benek might have signed that report, but he had recognized several of Dina's phrasings, distinctive word habits carried over from Dina's native Bulgarian to Czech, the ship's official common speech. He thought about that, his former lover helping another man arrange his destruction.

And how long *will* you grieve, Pov Janusz? He reached out a foot and pulled over a low padded bench, then settled more comfortably by propping up his feet. Wallowing, he thought, had its charm: it at least had the ease of familiarity. He sipped at his drink, making sure it went slowly. The vodka settled in his stomach with a warm glow, false but still warm.

"Good evening," a voice said immediately behind him, and Pov sloshed half his drink all over his lap. As he cursed and brushed at himself, Tully grinned and flopped down in the other chair in a lazy sprawl. "Don't you answer your doorchime now?"

"Didn't hear it—and you just shortened my life by a few days, thanks so much. Want a drink?"

"Sure." Pov got up to get a glass from the kitchen and washed his hands, then poured Tully a drink and brought it and the bottle back into the living room. "Good to keep the bottle in the kitchen," Tully advised judiciously, "not at your elbow."

"I'm not getting drunk, Tully. I'm just having a drink. There's a difference." He scowled ferociously at his friend, reproving him, then sat down again. "How'd the watch go?"

"Routine. Lots of unnecessary chattering among the techs. I had to comment officially to shut it up."

"And the verdict on the predictable topic?" Pov took another swallow, watching *Net*'s lights wink like fireflies, gold and red and bright blue.

"Pov . . ." Tully fell silent, long enough for Pov to finally glance at him. "You sound bitter. Is there real trouble?"

"Do I? I don't mean to. Don't worry about me, Tully. Captain Andreos has a plan, and Milo is no doubt conjuring clauses over his computer screen."

"And Rybak is sharpening his knife."

"Andreos knows that. So do I." He looked out the window and smiled. "I always think *Net* is beautiful. I just sit and watch, and find her exquisitely lovely, every time. Kate has her fancy piloting, Mother her traditions: I have the way *Net* looks to me. That isn't at risk, you know, however Rybak decides to carve me up. Negligence charges aren't enough to get me tossed off *Net* altogether if I don't want to go. So I'm sitting and watching *Net* tonight." He looked at Tully defiantly.

"And whatever you say about drunk and drink, you're smashed, sailmaster."

"Partly, only partly. This is good vodka. One of the better Russki inventions."

"Really. I'll inform Tania's Commodities Bureau when we get to Omsk. They'll be thrilled."

"Thanks for coming by, Tully."

"Anytime, you lush. Top off my glass, will you?" He held out his glass and Pov neatly filled it nearly to the brim, not spilling a drop. Tully raised a congratulating eyebrow. "They say the reflexes are the last to go," he said, "The mind melts first."

"Here's to melted minds."

"*Stin'ya saas*," Tully said in Greek, lifting his glass in a salute. "Cheers."

"*Sastimos*," Pov replied in Romany and saluted him back.

They sipped at their glasses and watched the lights blink, the farther dusting of stars against a wide blackness still partly obscured by comet gas. "How are you feeling?" Tully asked too casually some minutes later. Dr. Tully, Pov decided, out on night rounds.

"Confused. Wondering if Rybak's right. Wondering if it even matters who's right."

"The scuttlebutt is that you gave warning far earlier than some masters might have. Dust pockets are hard to see until they're practically swarming into your sails. You know that, Pov."

"Yeah."

"So why am I hearing a dirge in the background?"

"Milo believed it on the spot. Asked me how a sailmaster could screw up like that, practically before I could sit down. I nearly walked out."

"Hell, Pov. Milo is a cold-minded fish who hasn't had a native emotion since he got out of puberty." He waved at the window. "Milo never looks at *Net*, just to watch."

"True."

"So why care about a man who doesn't have a soul? What did Andreos say?"

"He has a plan." He smiled at Tully. "T Tauri. But keep that under your hat awhile. Andreos is planning it as an ambush on Rybak, maybe with Bukharin's help."

"The protostar?" Tully's eyebrows climbed.

"Rough environment for sails, maybe."

He saw Tully's eyes go abstracted as he thought about it, then watched the slow smile spread over Tully's face. "*Net*'s built for it. Hell, Pov, we could bring back a triple-rich cargo of radicals, maybe even a compartment of tritium. Imagine: an entire hold section filled with pure tritium. Tania's Ring couldn't take it all, even as fast as they're building reactors."

Pov nodded. "Better than that, friend. We could sell tritium all over the Hyades, maybe cut a wholesale deal with *Ishtar's Fan* just for old times' sake and watch Perikles get apoplexy at the markup Captain Janda will slap on it." He waved his glass expansively. "Hell, we could even dump part of it into Aldebaran and ruin those short-range carriers' market for years. And then, when we're rich, we buy out from *Dance* and tell Rybak what to do with himself." They both contemplated the prospect for a long moment. "Money is nice," Pov said.

"Amen," Tully responded fervently. "Of course, we could get fried, too. T Tauri isn't exactly stable. You got shock waves and UV bursts and unstable magnetic clumps. There're reasons why the probable profits have never justified the risk, not when you've got nice tame comets to chase."

"Well, that." Pov waved his glass dismissingly.

"And we've never done it before. Nobody in Taurus has."

"That, too. There's always a first time for everybody."

"Your calm alarms me for some reason. May I point out that Gray never redesigned *Arrow* to go farming protostars, and even so we didn't get *all* his sail modifications when *Dance* built *Net*. We could end up needing something badly we just don't have."

"True. Andreos wants specs. Why don't you think up some parameters and we'll do some dreaming?"

"That's okay." Tully laughed. "And I thought this was a wake."

He shrugged. "Maybe it is, but whatever happens, I can go along to T Tauri if I want to. I've been thinking about that, too." He raised an eyebrow at Tully. "And you might be sailmaster when we do, Tully. So climb off the ceiling and start worrying." Pov smiled genially at his friend, knowing he'd drunk too much vodka and not caring much that he had, either. Alcohol had a numbing effect he felt like appreciating tonight. "To T Tauri!" He raised his glass.

"You keep saying 'if you want to,'" Tully commented. "Sounds ominous."

"Never analyze a drunk's speech. There *is* no logic, only misfiring neurons. Makes a random brain plasma."

"Really."

"Pov's theory of higher thought. Professor Pov—now that's a label I could use."

"Well, Prof, can you navigate to bed?" Tully asked.

"Surely. This is a comfortable chair, though. And I'm not *that* drunk, Mr. Haralpos, thank you so much."

"Aren't you?"

"How many times have you seen me drunk?"

"That's the point. I haven't. Not even over Dina. Forget Milo, Pov. He's just a chaffer—what counts is what Sail Deck thinks, what Kate thinks, right? Who cares what a gaje chaffer cares about anything?"

"Andreos said I was shipmaster material."

"You are. What will you name her when you get your ship? And can I be sailmaster?"

"Sure." Pov smiled dreamily. "What would I name my ship? I don't know." He laughed self-consciously.

Tully sometimes surprised him with the oddest ideas. "I really hadn't thought about it. Besides, you know that's settled by committee, anyway."

"But if you had the choosing, Shipmaster?"

"I'm not shipmaster yet, you idiot."

"But."

Pov gave in and thought about it. "Well, let's see. It would be *Siduri* something, not something new. I like Siduri. She told Gilgamesh that a man finds his happiness in music and the dance, in a wife and children, not the immortality Gilgamesh wanted. But Gilgamesh wouldn't listen, the dope."

"Just as the Rom don't listen?" Tully was smiling at him, his face shadowed by the dim light from the window.

"Not at all. We take the music and love and family with us, and get the unending horizons, too. Gilgamesh just got the formula wrong—should have listened better. Comes with being a mythic hero type, I think."

"But you never find Siduri's island long enough to stay, Pov."

"Maybe not. Hard to drag an island with a wagon." He sat up a little straighter and tried to focus on Tully. "What kind of conversation is this, anyway?" he asked indignantly.

"Oh, just suggesting another horizon when even harvesting a protostar needs vodka to get a friend along."

"I'm all right."

"I beg to differ."

"I just . . ."

"What?"

"I just object to the methods. Milo thinks it's all proper sleight-of-hand—who cares what's the truth? Andreos plans ahead for countermoves, thinking he can finesse that to get this. Why doesn't anybody just stand up and tell Rybak it won't wash? Make him take his damage list and stuff it? Where's the truth, give it a capital T?"

"Maybe life isn't that simple."

"Why not, oh wise one?"

"Beats me. Why is Dina such a witch?"

"You and Kate—I don't want to talk about her. Okay?" Tully shut up and sipped at his glass, looking out the window at *Net*. "Sorry, Tully. I didn't mean to snap."

"She help Benek with that report?"

"You know about that?"

"This ship is a sieve—everybody knows about it by now."

"Great," he muttered.

"But, just to let you know, Benek won't last long on Sail Deck if this goes against you. Not even Slav connections can loft him over my seniority, not right away, and so I'll make sailmaster before he does. Greek feuds also have a tradition of centuries."

"Axing Benek won't put me back up in rank," Pov pointed out.

"True. Well, I thought I'd offer."

"I appreciate the loyalty, Tully, but if I lose sailmaster rank, not much else will matter, not even revenge." He looked at his glass. "But I appreciate it."

He sensed Tully watching him. "Why don't I put the rest of that bottle back in the kitchen?" Tully suggested.

"Am I that soused?"

"No, but you'll get there after I leave, I think."

"Likely so." He saluted Tully again with his glass and then drained it. "Point me at the bed, Tully old man."

"No way. You're coming with me."

"Where?"

"Well, Kate told me that Marina Slovnik just got her second pilot's bars and they're having a party on Pilot Deck, so you're going."

"Kate, huh? I should have guessed. No parties, Tully."

"Definitely parties. Music, dancing, weird jokes, getting sloshed, pilot panache. Maybe I can fix you up with a date if you cooperate. I've heard pilots are great in bed, especially the women." He spread his hands expressively. "See? The eventual object is still the same—bed. It's how you navigate there that matters, especially the celestial bodies who help you along."

"Irisa would love to hear this," Pov grunted.

"Irisa knows all about it. She merely insists on exclusivity." Tully grinned, then got up and pulled Pov to his feet. "Not that I argue with her—and you're not going to argue with me."

"You Greek," Pov said humorously, not resisting him much.

"That I am."

Pov set his empty glass down on the table. "Then lead on, sail. Chart the course."

"That's a deal."

Chapter 5

Pov woke up the following morning in a bed not his own. He opened his eyes and stared at the unfamiliar ceiling for a while, trying blearily to place himself in the universe, whatever spot this was, then fingered the silky patterned bedsheet on his chest. No clue there, except it definitely wasn't his bedroom. As he raised his head slightly to look over the room, a jabbing pain seized his temples. He dropped his head back on the pillow with a groan. There's a reason I don't drink often, he reminded himself. Really a good reason— why do I forget that?

With another groan he rolled himself to sit on the edge of the mattress and held his head for a while, then became aware of the shower running behind the bathroom door. He twisted around slowly to look at the other pillow, then saw the rumpled clothing on the floor beyond, his and definitely a hers. Well, he hadn't slept alone, and he wondered soggily what else he didn't remember. He looked down at himself and saw he was still wearing his shorts, but that clue was ambiguous at best. What a mess. The water stopped and he looked up as a towel-clad Avi Selenko stepped out through the door.

"Morning," she said brightly.

"Oh, God," Pov muttered and decided to hold his head some more. He heard her laugh softly, then the soft padding of her bare feet over to his side of the bed. He looked up as she touched his shoulder.

"I said, 'Morning,' Pov."

"Is it?" He looked up at her in despair.

"You passed out," she informed him, her eyes dancing. "Don't roll in the guilt quite yet."

"I did?" He straightened, feeling a stab of sharp relief, then saw her laugh at him because of it. Her long dark hair tumbled around her shoulders, dripping wet: on Sail Deck she always wore it up, prim and severe. He looked at it distractedly, then got distracted again by her towel. Brain plasma, indeed. "I'm sorry, Avi."

"For what? Passing out? So am I."

"No, not that. For this—" He gestured vaguely at the rumpled bed.

"Personally, sailmaster, I think you should have listened closer to Tully's prescription. Getting laid cures a lot of ills."

He smiled at her ruefully. "And you decided to be Dr. Selenko?"

"And I wasn't the only volunteer, sailmaster, sir." She bent and brushed his lips with hers, then walked toward the outer door. "Want some breakfast?"

"What time is it?"

"Early," she said over her shoulder. "Enough time for breakfast—and prescriptions, if you're interested." She didn't wait for a reaction, just sashayed out in her towel. He watched her go, then stared at nothing in particular for a few moments, dazed. He tried standing up, then made a second attempt and wobbled over to his clothes. Putting on his pants required a seat on the bed; he gave up on the shirt after he put his head through a sleeve twice. He walked out into Avi's outer apartment with half of him covered—it seemed all he was able to manage.

Avi was busy at the kitchenette on the far wall, fixing something on the stove. "Juice on the sideboard," she said. He walked over and picked up one of the glasses, took a swallow, then turned around and leaned on the counter for support.

"God, I feel awful."

"Ought to drink more often. Builds up your tolerance."

"Nuts."

She giggled and stirred vigorously at her pan for several seconds, then dropped the spoon abruptly and crossed the few steps between them. As she slipped her arms around his neck and pressed close, she looked up with a question in her face, a little uncertain. He smiled down at her and raised one hand to toy with a damp tendril of her hair for a moment, then gave in to the sweet impulse she invited and kissed her.

"Ah, nice," she sighed a minute later. "I always wondered how you kissed."

"In between or after you put me in my place on Sail Deck?"

"Both. Are you going to take me up on my offer?"

He sighed, sorely tempted, but suspected it would be a mistake he'd regret.

"You want to know reasons?" she asked. "Do you always need reasons, Pov?" She disengaged herself a little, and he was suddenly afraid he would wreck something he valued just because a hangover had leached his brains.

"I just don't want to lose your friendship, Avi. Sex changes a relationship."

"Don't confuse me with the likes of Dina Kozel, please. I'm unattached, not in love with anybody, somewhat plotzed on you, at least enough for me to notice it regularly, and when Tully brought you to the party last night you looked like death on legs. If an hour or two with me in bed helps, I'm offering. And change is a matter of choosing, right?" She touched his face, drawing her fingers lingeringly down his cheek. "Don't you sometimes let people help?" she asked softly. "Or is part of being gypsy always being self-sufficient, an island in the sea, no matter how much it hurts?"

"So they tell me." He slid his hand over the smooth

skin of her shoulder, taking his time at it, then tangled his fingers in the hair that tumbled down her back, caressing its damp length. She shivered. "I didn't know you had such pretty hair." He wrapped a frond around his finger and let it fall into a curl on her shoulder. "I'm still drunk, I think."

"That's on, sir. I don't mind." She pulled his lips down to hers and kissed him again, a long lingering kiss that didn't help the fogs in his mind. He felt her chuckle as he swayed off balance. She pushed him back upright and stretched out her other arm to pull the pan off the burner. "You just stay there a moment, sailmaster."

"Staying, ma'am." Then he let her lead him into the bedroom.

"It's always different," he said later.

"What?"

"Sex."

"Don't tell you're *analyzing*. Don't you ever stop?" She levered herself onto one elbow and glowered at him, her dark hair swinging to cover one breast. He caressed its silkiness gently, then cupped her breast.

"Appreciating. There's a difference."

"You do look more relaxed." She grinned at him impishly, pleased with herself. He smiled at her lazily.

"I may never move again. Thanks, Avi."

"Encores anytime, Pov. Just ask." She lay back and stretched out beside him, their bare skin touching from shoulder to ankle, a relaxed and easy feeling he liked. "And that's a serious offer," she said after a while. "As I told you, I am somewhat plotzed about you."

"Really."

"Can't imagine why," she teased.

"Neither can I." She chuckled low in her throat and turned on her side to trail her fingers down his chest, then walked them up again. He grabbed at them, missing badly. His reflexes were still shot, he decided. "What watch do you have today? I forget."

"Still beta watch. I'm on swing this month while beta gets upscale training."

"Hmmm. Today's a free day for me. Want to do something today?"

"Like what?"

"Kate's always nagging me to go skyriding with her for fun. She has this idea I don't have fun, silly as it sounds. Want to go out and look at *Net*?"

"Sure. Don't tell me we're starting a romance."

"I don't know. It's brain plasma—I developed this problem a while ago and my brains get short-circuited, so I don't know things I ought to." He hesitated, trying to see her face better in the shadowed bedroom. "Do you want to?"

She thought about it, then wrinkled her nose at him. "I don't know, either." They looked at each other and then laughed at the same time. "Well, store that for now," she said. "Let's go skyriding."

"That's on, sail."

Kate was agreeable, and Pov had a good morning watching the two women get better acquainted before Avi went off to beta watch. That night he took Avi out for drinks at the main companionway lounge, a nightspot frequented by pilot types with their rowdy ways. When the concessionaire had pointedly screened off a few alcoves from the noise, the skyriders merely elevated to steeper heights and ragged the poor man incessantly until Athena paid a surprise visit as stern pilotmaster, made the worst of the offenders ante up a penalty, and threatened terminal mayhem on the others if they didn't tone it down. Most of the skyriders cooperated good-naturedly, buying the proprietor several rounds of drinks from his own liquor whether he wanted them or not, and then helped him bodily toss out the one skyrider who drunkenly decided to test Athena's envelope. But the proprietor left up the screens, anyway, irritably daring the pilots to start anything. So far the skyriders had demurred.

As they walked into the low-ceilinged lounge, Pov glanced around the varied crowd scattered at the small tables, most of them people just off shift from the nearby decks. Along one long wall, a bar stretched its padded leather and polished studs for nearly ten meters, comfortable stools set at intervals for leaning, the traditional ranks of inverted glasses hanging from the hood above. The crystal sparkled in the muted light of the lounge, a subtle counterpoint to the table lights and decorative light-art on the opposite wall. Pov followed Avi to a corner alcove in the back, and they ordered drinks from the lighted tabletop's menu display.

Avi had dressed up in something silky, long, and red that set off her dark hair and figure nicely, then added some jeweled earrings that winked subtly in the soft light of the lounge as she looked around at the nearby tables. She looked back at him and smiled, then tipped her head. "Hungry? I haven't eaten yet."

"Not particularly. You go ahead." Avi tapped the table display and ordered some dinner, something salad and a light side dish. A minute later the automatic waiter opened, dispensing their drinks, and she slid his glass over to him, then half-turned in her seat to look over the lounge again, her earrings flashing against her pale skin. He sipped at his vodka cautiously, making himself a silent promise about smart, then watched Avi as she watched the crowd.

"Quiet tonight," she said.

"Skyrider inspections, Kate told me. It's always quiet here when Pilot Deck is busy."

Avi grinned. "True. What's it like having a skyrider for a sister?"

"Fun. Kate has good friends on Pilot Deck. They watch out for her when I can't."

"Is that part of being a brother, watching out?"

"Sure. Why not?" He looked at Avi quizzically.

"Seems a little old-fashioned to me. Kate doesn't seem the type to need the protection."

"Maybe not," he said agreeably, not wanting to argue about it. "How about your family on Tania's Ring? They have a co-op farm, don't they?"

"Yes, but I don't keep in touch." Avi fiddled with her glass uncomfortably. "Let's call it a mutual lack of interest. I tried, really tried, but finally I told Papa I had no intention of spending my life stamping around the family mud paddies, married to his brain-wipe of a son-in-law who was more interested in the Great Rodina and tannenberry graft-clones than in me. So I divorced Andreiy and got that tech posting on Omsk Station, then plumped for *Net* as soon as I could scrounge the buy-in fee. I've never looked back. They don't miss me and I certainly don't miss them." She scowled.

"Hard to not have family, Avi," he said sympathetically.

"Don't commiserate, Pov. I don't need it, okay?"

He raised his hands. "Sorry."

Avi flushed slightly, then shrugged an apology. "It's not something I like to talk about."

"So what's a better subject?" The waiter delivered her dinner in the slot and she pulled out the two plates and unwrapped her fork. She smiled.

"Sort of inverting this, aren't we?" she said, gesturing around at the darkened lounge. "Usually the mating rituals come first—you know, the dinner and conversation, being seen, seeing back, some slow dancing and maybe some extended groping in a dark corner. Then, after more deft maneuvering by both sides to the mutual object, comes bed. We seem to have it backward."

"You're the one who dragged me home. Not that I'm complaining."

"Neither am I." She winked at him and took a bite of her salad. "Sure you're not hungry?"

"I usually eat at my apartment or over at Kate's," he said, dogging some explanations he'd prefer not to make yet. He didn't know how much Avi knew about the Rom, and had enough history with Sergei's early incredulity about the Rom purity rules to avoid the topic with Avi for a while, at least until he and Avi felt more comfortable with each other.

He had grown up in a Rom household with its careful divisions between *wazho* and *marime*, the Rom words for purity and impurity that related closely to personal honor and one's identity as a Rom. Washing his hands after touching his lower body, dividing his laundry into separate washes for shirts and trousers, and not mixing certain foods in the same dish felt as natural to him as his sail patterns. As a scientist, he knew the purity rules were mere superstition from a primitive past, but they defined the Rom and he kept them as best he could without making an ostentatious issue of it among his gaje friends. Those who knew him well, like Tully and Irisa, interested themselves in the rules to keep him at ease and never mocked, and Tully had been so constantly around the Rom that he sometimes unconsciously hesitated before doing something *marime*, a problem in learned behavior that amused them both when it happened.

Still, sometimes Pov felt very aware of the difference, as he did now, and fretted about it. With Dina, he had chosen to forget *marime,* perhaps sensing instinctively through his haze his lover's probable reaction to something so completely outside Dina's own rigid patterns. At the time, keeping Dina was more important than everything else, even his Rom honor; it had been an uncomfortable choice he now regretted and preferred not to repeat with Avi.

"Hmm," Avi said absently and sampled her side dish. "I never do get used to real meat. This looks like chicken."

"Probably grouse. Tawnie says Biolab is experimenting with some genome ribbon samples *Dance* got from Perikles last year. She and another biotech decided to raise a flock of grouse for the commissary."

"Tawnie?"

"One of my younger cousins. I'll introduce you sometime."

"Sure."

Pov glanced around the lounge, looking at the people who chatted and relaxed over their drinks, then saw Benek walk in the outer door, neck craning as he looked for someone at the tables. "Excuse me a moment, will you, Avi?"

Avi looked up from her salad and smiled. "Of course, Pov."

Pov eased himself out of the booth and headed for Benek, and saw himself spotted when he had crossed half the lounge. Benek stared at Pov, then swallowed nervously and looked around, jarred toward flight at the mere sight of his sailmaster. Well, *Net*'s Fifth Sail had caused, Pov supposed.

"Benek!" he called as Benek turned to leave. "Wait up, will you?"

"I don't want to talk to you," Benek said, retreating a step. "Leave me alone."

Pov crossed the remaining distance in several long strides and caught at the man's sleeve. Benek shook him off angrily, then looked past Pov and gulped. Pov turned and saw Avi hurrying toward them with long strides, her expression hard.

"Go back to the table, Avi," Pov called. "I'll be along in a minute." Avi slowed in midstride and looked a question. "Please, Avi." Avi stopped, then complied reluctantly, looking back at them over her shoulder as she walked back to the table.

Pov turned back to Benek, very much aware that they had attracted attention from all over the lounge, enough to stop most of the table conversations. "I don't want to make a scene, Benek," he said, "so calm down. I just want to talk to you."

"Leave me alone!" Benek threw up his hands as if Pov had struck at him, his face contorted by fear.

"God Almighty, Benek, I'm not going to hit you. Will you calm down?"

Benek threw him a wild look and darted out of the lounge. Pov stared at the empty doorway a moment, then sighed and tugged at his ear in perplexity. Maybe some impulses weren't worth starting, he decided. Did Benek really think Pov would start a fistfight over Benek's sail report? Obviously. As if beating up Benek would solve anything, even if Pov felt inclined. He shrugged expressively for the benefit of the nearby tables and walked back to Avi.

"What was *that* for?" Avi asked as he sat down again.

"I wanted to talk to him, *mesh*, as Milo Cieslak calls it. Benek's still part of my sail staff, Avi."

"He's a sneak and a liar," Avi said angrily. "He—"

"Dear heart," Pov interrupted, cutting her off firmly, "I'm asking you to tone that down. I don't want any more scenes here or on Sail Deck about Benek." He moderated his voice, trying to take the sting out of a flat order. "Sailmaster talking here. I appreciate the defense, but I'm asking."

"I can't believe you," Avi said. "What he did was way out of line! What kind of noble act is this?" She stared at him incredulously.

Pov's jaw tightened. "So what would it solve to smash Benek's face? Am I supposed to toss him off Sail Deck because he made a report against me? He has a right to speak up, whatever his motives; so do you. This isn't an autocracy, and I'm not going to make it one. You don't command a deck that way, not if you want the best from your people."

"Sounds like pure Andreos to me," Avi said with a touch of sarcasm. It was not her most attractive point, he thought.

"You'd rather pure Rybak?"

Avi looked away unhappily, unable to meet his eyes. "I was just standing up for you," she said in a low voice.

"I know, but this won't help, Avi. Trust me, please. Let me deal with it."

"All right. I'm sorry, Pov."

"It's okay." They sat through an uncomfortable silence, Avi stabbing her salad uselessly with her fork and Pov busy with designs in the water rings from his vodka glass, then looked up at each other at the same moment. He saw her lips curve upward slowly, giving him a rueful smile, and he smiled back.

"I do like you," she said softly.

"You have a few sharp edges I didn't know about, Avi."

"And you get more righteous than I expected. Like in 'imperious.' "

"That's me, classic Rom male. Comes with the parcel."

"There'll be sparks, I think."

"Probably. Can you be patient?"

"You're asking *me* to be patient? After I jumped all over you about a simple question about my family, then barged over to interfere with Benek?" She laughed at herself, not very kindly, and it was not a happy sound. "He ran away from me, I think, not from you." She flushed and shook her head slightly, making her earrings glitter.

"Suits," he said casually. "I like those earrings; they look good on you. So does the dress."

"Thank you. And, yes, I miss my family." She looked at him defiantly, her chin up.

"Suits, Avi."

"You're too damn tolerant."

He grinned. "Not at all. You just don't know me well enough yet."

"And, no, after thinking it over, I don't miss them at all."

"Suits." He laughed as she pretended to glare at him, then watched her struggle to keep the glare. She lost it and clucked her tongue at him chidingly.

"You sod," she said.

"That's me," he agreed cheerfully.

She pushed her salad dish aside, then stacked the

other dish on top of it. "I'd like to dance, something slow and easy, then look for a dark corner somewhere. How's that sound? And you'd better say something else besides 'suits' or I'll brain you with my shot glass."

Pov opened his mouth and hesitated. "I can't think of anything else. Suits."

She sucked in a breath, then laughed. "Dance with me, sir," she demanded.

Dancing led to several dark corners on their way back to Pov's apartment, and the following morning he left Avi still sleeping to get up and dress for alpha watch. After he'd showered and dressed, he paused in the bedroom doorway and watched Avi for several minutes as she slept, her legs tangled around and about in the bedcovers, her hair streaming a dark cascade over the edge of the bed. It's always different, he thought, tempted to wake her and make himself very late on deck. And it's not fair to Avi to compare her to Dina, he reminded himself and walked on into the living room. Even when the comparison flattered, as it did. He wondered if she had loved her Andreiy once, and what Andreiy had done to lose her so thoroughly. He repressed an unprofessional wish to tap into Avi's confidential psych files, personal information that wasn't necessary to him as her sailmaster and even less as lover when she wasn't ready to tell.

He drank a glass of milk from the refrigerator and washed his hands in the sink, then walked over to the Rom shrine by the window. He made a vague plea to his ancestors about Avi, not knowing exactly what he wished but hoping they might fill in the gaps, assuming the Rom ancients even approved of a gaje lover for a righteous Rom. He studied the small saint's statue in the shrine alcove, a graceful carved figure he always thought more Siduri than the medieval lady she represented, then dropped some herbs in the censer. The herbs ignited on the glowing plate and sent a puff of vapor curling upward.

He turned to see Avi leaning in the doorway, watching him with alert interest. "Good morning," he said and crossed the room to give her a quick kiss. "I'm almost late for watch."

She looked past him at the shrine. "You're Catholic?" she asked uncertainly.

"Sort of, but I'm afraid the Pope would be scandalized at what the Rom do with his saints. We've invented a few extra ones to suit some better ideas, and their feast days are three-day parties with lots of liquor and loud songs, enough to annoy any gaje in the neighborhood. Some of Kate's skyrider antics probably come naturally."

"Well, I saw another sample the other night." She dimpled as he made a face. "You were *very* drunk."

"Don't tell me the details," he warned. "I don't want to know."

"Who is she?" Avi asked, nodding at the saint in the alcove.

"Siduri, of course. Who else?"

"You're right. The Pope would wonder. A Babylonian goddess?"

"So don't tell him, either." He kissed her again, and she surprised him by clinging hard before she reluctantly let him go. "See you tonight?" he asked her in a low voice, responding to her intensity.

"Yes. Take me dancing again, with corners after, will you? I'd like that."

"Suits," he teased.

"Soar off," she announced and turned back into the bedroom. As he left the apartment, he heard her chuckling softly to herself, a sound that pleased him.

In the afternoon after watch Pov went outboard again with Kate to watch *Dance* limp out of the comet's tail. As the two cloudships had sailed slowly out of the gas stream to open space, *Dance* had followed as closely behind *Net* as she dared, balancing the extra safety inside *Net*'s bow wave with the risks of *Net*'s engine exhaust directly into her crippled sails. Athena had lent a chevron of *Net*'s skyriders to *Dance*, and two of the combined chevrons flew in curving formations along the edges of *Net*'s bow wave, extending *Dance*'s zone of safety. A shorter skyrider line had been equipped with heavier sails and flew between the two ships, diverting the worst of *Net*'s engine exhaust. It had worked, though either placement was a rough environment for the skyriders who had volunteered for the duty.

As *Dance* reached clear space, the outlying skyriders wearily broke formation and dropped below *Dance*'s hull in a ragged line, heading inboard. A few minutes later *Dance* slowed speed, increasing the distance between the ships, and the central chevron also broke formation and split off into two curving lines, one for *Dance*, another for *Net*. Kate sighed softly.

"Hard duty," she murmured sympathetically, then clicked her tongue as Epsilon's starlight finally revealed the full damage to *Dance*.

The dust storm had torn large holes in the lower starboard wing, venting several hold compartments in the lower tier. Some of the ragged gaps were several meters wide, a microscopic hole torn immensely larger by the stress of the plasma impacting directly on the metal. Though the other sails had kept partial integrity, thanks to Ceverny and only to Ceverny, half the topmost radio assembly was gone, other fragile bridges bent askew and twisted. The damage gave *Dance* a ragged appearance, like a space-torn derelict empty and forlorn. They watched silently as *Dance* tried to extend its spinnakers and top skysail. Pov winced as the entire structure collapsed.

"Ouch," he muttered.

"If that had been us," Kate asked, subdued, "would we have that kind of damage?"

"Probably. They were lucky to get away with as

little damage as they did. That dust storm could have killed half the crew."

"Smart Ceverny. It was him, wasn't it?"

"Yeah. He knows more about sails than any other man alive, I think. He couldn't stop the dust, so he controlled the flow with the sails he had left, then spun most of it into the bow wave. Saved the ship, maybe single-handedly. If it had been us, *chavali*, I wouldn't have been that good" As they watched, *Dance*'s sails collapsed again. "Christ," Pov swore softly.

"It's part of the risk," Kate said briskly. "I don't plan to stay here for forty years to get perfect info on Epsilon's short-term comets."

"True."

"Right," Kate said, her shoulders sagging. "So why do I wish we had that forty years, whatever I say? I feel just like *Dance*'s skyriders do—this *rage* that this happened to a beautiful ship like *Dance*." Kate pounded her fist hard on her console. "It's not *fair*. It's not right, it just isn't." She massaged her hand tiredly and then sighed. "But it'll be easy for them to blame us, too easy. It has to be somebody's fault, right?" She glanced at him in sympathy.

"So they'll say."

Pov scowled at *Dance*, torn between his outrage at Rybak's blame-shifting and his concern for the older ship. With this kind of damage, *Dance* would spend months in drydock, caught between the delays of its limited repair crew against paying premium wages to Omsk Station repairmen, leaking profits all the way the longer she stayed in-system. Even if Rybak borrowed repair crews from *Net*, he would still have to pay for the labor. Under the circumstances, it was unlikely *Net* would offer for free.

I wish we would offer, he thought sadly, knowing the idea was idiotic in a dozen ways but still wishing, anyway. You wish too much, he told himself, idiot wishes. But he had grown up on *Dance* and knew her as well as he knew *Net*, with a thousand associations and memories bound to the ship and its people: how had matters soured this way? Would that he could bring it all back again, all the good memories before *Net* became a rival to *Dance*. I wish I had St. Serena's magic wand, he thought, bong I'm forever sailmaster, bong *Dance* forgives us for being young, bong Tania's Ring doesn't win and we lose. As they watched, the *Dance* skysail extended halfway and then collapsed on itself a third time.

Pov could have watched *Dance* from Sail Deck or on any other of a half-dozen screens aboard ship, but had come out with Kate in the skyrider to give them more time together. He looked at Kate, worried for her. Though his sister had shown polite interest in Avi, she had been badly preoccupied on both outboard trips, talking less than usual on their first ride "for fun," and talking even less on this one. He had expected Kate to hit the ceiling when the lot hadn't chosen her for this latest skyrider duty, but he saw no sign of that, just the preoccupation. Odd. He looked at her more closely.

"Kate?" he asked.

"Don't ask, Pov. Okay?" Kate suddenly engaged the skyrider engines and took them through a wide trajectory over *Net* central bridges, a dizzying swoop that buzzed the chemistry labs by a few scant meters.

"Kate ..."

Kate muttered indistinctly and hunched her shoulders.

"Shall I guess, then?" he demanded.

"Listen, I'm not meddling about Avi. Why don't you return the favor?"

Pov humphed and decided not. Her mention of Avi gave him a clue: and nothing could really dent Kate's spirits except the ever-present issue about Sergei. "Mother's convening a *kris*," he guessed.

"Not yet, thank God." She gave him a daunting frown over her shoulder.

Pov tried to imagine something worse and thought of an absurd possibility, then decided to use it to cajole Kate out of her mood, if he could. "You're pregnant," he announced and then waited, half-smiling, for Kate to react to the joke. Kate's jaw dropped and she swiveled toward him.

"How'd you ..." She saw his stunned face and snapped her jaw shut. "Blast you, Pov. You were guessing, weren't you?"

"You *are*?" Pov goggled at her. "How'd that happen?"

"The usual way. What do you think?" They stared at each other a moment, then Kate laughed bitterly. "Right."

"And you're going to keep the baby," Pov said slowly, reading the stubbornness in her expression, a determined choice as hard as their mother's certain displeasure. Kate looked away unhappily, unable to meet his eyes.

"Damn right I am," she said fiercely, but would not look at him.

Pov stared at his sister's averted face, appalled. Their mother would not accept a half-gaje child, not when Kate might inherit her rank of *puri dai*. That choice of leadership lay by the Rom's collective vote, and Margareta Janusz would not risk the leadership passing from her line, not when the only obstacle was a willful daughter and a child easily aborted. Gypsy families ran large, when pregnancies were successful: Kate could have other children, their mother would think, giving the Janusz elders more time to shift Kate to a proper Rom husband. And their mother had miscarried several times on Perikles, accepting the loss each time after her grieving: she would not understand how Kate would tear herself apart over one lost pregnancy, would not see the difference she imposed if she forced Kate into it. He looked at Kate's stubborn profile and knew she'd never agree, whatever the penalty to herself and her baby.

Kate punched at her board, rotating the ship quickly until *Dance* was wrong side up, making *Dance* a cloudship indifferent to arbitrary orientations imposed by lesser mortals. "Easier to watch this way," Kate said.

"Sure it is. Swing us back around, skyrider. I already know you're a hot pilot." Kate complied, then put them on automatics and fiddled busily with other dials, but he wouldn't be so easily diverted.

He tried to orient himself to the sudden prospect of being an uncle, something he hadn't expected for a few years yet. It was startling enough to distract him wholly away from *Dance*'s problems, something he hadn't thought possible. "Uh, should you be out here in your condition?"

"We are fully shielded, thank you, and well within the ship field besides. Don't you dare turn into that kind of brother, hovering and smothering and asking embarrassing questions. I'm fine. Sergei's happy. So am I." She looked at Pov defiantly.

"If the *kris* boots you out of the Rom for it, Kate, I'm coming with you."

"Pov!" Kate was aghast.

He shrugged. "I've gotten more support from the gaje the last few days than from any of the Rom." He gestured at *Dance*. "There sit nine cousins, family all my life, and not one word of support even before *Dance* stopped talking to *Net*. Even Mother hasn't talked to me much, just a shrug and a few words. It was Tully that came and sat with me that first night, and it's Athena who's stomping around cursing *Dance* while Andreos schemes. All gaje."

"And Avi?" Kate blurted, then looked upset at herself for mentioning it. She scowled at him ferociously.

"And don't be that kind of sister, snide and jealous and arch. I admit you were right about Dina, but Avi's different. She's my friend and I like her. She's like Sergei in a lot of ways." Kate hunched her shoulders a little, then glanced at him probably sorting half a dozen things to say before nixing each of them. "Come on, Kate. Jealousy doesn't suit you."

"Oh, hell."

"Damnation," Pov agreed. Pov leaned back in his chair and rocked it slightly back and forth. "I've been looking for gypsy tokens in the corridors. Remember how we always find the little messages up above eye level that only a Rom recognizes, a tuft of fabric, a few beads, tied around with golden thread, the way the gypsies on Earth used to leave messages for each other along the road. 'Meet us at Dijon.' 'Savi's getting married on Hallows' Day.' It was a nice tradition, one of my favorites, having us all over the ship. You used feathers from God knows where."

"Biolab. I assaulted the parakeets."

"Humph. I admit I wondered. But I haven't seen any tokens left for me lately. It hurts."

"They don't care about gaje honors, Pov. It's only that."

"But *I* care. Like you care for Sergei. Doesn't that count? What do they want? Do they want me disranked?" Kate said nothing, and Pov felt suddenly coldly still inside. "What have you heard, Kate?"

"Nothing."

"I don't believe you. You've been talking to *Dance*'s skyriders. What have you heard?"

"Truly nothing, Pov. Honestly." She looked at Pov unhappily. "The geno-test says it's a girl, a little girl. If it had been a boy, I might have skated through: but a girl can become *puri dai*, and that's an overt threat to Mother. You know that."

Pov nodded. "So did you, Kate."

"Yes, I did," she acknowledged candidly. "I've been thinking a lot lately about how a Janusz girl gets raised. Mother tolerated you and Dina, just grumbling a little now and then, but wages outright war on Sergei. What's the difference? You're a son and somebody has to marry outside the tribe: even Mother sometimes admits that. Now you're getting involved with Avi, and she won't complain—but she's been closeted twice with Uncle Damek and talks to the others behind my back, all about me. Why are girls treated like owned things? Why is it different just because I'm the daughter of the *puri dai*? Why am I considered polluted because I make love with a gaje and you're not?"

"Polluted? Who called you that?"

"You weren't there during *that* particular argument. It was one of the rougher ones with Mother and Uncle Damek a few months ago. And now I'm pregnant and all the 'shame' will be known, to use the traditional interpretation. It's just awful." Kate's eyes shone with tears and she ducked her head, hiding them. "I thought that if I had a baby maybe things would change.... Now that it's real and it's a girl, I realize what a fool I was. I should have waited. I shouldn't have tried to force the issue."

"You won't lose the skyriders," he pointed out. "Nor *Net*—nor me. And you're not forcing the choice; Mother is."

Pov looked out the viewscreen at *Dance*, feeling a wash of disappointment and loss. What had he told Tully the other night? *We take the music and family with us.* But even a Rom could pay a price, it appeared, when a greater love became a rival, Sergei for Kate, Sail Deck for himself. He might lose sail rank, breath itself to him, and his family seemed to welcome the loss; now he might lose the Rom altogether for Kate's sake. Without Sail Deck, without the Rom: the thought of that loss swept him empty inside, leaving nothing but empty echoes. He tried to shrug it away, denying the fear it brought him like a cold wash of water.

"And I thought life was easy," he said aloud, then smiled at Kate as she looked at him in surprise, tears on her face. She blinked, sending more tears down her cheeks, then straightened in her seat as she tried raggedly to pull herself together. Her effort tore at his heart.

He leaned forward and tugged at her sleeve hard. "When I'm an uncle," he said, pretending outrage that she might refuse him, "can I baby-sit?" His teasing made her smile wanly.

"She'll be a darkish blonde, the test says. Sergei's genes won that war." Kate took a deep breath. "A blond gypsy. Can you believe it?"

"She'll be beautiful, Kate. Just wait and see."

Kate drew her hand across her face, then sniffled. "I hate snively women."

"Oh, they're okay. Let's go inboard. I've seen enough of *Dance*'s problems for today."

"You'll get to see more, I'll hazard. I did pick up some news. Mika says Ceverny's planning to come over and climb you like a tree when we get back to Omsk. He is one *mad* sailmaster, this Mika says. He says it's truly awesome to see how mad. And Ceverny's mostly mad at you, as in personally, with Rybak egging him on every chance he's got." Kate flipped a disdainful gesture at *Dance*.

Pov sighed. "Mika says far too much, I agree." He watched *Dance*'s sails collapse again, folding over each other like a shuttering fan. "Hmmph. Another week of that happening over and over again, and he'll probably skip the talking and shoot me on sight. And I was feeling mournful I hadn't heard from him."

"Consider it a favor, I'd say."

"I agree. Let's go inboard, *chavali*."

Chapter 6

He left Kate to her skyrider checkdown and took a short elevator trip upward to the starboard companionway, then turned left away from Sail Deck toward his apartment, thinking better of his first impulse to confront his mother. His mother too easily used his temper as a weapon against Kate, and she'd see his anger on his face, there to use again. The worry about Kate pricked at him, anyway, making a muddle with Ceverny's bad opinion and his personal future as sailmaster. He let the pattern of his footsteps calm him, nodding pleasantly as people greeted him in the hallways.

Pov keyed himself into his apartment and turned on the ceiling lights, then turned on his computer in the alcove off the bedroom. He could run the T Tauri specs in his office on Sail Deck, but his apartment computer had similar access and he preferred some dream-spinning without interruptions—or inconvenient noticing by his sail staff. There was also the chore of preparing for the intership hearing, something he did not relish. He swore feelingly in Romany—it always felt better in Romany—then gave into the necessity. Duty, Pov.

He got some juice from the refrigerator and sat down at his computer station, then called up several access codes into the library reserves, his sail simulations, *Net's* official records of the last sail run, and Benek's last efficiency reports. He scooted the labels around on his screen, tinkering with a tentative order, then gave in to his impulse and accessed Sail Records about Benek. The computer asked for security codes, which he supplied—an advantage of being sailmaster, he reminded himself—then opened to the first screen about his Fifth Sail.

First-Ship Czech, the file read, a grandson of one of the original signatories of *Ishtar's Fan*. That explained the early promotion: First-Ship rank didn't go much higher than that. Marginal competence in several areas, though Benek tried hard: Benek had poor spatial understanding and a pronounced weakness in mathematics, however doggedly he tried to overcome his limitations. But he did try, stolidly plodding forward, awkward and determined. It was that effort which led Pov and Tully to overlook the deficiencies, and that fact which bothered Pov now. Benek tried so damn hard. He wasn't the type for cheap politics, even bedazzled by Dina.

Pov clicked through the last several efficiency reports, the staff interviews, routine random monitoring by the sail computer during Benek's watch, Benek's sail reports, Tully's own assessments that agreed with his own. Likely Benek would never rise above his present rank, and that posting somewhat exceeded his competence, but he had steadily improved, despite his limitations. Pov scowled, trying to identify what was twigging his uneasiness, the *something* that didn't fit. What was it?

Worse, Benek wasn't the only anomaly in the recent accident. When a comet spun off bad dust, the sample data did not spin up in a sudden surge: it curved in predictable patterns, a phenomenon bound by the basic physics of a charged cloud and the solar energy that melted out a dust pocket. He might doubt his motives in questioning Benek, but such reasons didn't apply to a comet not behaving as it should.

He stored Benek's file to a downward corner, then opened *Net*'s data records of the last run, clicking through to Benek's UV station file. In a comet cloud, ultraviolet wasn't an active consideration—dust ran to infrared and most particles to visible light—and so Benek's station got sampling and some other chores during a comet run. He studied Benek's sample data on the screen, scowling more deeply, then clicked over to the videotape to hear the audible report by Benek. It matched.

But it doesn't make sense, he thought, baffled. On the other hand, just because dust usually sent signals ahead didn't mean it had to. He clicked through other data related to the run, looking for some factor that supported the low dust count: no marked flare in the solar wind that might send a dust explosion out of parameters, no particular rise in carbon monoxide, though that sometimes hid itself in carbon-binding when comet ice was heavily contaminated by other heavier elements. Carbon bound with all kinds of things that scooted by, and this pocket of ice had higher than normal nitrogen and sulfides, lower free oxygen, enough to mix up the proportions. The late CO reading fit, assuming. But there should have been more dust in that sample.

Why wasn't it there? When Captain Rybak could rearrange the composition of a comet at will, Pov would toss in his hat, but he doubted Rybak had quite managed that edge on divinity, at least not yet.

There should have been more dust. He smiled ironically as he realized he felt more *offended* by the comet-data anomaly than anything else. What's the point of physical laws if the universe decides to go uncertain? Well, more uncertain than usual, he amended. At subatomic levels, reality lost most of its larger rules, becoming a cosmic buzz of particles that were likely never where they ought to be, as if God were humming randomly while He worked on His next creation. Even so, comet phenomena didn't get as doubtful as subatomic realities. Comets had rules.

He crossed his arms and stared at the screen, half inclined to prod himself into the other work this morning, but stubborn about that dust count. Maybe it wasn't low, whatever the screen said. Maybe the record was wrong. He began a data scan of the computer log for the sample, using his sailmaster security codes to go deeper into the programming, then tracked patiently into the computer data log with its tedious attention to everything a computer found interesting down to the microchip. A few of the codes he had to look up by rummaging in his side drawer for the small code notebook: it had been a while since he'd used them. Sample taken at 10:42:32 ship time, reading intersected into records at 10:42:57, incorporated in permanent record at 10:52:12. . . . He flipped his cursor back to that line and studied it. Data transcription was virtually instantaneous, limited only by the double-check programs that created backup copies and checked for errors. Ten minutes difference? Not hardly, and only if what went into the permanent record was something else. He pursed his lips and blew a long soft whistle, then sat back in his chair.

The tampering was nearly traceless, limited only by the inevitable cascade from fooling with the computer's time clock. A computer got insecure when it lost track of time: shifting the time-set would ring bells everywhere throughout Sail Deck's data programs, then spread an alarm like sifting ink through *Net*'s entire database, alerting everyone to a virus the system would not accept and was designed to warn against. Somehow Dina had skirted the other program safeguards—it had to be Dina, Benek hadn't the computer skills—but time had defeated her, if only because she hadn't time to find a safe way around the clock program before somebody surely looked at the data. A nice irony.

But how had she got his sailmaster codes? he wondered, puzzled. For the sake of system integrity, only the computer chief himself and the captains had the last four codes. . . . His eyes fell on his code notebook in the half-open drawer. Ah, Dina, he thought. What other rummaging did you do while I was asleep? It made him feel violated, though likely her snooping had more to do with curiosity than an outright plot against him, at least back then.

What had the sample reading really shown? Benek sometimes had trouble reading his displays when he got nervous, as he would when things on Sail Deck got tense. He imagined himself as Benek right then, sorting mentally through Dina's many whispered instructions, knowing he hadn't the talent for quick thinking, wanting to please her desperately, growing more and more confused, maybe enough to misread a sample screen when the tension went sky-high all around him. Had he? Called out the wrong percentage, then looked back at the screen after events had gone inevitably to their conclusion and realized his mistake? What then? Pov navigated into message traffic data and hunted for Benek's cry for help to Dina— one of Dina's whispered instructions? *Call me if you see a chance.* Or had Dina been monitoring Sail Deck through the real-time programming? *Benek, you fool! Now listen carefully....* He checked the shift roster for Computer Deck: she'd been there, but of message or monitor there was no trace. Deft Dina.

He scowled and pulled a slip of paper from a drawer, then wrote down the computer location of the time for Andreos' reference, then thought even better and ran a printout of the screen in case Dina kept on thinking about a certain problem. Then he folded both slip and page into a tight packet and put it in his tunic pocket. He also locked his desk drawer, a bit late, true.

Is that why you ran away from me, Benek, he thought, knowing you're a decent man who would say, knowing it was more your fault than mine, if there was fault—but *wanting* her so much that you'd take the pain, the dishonor, the memory all your life just to keep her? Were you afraid to tell me? Benek might lose everything he loved in Sail Deck through this one mistake, as entangled in a web as hard as Pov's own. Do you know what you've done? Do you know even now?

If Benek had given a wrong dust reading, *Dance* had the trajectory it wanted to dump everything on *Net*—if *Dance* found out. *Net* could argue that it wouldn't have made much difference, how fast it happened, how *Dance* should have been looking, too. And Rybak would smirk and ask pointedly why *Net* had erased the data if it meant nothing. Right.

It's always the people who drive events, he thought—Andreos had the truth of that. Dina's ambition, Benek's star-struck emotions, Rybak's arrogance and fear—and a gypsy sailmaster who might have to give up a few pet preferences to save his ship's fortunes. God, how we'll lie, smiling our innocent smiles.

Where is the fault? Who has the responsibility? Somehow the issue didn't stay stuck at that. He hesitated, then shrugged resignedly. He didn't like it, but it would have to do until he thought of something better.

He closed the windows on Benek's file and the Sail Deck records, then clicked back into the library to hunt up data on T Tauri. The computer looked awhile, then suddenly flashed a neon message in the middle of his screen, nicely actinic blue and decorated with Doric columns and a Grecian lady throwing flowers at a three-headed dog. *Database glommed,* the screen said. *If you want to see it, you come up here.* The message flashed at him a few times, then the dog opened and closed its mouths at the Muse. *Bark, bark*[3], the screen said helpfully.

Pov leaned his forehead on the monitor and sighed. Greeks: God save me from Greeks. He shut down the computer with a snap and headed for Sail Deck.

When he walked on deck, he found Benek sitting stiffly on temporary duty at the command console, looking more uncomfortable than pleased by Tully's handing him beta watch so Tully could go downstairs and play with sail's computers.

"Hello, Benek," Pov said mildly.

Benek nodded his head jerkily, flushing crimson from his collar to his hairline, then half-flinched as Pov stopped beside his chair. Pov repressed a sigh, then saw Benek's expression change to puzzlement at whatever he saw in Pov's face. Pov looked away at the sail display on the wallscreen, not knowing what to do about Benek.

If only everything were as easy and lovely as sails, he thought.

In open space *Net* carried minimal sail, just enough to deflect the isolated atoms of Epsilon's intraplanetary haze and add a trickle to *Net*'s engine-fuel stores. Even at the low concentration, he saw, *Dance* had moved prudently into *Net*'s sun shadow, shielding herself from Epsilon's active radiation to help conserve her tattered sails. No problem, he decided in a glance, not minding *Net*'s favor to *Dance*. Maybe someone over there might even appreciate it.

He walked over to check the UV flux over Celka's shoulder and frowned at the UV level. During this last run into the tail, the comet and the two ships had passed the second planet's orbit, uncomfortably close to the star. Usually the ships broke off the chase sooner: comet instability tracked predictably with the rise in solar radiation as the comet got closer to the sun. Was that the difference in the dust count? he wondered, still testing his ideas.

"Watch the wind activity, Benek," he said to Benek. "I see *Dance* has moved into our shadow."

"Yes, sir," Benek muttered and shifted uneasily.

"That ought to help *Dance*." Pov turned and smiled deliberately at the man, keeping it neutral yet calm, positive yet not inviting, then smiled more genuinely as Avi sneaked a glance around from comm. Benek abruptly gulped, like a chicken eying a cobra on the advance.

"I haven't done anything at all," Avi declared stoutly to Pov.

"Good," Pov said.

"Sir?" Benek asked confusedly.

"Just keep the watch, Benek. I'll be downstairs with Tully." He walked down the stairs into the computer room.

Tully had chased two of the four computer techs on duty to the other side of the room, then had sat down in a station chair for its inconvenient angles to any spying. The move had promptly attracted interested attention from all four techs, and the boldest, Lev Marska, had turned his chair directly at Tully, crossed his arms, and now watched Tully unabashedly. As Pov stepped off the ladder, Lev glanced over and grimaced.

"Big chief arrives," Pov agreed. "Lev, I think you're annoying Second Sail."

"What's up, sir?" Lev said impudently. "*He* won't say." Lev stabbed his finger at Tully accusingly, who grunted back, unmoved. So much for secret studies, Pov thought: he wished Tully had thought of that before he staked out a Sail Deck computer. Lev was bright and ambitious, alert to everything, and loved intrigue. I wish you'd thought, Tully.

"It's a secret," Tully said sternly as Pov sat down.

"*That* I figured out myself, sir."

"Tully and I can always move up to another computer," Pov warned, "and then you guys won't even get a chance to peek." Lev shrugged good-humoredly and threw an expressive glance at his fellows.

"That's on, sir—I guess."

"Thank you—I think," Pov retorted. "I'm asking you four to keep this quiet, by the way. It *is* a secret for now, for ship's reasons you'll understand later. Andreos's orders."

"Yes, sir," Lev said dutifully, then grinned and turned back to his screen.

Pov scowled at the four techs. He was very aware that a loose word spread to *Dance*, even unintended, could ruin Andreos's advantage. Sailmaster codes would protect *Net* against an easy discovery of Dina's tampering, but sailmaster scheming was a little too visible today with Lev watching.

"Maybe we ought to move upstairs to my office," he said reproachfully to Tully.

"Bark, bark," Tully retorted, then added in Greek, "I've been considering strategies." Pov blinked, then looked again at the four techs, all Slavs, a point Pov hadn't noticed. Tully had, probably checking out a hunch in the four's personnel files.

Tully smiled and wiggled his eyebrows craftily, confirming it. Out of the corner of his eye, Pov caught a dismayed look from Lev, then saw the man shrug disgustedly at the other techs.

"Not today, Lev," he said in ship-Czech. "You've been outmaneuvered."

"Hell, sir," Lev retorted.

Tully smiled his Cheshire grin. "The Trojan Horse, Perseus and the Minotaur, the Argonauts: it gives one a certain range on tactics."

"You forgot Xerxes and the dead Greeks at Marathon," Pov retorted in Greek. "Just keep it slow: I'm a little rusty."

"We can use Romany to help you out," Tully suggested. Pov gave him a genial glare.

"Don't show off. So I'm here. 'Bark, bark' yourself. What kind of info do we have?"

Tully brought up a historical display on his screen. "Before we discuss T Tauri in terms of Marathon, why don't we look over Troy and its fabled riches?" Tully sketched the screen with his stylo, windowing up more details from the coded list. "Last year we bought the latest generic data dump from Aldebaran, as usual, and it had some miscellaneous probe data in the right direction. Ashkelon sent a search probe to the Outer Hyades last year to find some more habitable systems—are they thinking of expansion already?"

"They *always* think of expansion. It's in the Koran somewhere, I think." Theta Tauri's Arabs liked gran-

diose statements about their Islamic destiny in all of
Allah's Heaven, including the parts already occupied
by somebody else. It made colony discussions interesting. "It's better than an immediate sweeping conquest
of nearby worlds, you'll agree," Pov said, then threatened Lev with a half-turn of his chair. Lev hurriedly
went back to his computer-punching.

"True, though likely that comes later when they
sweep *back*," Tully said absently, distracted by Lev's
game-playing. Tully scowled irritably, then windowed
more with his stylus. "Anyway, the probe took some
long-distance readings of T Tauri, enough to update
the data Earth has been catching for a couple of centuries." He keyed to another screen and clicked
through several tables of data to a graphic. "They also
surveyed a few of the other protostars along the probe
track. Several of the star stream protostars have companions, like T Tauri does, which'll help our data
profiles."

On the screen, a miniature latticed starpoint embed-
ded in an oval disk turned slowly in space, connected
by light lines to two smaller ovals that hurtled away
in opposite directions. As a gascloud collapsed, its rotation speed increased exponentially, like an ice skater
pulling in her arms during a spin. Unless the cloud
could shed the excess momentum, eventually centrifu-
gal forces overbalanced gravity and tore the cloud
apart again. And so infant stars shed momentum in
various ways, first by spinning a planetary disk, then
by ejecting high-speed gas from its poles or dividing
into multiple stars. T Tauri had apparently done all
three.

"T Tauri ejected its two companions about a hundred thousand years ago," Tully said. "Both are still
moving straight out from the poles at high speed with
these gas streams between." Tully touched the screen
with his stylus, and the computer slowly turned the
graphic in three dimensions, rotating the three-star
system through a steadily shifting angle. "Until T

Tauri collapses some more mass and ignites its nuclear fuel, it won't have enough gravity to pull the others into a mutual orbit. Maybe in another hundred thousand years, and even then one of the companions might escape. Until then, we've got this."

"Hmmm. How fast is that gas flow?" Pov asked, tapping his finger on the gas jet linking the primary with its northern companion.

"Not clear—it's too far away for Doppler scans to be specific. Probably an order of magnitude or two faster than comet flow, with a lot more energy flowing into the phenomena. There's a hint of protoplanets in the outer dust shell, but most of the planetary disk is still scattered debris falling inward to T Tauri."

"Hmmm." Pov took the stylus and windowed up an analysis program and punched in the general parameters of the system from Ashkelon's data, trying to get an estimate of the energy levels building up as T Tauri's gascloud continued its collapse, then frowned as the computer shrugged ignorance. "Undetermined," he muttered. "Big help." Earth might have finally built computers big enough to solve most of a planet's weather system, but even Earth's astronometrical computers couldn't completely solve a star-system like T Tauri. The phenomena were too massive and complex.

"Angular momentum translates into magnetic flux," Tully commented. "Now that T Tauri has ejected its companions, the gas jets might be freezing their magnetic flux, however that happens. But so goes the theory, and if it's right, we may hit one of those, and we won't bounce. That's the Marathon part of this venture, I think."

Pov scowled, then grunted noncommittally and clicked back to the ultraviolet readings, then x-ray. The shorter wavelengths were higher than normal, even through the enshrouding dust. Dust that heavy often absorbed ninety percent of the higher wavelengths, yet still T Tauri showed a broad spectrum:

who knew what kind of maelstrom raged inside T Tauri's planetary disk? The star's light curve also suggested flares, some into x-ray from massive plasma explosions as matter fell onto the star's surface. *Net* didn't dare enter that kind of energy storm. "Humph," he said, disappointed.

"As I told you the other night," Tully agreed, "we could get fried. A protostar during infall can get as active as a flare star, sometimes worse, and T Tauri is still a very young star. Some of its flares might radiate through the entire planetary disk, just punching through the dust and maybe us."

"Not as fast as a flare star, though. We'd have some time to dodge—maybe."

"I like your optimism. Let's hope T Tauri does."

"You think it's impossible, Tully?" Pov asked, raising an eyebrow at his friend. Tully took a deep breath and thought about it, scowling at the computer screen.

"Well, let's say I'd prefer to have a comet fall apart in my face. We don't know these radiation parameters, Pov. A comet is just sublimating ice, not a radiating source: it simplifies things for the computers. I'm afraid the data capacity might get beyond us. It took a Cray Nineteen to finally solve Earth's weather patterns: T Tauri is a thousand times more complex, with maybe weird matter powered by all that energy and making up its own rules. I've hunted through our entire database, and I can't find any close-up studies: it's all observatory and long-range probe stuff." He scowled. "This might be a bit too much as it used to be against wind and wave, as much instinct and luck as concrete knowledge. That kind of energy can tear a cloudship apart. Is not being bought by Tania's Ring worth everyone's death? We could lose everything, you know, including our lives. I was thinking about that this morning at breakfast with Irisa and the kids." He shook his head in perplexity.

"We could leave the children behind at Omsk Station," Pov argued. "Or maybe *Dance* would take some of them for the interim."

"I don't like that, either, but I admit the ship will have to think about options. We put the kids at risk whenever we sail a comet. It's part of what we choose when we join a cloudship, but this . . ." He waved his hand at the screen. "I think it's too dangerous."

"What about another protostar? One that's younger?" Pov pulled up the star trace data of the objects near T Tauri and studied the possibilities. "There's an early sibling moving away from T Tauri, still in the cloudlet stage. Probably too small to ever form a star, even with more infall from the nebula."

"Bad weather to sail, small or not."

"Weather we can handle." He pulled up a star map of the immediate region, still in photonegative black points on white from the original observatory photographs. "How about DD Tauri? Or the open reaches of Hind's Nebula itself? Or, if that's too thin, this wisp over here? We've got a whole star nursery to explore, Tully."

Tully smiled. "You're determined, aren't you?"

"Yeah, and wondering how much of it is just concern for personal fortunes, maybe." He shrugged. "I mean, if we go, I keep my sailmaster rank for a while. Maybe I shouldn't make this decision."

"If Andreos was bothered by that, he'd tell you. I'm not, so trust your Greeks. After all, we're the ones who thought up the Trojan Horse, right?"

"Now that's a comfort."

Tully smiled. "Okay, I agree we've got more possibilities than T Tauri. Maybe even the T Tauri data will look better up close."

Pov looked at Tully quizzically. "I love the way your opinions stay in place, Tully."

"This is dreaming, right? Who expects dreams to be logical—or to stay in place? Excuse me, Pov, I get unnerved when I see that much energy twirling in one place, especially when we're thinking of visiting the neighborhood."

"Write up your negative recommendation for Andreos, anyway. It's only fair to give him both sides of the risk before we commit ourselves." Pov frowned. "I doubt he'll give this to the other captains for decision: it's a shipmaster's choice."

"With his captains' votes all too predictable: Milo no, Athena yes, Janina on the fence, you worrying about how much is Pov and how much is *Net*."

"I could believe you've been at the meetings recently," Pov said ruefully. "But you're right: whatever he does, the decision belongs to Andreos. So let's write it up with that in mind, configured with T Tauri as worst and that ejected cloudlet and open nebula as best."

"That's a deal, Pov. Are *you* going to menace?" he asked, looking past Pov again. Pov looked around and saw Lev's interested clever eyes.

"You just record all this, Lev?" he asked in Czech, and saw the quick flash of uncertainty in Lev's eyes and knew Lev had done just that. Pov leaned back in his chair and looked Lev over for a long moment. "Why do you think?" he asked Tully, making it Czech so Lev got every word. "Does he scent blood from a certain gypsy sailmaster? Or is he just pushing the envelope on ambition and disobeying orders?"

"Either," Tully said disgustedly.

"Do you think he'd really sell out *Net*?" Pov asked, making it loud enough now for all the techs to hear. "What kind of family links does he have to *Dance*?" The other three techs looked around, wide-eyed. Lev was struck dumb, his mouth flapping.

"Hmmm." Tully thought about it. "I don't quite remember. A mother, I think, on their chaffer staff. He could feed the pipeline right into Molnar, tell Rybak everything."

"He'd surely get a reward. What do you think they'd give him?"

"Well, the sail ranks are filled up on *Dance*. Probably just money until *Dance* builds a new ship. A man can always use money."

"Sir!" Lev blurted at last.

"What?" Pov stared at him challengingly.

Lev's surprise changed abruptly to anger. "I'd never sell out *Net*. How can you say that?" He started to get out of his chair, whether to stomp out or trounce Pov, probably even Lev didn't know. Pov remembered that Lev had a temper, as well as being sly, but remembered other better things, too. He had worked with the man for three years, thought he had earned some loyalty. On the other hand, Pov had thought a lot of other things until lately.

"Sit down," he ordered coldly, then waited until Lev complied. The other techs had now frozen in place, not sure whether to look or pretend nothing was happening and caught somewhere between.

"Sir . . ."

"Shut up. If you had used your brain instead of congratulating yourself on how cleverly you can find out things, you'd already guess why Tully and I are down here. I told you to butt out, and if this weren't a time when the ship's fortune *is* at stake, I'd probably ignore your games as I usually do. If this information gets back to *Dance* too soon, we get sold to Tania's Ring. Do you understand?"

"I'm not a traitor," Lev protested. "I—"

"You talk too much," Pov said flatly. "You get tempted to parade what you know." Lev's mouth worked open and shut, then closed uselessly. He flushed to his collar, then looked away, his jaw muscles working. "So what do I do, Lev?" Pov asked angrily. "Do I cajole you and push your loyalty buttons? Do I flatter, admiring how clever you are? Or do I call you on a dumb-ass maneuver and dump you off Sail Deck so fast your head'll spin?" Pov jerked to his feet but stopped himself with an effort, trying hard to keep his control as it slipped too close to outright rage. "How *dare* you risk *Siduri's Net*? How *dare* you?"

"Pov," Tully said quietly, catching him.

Pov reseated himself with an effort, trembling. "So much for command technique," he muttered. Tully laughed, and Pov looked at him incredulously. "What's that for?" he demanded.

"Ah, hell, Pov. So who says the sailmaster can't want to punch out a sail tech—or vice versa? Not that the punching ever solves much, and *Dance* would love it all." He spread his hands and spoke directly to the techs. "Gentlemen, the cloudship wars have just turned nasty, and we are polishing our weapons. We are going to T Tauri to make money, lots and lots of money—assuming we don't get fried while we're doing it—and then we're going to make *Dance* very sorry we have all that cash. Andreos wants to spring it on *Dance* unawares so they don't have time to say no. Does that fill in some gaps, Lev?"

Lev looked down at his hands, visibly uncomfortable. "I'm sorry," he said, abashed.

"I'm sure you are. A certain sailmaster has taken a lot of dust lately and doesn't know whom to believe. He keeps trying to trust, like the loyal dutiful dope we know and love, but now he thinks he's a fool to do it, probably."

"God Almighty, Tully," Pov protested weakly.

"Command technique," Tully said, winking at him. "Lev got cute at the wrong time, but I think Lev knows what to do with that tape of his. Don't you, Lev?"

"Yes, sir." Lev smiled.

Tully pointed an imperious finger at all four techs. "And Sail, you put together three years with Pov Janusz as sailmaster and use those brains of yours to figure how much you're really at risk of getting tossed off Sail Deck, whatever he just said. This dutiful dope was overheard defending Benek's right to trash him in front of Captain Andreos, of all things."

"Tully . . ."

"*And* he pulled off Avi from doing mayhem to Benek," Tully barged on, "and so impressed her with his dutiful dopiness that she got Celka to leave him alone, too." Tully spread his hands in mock bewilderment. "What can I say?" he asked the open air.

"You've said enough," Pov informed him.

"So toss me off Sail Deck, too. I can handle it." He grinned wickedly. "Just giving Lev some better news to spread. Right, Lev?"

"Right, sir," Lev pronounced stoutly.

Pov looked at the open grins on all five faces and shook his head in bewilderment, then scowled at the laughter that answered. "I *should* dump you all off deck, you null zeroes."

"That's on, sir," Lev agreed. "I *am* sorry, sir."

"It's just that it's important, Lev."

Lev nodded. "Yes, sir." Pov looked at his earnest face and hoped that Tully's instincts were right, however oddly he chose to apply them. "Could you use some help?" Lev asked. Pov hesitated, still inclined to doubt Lev's motives, and it must have shown. Lev made a face, then sent an appealing glance to Tully. "Please, sir?"

"It *would* be a help," Tully commented. "We've got a lot of modeling with parameters this wide, more than I expected."

"All right," Pov said. "But put it under a new security code, including the library access. Keep it tight."

"What's wrong with our current sail codes?" Tully asked in surprise, then backed off as Pov shot him a warning glance.

"Just do it, Tully."

"Yes, sir. Uh, sir, I have some confidential data I need to discuss with you."

"Okay. Come up to my office."

Talk about signals, Pov thought, knowing they'd just given Lev a whole new topic to maybe snoop. He led the way up-level, waved Tully into his sailmaster office off the lounge, then shut the door. "What the hell was that about, Tully?" he exploded.

Tully put his hands in his pockets and leaned against Pov's desk, smiling oddly. Then he laughed again. Pov crossed his arms and glared, half convinced Tully *had* lost his mind.

"Ah, hell, Pov," Tully said. "Lev would have started snooping the second he had a mystery on—and us too busy elsewhere was a clue just in itself. So I set up the situation so you'd explode at him and stomp it."

"All that was deliberate?" Pov asked tightly.

Tully straightened, still grinning. "Hey, coz," he said softly in Romany. "You have to ask? The gaje got your brains, I'll hazard."

"They do not," Pov said automatically.

"I beg to differ. What's the matter with the codes?"

"Dina tampered with the sail report, maybe. Got the codes from my apartment drawer, maybe. There's a time slip in the record encoding."

"Are you *serious*?" Tully asked increduously.

"Absolutely. I think Benek goofed the dust sample and Dina covered it up. You're not the only one with fancy footwork, friend." Pov sat down heavily at his desk.

"And you *defended* Benek?"

"I didn't know it then—and I'd defend him, anyway, for a couple of good reasons. Think about it."

Tully did. "Hell," he said.

"You're so right. And you're down there playing stealth games with Lev."

"Lev won't do anything against *Net*," Tully said confidently, "and he doesn't blab *all* the time."

Pov hoped he was right, probably was. "Even so," Pov said, "I think we ought to ask the computer chief to change the sailmaster codes, in case Dina isn't the only tech with itchy fingers. And I've got to tell Andreos about this."

"What do you think he'll do with it?"

"I don't know. If we admit the error, we lose *Net*."

"So we don't admit it. Easy." Pov scowled, making Tully smile. "The truth of the sails? You do stay consistent."

"Probably we'll pick lies," he admitted, unhappy with it and knowing Tully knew it. It was smart to lie: Pov knew it was smart, but it still offended his personal sense of *rightness*. Righteous Rom, indeed.

"For *Net*'s sake, Pov," Tully said softly.

"So you say. I hope you're right."

Chapter 7

A week later, *Net* and *Dance* arrived at Tania's Ring, docking at the planet's massive space station. Tania's circumpolar complex, Omsk Station, was a massive structure kilometers long in several dimensions, a boxy, disk-shaped construction of gray metal and ceramic, added to every year with new offlinks, habitats, laboratories, and power stations. Tania's Ring intended to own the best and biggest of everything, and its space station was her principal jewel for impressing visitors of any stripe. As the cloudships descended from higher orbit to dock at the station, *Net* in the lead, Pov and Athena watched the approach from the prow window on captains' level, and it was Athena's quick eyes that spotted the Aldebaran markings on a small cruiser in a nearby docking bay.

"Short-range carrier," Pov grunted as she pointed. "The vendor's back again."

"Bukharin always arranges deftly—though who's he hinting at, do you think, that vendor or us?"

"Both, of course. Omsk has forty docking bays, but he puts that Aldebaran vendor just a few slots down from ours. 'See?' he says to us. 'I don't need you.'"

"And we ignore it loftily, saying, 'See, we don't need you, either.' But everybody's seen and heard quite well." Athena chuckled. "Don't I wish? God, I'd like to get away from this politicking." She sighed and turned away from the window, took a step towards the elevator, then stepped firmly back. "No, I promised myself to let Stefania alone. Didn't I?"

"Docking isn't that hard. She's probably done it in simulation a couple thousand times and watched you for three years besides. And Berka's watching, you mother hen."

"And if she smashes us into Omsk, we can get *two* repair bills. Wonderful." Athena bit on her lip as *Net* eased closer to the station, then walked around Pov for a few strolling circuits as the ship crept agonizingly closer to immovable metal. "I can't look."

"I told you to practice by giving her half-watches and a few odd ship maneuvers without you hovering, as I did with Roja last year." He stretched his shoulders casually. "Look at me, calm and relaxed, not a worry. It's your own fault."

"Don't say 'I told you so.' It's not polite."

"I told you so." She menaced him with a growl, then strolled another circle. *Net* slowly eased into its dock connections and stopped. "We've arrived, Athena," Pov said, amused. "You can look now."

"We have?" Athena said, affecting one of Stefania's breathless squeaks. Pov grinned, then laughed as Athena grimaced and looked guilty. "Sorry. I shouldn't. Stefania does okay."

"Yeah. You can't help nerves." That got him a hard thump on the arm and a fearsome scowl, then Athena laughed despite herself.

"Aren't we a pair? Now don't you ever tell anybody I admitted anything about Stefania. She's good at helm, whatever the sound effects."

"If you say so." He shifted uneasily, reminded again of the intership hearing when he'd rather not think about it, at least not for the half hour of grace he had left. In the past week he'd occasionally managed for an hour or two at a time to not think about it at all, at another dinner with Kate, often with Avi under her flowered sheets. He smiled to himself, then took in a deep breath and looked over the spreading length of Omsk Station, conscious of Athena watching him.

"You look good in uniform, Pov," Athena said,

brushing imaginary dust off his shoulders, then stepped back to tip her head and inspect. *Net*'s formal uniform, a smartly tailored dark-gray tunic and trousers, was optional on all watches, and Pov wore his seldom enough that dressing up for formal sail inspections got good attention from his staff. Athena was as casual, with similar uses for the formalities. He fingered *Net*'s woven-gold emblem on his sleeve, a graceful hand casting a net on a dark-gray sea, then let his hand drop.

"Not as good as you. I don't have the right curves." He inspected her back. "Why do pretty women always pretend they don't like men noticing?"

"Who's pretending, sir? I like it just fine." She slid her hands down her hips and wriggled, showing off. "And after three kids, too. Noticing's for free—and I'm glad to see you're doing it again, to add my out-of-line comment. Avi's a good woman."

"This ship is a sieve," Pov muttered. "Though we haven't been exactly hiding it, I guess."

"A sieve it is. And I hope you've been hearing the support, Pov, as well as the other."

"Yes, I have. Thanks, Athena." She pulled down his head and laid her cheek against his for a moment, then pressed his arms tightly as she looked up at him fiercely.

"Luck, Pov," she said, using the Romany word.

"Thanks, Athena," he said, guessing she'd asked Kate for the word just for this moment. A good friend, the best. He took a deep breath and turned to face the window again and its view of the Russki station. "Well, let's go see what *Dance* wants to say about needing Pov Janusz."

They went down-level together to join the others waiting to leave *Net*. Besides the captains, Milo had brought along Pov's beta sail watch as possible witnesses. All watched as Andreos exchanged courtesies with Tania's Trade Bureau chief, Nicolay Bukharin, by the off-access portal. The Russian, a portly, gregarious man in a black jumpsuit that little flattered his pear-shaped form, greeted them expansively, chuckling and winking his goodwill, then turned to welcome Rybak and his contingent as they entered through another door from the next dock bay, his charm impervious to the grim scowls that surrounded him.

"Captain Rybak!" he declared and rushed over to give the autocratic Rybak an enormous hug and kisses on both cheeks, followed by a running burbling joy of greeting. Rybak's expression at such manhandling forced Pov to turn away to hide a grin, and he saw Athena's eyes dancing.

"Please, Mr. Bukharin," Rybak said, setting the enthusiastic Russki firmly back a pace. "This is a serious matter."

"Yes, I saw your damage." Bukharin tsked, his black eyes hard for an instant as that clever mind gloated just a little and let Rybak see it. "My regrets, captain."

"Yes," Rybak said shortly and shot a bitter glance at Pov.

Behind Rybak, Sailmaster Ceverny tiredly studied his boots, his tall lean figure slumped with fatigue. When Ceverny looked up, his glance slid over Pov as if *Net*'s sailmaster weren't even there, his emotions about the encounter showing only in the slow jerking of a muscle in his cheek. By now Rybak's convinced him of everything, Pov thought, and gave Rybak a resentful stare.

Captain Rybak dismissed him with a snort. "Shall we begin?"

Bukharin waved them toward the interior corridor and led the way to the well-appointed conference room off the main lounge. Bukharin had set his stage well. With great affability, he arranged the five *Dance* captains in a semicircle around one end of the large table. *Net*'s captains got the other end of the table, with Bukharin and his two aides in between, as Bukharin no doubt wished for other ways with all the fervency of his Russki heart. Pov stored his sail staff in hallway chairs and took his chair with *Net*'s captains.

"In that Sailmaster Janusz is here as a witness," Rybak said sourly, "I suggest he also wait outside."

"In that Sailmaster Janusz is here as a *Net* captain," Andreos countered firmly, "I insist that he remain."

Captain Rybak scowled and conferred in whispers with Molnar, a long and serious consultation that left everyone else to watch the ceiling lights, the tabletop, or any wall. As the whispered discussion went on and on, Pov raised an eyebrow at Andreos and got quieted with a glance. Pov intertwined his fingers on the table in front of him and tried to copy Andreos' bland stare, his heartbeat a steady fast thumping in his chest and ears.

Across the table, Ceverny shot Pov a short bitter glance that chilled Pov to the bone, then Ceverny, too, pointedly watched Rybak, his long face settled into lines of grief and strain. What is he thinking? Pov wondered, remembering all the years he had served on *Dance*'s sail staff under this grand old man, all the help Ceverny had given freely to Pov during *Net*'s first months on her shakedown cruise. Miska Ceverny did not tolerate fools easily, disdained politics as idiotic, and said whatever he thought, blandly ignoring the resultant sputtering from lesser types: Ceverny knew his value and its privileges. In return, he gave his ship everything he had. Without Ceverny, Pov had no doubt, *Dance* would not have survived. Without Ceverny ... What was he thinking now?

Rybak conferred, Molnar listened; Molnar advised, Rybak scowled. Finally Rybak left off with his whispering and, after a sour glance at Bukharin, touched an electronic stud in front of him; a mellow chime issued from the intercom speakers. "This hearing is now invoked and is being recorded," Rybak said formally, neatly skipping over Andreos' challenge. "Charges are laid of ship's negligence by *Siduri's Net*,

causing severe damage to *Siduri's Dance*, in violation
of intership contract, Protocol Alpha 29, clause 42.
Present are the command staffs of both ships; witnesses will be called to establish the facts. After testi-
mony is presented, damages will be assessed per ship
contract."

"That assumes," Andreos said, "that *Net* is found
to be at fault. Let's not rush things, Sandor."

Rybak scowled at the familiarity. "It is obvious, sir."

"Not to me nor to *Net*. Call your first witness."

Rybak hesitated, then glanced his permission at
Molnar. The *Dance* chaffer cleared his throat.

"Our first witness," Molnar said, his tone carefully
neutral, "is the *Net* Sail Deck record. Your attention,
gentlemen and ladies, to the main viewscreen."

One of Bukharin's Russki assistants dimmed the
room lights, and Pov watched himself on the wallscreen, a foreshortened figure on a wide deck, as Molnar ran the data scan. Strange to see himself from a
distance; he tried to be objective, critiquing that sailmaster's work performance as he had so often cri-
tiqued each member of his sail crew, very conscious
of the rapt attention of Bukharin. He noticed Andreos
stir in protest as Molnar allowed the tape to run past
and through Benek's accusation, but all of *Net*'s captains sat patiently through to the end. When the room
lights went up, Andreos was tapping his fingers irritably on the table.

"We call Benek Zukor, *Net*'s Fifth Sail," Molnar
announced.

"A point of order," Andreos interrupted. "Since we
are viewing the basic data of sail records, I ask that
Dance display its contemporaneous records from her
Sail Deck."

"Not relevant," Rybak said immediately.

"Oh, definitely relevant, shipmaster. Mr. Janusz's
warning was sent in due course, as we all just saw on
Net's record; I want to see how and when it was
received."

Sailmaster Ceverny flushed angrily but determinedly set his jaw against any protest. It had been years since anyone had challenged the competence of *Dance*'s sailmaster, if anyone ever had. Had Molnar given Ceverny his own set of chaffer's cautions? *Watch your anger, Miska: Andreos is tricky.* God, it's inhuman, Pov thought, knowing that Ceverny had gone through the same anguished self-appraisal as he had. Yet now, after he saves the ship and after all that had happened since, *Net* tosses the blame back at him. Their eyes suddenly met again, and Pov saw the pain in Ceverny's eyes, the surprise as they shared it, the sudden empathy of sail rank that flashed between them.

"*Net* may present evidence in its own turn," Molnar said sourly.

"*Net* protests," Milo replied snidely, pounding on the weak protest. "The rules of evidence require similar records to be viewed together, Protocol 72, clause 12. I make formal objection, and failure to yield will result in automatic appeal to the Tania's Ring arbiter, Mr. Bukharin, Protocol 123, clause 16. Do you really want that, Antek?" he added quietly. "It's rather early to toss it into Nikolay's lap."

"Is that the way it'll be?" Molnar asked. "Do it our way or we'll hand it to Bukharin?"

"Gentlemen, please," Bukharin said, his voice loaded with sensible reason and wisdom. The two chaffers sublimely ignored him, their eyes locked for several seconds. Then Milo tapped his pen on the table and bared his teeth. "I'm just reciting contract provisions, chaffer. And yes, that's exactly what I'm saying. This hearing will be by the rules, I assure you. We want *Dance*'s tape." Ceverny swept to his feet and stalked out of the meeting room in long, angry strides. Milo smiled slightly, no doubt liking the effect.

"Perhaps a brief recess?" Andreos suggested smoothly to Bukharin. "So that *Dance* may consult with her sailmaster?"

"Certainly, certainly." Bukharin smiled. "Mr. Molnar?"

Molnar nodded reluctantly, then left the room in pursuit of Ceverny. As Milo stood, he gestured to Pov. Pov followed him out of the meeting room to a small sideroom far down the corridor outside. Milo waved him into the room and then shut the door behind them. A few moments later, Andreos tapped and Milo admitted him, then resignedly opened the door again for *Net*'s lady captains. "All of us huddling together is a signal, ladies," Milo chided.

"Signal away, Milo," Athena said, tossing her curls, and sat down in one of the chairs by the wall. Janina sat down, too, and crossed her arms across her ample middle. "If you two get to listen, so do we. Right, shipmaster?" Milo scowled, then gave it away with a shrug and turned to Pov.

"Remind me, Pov, of the Sail Deck procedure when a dust warning is received. What was Ceverny supposed to do?"

Pov hesitated. Andreos had elected not to tell Milo about Dina's tampering, and likely Andreos had his good reasons, chiefly Milo. Milo did best when he thought he had the other side pinned flat, and knowing about Dina might loosen a few of Milo's gears. The chaffer tapped his pen impatiently, then raised an eyebrow, prompting at him.

Pov glanced at the utterly bland Andreos, getting no help at all, and cleared his throat. "Supposed to do? If you're riding the bow wave of another cloudship, immediate evasion. If a full dust pocket just blew off the comet, you could get punched hard before you knew it."

"Avi had trouble putting her signal through to *Dance*," Milo pointed out. "Why was that?"

"That's usual in plasma stream. You need to allow time for it, especially when the infrared starts to go up."

"Could this be going the way I think it is?" Athena asked. "Was Ceverny at fault?"

"Probably not," Milo judged. "If Ceverny was outright negligent, we wouldn't be having this hearing—Rybak wouldn't risk it."

"What if Rybak assumed," Janina suggested, "and started it in motion before he talked to Ceverny?"

Milo shook his head firmly. "It's still too big a risk. He'd have discovered that by now and found some way to tone all this down. I doubt if we'll find much on *Dance*'s own tape." Milo pointed at Pov. "True, you could have been at your command console and seen those readings earlier. True, you could have sent the warning before you had reasonable data from the probe, right?"

"That's right," Pov agreed. "And *Dance* would have screamed if I sent a false warning and made them pull out of trajectory."

"Also true. Reasonable risk balanced by reasonable prudence. I think both you and Ceverny got caught in a bad draw of the risk. *Dance* is trying to shovel all the load on *Net*'s reasonable error."

"Error?" Pov asked tightly.

"Oh, hell, Pov," Milo said impatiently. "It's an uncertain universe. Ship's duty requires only reasonable prudence, not infallibility. You could have sent the warning earlier to follow up your outright advice against slip course."

"Right." Pov clenched his jaws and studied his hands again.

"And I think," Milo continued, confident of his logic, "that we'll find Ceverny could have listened sooner. And he's not liking to admit it any more than you are." Pov flushed and said nothing.

"They'll still push it, no matter what *Dance*'s Sail Deck record," Janina said. "As we know so thoroughly by now, *Dance* is in bad shape, sirs. The holdmaster report I've seen has enough to wipe out this run's profit and the last two as well—and repairs always go overbudget at Omsk. Bukharin will see to that, especially when he scents blood." She looked quietly worried, her plain face distressed. "I'm surprised how blatant Rybak is acting in front of the Russkis. Where's his advantage?"

"How much are they at risk from Tania's Ring?" Andreos asked.

"Not enough for Bukharin to buy *Dance* as a personal toy, however he'd like—not yet. Another bad sail run and matters are much worse." She spread her hands and shrugged. "*Ishtar's Fan* has skirted bankruptcy for years, and Perikles is far more aggressive than Tania's Ring. *Dance* can skate by this, with a good run and our contributions in profit share, but there won't be any new daughter ship for a while if *Net* is sold. It might be fifteen years before *Dance* can build again, fifteen years of skating the edge on every comet run."

"This is going to go to Bukharin, isn't it?" Athena asked. "No matter what happens today. Since when do we have to air our linen to Tania's Ring? I don't like that."

"Are you suggesting we just roll over and give in?" Milo asked.

"No. But lay off on the 'error' labels, Milo, will you? Plasma runs are a risky business, and all the contracts in humanity's devising won't make dust damage a hundred percent avoidable. Pov did okay."

"Thank you for your expert opinion, Pilotmaster," Milo said sarcastically.

"You're a cold-minded lizard, Milo, like all chaffers," Athena retorted. "Someday a jungle hunter might come along and stab you with a stick to cook you."

"That's enough, Athena," Andreos said mildly.

Athena bristled. "I just don't like his attitude, sir, and I know you don't, either. Look how much of this discussion divides along Slav and non-Slav lines. If we voted right now about whether Pov was negligent or not, do you have any doubts about how the vote would run?" She pointed dramatically at Milo and Janina, then at Andreos and herself. "Even when we all *know* the tape is ambiguous? The whole ship is talking about it. I've heard about the talk on Hold Deck, and my skyriders are split along the predictable lines, too. And we all know what Dina Kozel has been saying."

"Saying what?" Pov asked.

"Not to much effect, I think." She smiled at him sympathetically. "My point, sir, is that we're a new ship, with a new chance to shake off the old prejudices about First-Ship and newcomers. A cloudship needs new people for their fresh point of view, their different skills, and mostly the change they bring. Organize a ship by ancestry and we're finished. So even if we win this particular fight with *Dance*, the consequences to *Net* are already there in the divisions. Milo can scheme about his contract clauses and you can arrange whatever startling surprise you probably have in mind, but I see the people of *Net* divided by this. This is a wider issue than Pov: this incident can set our ship policy, unofficial or otherwise, for a generation."

"I'm aware of the consequences," Andreos said smoothly, but Athena shook her head impatiently at him.

"Did you know that *Dance* refused five pilot applications from Omsk Station last year? They haven't accepted any new Russkis for nearly two years, except that specialist on carbon chemistry. Haven't you noticed that all the principal Greeks in the command cadre—you, me, Stefania, for instance—were transferred to *Net* when Rybak approved the crew list? I've been thinking about that for a while, and I don't like it. I don't like this whole situation, being dragged over here like schoolchildren off to detention. I don't like a lot of things." Athena crossed her arms and glared at Milo. "This reeks."

"What do you suggest, Athena?" Andreos asked.

"Is that a serious question, captain?"

"Yes."

"Let's go back to *Net* and tell *Dance* to stuff their hearing. Since this is going to get appealed to Bukharin, anyway, why go through the aggravation? I don't like feeling this angry at Milo, as richly as he deserves it; I've forgiven him before and I'll do it again, but right now he's at risk himself, and not from dust damage. I don't see why Pov should go through the humiliation, however well he's trying to hide what he's feeling right now. I think *Net*'s people are more important than Rybak's getting in his drubs at our expense. Turn it over to Bukharin: he'll love the circus." She smiled slightly. "End of speech, sir."

"Milo? Does our contract permit it?"

"Allegation of breach invokes mandatory arbitration," Milo protested. "The contract requires this intership hearing to settle the dispute."

Andreos considered it, tapping his long fingers on the table. "But the contract doesn't say *when* we have to have a hearing, right?"

Milo scowled, then shot a suspicious look at Athena. "Within a 'reasonable time.' You've been studying up, sir," he said in an accusing tone.

"Cross-training is always useful. And, no, I didn't conspire with Athena. I think we've learned what we wanted to know from Ceverny, and I'd like to see *Dance*'s Sail Deck tape without the to-and-fro of *Dance* watching us when we do. Can we get the tape beforehand if we insist on a postponement?"

"Maybe. They'll contest it."

"Bukharin will have a lot of items on his agenda, won't he?"

Milo shrugged. "If you've obviously made up your mind, sir . . ."

"I will listen to your judgment, Milo. You're *Net*'s chaffer: you make a call."

Milo glanced at Pov, then locked eyes with Athena.

He quirked his lips, then laughed softly. "If I say go on with the hearing, do I still get forgiven, Athena?"

"I'll take it under advisement," Athena retorted. "Come on, Milo. What's the point?"

Milo pursed his lips, giving her the grace of thinking about it. "It would mix things up considerably. *Dance* would consider it a hostile act."

"So? Isn't it?" Athena's eyes narrowed. "I am sick and tired of Rybak's arrogance: his jinking during Pov's sail inspection was out of line, even without the sail fault. You *know* that, Milo. You can wave your contract clauses and shrug and sigh, but I don't care about contract niceties. Just because you can do it legally doesn't mean it's right, no?"

"Morality has plagued jurisprudence for centuries, I agree."

"And bloodless lawyers push it as far as it'll go, too."

Milo scowled impatiently. "Soar off, Helm. You have one role on *Net* with dash and flair and hot-jet pilot types to manage: I have another. Passion and judgment—is that a fair summary? Pov has another role, Janina yet another, and Captain Andreos is the mom managing the store. Our division of command has worked for decades: it's our strength."

"So is cross-crew, Slavs *and* Greeks." Athena crossed her arms and looked away rebelliously.

Milo scowled more fiercely at her, not at all pleased. "And I won't be railroaded into a profitless insult to *Dance* just because you're annoyed at Rybak."

"Have you heard *anything* I've said?"

"Athena," Andreos said quietly and waited until he had her full attention. "How much of this is 'passion' and how much is defending Pov?"

"Maybe there's more than just either, sir. This is not a short-term concern. Rybak started it when we were building *Net*, little jinks there, little sniffs here, little contract phrases that got pushed to the limit. Unfortunately, his current target is Pov: Rybak is good at detecting vulnerability. Everyone in command has a few ship connections to explain why we got our posts on *Net* even without Slav ancestry: you served under Rybak for twenty years, and my family joined *Fan* on her first voyage at Perikles. All the rest of us have the Slav connections to fluff over occasional mistakes. Pov won his by sheer ability, and he doesn't have those protections, with the gypsy on top of it." She turned to Pov and shrugged. "I'm sorry, Pov. Fact of life." She spread her hands. "And so Rybak will make Pov a scapegoat for this: he'll make it a choice between Ceverny and Pov and force both ships to choose it his way. *Dance* has too much damage. Milo just looks at the contract language, thinking it imposes safety in its limitations; I suggest that the safety is an illusion."

"Janina?" Andreos asked. "What's your opinion?"

"I agree with Athena," the older woman said slowly. "I admit I've felt very troubled. I don't understand too many things behind the scenes; I'm not even sure there's a logical consistency—which means the source is likely emotion and ranking and convenience, not rational economics." She gave Athena an unhappy glance, then sighed. "I vote to not make Pov expendable; I vote for a visible statement that draws the line clearly." She smiled a small wintry smile. "Sometimes, my friend Milo, playing by the rules sets you up to lose."

"But Pov should have sent an earlier warning!" Milo protested.

"This isn't about warnings, Milo," Janina retorted. "Athena's right. This is about *Net* and the ship we'll be in the future." She looked around at their faces. "Look at us now, quarreling like this, and magnify that a hundredfold aboard *Net*. Whether we like it or not, the charges against Pov have become significant to all the non-Slavs aboard *Net*. We must choose wisely here."

"I don't see that kind of problem," Milo said resistantly.

"That is obvious," Janina said with a sad smile. "We have listened to you many times, Milo, trusting your judgment as *Net*'s chaffer. In this, please listen to ours." Milo stared at her for several moments, then shrugged indifferently. "More than that, please," Janina added with some asperity.

"All right." Milo stood up. "I'll inform Molnar."

"Sit down, Milo," Andreos said. "We aren't done yet."

"Aha!" Athena exclaimed. "Here it comes! I knew you had something up your sleeve!"

Andreos pointed a long finger at her. "Baffle that, pilotmaster," he said irritably. "If you'd had your spies out properly, you'd already know what's up, but you've been too busy reacting to *Dance* and Milo. After this is over, we will discuss you and Milo. I will not tolerate open hostility between my captains, and I blame you both for it. Is that understood?" Milo flushed and sat down, then twiddled with his pen.

"Sorry, sir," Athena mumbled, her own color rising.

"Now that you both feel like abashed children, may I have your attention? Thank you. Not that I appreciate being put in the position of reproving father—which we will also discuss later. I agree with Athena that this has implications for *Net*, and I agree this is our ship's history. Walking out on *Dance* would be very satisfying—and it would be consistent. But we don't have the capital to go independent, and *Dance* doesn't have the capital to repair itself without severe financial peril from Tania's Ring. *Dance* wants the money from us: I propose we go get it."

"Sir?" Athena blurted.

Andreos smiled thinly. "Normally I would have presented this at a captain's meeting before now, but you and Milo were so aptly serving our purpose in your acting off in front of *Dance*, I let you spin in orbit."

"A matter to discuss later, sir?" Athena asked, batting her eyelashes at him. Andreos shook his head and appealed to the ceiling.

"Pilots," he said disgustedly. Everyone laughed in response, and abruptly the tension that had gripped them all eased to their usual familiarity. Deft, Pov thought in admiration.

"T Tauri," Andreos said. Athena's jaw dropped.

"Tritium by the holdful," Janina breathed, her eyes widening. Milo looked stunned and a little hurt that Andreos had cut him out. Discussions indeed, Pov thought, watching the expressions shift quickly across the chaffer's face. Little do you know, Milo.

"Money," Andreos agreed. "Lots of money, enough to repair *Dance*, give those short-term carriers a setback, enough to buy us free."

"Free?" Milo asked. "To do what? Go where?"

Athena thumped on Milo's arm hard. "Where do you think, you idiot?" she said, then smiled delightedly at Andreos. "Oh, this is good, sir. I like it. I like it lots. But how will you get Rybak to go along?"

"Care to watch, captains?"

"Oh, yes!"

"Milo?" Andreos prompted.

"I'm obviously outvoted," Milo said sourly, then shook himself like a spaniel shedding water. "Not that I'd necessarily vote against it, I guess. I'd want to study it first."

"Study it later," Janina said. "Are you seriously opposed?"

"Well, considering the alternative ..." Milo shot a glance at Athena. "No, sir."

"Then let's go."

Andreos stood up and led them all back to the main conference room, watched by a half-dozen pairs of fascinated eyes as *Net*'s captains strolled past the sail crew sitting in the corridor chairs. Avi looked up at Pov, her anxiety plain on her face as he approached; he glanced down the corridor to see if anyone but his sail crew was looking, then bent to kiss her quickly to reassure her. Avi stood up and made the kiss more spectacular than he had intended, enough to make Pov stagger slightly as she released him.

"Next is *my* turn," Celka announced loudly.

"Want to lose an arm?" Avi asked her with sweet malice. "That's the way to try." Celka snickered, undented, and everyone except a very sour Benek grinned broadly. Pov opened his mouth and couldn't think of a single appropriate thing to say, then let them laugh as he walked off to catch up with Andreos.

The *Net* captains arranged themselves at their end of the table, watched by Bukharin's alert black eyes. The Russian frowned slightly, his infallible instincts sniffing something on the station ventilator currents and not liking the smell. Andreos smiled at him affably, which lowered Bukharin's eyebrows another few millimeters. A few minutes later *Dance*'s captains reentered the room and also took their chairs. Captain Rybak glanced around the room, then cleared his throat.

"We will now resume the hearing," he announced. "On the point raised—"

"One moment, captain," Andreos interrupted. "I have a counterproposal and suggest we continue the suspension of these proceedings so that the cloudships can confer in private." He glanced at Bukharin politely.

Rybak lowered his eyebrows. "The arbiter is present so that he can witness any matters which may require his ruling."

"Since we are suspended, our discussion will not require rulings. Off the record, Sandor. Will you listen?" Andreos turned to Bukharin. "I intend no disrespect, sir, but I have a matter between ships to discuss. We request privacy." Bukharin affected mild offense but nodded, then waved himself and his two aides out of the room. Andreos watched him leave, then shrugged at Rybak. "Such easy agreement by our Russki host suggests a video monitor in this room, audio at a minimum. Not that it matters. By the time Bukharin knows, it'll be too late."

That last comment got Rybak's attention, and the older captain eyed Andreos for several seconds, then each of *Net*'s captains in turn, a slow scrutiny that showed all the clever rapacity that had won Rybak his bonuses at Tania's Ring and a daughtership he wanted to keep. His lined face still showed its displeasure and pride, but when Molnar stirred restlessly, Rybak waved him silent with an arrogance that would have had Milo stomping out of the room. "Your item off the record, *Net*?"

"*Net* does not concede fault in this matter. If there was fault, and we do not concede there even *was* fault in this accident, the fault is shared by both ships." Ceverny stirred restlessly, but Andreos quieted him with a quick gesture. "Wait, Miska. You'll like this."

"Your sailmaster—" Rybak began angrily. Andreos cut him off with another gesture.

"Let me finish, please. If we wished, we could both shift blame to Tania's Ring for its inaccurate comet data. This was not a young comet, whatever Omsk's observatory thought, but a comet that had aged through hundreds of orbits and, as we know, fell apart in our faces. That error led to the dust storm with atypical readings that did not fit our models: both ships were caught off guard. I suggest, however, that the issue at hand is not who was at fault, but how to repair *Dance*."

"We have presented our repair list," Molnar said coldly.

"That you have. *Net* proposes to pay it, captains, but I suggest not by whatever arrangement you're looking for with Bukharin. If Bukharin rules *Net* at fault, you get your list. But the only way *Net* can pay is to sell itself to Tania's Ring. *Dance* is repaired, but loses its daughter ship, setting up its own competitor in this system. Do you really want to go sailing with us, captains, when we're owned by the colony that would love to own you, too?"

"There are other star systems," Rybak said loftily.

Andreos stared at him, a great sadness washing across his face, quickly concealed. "I see. *Net* proposes a cloud run to T Tauri, captains. We have the sail capacity to bring back a hold or two of tritium that will more than pay for *Dance*'s damage, your new sails, and whatever else is on your wish list."

"And buy out?" Molnar said snidely.

"Almost certainly," Andreos replied coldly. "After *Dance*'s openly hostile actions against *Net* in this affair, ship's loyalty has become irrelevant. Under our contract, you have titular control over *Net*'s proposed operations. Accordingly, as *Net*'s shipmaster, I am formally asking permission for a cloud run at T Tauri."

Rybak stared at Andreos. "And if you fail . . ."

"You can still sell us to Tania's Ring. Just make sure the price is enough when you do, Sandor. Will you agree?"

Rybak drummed his fingers on the tabletop, then glanced at Molnar. "If *Net* accepts fault . . ." he hedged.

"No. This is an offer without concessions of any kind. If we come back from T Tauri without a successful cargo, this intership hearing starts all over again. No concessions. My sailmaster will not concede fault, and so neither does *Net*."

Ceverny stirred restlessly in his chair. "T Tauri is a protostar. Your sails are not designed for—"

"That is *Net*'s affair," Andreos said coldly, including Ceverny in *Net*'s intense displeasure. "Does *Dance* agree?"

Rybak looked it over, obviously tempted but prudently wary of lurking side slips *Dance* might not like later. He scowled.

"I need time to . . ." he hedged.

"*Now*, Captain," Andreos said. "I insist. Our contract requires us to ask, but *Net* is going to T Tauri, legally or otherwise. You choose what it'll be."

"You'd break contract?" Molnar asked incredulously.

Andreos smiled like a wolf, letting *Dance* stew in the possibility. Molnar looked wildly at Rybak.

"We agree," Rybak said abruptly, without consulting his captains. None of the others objected to the presumption, Pov noted, though Molnar did shut himself up with an effort. Different, indeed.

"Very well," Andreos said into the silence that followed, a tense and acrimonious silence between ships that had once been allied. "Begin your repairs, *Dance*. We will advise you when we depart for T Tauri."

They all stood up, and *Net* left first.

Chapter 8

Net's captains and sail beta watch walked through the tubeway connecting Omsk's docking lounge to *Net*'s access port on the lower hull, then split up quickly, the sail staff scattering until beta watch in an hour or so and the captains lingering briefly in the ship's dock lounge to talk. Pov didn't have much to say on any topic, and so chose to watch the blank walls of Omsk Station through the lounge window. After a few minutes, Athena joined him and made her point by putting on a vapid expression, mouth slightly open, eyes a-bugged, mesmerized by rivets and blank metal. He shifted his boot onto hers and leaned.

"Off, sir," she said and elbowed him hard.

"Stop that, then. I can look at anything I want, thank you."

"Stop what?" Athena asked innocently.

She glanced around at Andreos and Milo, now engaged in an intense muttered discussion by the elevator. The two left, still talking. Let's mesh, Pov thought sourly, watching them go. Athena waved casually as Janina moved off, too, then frowned as Janina disappeared through the connecting tubeway to the holds. "At least she could have come to you and said something."

"She thinks it's my fault, just as Milo does." Pov turned back around to look at rivets again.

"Janina isn't biased that way, Pov."

"Oh? She's still Slav. You get raised a certain way." Athena tipped her head and eyed him. "I don't believe that such things get fixed in concrete. And don't say, 'You're Greek and don't have to.' We Greeks still have to push and shove, whatever the contract guarantees we wrote in when we joined *Dance*."

He shrugged, accepting it.

"Then what is it?" she demanded. "We got T Tauri—and you didn't tell me about that, with discussions to come, you traitor, but ah, well. You're acting as if somebody died."

"Leave it alone, Athena. Please."

"Pov, what *is* the matter?" He shrugged vaguely, wishing she would let it be, knew enough to guess she wouldn't. "Do I have to get Kate to wheedle?" Athena demanded. "I will, if I have to."

"Please don't." He turned to face Athena, saw the alarm in her dark eyes, the genuine concern. "You're a good friend, but I have to work this out myself. It's nothing world-shaking, don't worry, just a lot of disruption lately. Family problems, ship problems, Sail Deck problems ... problems, problems. Life used to be easy. Everything was clear."

Athena slipped her arm through his, a companionly gesture that gave him comfort. He sighed and bowed his head, very aware of another Greek he valued.

"I meant what I said to Milo over there," she said quietly. "This choosing is for the future, Slavs and Greeks and Rom. I think I'm the only captain who really sees it, and I worry about that. If we're each too busy pursuing our own agendas, we might hand the best of *Net* away. You're connected in that somehow, Pov."

"But what if *Net* really was at fault, Athena? How does that fit in?"

"Don't listen to Milo, Pov. You weren't—"

"No, I mean in another way, something else that's clearer," he said. "Wouldn't that change things?"

Athena raised an eyebrow in surprise, then thought about it. "Not really. *Dance* still wants to strangle us. If we *were* at fault, it still shouldn't be opportunity to sacrifice *Net*. That's the difference. It's a sickness in the Slav ships, this politicking by race and advantage, a sickness we brought with us from Old Europe." She waved at the Omsk walls. "And there's the same sickness, Bukharin's New Rodina that restricts immigration to proper Russki credentials, keeps out the outsider peoples who don't fit into their Great Plan. And the Slavs aren't the only colony people who want monotony—Ashkelon's Arabs like their rules, too—but it's hurting us now. We Perikles Greeks started *Dance*'s personnel crisis when we joined *Dance*. Rybak has managed to dodge a lot of it, but now he can't avoid it. But it wasn't a Greek he chose as the scapegoat; it was you. I can't figure that."

"You *said* the reason in the meeting over there," he said, pointing at Omsk Station.

"Because you're gypsy? I do *not* believe most of the Slavs share that bias. Kate's as popular as any of my pilots, and your cousins have good positions on both ships. The Rom are part of us all."

"Rybak doesn't feel that way."

"Rybak's feelings run more to greed and power, and I do not accept his ordering of the priorities." Her dark eyes flashed with anger. "I don't know what he intended, but he surely got more than he expected—and we can expect him to entrench now. He is the enemy, Pov: don't forget that. Don't expect fairness and truth, not now. This is truly war."

"You're convinced of that?" Pov asked slowly.

"Absolutely. Andreos can chide me about not picking up rumors, but he's mistaken about the rumors in which I'm interested and the tools I have in my skyriders. This attack against you was deliberate, hatched by Rybak or one of his officers—but not Ceverny," she added quickly. "I know how you feel about him, Pov. But Ceverny surely knows about it now, and he did not speak for you. You should think about that."

"I don't like it, none of it."

"You don't like to lie," she said, smiling at him.

"You're half Rom, half sail: it creates some conflicts. Since when does a gypsy worry about lying to the gaje? It's part of the game, part of survival. But you *do* care—that's the half sail. Not easy." She clucked her tongue. "So Andreos is hiding something else, whatever it was you just hinted. And I thought he'd emptied the bag. Has he told Milo or Janina?"

"No. And don't wheedle at me about what it is."

"Oh, I've got enough of a clue to add it to other things I know." She tipped her head and looked at him blandly, just as Kate did when she felt especially sly.

"Great," he said. "And what will you do with it? Play games like everybody else? Just add it in?" He disengaged her arm and took a step away. Athena promptly stepped over and reattached herself, then entwined her fingers in his with a tight grip.

"You're not losing me so easily, Pov. Don't even try."

He grimaced. "I don't know what you want of me," he said helplessly.

"Ah, Pov. Do you really feel that alone?"

He said nothing for a moment, then looked at her bleakly. "Yes, I do."

She smiled and shook her curls. "So go look for the connections. Go back up to Sail Deck right now, let yourself be seen. Put our talk on hold. Go find *Net*."

"Mother Athena."

She grinned, openly amused. "Goddess of wisdom, that's me—and a willing companion to Truth, the shining god Apollo. I'm sorry: I didn't realize you were this vulnerable. I didn't know this other, whatever it is, and so barged. Will you come ask when I can help?"

"Yes."

"Good." She released him and stepped back, then clicked her heels in a salute, as if he were a lofty shipmaster and not a very confused Pov Janusz. Maybe the gaje did have his soul, for him to worry about the purity of *Net*'s truth, but he didn't mind

Athena's part in the sharing. "Sir," she said, giving him a wide grin. Then she moved off, striding along on her long legs. He watched her disappear into the same Hold Deck tubeway as Janina, taking the shortcut to Pilot Deck.

He turned back to the window and hesitated, inclined to stay in his mood despite her advice, then, nothing resolved, wandered out of the lounge. He took the elevator up toward Sail Deck, then thought of doubling back to his apartment, perhaps, or maybe Avi's apartment—though she was almost on duty, he belatedly remembered. Well, maybe he could wait for her there. For eight hours? The elevator continued its ascent while he was debating and delivered him, still debating, to Sail Deck.

I am a chunk of wood bobbing in a river, he told himself. I am out of my mind.

He walked onto Sail Deck and sat down in the second console chair beside Tully, glomming onto Tully's watch again. Tully grunted at him, choosing to be unimpressed, and they silently watched the staff run simulated sail drills for a while, an unexciting affair: computer drills with *Net* docked at Omsk were a tame ritual compared to the real thing. He noticed that his appearance on deck visibly reduced the recent tension among the alpha watch techs, and then realized he had signaled a good result just by showing up on deck, not that he had exactly intended that. Or had he? He puzzled about it, wondering if it was command instinct or personal self-reassurance—and glad to think of something different from the constant topic the last several days.

So we lied. Was Athena right? Is it *that* important? Why don't you store it for a while, look at it tomorrow or next week? He felt his troubled mind ease a little and looked around Sail Deck possessively. Mine, he thought, aware of Tully's covert attention.

Avi came in early as the watch began to change and relieved the tech covering her station. He looked at her until she glanced at him. They sent telepathic signals to each other for a while, a regrettable inattention to duty on both sides that Pov rather enjoyed—not that anything was happening much on deck—until Avi laughed aloud and forced Tully to notice.

Tully raised an eyebrow at Avi. "I've heard pilots are better," he informed her severely.

"Permission to brain Second Sail, sir," Avi retorted.

"Granted," Pov said. "Butt out, Tully."

"This is *my* deck on this watch, not yours," Tully said. "If you want to poach by sitting there like a gypsy horse trader, sending your secret signals to certain spies and oozing away my authority, I demand better attention to what matters, that is, *my* sail drills. At least try to pretend it's important." He yawned dramatically, then closed his mouth with a snap. "The hearing went well? Are you going to tell us or do I have to wheedle?"

"On the green, Sail."

Tully smiled a big smile. "And you're still sailmaster, I assume?" He made it loud enough for everyone to hear, tinkering again with his own brand of command technique. Pov looked at him indulgently.

"Theoretically. When it's not beta watch and a certain Greek with delusions about himself makes irrelevant comments—yes. Andreos did say *Net* stood by her sailmaster. I appreciated that." He stretched his shoulders and rocked his chair a little. "Avi kissed me in front of everybody and made me gape like a fool. Another of those risk-benefit balances, I guess." He smiled at the dirty look Avi gave him, and stretched his shoulders again. "Want to check the T Tauri specs?" he suggested to Tully.

"We've checked the specs a couple dozen times already," Tully said rudely. "I'm busy. And don't bother Roja when he shows up, either—he's got work to do. Why don't you wander away until it's *your* watch?"

"Maybe we could undock for a few hours and try

some real sail extensions. After all, it's not a secret anymore."

"I've got Lev touring Omsk Station, checking the libraries for more data on protostars, and likely a few other people are touring, too, enriching the Russkis by wasting good money on things they don't need. Ask Avi: she knows all about Russkis."

"We'll send a skyrider over for Lev if he'll be late for watch—and hell, we'll come back. Why the argument?"

Tully wiggled his eyebrows some more. "I have spies, too. After Dina recultivated some friends on *Dance*'s Sail Deck, so did I. Just sit for a while." Tully slouched deeper in his chair. "Simulation's going well," he mused. "Look at that," he said grandly, waving his hand at the wallscreen. "Perfect extension, just like it looks on the computer."

"That *is* the computer, you cretin, ho-ho. Let's go do something real. All we have to do is call up Captain Andreos and ask. Or do I have to wheedle now?"

"Yes. Shut up, Sailmaster, sir. This is my watch and I'm the king who rules."

"King Tully."

"You got it." He smiled again.

Pov gave it up and waited, amused, for whatever Tully's "spies" had told him. After a time, an alert light lit on the console, the light usually used for massive hold breach and other mayhem. Tully had his own particular sense of humor.

"Here he comes," Tully announced.

"Who?" Pov asked indulgently. "Hold Deck just vented to open space, by the way."

"That's okay. We don't need all that air, anyway."

"*Who*, Tully?"

"Well, according to my infallible spies, he had a big fight with Captain Rybak after they got back to *Dance*, with all kinds of shouting around about Rybak's accusations against you. In full view of *Dance*'s sail staff, too. Rybak finally threatened to disrank him for insubordination, also in full view of the staff. Must have been a treat: that kind of stuff *never* happens on *Dance*, not if Rybak can help it. Undermines morale or something." Tully smiled at him, then rocked his chair to time it. "Must be an occupational disease for sailmasters right now, skirting around getting disranked."

"Ceverny?" Pov asked increduously.

"Yeah. I asked the security chief to let me know when he came aboard. Somehow I don't think he's over here with Rybak's approval, so everybody's pretending he's a hold tech."

"Why would he come over here? We're not talking to *Dance*."

"So ask him. Apparently *Dance* wants to talk to you, at least part of it does." Tully's smile broadened; *Net*'s Second Sail was obviously pleased. "Remember what you said about truth?"

"Hmmm?"

"*Are* you present?" Tully asked with asperity. "Didn't you hear what I said?"

"Yeah. At least I'm still in uniform."

"God, the things you worry about, Pov. Why not ease up a little?"

"Grandmam Tully."

"That, too."

The elevator chimed softly and Pov turned his chair around. As the doors opened, Sailmaster Ceverny hesitated a moment, then stepped out firmly onto Sail Deck. He glanced around in obvious interest—but mildly, not a judge ready to criticize, and not the angry man who had earlier stormed out of the intership hearing. Even so, he looked vaguely uncomfortable as he stood there—and Pov did not remember ever seeing Sailmaster Ceverny unassured about anything, not on a Sail Deck.

Pov stood up and walked to meet him, offering his hand. "Good afternoon, sir."

"Mr. Janusz," Ceverny answered and grasped his

hand back firmly. "I had forgotten how new *Net* looks."

"Sir, welcome aboard."

Ceverny hesitated, his face troubled as much as he tried to conceal it, and seemed to struggle for some other inanity to say. His eyes flicked to Tully and the sail techs at their stations, aware of the intense interest focused on them both.

"Why don't you come into my office?" Pov suggested, gesturing at the lounge door and the suites inside. "Maybe I could run the T Tauri specs for you. I'd like your advice."

"Good idea," Ceverny said, a little too eagerly. "Lead on."

They walked into Pov's office, and Pov dragged a chair around his desk so that Ceverny could see the computer monitor. The older sailmaster sat down, then stretched out his legs slowly, wincing.

"God, I'm tired," he muttered. He rubbed his face, then blinked dazedly at Pov.

"Have you rested since we got in, sir? You look awful."

Ceverny quirked his mouth. "Thanks, but I already know that. No, I haven't rested well. *Dance*'s sails are in shreds, dust damage all over the ship, Medical's full of injured people, and I had the devil of a time trying to get something up in sails, something.... *Net* helped greatly, running draft for us out of the tail. I must thank Athena for her steady helm, thank the *Net* sky-riders who helped, too. I must ..." He trailed off and rubbed his face again. "I wish I could sleep," he said.

He sagged deeper in the chair, his long face nearly gray with exhaustion. The fight with Rybak must have drained what little strength Ceverny had left, leaving him a pale shell of himself. Ceverny's rare towering rages, when he had them, were indeed awesome: *Dance*'s gossipy pilot had the truth of that. Now it had taken a toll Pov regretted to see, that and the week of strain to bring *Dance* home and the damage to

Dance and now this very public fight between their ships.

Pov stood up. "Come on. We're going somewhere."

"Where?" Ceverny asked, looking confused and a little lost. "I thought we were going to look at specs."

"We can look at specs later," Pov said firmly.

He grasped Ceverny's arm and waited for his cooperation about getting up, then got the older sailmaster into motion. A dozen interested eyes watched them leave Sail Deck, and Pov left them frustrated about where two sailmasters might be going now. Inside the elevator, Ceverny leaned against the wall and closed his eyes. "Where are we going?" he growled. "Just to know a fact or two."

"You've got a choice, sir. Bed or food or sitting around in a daze."

Ceverny thought about it. "I'd rather look at specs."

"You're as bad as I am," Pov said with some disgust. Ceverny opened his eyes and gave him a tired smile. "Choose, sir. And no specs."

"Anywhere we go, we'll be noticed."

"You've already been noticed, quite well. And I'm not going to ask why you're here, either." He smiled. "I'm just glad you are, sir."

"*I'm* not sure why I'm here, Mr. Janusz, so I couldn't fill you in much. I thought ... I thought maybe I could help with the T Tauri specs. That kind of energy flow could be ..."

"Sir, store that."

Ceverny sighed and sagged even more, his legs trembling slightly as he tried to keep himself erect. Pov clucked his tongue in dismay and keyed the elevator downward, then took Ceverny to his apartment and installed him in bed. Ceverny was asleep within seconds, his snores loud enough to rattle the glassware in the kitchen. Pov called Sail Deck and told Tully where they were, then walked quietly back through the bedroom and sat down at his computer. He windowed into the T Tauri specs and continued on with the modeling, listening to Ceverny's exhausted snores as the man slept.

Two hours later he heard Ceverny stir, then the thud of his feet as he sat up. Pov leaned backward to look around the corner, and watched Ceverny blink dazedly at the unfamiliar bedroom, then notice Pov in the alcove.

"That's not enough sleep," Pov said flatly.

"Mr. Janusz," Ceverny said, "you are not my wife and I refuse to be chided in that fashion." He ran his hand over his chin, then straightened his shoulders. "But I do feel better. Good definitive action on your part, though I can't imagine why my dignity failed me enough to allow it."

"Nuts, sir." Pov smiled, pleased by the renewed vigor in Ceverny's face. Ceverny noticed and smiled wanly, then stood up and walked over.

"Show me your specs," he demanded.

"You *are* determined."

"Of course."

"There's an extra chair in the kitchen."

Ceverny ambled out and snagged a chair, then sat down in it behind Pov. Pov saved his latest modeling program and clicked back to the main specs window, then traded chairs. Ceverny began clicking through the several screens of summaries.

"Have you run simulations?" he asked absently, frowning slightly as he traced the sail designs with his eyes.

"Dozens of them," Pov said feelingly, "but we need better astronomical data. My sail tech's visiting the Omsk observatory to wheedle the latest scans on T Tauri."

"In Bukharin's mood, you'll have to pay for them."

"Suits, sir. Unfortunately, the nearest star probe was just a bypass scan a hundred light-years out some time back: the colony governments aren't much interested in a system without terra firma, much less a fully working sun. T Tauri hasn't ignited its hydrogen core yet."

He leaned around Ceverny and took the stylus, then brought up another section of the programming. "We do have the last several decades of light-curve readings, though a protostar hasn't many definable patterns."

Ceverny grunted. "Typical variability won't help much," he warned. "Protostar collapse is strictly a gravity phenomenon, not hydrogen burning. We can't assume too much." Pov watched as Ceverny clicked through the light readings again, then accessed the star graphics. "Hmm," Ceverny said reflectively. "Triple star."

"Yes, sir. We thought we'd focus on the primary, maybe try to harvest something from the gas jet."

"Possible." Ceverny clicked to another screen and examined the spectrum of the entire system, then requested a spectrum on the center star alone. He shook his head. "Look at those emission lines! X-rays through that kind of dust! With the intensity of those flares, she's active enough to send shock waves through the entire disk."

"Yes, sir. That's our chief hazard. It's hard to see a shock wave coming." It was an elliptical reference to *Dance*'s own accident that Pov instantly regretted, but Ceverny didn't seem to notice, his attention fully on the data. Ceverny clicked back to their sail designs and watched several rotate through a graphic, looking at two of them a second time.

"These designs fit an unstable medium well," he said approvingly. "You plan to enter the T Tauri system itself? Why not just cruise Hind's Nebula?" He accessed the star map and tapped on the screen. "There's another cloudlet less than two lights away. You could skim off the edges of its cloud system." It was an odd reversal on Pov's first argument with Tully, but Ceverny's identical track into the data was reassuring.

"We thought about that, but we're hoping the more condensed gas of an established star means more tri-

tium. Established protostars are also high in lithium—
with those high-energy parameters, a lot of that lithium may break down into valuable isotopes. Another theory."

"Iffy theory," Ceverny grunted, "though I'll admit
the lithium is a draw." He straightened in his chair
and looked at Pov, one corner of his mouth turned
up. "And sailing a bare medium, nebula or not, isn't
as fun?"

"Fun, sir?"

"Fun, Mr. Janusz. I was young once, too." The older
man's smile broadened. "I'd look for lanthanides and
the heavier carbon-60 molecules, too, if you can find
something along the edges of the dust shell without
getting hulled. You might find some interesting
product."

"Janina is looking at that, too" Pov said. "We might
even find some new petrochemicals."

"I'd just survey this trip, get samples, a composition
scan. A good hold of tritium could finance two, three
more trips for the vest-pocket products."

"Yes, sir."

"Good designs—considering your imperfect data on
conditions. Get better data before you start the runs
into that gas jet: something could walk up and bite
you." Ceverny clicked through Pov's primary sail extension again, watching the shapes slowly curve on the
screen as the sails extended in front of a tiny ship
model. "Strange to see the sails that far forward. I
look forward to getting new sails with the same capacity, though I wonder if Captain Rybak will ever interest himself in *Dance*'s own runs out there. I remember
someone on Helm Deck suggested it once, but the
hazards didn't justify the risk. Easier to farm comets."
Ceverny made a face, then turned his chair to face
Pov. "When is *Net* planning to leave?"

"In two days or so, after we settle some crew issues.
We may leave our children behind with *Dance*, each
family to decide for themselves, I think. Some crew

may wish to off-ship, too, no penalty, and stay the duration on Omsk. It'll be a voluntary choice for everybody. We thought that was best, considering the risks."

"Prudent." Ceverny hesitated, suddenly awkward again. "For the record, Pov, I want to apologize for some of my thoughts about you in recent days. It's not common for a master to apologize to a junior, but you deserve it. You could have warned me sooner than you did, but I could have been more alert myself. I now think both ships contributed, as Captain Andreos suggested, and that our mutual fault is much less than I had thought. I don't know if that's a relief or not: *Dance*'s sails are still in shreds."

"Atypical readings are hard to scan, sir," Pov said.

"Especially when a comet disintegrates in your face," Ceverny said ironically. "But we should have foreseen it." He pointed a finger at Pov's chest. "As you should expect any foreseeable danger, however remote, at T Tauri. Be prepared for everything. Don't get entranced by using *Net* for what she was built for—protect those extra sail extensions. It'll do you no good to wreck your sails."

"Yes, sir."

"Just remember it. When you put your sails out farther, you loop in more material that can hit your ship, and the more complicated the plasma inflow, the more stress on the sails. Don't assume the limits in the specs are right: you won't be using the designs for the same conditions that tested them. Not even Gray has fiddled with protostars, not that he needs to where *Arrow* is."

"Yes, sir," Pov said again, then smiled ruefully as he found himself sitting at attention. Old habits died hard.

Ceverny grinned back. "I do hector, don't I? I wish we'd had time to talk with *Arrow* and ask if they've tried these different parameters—provided they'd help us, of course." Ceverny shrugged. "Well, probably not. Old rivalries take a while to fade."

"Even now, sir? After forty years? There aren't any American versus Slav cloudships anymore, just cloudships together—or so we can hope."

"Instead it's ruthless commercial competition, ship against ship, and who cares if we're cloudships together? There are reasons why Captain Rybak has resisted taking us to the Pleiades, young man, whatever you younger types think." Pov repressed a comment, wanting to keep the unexpected accord with Ceverny, but the senior sailmaster saw the effort. He looked saddened. "This isn't what you think, Pov, *Dance* coldly moving against *Net*: this is *Dance*'s fear. Sandor feels old; so do I, and the old tend to hesitate, to hold on to what they value—and so drive away the children by seizing too hard. But I think you understand that." He studied Pov's face.

"I'm just glad you're here, sir."

"And surprised by it, I'll hazard."

"Not so much. After all, you're a sailmaster." He smiled at Ceverny. "Sailmasters have a simpler universe."

"That would be nice—but it's not exactly true. Even oldsters keep learning that." He gripped Pov's arm and stood up. "Good faring, *Net*. Come back to us." He hesitated, as if to say something else, then shook his head slightly. "If you have time, come over to *Dance*. I'd like your opinion of my sail damage."

It was a gentleman's gesture, and Pov's answering smile was without strain. Sailmasters did have a simpler universe, though he admitted Ceverny had not gone the extra step of warning a gypsy sailmaster of a gaje captain's plot against him. If Athena's spies were right, if this affair had any coherent reality behind it, if Ceverny even knew. But he would take what had been given.

"I'll try, sir."

"I've got to get back to *Dance*. Thanks for the nap."

He smiled, looking ten years younger after rest. "Download me a copy of your specs; I'll go up and chat with Tully, then take it with me."

"Thank you, sir."

Ceverny took the chair back into the kitchen and left the apartment, heading back to Sail Deck. Pov rummaged in his cabinet and found a data carrier, then downloaded the sail program, pleased that Ceverny had offered, thoughtful about what lay behind Ceverny's visit. It had surprised him, made things more complicated. It was easier to stay angry, he thought ruefully. It made clearer choices. He waited patiently for five minutes as the program downloaded, then picked up the data carrier and went upship to see Ceverny off.

The next day, the three sail chiefs switched watches around again and Tully came to take the beta watch at the change of shift. Pov went looking for Avi, who was now assigned to Roja's night watch as Roja's group began the upscale training that had put Avi on swing for a few weeks. She didn't seem to mind the turnabout—lesser sail ranks, like Pov in his early days, learned to put up with the injustice of watch changing—though half the time she seemed hardly awake.

To his mild irritation, Avi was still asleep with a not-on-your-life message on her doorlock, so he wandered the corridors for a while, then drifted in the general direction of his own quarters. Everyone he passed seemed keyed up, talking a bit more loudly, moving a bit more energetically. The feedback from *Net*'s people, considering Andreos was risking their profit shares, too, was generally favorable, though a few groused, spinning out their own opinions about how *Net*'s captains should have maneuvered. And he picked up a rumor here and there that a few still blamed Pov, negligent or not, for the end of *Net*'s easy life drifting after comets. Pov shook his head, wondering if a captain ever controlled all the nuances on his ship—and whether he had to. But most of *Net* trusted Andreos, a trust earned by three years of good captaincy.

The formal ship choice was set for the afternoon, with the issues of *Net*'s kids and some off-shipping of other crew to be decided. True, the ship could vote against the T Tauri voyage altogether if enough people rallied enough noise. *Net*'s contract gave the crew the power to head off "dire peril, unjustified" and other chaffer-speak amounting to idiot idea—but everyone knew that was unlikely under Andreos. A shipmaster won his leadership day to day, not in sudden crises: as he saw *Net* argue about the captains' proposal, pro and con, his own doubts about Andreos, which still lingered a little, steadily eased. He saw the trust, saw the excitement: however Andreos had achieved the chance, the people of *Net* would seize it. People and ship: it put a lot of responsibility on his and Tully's shoulders, but *Net* would follow Andreos.

He had just keyed open his apartment door when someone called his name. He turned and saw a security officer hurrying toward him at a fast walk, his expression intent. "What is it?" Pov asked.

"Please come with me, sir. Right away."

"Why?" The man grabbed Pov's arm and pulled hard to get Pov into motion down the hallway. Pov planted his feet and yanked back hard, freeing himself from the man's grip. "I said *why*?" he repeated coldly.

"I'm sorry, sir. Please excuse me." The security man looked abashed, but stood his ground. "You'll understand when you get down to the docking lounge. Captain Andreos asked me to find you, wants you there right away. Rybak's having Sailmaster Ceverny arrested."

"What?" Pov's mouth dropped open.

"Yes, sir."

"When did this start?" Pov strode on past him, and the security man had to run a few steps to catch up.

"Just a few minutes ago, sir. Ceverny showed up

and three of *Dance*'s security men came in right after him, insisting he go back to *Dance*, then said they'd arrest him if he didn't. Our security chief called Captain Andreos, and he sent me to get you.''

Pov hurried down the corridor, then broke into a run on the main companionway, the security man pelting along behind him. A little out of breath, he arrived in *Net*'s docking lounge on Milo's heels. They both pulled up short when they saw the tableau in the lounge. *Dance*'s sailmaster stood in the far corner, defiantly facing off *Dance*'s security chief and two of his security men. Pov's eyes widened as he saw all three security men carried sidearms. Andreos stood nearby, his expression thunderous, with two of *Net*'s own security people standing behind him.

"You tell Captain Rybak," Ceverny was bellowing, "that I can take my vacation time anywhere I please! God knows I have enough racked up by now. If I choose to spend it aboard *Net* at T Tauri, I will. How *dare* you threaten to arrest me!"

"Sir, I have orders from Captain Rybak himself," the *Dance* security chief said tightly. "I understand you also received that order, and that order will be enforced. Shall I recite the contract clause again?"

"The anticompetition clause? Are you out of your mind, Brodsky? That applies to ships owned by Tania's Ring and you know it!"

"It's standard personnel contract, sir," the other replied stubbornly. "Captain Rybak says it applies here."

"I'll just bet he does," Ceverny said savagely. He turned to Andreos. "I have come to offer my help at T Tauri, if Pov is agreeable. I *will* offer that help, and I *will* go." He glared at *Dance*'s security men. Chief Brodsky drew his sidearm and took a menacing step forward.

"That's enough," Andreos said. "Chief, you will step away from Mr. Ceverny."

"I have orders—" the man protested.

"Step back," Andreos repeated icily. "That is an order from *this* shipmaster, which you will obey while you are standing on *Siduri's Net.*" The man hesitated uncertainly, his eyes flicking from Andreos to Ceverny and back again. *"Now!"* Andreos shouted.

Brodsky hastily stepped back, bumping into one of his men. "Yes, sir," he muttered rebelliously.

"And holster that sidearm," Andreos ordered. "I will not have guns waved around on my ship."

Chief Brodsky flushed, but he obeyed. "Sir, I have orders—" he began again.

"*That* we understand quite well. What's next, Brodsky? Bukharin's station force with laser rifles?"

Brodsky's eyes shifted uneasily. "I don't know anything about that," he said.

Andreos pointed at the door to Omsk. "Wait outside."

"Sir! I can't—"

"We'll give him back, Chief," Andreos said heavily. "Just wait outside so I can talk to him first."

Brodsky hesitated, staring at Andreos' face, then flicked his eyes over the others in the lounge. Then he abruptly gestured to his men and walked out, the other two following after. Captain Andreos turned to Ceverny.

"It won't work, Miska. I wouldn't put it past Rybak to get Omsk involved, not when he's rattled Brodsky into acting this aggressively."

"It's a stupid excuse," Ceverny sputtered. "Hell, I have four *years* of vacation time owed me."

"This isn't about vacation time."

Ceverny sat down on a couch and sagged into the cushions. "A dozen of *Dance*'s techs have asked to go with *Net*. He said no to all of them."

"Predictable." Andreos sat down on the couch facing Ceverny, then beckoned to Pov and Milo. *Net*'s security men retreated to the lounge's outer doorway, watching Brodsky through the open port.

Milo walked over and sat down by Andreos, his

expression profoundly noncommittal. Pov stayed where he was, his hands thrust into his pockets. He could hear just as well from where he stood. What a mess, he thought.

"We could help," Ceverny protested. "Most of our senior expertise is still on *Dance*: the officers who had to cope with *Fan*'s early sails and the chiefs who sailed at Perikles have thirty *years* of accumulated experience. It's not that Pov can't manage, but he *is* a junior officer." Ceverny glanced at Pov in awkward apology.

"That I am, sir," Pov said. "I'm sorry, too. I would have welcomed you aboard." As Ceverny hesitated, Pov smiled. "It's all right, sir."

Ceverny blew out a breath and looked old. "I don't understand this. I don't understand *any* of it," he said, his voice ragged with frustration. "It's *Dance*'s fortune, too."

"That anticomp clause *could* be interpreted to bar *Net* service," Milo offered judiciously. Andreos's head swiveled to look at him. "Well, it could, sir. It doesn't say anything about *what* ships are prohibited. After all . . ." His voice trailed off uncomfortably as Andreos just looked at him.

"Store that, please," Andreos said. "This isn't about clauses, either." Milo flushed darkly at the reproof in front of the others.

"I'm only offering my opinion as chaffer, sir," he said stiffly.

"Your opinion is noted." Captain Andreos turned back to Ceverny. "Miska, this won't work, not with Rybak shouting about 'defection.' I'm sure that word's been used, along with 'treachery' and the like. It's his mind-set right now, and it can't be argued away. So go back to *Dance*. Make her space-ready. You'll help us best that way. And—" He stopped, frowning to himself.

Ceverny looked up. "And what?"

"Don't trust Bukharin. Chief Brodsky's hesitation about Bukharin's police was rather telling: Brodsky's seen or heard something that made him wonder." Andreos spread his long hands. "I don't expect you to share captains' strategy with me, Miska, or tell me about *Dance*'s recent huddling with Tania's Ring, but I can guess. I think Rybak's flirting with Bukharin is dangerous to both ships, and especially to *Dance*, not us, whatever Captain Rybak thinks. *Fan* never made that kind of mistake at Perikles, despite her other troubles." He leaned forward, clasping his hands in front of him. "So go back to *Dance*, Miska," he urged softly. "Go back and protect *Dance*. We'll take care of *Net*."

Ceverny gave him a long look, considering it. "If you think so," he said reluctantly.

"I do."

Ceverny scowled, then got up slowly. "Well, it was worth a try." He sighed heavily, then looked over at Pov and nodded, gave him a brief smile. "I envy you," he said simply. He shook his head, then walked out of the lounge.

"Sir," Pov whispered, watching him leave.

Milo sighed feelingly, then shook himself briskly. "Whew. That was too close to contract breach, captain. If we give *Dance* one call on us, one opening . . ."

"Milo, this wasn't about contracts," Andreos said patiently. "We could have used Ceverny's help, more than you know—with no insult to Pov in thinking so. That little problem pales, however, against what Rybak just bought for himself by insisting Ceverny stay." Milo scowled, still confused. Andreos shook his head and sighed, then stood up. "You're both dismissed. Let's make ready for departure and get away from here." He dismissed the security men with a nod and walked out of the lounge.

Pov and Milo followed, going their separate ways.

Chapter 9

The next morning *Net* completed her preparations and undocked from Omsk Station. As it turned out, few of *Net*'s parents chose to leave their children behind, and barely a dozen adults, mostly recent transfers from *Dance*, went off-ship to stay on *Dance* or rent quarters on Omsk until *Net* returned. Pov left Tully on Sail Deck to finish rigging the touring sails, the heavy short-field sails that would protect *Net* during her out-system acceleration, and looked briefly for Avi but couldn't find her, then went down to the central companionway to watch *Net* leave Omsk. The long amidships bridge with its double array of windows gave a great view, and over fifty people had had the same good idea, standing in small groups to talk as they waited.

On the companionway, the wide metal bulk of Omsk Station's dock bay loomed on both sides, shadowing the bay and blocking any view of space. Slowly, at long last, the bay walls began to slide backward as *Net* undocked. Pov put his hands in his pockets and slouched comfortably, watching, then smiled at Kate as she slipped her arm through his.

"Here we go, Kate," he said in Romany.

"I always approve of a new road, one with new turnings," she replied. She lifted her face and smiled at him. "What would Dad have thought of all this?"

"I think he'd approve," Pov said slowly, thinking of a father he only barely remembered, and whom Kate had never known at all. "I'm not really sure."

"He would," she said confidently.

As *Net* cleared the docking bay, Tania's Ring appeared far beneath them beyond Omsk, a blue-and-golden crescent just turning into the station's dawn. Pov and Kate watched a few minutes longer as *Net* began a slow spiral away from Omsk, then separated as Kate walked off toward skydeck and he took the elevator up to Helm, as Athena had asked earlier that morning.

Athena's Helm Deck stretched twice as wide as his own Sail Deck, with a half-dozen extra stations and a wall-sized window dominating the forward section of the deck. As he walked out of the elevator, Athena spotted him and waved him over. She was bending over Stefania's chair at a side station, looking at the screen on the console. As Pov walked up, both women swiveled abruptly toward him, making him hesitate in midstep. Athena snickered.

"Wondering what you've done now, Sail?"

"Have I done something, Helm?" he asked mildly and strolled over, then smiled down at Stefania. "Hi, Stef."

"Pov." Stefania smiled up at him, tense but in control. "We're looking at the fuel-consumption curve again. Are you sure about the sail data during transit?"

"Yes, I am."

Stefania sighed and glanced at Athena. "Now, Pov, this is our first interstar—" she started.

"The data's based on *Dance*'s jump from Perikles," Pov interrupted, a little annoyed with the byplay. Did Stefania expect him to change physical laws? "Go argue with *Dance*, Helm. It's their data."

"We did," Stefania said. "No matter how we jiggle the figures, *Net* still arrives at T Tauri bone-dry. Not good." She straightened and sighed, then exchanged another look with Athena.

Net had kept its tritium harvest from the recent comet run and had borrowed heavily from *Dance*'s fuel reserves, storing the tritium fuel in extra baffled holds near the engines. Though the Leland drive skirted most of the time slippage mandated by Einstein, a decent speed required adequate reaction mass, first to accelerate to light speed and the singularity jump, then to decelerate into real-time space. Even after three centuries in space, interstellar travel was still cruelly expensive in a too-rare product. Pov sat down in a nearby chair and stretched out his legs.

"We're going into a nebula. Hydrogen concentrations will be way above normal as we decelerate, and our touring sails will catch the higher flow—not as much as full sail, but enough for maneuvering."

"You don't *know* that," Stefania said.

"As a matter of fact," Pov said firmly, "I do know that. It's called long-range radio waves. That's how we detect hydrogen in nebulas, Stefania." He gave her a glare and saw her bristle in response. Athena quietly laid her hand on Stefania's shoulder.

"You guys want to go in the next room?" she asked. "Pistols at two paces, maybe?" Stefania flushed and looked away.

Pov added the angry flush to some overheard talk the last few days, and suddenly understood why Stefania was mad at him. Rybak's brush must have swept a little too far, pulling her into the gossip, too. He sighed. He regretted this. "I don't blame *you* for what happened, Stefania," he said quietly. "When have I said I did?"

Stefania looked back at him, her pretty face remote. "You're an arrogant so-and-so, Pov Janusz."

"True." He held out his hand, offering. "And you squeak when you get insecure. Peace, Stef?" Stefania hesitated. "Talk like that hurts; I ought to know. About me, it was fair, I suppose, but who's been saying you were involved?"

"A few. The skyriders told me."

"Skyriders talk far too much," he said tiredly. As he started to withdraw his hand, Stefania reached out and caught it, squeezing his fingers. "You don't blame me, Pov?"

"Hell, no."

Stefania pressed his fingers and let her hand drop. "Okay." She took a deep breath, then smiled. "I still don't like you very much."

"I don't like you, either. You drive me crazy."

Athena rolled her eyes. "*When* you two are done exchanging your insults," she advised ironically, "I suggest we start lining up for T Tauri. Stefania?"

"Yes, Helm." Stefania turned her chair and began typing on her console, loading the helm screens one by one. Pov saw the wallscreens begin to change as the helm computers built their maps, laying the course ahead. The ship swung in space, lining up on a distant star not visible in the starfield, not yet.

" 'And Odysseus set his course by a single star,' " Athena quoted softly, smiling at the array of stars ahead, " 'a star low over the island, a star that beckoned with a pallid gleam.' "

"He was a great voyager, Athena," Pov said. "One of the best."

"So are we, my friend. So are we." She waited a moment longer, watching the screens. "Open the all-ship channel, please."

"Channel open," Stefania replied quietly. "*Net*, this is Helm. Prepare for course. Helm, you are on all-ship." She turned around to watch Athena, her eyes shining.

Athena set her feet apart and lifted her head proudly. "The course is set," she called out, lifting her voice so that it rang through Helm Deck and all the ship. "Lock down!"

"Locked down!" a tech called back.

"Trim the ship for course!"

"Ship is ready!"

"Launch!" Athena called out, and *Net* began to accelerate, its engines blazing. As *Net* surged forward, a shout went up on Helm Deck, echoed by other shouts over the all-ship channel. Pov found himself on his feet, caught by the exultation that swept over the deck, bringing the others to their feet, too, all clapping their hands in enthusiastic applause. Over the all-ship circuit, he heard the babble of other cheers, of voices excited and happy. Pov grinned as Athena turned to look at him, her face ecstatic.

"Hot jets, Helm," he said.

"That we've got," Athena said with satisfaction. "All the way to T Tauri!"

Afterward, Pov went back to Sail Deck, glomming onto Tully's duty to watch awhile longer on Sail Deck's own screens.

"Well?" Tully prompted as he sat down.

"Well, what?" Pov stretched out his legs, then laced his fingers comfortably on his stomach.

"Did you and Stefania kiss and make up?"

"How'd you . . . ?" Pov tsked at him in exasperation. "Sometimes I think certain people have secret eye beams that let you see things lesser mortals don't. How do you pick up stuff so fast?"

"With secret eye beams." Tully snickered at Pov's expression, then rocked his chair, looking smug.

"So who suggested it, you or Athena?"

"Suggested what?" Tully asked innocently.

Roja had come in for beta watch and hovered in the corner, eyeing Tully, then Pov, fidgeting as his two seniors glommed his watch. Roja was still new enough at sail command to feel slightly threatened whenever his seniors lingered too long. Pov and Tully shifted genially to two side chairs, letting Roja take the watch. Pov noticed that Benek's station was empty, though the watch had changed a half hour before. He frowned.

"Where's Benek, damn it?" Pov said abruptly. "He's late again."

"Permanently late," Tully said with some satisfaction. "Andreos kicked him off *Net* back to *Dance* just before we undocked, him and Dina both."

"What?"

"Come on, Pov. Stop defending him. He doesn't deserve it."

"Why wasn't I asked?"

"Andreos' prerogative, I guess. Let it go, Pov."

"I'll be back."

Pov got up without another word and walked off deck to look for Andreos. He found the shipmaster in his office, his computer opened to Pov's sail programs. Pov stepped into the office and stood in front of the desk, not sure what he wanted to say. He could guess some of Andreos' reasons, even the one for excluding Pov, but still ... Andreos lifted his eyes, took a quick glance that probably read everything in Pov's face, then looked back at the specs.

"This larger sail extension. Are you sure it's safe in a gas jet?"

Pov sat down. "I just heard you off-shipped Benek. Why wasn't I consulted?"

Andreos leaned back in his chair and sighed. "My choice. Easier for you to not be involved."

"But, sir ..." Pov fumbled to a stop. "I just want to know your reasons. I think I can see them, but I wanted to ask."

Andreos took his time folding the data sheets on his desk into neater piles, then rearranged them again. Pov waited patiently, his eyes on Andreos' tired face. "You're not angry at me?" Andreos asked.

"Angry, sir? When have I ever been angry at you?"

Andreos snorted his opinion of that idea, then leaned back in his chair with a sigh. "Oh, I remember a few times, now and then. I've told you the fundamental, Pov. In a choice between people and the ship, the ship must come first. At T Tauri I need a reliable crew: there's too much at stake."

"Just because Benek made one mistake?"

"It's more than 'just a mistake,' and you know it.

He let himself be manipulated by First-Ship politics and moved against his sailmaster."

"All through the hearing," Pov said, "all I heard was that invisible fact, the lie we made. Then Sailmaster Ceverny comes over and apologizes and then has that fight with Rybak for our sake—and here we sit with a secret like that, one that exonerates him, gives his ship a fortune by selling us." Pov stopped, then grimaced. "He knew something about the plot against *Net* and me, probably; we know about Dina. Maybe that balances." Andreos nodded, his lips quirked in a slight smile. "Not that I like it, sir," Pov added stubbornly.

"And?" Andreos prompted, when Pov fell silent again as he puzzled at it.

"But still ..." Pov smiled and spread his hands. "But I agree it had to be hidden, for *Net*'s sake. I concede that, even if I don't like it. But, sir, why punish Benek publicly like this, without giving him a chance? He might have told in time, might have realized what he's done."

Andreos rubbed his nose tiredly. "True. But Benek's caught in a web now, though not entirely of his making. And Ceverny's fight with Rybak has just tightened it into a noose. If he wants Dina, he can't have us, but he wouldn't see that right away. I just made it easier for him by making the choice, not that my action was entirely benevolent in its motives. Booting him and Dina back to *Dance* was a message I wanted to send to Captain Rybak. Maybe it'll make him think a little, too."

"You really think Rybak's made a fatal mistake for *Dance*?"

"Maybe. We'll see." Andreos grimaced sadly. "I worry for *Dance*. Does that sound odd to you?"

"Not at all, sir." Pov smiled.

Andreos grunted. "So you feel it, too. How we get entangled, when it's smarter not to care. I was Captain Rybak's holdmaster for years, and one of the reasons

I command the way I do is the way he does, if you get my drift. Ceverny is a proud old man, with personal truths as strong as the ones that conflict you: he's also one of *Dance*'s most important assets, and the single-handed reason why *Dance* made it back to Omsk. Yet when Ceverny *dares* to lose his temper at Rybak in public, from exhaustion, from self-doubt, from grief, Rybak hits back *hard*." Andreos raised his hand and clenched a fist tightly. "All Rybak sees is the challenge to his authority. He crushes, because all that counts is his authority as shipmaster, his right to rule."

"Miska Ceverny doesn't crush easily."

"True. But Rybak's fallacy is thinking that the shipmaster is the ship. He's not. I keep giving you this rule that the ship is more important than its people, but the people also *are* the ship. Captain Rybak forgets that." Andreos smiled wryly. "I sometimes worry that I'll overreact by remembering it too well, and so I worry I might make a terrible error because of it, something that hurts *Net* badly. You might take that into account when I zig in a direction you don't expect."

"Hmm." Pov frowned.

"Defending Benek was a good action, Pov—it's part of strong command, that trust in your people. If you don't give that kind of loyalty, you won't get it back and the ship suffers because of it—and sometimes it never heals." Andreos leaned back in his chair and stretched a moment, then let his hands fall loosely into his lap. "When I was a young man on Hold Deck, about your age, actually, I sorted some radioactive carbon into a tritium container. I never heard so many alarms go off at once. Wasn't my fault: a Perikles tritium firm put a computer virus into some data they sold to a rival company, and the rival sold it to us, probably guessing what it had in it. The virus sneaked around *Dance*'s computers awhile, then finally exploded in my hold program."

"God, sir," Pov said.

Andreos shrugged ironically. "We didn't know that right away, of course, and Ryback was *convinced* it was my goof-up. Full ship hearing, averted stares, Rybak's lofty scorn for incompetents loudly announced, gossip all over the ship: I was three days from being off-loaded back to Perikles when *Dance*'s computer chief found the virus trace. And so I was saved. Of course," he said dryly, "later I learned the *real* consequence of that hold accident when Sophia and I couldn't conceive a child, but that was much later. At the time, I got a stiff little apology from Rybak, a little citation, a fragment of profit share, backslaps all around from my fellows in Hold. But Rybak had believed it, believed it in an instant. And I had loved him as I loved my own father. All the apologies couldn't erase that *first* fact." His eyes glittered a moment with the memory, then he lost the anger with a fatalistic shrug. "Old history, true, but we don't forget."

"I'm sorry for you, sir."

Pov hesitated, not sure what else to say, not sure what Andreos needed from him. He wasn't used to this confessional side of Andreos. He had seen Andreos in a dozen different moods, worried, elated, angry, mellow, but all had been tempered by Andreos' secure confidence in his clever mind. Perhaps Andreos' fear looked like this, that and the sense of growing old. How would I feel, Pov wondered, if Ceverny had truly acted against me? He frowned, and looked up to see Andreos watching him benignly, his eyes alight with an open affection.

"Sir." Pov said, answering the look, and smiled at his captain.

Andreos' smile broadened. "I don't have any sons, Pov, but, having none, I can find my sons where I choose to find them. I love the cloudships as much as you do. Life itself to me. And a greater part of the love as we get older is training the young and ensuring a future. Aside from some pointed empathy from personal experience, I defended you for *Net*'s sake, for the legacy I want to pass to you. And, for the sake of that legacy, I cannot have Dina on this ship when we go to T Tauri, and Benek won't leave her, not yet. So he had to go, too. But when we come back from T Tauri, you can invite him back—if he'll come without Dina. Does that satisfy you?"

"Thank you, sir. Uh, I'll think about it."

Andreos raised an eyebrow. "No automatic 'of course I'll invite him'?"

Pov shrugged back. "I'd have to talk to him, and, yes, I'm starting to get the drift of all this advice you've been handing out recently. So sit there and look reassured all you want." Andreos rocked his chair, smiling. "You realize Dina might tell Rybak?"

"That's part of the risk." Andreos smiled with smug satisfaction. "To lessen the risk, I ambushed her. I had her escorted off the ship by Security, and the chief watched her like a hawk every moment—then walked her through a magnetic field as she left. It trashed her music tapes and some family letters, but it also got any data-scan copy she might have hidden on her personal tapes. She certainly didn't take anything from Central Records and hadn't time to download a copy from the main computer banks. Wherever she hid it, it's still there. The computer chief is looking."

"The computer chief knows, too?"

"I needed some expert help."

"Have you told Milo yet? Athena has a hint, by the way."

"I expected that: Athena believes in good spies. You might copy her and Tully sometimes. I haven't decided about Milo: he'll keep."

"Division of command, sir? Not very smart—nor fair to Milo."

"It's *my* job to recite the rules, not yours, young man. Please let my instructions stick a little before you start peeling them off. I'm thinking about Milo."

Andreos looked stubborn. "Janina won't care about being left out: she's happy with her hold rank and uninterested in higher captains' affairs. But Milo . . ." Andreos scowled.

"He doesn't like me."

"It's not personal to you, whatever his gauche opinions about gypsies fed to him in the cradle. He's jealous of you."

"Jealous?" Pov asked with surprise. Andreos chuckled, genuinely amused and showing it. "Am I that dim?" Pov demanded.

"No. You just choose not to notice what you think is unimportant. Why should you care about what you are, what other people think you are? You're a Rom. That answers a certain question so thoroughly you don't need to worry about it. Milo does. Every time I show approval of you, it's like a needle in his skin, jab, jab. Would I have protected Milo as I protected you? He doesn't know. I would, of course, but *he* doesn't know that. So he worries about things a Rom doesn't have to."

"Like Greeks don't worry?"

"Something like that. Hard to be a Slav." Andreos smiled contentedly, the lines of his face deepening. "Easier to be younger on the ships."

"I'll say. Why are you so sure I didn't worry?"

"Did you?" Andreos affected surprise.

"Hell, sir," Pov said disgustedly. Andreos laughed.

"I wanted some wiggle room for *Net*, and we have that now." He shrugged fatalistically. "I don't expect it to last. One thing at a time." Then his expression changed and he swiveled his chair back to his computer. "Speaking of the other, I want you to explain some of these T Tauri specs to me." He paused, shooting a quick glance at Pov. "Assuming we've settled Topic One?"

Pov hesitated.

"Have we?" Andreos prompted softly, turning back to him. Captain Andreos folded his hands on his desk and waited, not pushing, just asking. It was that patience that Pov trusted: it had never failed him, not in three years under *Net*'s clever shipmaster. Can a captain be too clever?

Pov took a deep breath, and decided to choose the trust. Consistent, Andreos called him: well, that's what he was.

"Suits then, sir: what do you want to know?"

Pov finally caught up with Avi in the corridor near her apartment, and stopped a few paces away, looking at her reproachfully. He'd looked for her all day, not knowing if she was avoiding him, or if she was, why. She stepped closer and touched his face.

"Missing me, Pov?" she asked softly.

"Hmmm. Want to come to dinner? My treat."

"You've never let me cook since that first morning. Why is that?"

He quirked his mouth. "It's Rom choice. I've been reminded a lot lately about those connections." He hesitated, caught in his habit of keeping the secrets. Rom secretiveness had protected their way of life for centuries, and every Rom child was raised to keep the practice of fooling the gaje. But this was Avi. He looked down at her, probably showing his perplexity.

"Your purity rules, I suppose," she said. "Like Kate never walking in front of you when you're sitting and your throwing away something perfectly serviceable because it touched the floor? I've noticed more since I've been around you, when you're not on Sail Deck. Don't you think some of the rules are a little archaic?" She tipped her head and gave him a quizzical look. "You don't do any of those things when you're on duty. Movable rules?"

"It's a private thing. It doesn't fit on deck, so I don't show off. Personal choice."

"Don't you get into trouble with people being offended?"

Pov twisted his mouth. "In Rom eyes, Avi, gaje

offense doesn't matter." He looked away, feeling uncomfortable, but knew they'd have to discuss this. "*Will* you come to dinner?"

"If the Rom are so pure, how can you sleep with a gaje woman and not get polluted?" She spread her hands. "See, I've been reading up on gypsies." He saw the shadow in her eyes and abruptly knew why they were talking about "offense."

"Reading *what*?"

"Oh, I did some research in Omsk's library." She waved her hand airily.

"Those Russki studies about the Rom? Hell, Avi, those studies are drift gas. Mother Russia's never been interested in assimilating us, and after the political camps, we were never interested in cooperating. Most of the gypsies left Russia in the twenty-first century and never went back."

She tossed her head. "Even so, some of the words are very interesting: secretive, deceitful, fleecing the gaje, antisocial, ancestor worship. I especially like the rule about women being more polluted than men. In this day and age? I'm surprised Kate puts up with it." Pov looked at her, feeling frustrated by the anger in her eyes.

"It's not like that."

"As a Rom male, of course you would say so."

He bit his lip to hold his temper. "Listen, Avi, you can either listen to those gaje tapes talk about us or you can listen to the Rom talk about the way it really is. I *live* the life; I was raised in it."

"So why haven't the Rom ever told it 'like it is'? None of those scientists were Rom."

"The Rom don't feel any great mission to convert the gaje. The Rom way of life has endured for twelve centuries."

"So did slavery," she snapped. "How is *that* an argument for intrinsic value?"

"You aren't being fair."

"Fair?" Avi's eyes flashed. "Maybe I'm just asking questions you don't want to hear."

"No, you just want to fight. You don't want to come to dinner, fine. You have second thoughts about anything with me, fine. Let me know if things change." He turned on his heel and walked away from her.

"Don't you dare walk out on me!"

He turned and glared at her. "You want to start a fight, do it. But don't recite those stupid gaje studies at me and think it's the final word. I'm not going to cringe and blush about what I am—you don't even know *what* I am as a Rom. You haven't asked."

She hesitated, shifting from one foot to another. "Then let me cook," she said, crooking her lips into a ghastly smile.

He shook his head sadly. "Why should I prove that kind of point, breaking my purity just to please you? I'm sorry." He turned and headed off, then heard her hurry to catch up with him. A moment later, she slipped her hand tightly into his, her eyes pleading. He looked down at their hands then pressed her fingers with a sigh.

"One of the studies says a favorite Rom dish is hedgehog," Avi said. She wrinkled her nose.

"Used to be—when we had hedgehogs about. Easy to catch along the road, nice with peppers."

"Another says the average intelligence of a gypsy is that of a ten-year-old because of all the inbreeding."

"It's one of the better gypsy dodges, I think: just look vacant, maybe drool a little, then twitch. It makes the guy with the tapecorder go away real fast."

"Or toss back snippy comments that defy sense," she said, standing her ground.

"That works, too," Pov agreed, "for both Rom *and* gaje."

"I'm sorry, Pov. You wouldn't believe how wide my eyes got reading that stuff."

"I can believe it, though I'm sorry you were so quick to think it might be true." She winced, and he felt the gulf between them. "Some of it's true," he admitted, "but there's a balance they leave out."

"All those don't-touch rules about women?" she asked increduously. "Make them drink downstream, *below* the horses? Throwing away anything she touches during her period? Calling the lower body *dirty*? Are you kidding?"

"Avi, Rom society is South Asian, not European. It's not like that, not really: our women aren't devalued by that kind of thinking. Rom women can rule as much as Hindu wives do—and both sexes rule as tribal elders. And the purity rules protect women as well as confine them. As I said, there's a balance they leave out, something gaje never see, even when we show it to them." As Avi wasn't seeing, he thought. Did she even want to see?

They turned the corridor bend and passed a couple walking the other way, hands also linked; the woman smiled and nodded genially to both Avi and Pov. "Protect?" Avi asked, confused.

"Purity works both ways, Avi. If a man oppresses a woman, all she has to do is threaten to pollute him. Touch him with her skirts, feed him food that's touched the floor, mix up his clothes in the washing: all it takes is the threat and he backs off fast, believe me. In the old days, the tribe might *expel* a Rom for that kind of minor impurity. They usually let you back in later if the offense wasn't too bad and you'd reacquired your purity and groveled to the elders, but still you got kicked out for a while, had to go on the road. It was a good release for social tensions. So if a new wife is badly treated by her in-laws, all she has to do is accuse one of them of something *marime*, like saying her father-in-law touched her wrong, maybe even tried to seduce her. It doesn't matter if it's true or not."

"She lies?" Avi wrinkled her nose again.

"Sure. Lies are easier." He looked at her, upset by the obvious distaste he saw in her face. This was not going well, not well at all. Pov felt a wave of the old despair he'd almost forgotten, before he was a man and the gaje boys had pointed their fingers and mocked what he told them. He hadn't expected this from Avi. It's stupid to trust the gaje, the Rom said, he reminded himself.

But he tried again, watching her face as they walked. "All that counts is *marime*, Avi. *Marime* protects her. Even if everybody knows it's a lie, the in-laws are still disgraced and she gets to go home and get out of a rotten marriage if she wants, then gets to gloat as her in-laws scramble to erase the taint, maybe even have to leave town. Then, sometimes, when they come back, things are patched up and she goes back to live with them and things are easier. And you think that's not *power*?"

Avi scowled and looked unconvinced.

"What counts is the family, nothing else. The family finds the way to endure—by using the rules to keep a balance." They reached his apartment door, and he keyed it open, then looked at her. "You don't have to come in, Avi."

She stepped past him firmly, and preceded him into his apartment. "Does Sergei keep the purity rules?"

"Yes."

"But how does Kate feel about being called less than a man?"

"Not less—just more vulnerable to impurity. And if she keeps the rules faultlessly, she can be purer than a man, have more status. Balance again."

Avi shook her head, then smiled at him ruefully. She shrugged. "It's still female labeling."

"True. Everybody gets labeled one way or the other."

"Fatuous comment, Pov."

"I'm a fatuous man."

"No, you're not." Avi strolled around the room, then stopped in front of the saint's shrine in the corner. She bent forward to look at the statue and tiny shrine lights, but did not touch. "Ancestor worship? Like dead people turn into gods?"

She meant to hurt him now, and he retreated emotionally into a safer place, barricading away the pain. "No, not really." He sat down in one of the window chairs and turned it to face her. "Reminding. And every people has ghost stories. For us, every Rom sees a ghost at least once, maybe hovering over the grave, maybe along the road, a spirit wanting to meddle in his life for good or bad. Every Rom knows the ward spells and the risks in offending the departed. I saw my father's ghost when I was a boy; so did Karoly. He hadn't been dead long, and a ghost lingers longer when the death is sudden."

She turned. "But you're a scientist, Pov."

"That I am."

"Ghosts?"

"Rom religion." Avi threw up her hands.

"Atheism is easier." She sat down in the other chair and curled her fingers over the chair arms, then picked at a loose thread in the weave. "If we end up where Sergei and Kate are, will I have to become Rom?"

"I would ask that, I think," he said slowly. If he asked, he thought, and looked away from her.

"Sergei believes?" She sounded incredulous.

"No. But he does it for Kate, and tries to see the value. I don't think he does quite yet, except that it makes Kate happy and deepens what they share. All mixed marriages are like that, aren't they? But isn't this a little premature? I thought we hadn't even decided if we were having a romance."

She smiled then, without discomfort. "Well, after all the times we've been in bed so far, I'd say it's a romance. Don't you get lonely, being apart?"

"Apart from whom?" He raised an eyebrow. "The rules make me Rom."

"Don't you want more than the Rom?"

"I have more. I have Sail Deck and Tully, I have *Net*

. . . and you, I thought." He shrugged. "It's not an easy balance, and my mother and I are arguing about it."

"But she doesn't object to me—or does she?"

Pov looked at her sadly. "To my mother, sweet Avi, you really aren't a person. You're a gaje and so you don't count. She doesn't like the fact we're sleeping together, if she knows about that; she doesn't like my ignoring marime on Sail Deck, but she accepts it. All that counts is the private life inside the family, and then only the part that's publicly admitted to other Rom. If I wanted to marry you, she'd have some insistences, but *gaji romni*—our label for such brides—are permitted, if the couple wishes. You would never really be a gypsy, but everyone might pretend nicely. Maybe. And likely she'd be a typical Rom mother-in-law, putting you in your place and hoping maybe she could break us up by harassing you with it. I'm not saying that *all* of the Rom way is a good way."

Avi looked at him for a long moment, her face unreadable, then she took a deep breath. Her fingers tightened on the chair arms, then relaxed. "All of a sudden this has gotten too serious. But I guess eventually you deal with the whole man, right?"

"Or the whole woman. Do you want to go back to just Sailmaster Pov?"

She smiled. "Not really, but let me take the Rom in stages, okay? And I'll always be your friend, Pov."

He heard the touch of a tentative farewell in the assurance, but it was gentle enough not to hurt as much as he thought it might. He got up and bent to kiss her.

She clung to him hard, kissing him back, but he noticed that she skipped dinner, choosing to lose herself in extended sex, a last desperate joining. After she had dressed and left a few hours later, not staying the night, he lay on the bed naked, conscious of the ventilator currents breathing across his body.

Avi avoided him the next few days as *Net* continued its steady acceleration to jump point. When they shared the second day's watch on Sail Deck, he watched her covertly, not knowing what to do and seeing the same misery in her dark eyes whenever she glanced at him. But she kept her distance, avoiding him, running away.

Do you blame her? he asked himself, trying to be fair, not wanting to be fair. In the end, he stored the pain as best he could and focused on his work as *Net*'s sailmaster, a role he knew, one with fewer doubts.

By the fourth day, *Net*'s speed had distorted his sail screens' light readings into an incomprehensible blur, making the sail screens a painful glare to watch. Pov shut them down and tightened the touring sails, channeling as much hydrogen into the engines as possible as *Net* edged closer and closer to light speed. *Net* held its collective breath as the dials counted off the last decimal nines, edging closer to Einstein's limit. Then, between one moment and the next, the ship singularized and jolted into nonspace, jumping three hundred light-years in a convulsive instant. Andreos had the chiefs spend an hour double-checking that *Net* had arrived intact, then ordered Athena to reverse ship. *Net* slowly swung around, her engines now retrojets to slow her speed.

It took still another full day for the light readings to stabilize and give *Net* her first look at T Tauri, though the ship was still going too fast to make much sense of the data. By the third day after jump, *Net* had slowed to one-quarter light speed and Athena turned the ship again, allowing the sails to replenish some of *Net*'s expended fuel. The particle count on *Net*'s sensors rose dramatically as the free-floating hydrogen of the nebula impacted the sails, slowing *Net* still further. They had entered real space safely distant from the rotating dust cloud that shielded the central star. As *Net* plunged into the star system, she skimmed across the outer edge of the dust cloud, allowing Janina to take particle samples of T Tauri's dust, then swung outward to take a long and better look at the star system.

Then, when *Net* reached the far lip of T Tauri's gravity well, Athena and Captain Andreos began mapping the star system with fast probes. Some probes plunged into the dust cloud around the central star, taking a few samples before the heavy dust pounded them to scrap. Other probes sped after T Tauri's two companions that hurtled outward, each a slightly flattened globe of reddish gas already beginning the slow assembly into a star. Still other probes plunged into the incandescent gas jets that linked the three stars, collecting data on particle strength, magnetic field lines, and radiation wavelengths. Most of the gas-jet probes were almost immediately lost, torn apart by the jet's maelstrom of energy, but enough survived just long enough to give *Net* a sketchy analysis.

The results did not please Andreos. T Tauri was busy redesigning its territory, and apparently prone to change its mind in unpredictable ways. Pov found anomalies in the gas jets not even hinted at in Ashkelon's long-distance readings or the centuries of Earth's observations, anomalies that defied explanation, at least yet. In T Tauri's dust cocoon, energy seemed to appear and disappear at random, the product of unknown phase sequences between dust and gas that the cloudships had never documented. The dust cocoon was a maelstrom *Net* would avoid carefully. Well, he hadn't expected to try the dust cloud.

"The gas jet," Pov insisted at the chiefs' meeting that followed. "I'd like to give it a try."

Andreos looked over the twenty-odd chiefs assembled in the main admin lounge, getting a probe reading of his own. "The parameters are off by twenty percent," he hedged. "And that's only our preliminary analysis."

"Twenty percent isn't enough, sir."

"Not enough? What d'you mean, 'not enough'?" He scowled genially at Pov.

"Let's vote," Athena said and stood up, turning to the assembled chiefs. "Everybody who wants to try the gas jet, raise your hand."

"Athena!" Andreos chided.

"Otherwise," she said, blithely ignoring *Net*'s ship-master, "we can sit and talk here on and on and on." She turned and looked at Andreos challengingly.

Andreos harrumphed and pulled at his chin, eyeing her for a long moment, then took another reading on the group. "Okay," he grumped, "raise your hands."

He looked over the result. "I see our sailmaster has deftly spread his bribes—or was it Helm's arm-twisting extortions?" They grinned back at him. "The gas jet it is. Pick us a good trajectory, Helm."

"That's *on*, sir!"

Andreos took a deep breath and blew it out dramatically, scowling at them all, then smiled as an overenthusiastic hold chief stood up and started waltzing with himself, playing a sad violin to Andreos and his tut-tutting. "That's enough, you null-brain," he growled.

When *everyone* stood up and waltzed the violin, Andreos tipped back his head and laughed out loud.

Chapter 10

Throughout the next day, Athena took *Net* on a high curving trajectory across the planetary cloud disk toward the northern gas jet, using T Tauri's gravity as a sling to control the last of *Net*'s jump acceleration into a smooth curve. Ahead, at the center of the vast disk, the gas jet made a twisting, glowing river of gas that stretched across millions of kilometers, linking the enshrouded primary star and the smaller brilliant cloudlet of its northern companion. Pov had chosen the northern gas jet as *Net*'s sea to fish, and he watched anxiously as *Net* sent new drones plunging into the wild energies that dominated the gas stream. As the probes disappeared from view into the gas jet, the entire array blipped out, smashed by something in the jet.

"What happened?" Pov asked, startled. "What could they hit in plasma?"

"Let's try when we're closer," Athena suggested.

"We need composition data," Andreos warned. "We can't choose a trajectory into the jet without it."

"We'll get it, sir," Athena said.

As *Net* came closer, Athena sent out a new series of drones, aiming them at a less turbulent area. This time the drones survived the entry and sped inward, lasting long enough to send back the gas-composition readings Andreos wanted—not much, but enough. With some clue to the atomic source of several anomalous light readings, all of it boosted to a blinding glare, Pov's computer techs started mapping the slow turning of the spiraling gas and the several cyclical pulses that shuddered up the jet.

At its edges, the jet flowed in small eddies and spirals that looked possible, each a dozen times larger than *Net* but not wide enough for an adequate collecting run. Cautiously, *Net* approached the jet from the side and slowly drifted downward, paralleling the gas jet, studying the whorls and twisting energy of the jet. To fill her holds, first to refuel her empty reserves and then harvest a cargo of tritium for Tania's Ring, *Net* needed a long smooth trajectory through the gas stream. If they could find it. If it was there.

At midwatch he left Tully and Roja in charge of the main Sail Deck and went into the Sail Deck lounge nearby. There he would interlink by computer and video with *Net*'s other captains as *Net* made its first trial of the conditions at the jet's edge. Because of the dangers, Andreos had adopted the captain interlink regularly practiced by *Arrow* in the Pleiades gasclouds; it provided a degree of coordination rarely needed in the tamer conditions of Tauri comets. During interlink, each captain handed the deck's immediate concerns to his second officer, allowing the four captains to focus on coordinating the run without the distractions of direct command. The captains had practiced the interlink with computer simulations during jump transit and then with the reality of the probe launches, but the new procedure still felt strange to Pov. He was used to sitting on Sail Deck.

The interlink adaptation to Sail Deck's computer communications had made a mess of Pov's sail lounge that the computer staff still hadn't entirely put to rights. He picked his way through the loose cables and banks of support hardware to the padded chair in mid-room. His chair faced a curving half-wall of monitor screens, a few central monitors for video link to the other captains, the uppermost and side-tier screens for direct feed from the sail computers and the other decks. He sat down and began powering up the complex computer station, first connecting his station to each of the other decks by lighting a row of monitors along the lower row of central screens.

In the video screen on the right, Janina sat at a similar hold console, her broad face intent as she went through the same uplink procedure as Pov. She looked up and gave him a quick smile. In the screen next to her, Athena lounged sideways in her chair at a helm alcove station, watching her crew over her shoulder through the open doorway behind her. Andreos keyed in on a third screen, sitting at his office desk, then cleared his throat pointedly to get Athena's attention. Athena swung around and raised an eyebrow, then abruptly leaned sideways over the edge of her chair to reach for something. When she straightened, she brought up Pov's shrine statue of St. Serena and placed the small figure on the table in front of her with great ceremony, then turned it to face the other captains on her screens.

"Hey!" Pov objected. "What is this, breaking and entering?"

"Theft, I admit." Athena shook her curls. "I figure Siduri should watch this crazy adventure from the front row, just to plotz in a little magic when needed. We might need the help." She chuckled at Pov's expression. "Is it okay, Pov?"

"Yeah, I guess."

"You're so gracious, Sail." Athena moved the statue slightly to the side, using arcane Athena standards for picking the best spot.

Other monitors flicked on as the computer chief continued the rest of the interlink, binding the four command decks together. As part of the interlink, the chief also fed the outship views to wide viewscreens in the lounges throughout the ship, with voiceover feed from the captains. All of *Net* not on other duty would watch, with the children and those in hospital safeguarded in sections farthest aft of the prow, shielded by *Net*'s bulk and interior magnetics. *Net* would risk its vulnerable ones in this venture, as a cloudship always did when it sailed a plasma stream, but her captains had ordered whatever extra safety they could build within *Net* against T Tauri's greater hazards. Kate had disliked being included in that group, though she admitted its necessity—and at least she could watch.

As the computer chief completed the in-ship links, Athena leaned forward and keyed on the uplink to the skyriders outside. "Adding chevron, Stefania. Pipe the link to me, please."

"Adding chevron," Stefania replied from her station on Helm's main deck. In a fourth central screen, a picture flickered on to show the small cabin of the lead skyrider. The pilot touched his helmet in a brief salute as they linked, then split his face in a wide grin.

"Hot jets, Helm," he said exuberantly.

"Not this run, Josef," Athena retorted firmly. "You do what I tell you to do, or that gas jet will fry you. Or *I* will if the jet misses when you goof up. Understand me?"

"Yes, ma'am." Josef grinned, mostly undented. He punched buttons on his own board and one of the side screens on Pov's board lit with a graphic, projecting the six skyriders against a graph centered on *Net*. The small row of icons took position directly below *Net*'s hull, still shielded by the skysail. "Chevron in position," Josef said. "Awaiting orders."

"Acknowledged."

"Helm," Andreos prompted.

"Tracking," Stefania said over the audio link. "Interlink completed. Program running."

"Janina?" Pov felt his heartbeat accelerate, then quietly signed Rom luck to himself, choosing all his available omens today.

"All ready, sir," Janina replied smoothly.

"On the green, Sail?"

"Sails in optimum setting, first configuration," Pov said. "Let's go."

"Which eddy do you want, Captain?" Athena asked.

"First, let's look them over a little. Keep the chevron in our lee."

"Yes, sir."

The nearby tendrils of gas swirled as *Net* slowly sailed nearby. Pov keyed an analysis of the light readings from Sail Deck, then muttered to himself as something phased outward from the jet, whatever it was, and lit up a nearby eddy in x-ray. Andreos saw it, too, and his scowl deepened. The phenomenon faded, and Andreos waited a few minutes more, hoping for better stability. *Net* drifted slowly inward.

"That eddy at seventy-five degrees, five kilometers ahead," Andreos decided. "Helm to port. Let's ease in slowly."

"Helm to port," Athena acknowledged. "Slowing speed as we turn. Entering program."

"Extending the skysail," Pov said. "Spinnakers at half extension."

Pov looked up at the outship viewscreen and the glowing river directly ahead, a swirling mass of yellowish gas that dwarfed *Net*. A subsidiary screen read off the spectra of the ions and free hydrogen that made up the eddy, high in lithium and slightly heavier elements but still predominantly hydrogen—of which Pov hoped a reasonable proportion was the heaviest of all hydrogen isotopes, the tritium that had brought them here. Janina's early readings suggested high tritium, but the light readings fluxed badly enough to confuse the computer's analysis, a defect in their computer program the chief was still trying to fix.

Athena brought them into the jet at an oblique angle, allowing Pov to adjust his sail configuration as the gas began flowing more strongly into the sails. The outship viewscreen diffused into a featureless bright glow as *Net* slipped into the edge of the eddy. The screen cleared slightly as they moved farther inward, then blanked again.

"Skyriders move out," Athena ordered. "God, this is a soup. Josef, you keep alert."

"Yes, Helm."

"I read ninety-eight percent hydrogen, high isotope differential," Janina said as she took samples from the gas beginning to flow into her holds. She raised her eyes and smiled at the other captains. "*And* I'm reading twenty percent higher tritium and deuterium, with some helium-3 and lithium-6, too. Do you want me to separate out the other components?"

"Just bottle it for now, Janina," Andreos said. "We'll sort after the run."

"That's on, sir." She frowned slightly. "Higher radioactivity levels than usual: flowing some product into shielded holds."

"I've got radiation cascades inside my holds," Janina said a minute later. "Lots of fragment atoms, weird stuff. It's . . ." She frowned. "Blast! Vent Hold Container Six, Marcos—it's got a critical mass." She blew out a breath as *Net* ejected a hold container. "My God, that was fast, whatever it was. This material is *active*, captains."

"How's the tritium level?" Andreos asked.

"I'm too busy watching the other stuff, sir. Tritium won't blow up in our faces like whatever that was." She paused. "Venting *another* hold now. What in the hell are we picking up?"

"Maybe transuranics?" Pov suggested. "Supernovas make heavier elements, and this cloud is second-generation gas from the Geminga starbursts."

"Maybe," Janina said absently. "I'm still trying to analyze it."

Pov tapped the comm-link to *Net*'s chemlab. "Chief?"

"Yes, sir," a deep voice answered on the audio channel.

"What do you see in your particle chambers?"

The chemlab chief hesitated. "Weird matter, sir: Hold has the right of that. A few transuranic atoms, but most of the weight comes from subatomics. I've got spirals and zigs I've never seen in Epsilon's solar wind, massive particles we've made maybe twice in the big supercolliders on Earth. No wonder Janina's concentrations are reacting: there's a lot of energy inside a few of those atoms we're collecting."

"High radiation count outside, too." Athena said, worrying for her skyriders. Pov glanced at the subsidiary screen feeding from the skyrider's radiation counters, then whistled. Athena had cause to worry: the monitors showed high radiation in all the skyrider cabins. "Where's it coming from?" Athena asked, bewildered. "Sails ought to keep that out."

"Secondary cascades," Janina said. "Those heavier particles are penetrating the sails and breaking up when they hit the skyrider hulls."

"We're okay, Helm," Josef said from his skyrider.

"You remember my rule, Josef," Athena warned. "I'll fry you."

"That's on, Helm." Josef grinned.

Pov saw his readings change on the ultraviolet scale and bent forward to study the curves. "Change in gas flux, sir. We may be crossing a magnetic field line. Not a big one," he added judiciously.

"Out here?" Andreos demanded.

"Data confirms a spiral, sir," Pov said a few moments later. "The eddy is definitely spiraling and the field lines with it." He glanced at Andreos. "Angular momentum, sir. T Tauri's unwinding her top, right at us."

"Hmmph. Watch those angles, Sail." Andreos scowled, watching the same data on his desk screen, then keyed up other data. "What's your other probe data, Athena?"

"Monitors on the star show a steady infalling of matter, sir. No shock waves expected." A thin line appeared between Athena's eyebrows, and she tapped the arm of her chair irritably. "Suggest we not push our luck, sir, Janina."

"Holds two percent full," Janina said placidly. "Keep your belt tight, helm."

"It's not my belt I'm worried about." She tapped her fingers on her desk. "I wish we'd had more time for shielding—and the thought to do it before we got here."

"Add it to the specs," Andreos responded. "We'll remember next time."

"More turbulence, sir," Pov said. "Another field line, and out of place. We've got some space compression here."

"Take us out of the jet, Athena," Andreos decided abruptly. "Starboard and make it smooth."

"Yes, sir. Skyriders, under our lee. Sail, if you please."

"Extending the spinnakers over the skyrider line," Tully responded, his voice tense. The chevron scattered and darted back to safety behind *Net*'s skysail. Pov waited until the main viewscreen began to clear, showing the darkness and scattered stars of open space, then let himself relax a little. One of the spinnakers bowed inward as it brushed another magnetic field line—strange that they could be that rigid, he thought. He watched as Tully quickly corrected, then *Net* was clear. The ship soared outward.

Athena sat back in her chair and scowled, then gave St. Serena a dirty look. "Some help you were. Pov, you need a new statue. This one doesn't work."

"We got something in the holds," Pov argued.

"Yeah," she groused, "more than we wanted." She thumped her hand on the desk. "So how come we can't see those heavier particles before they hit our sails? Why don't they decay inside the jet?"

"Field flux, maybe," Pov said. "Ask the magnetics."

"That's jargon and you know it, sail. What is *feeding* that thing? It's right off the scale."

"I got less than five percent in our holds," Janina rumbled. "And I don't have hold containers to waste just because one wants to start a chain reaction."

"We got out without getting flattened," Captain Andreos pointed out. "Let's run an analysis and fine-tune while you sort, Janina."

"Yes, sir," Janina said, sounding subdued.

"We need more shielding on the skyriders," Athena insisted.

"How long to do that?"

"A week to fabricate and modify six skyriders." She thought about it. "Maybe. I'll have to check where exactly we could put it without unhooking some essential parts. I'd like to talk to Pov about enhancing the skyrider sails, too."

"Heavier sails won't keep cascade particles out," Janina said. "The heavy particles will still get through."

"I know, but I'd like to try." Athena scowled, then pounded her chair arm. "Captain Andreos, I respectfully request that—"

"Granted, mother hen. Wrap your children in bunting as much as you please."

Even so, Andreos looked gravely disappointed in *Net*'s first attempt, a disappointment shared by all her captains. Five percent into the holds was not worth the radiation taken by the skyriders. Five percent was not enough fuel to get home, either. The computer chief began shutting down the uplink, leaving *Net* to scan some better ideas before a new attempt.

"Pov?" Athena said. "Will you come down?"

"Coming, Athena." Pov walked out onto the main Sail Deck and watched briefly over Tully's shoulder as his Second Sail began the data analyses, then took the elevator downward to Helm. Athena had moved to another side station on the main Helm Deck, where she was scowling over the initial skyrider reports from the skydock.

"Look at that!" she exclaimed, waving her hand at the radiation levels on the screen. "God Almighty! One of the ships is actually radioactive. It *glows* in the dark. This is *not* acceptable."

Pov sat down in the chair beside her. "Risk is part of any venture." As Athena swung toward him, her eyes flashing dangerously, he pretended to ward her off with his hands. "Calm down, Athena. Captain Andreos let you stop the run early: he thinks of benefit, too."

Athena pushed back her hair and blew out a quick breath. "Sometimes I'm hard to be around."

"Suits." Pov scanned the radiation level in the offending skyrider and let out a low whistle. "I take that back. That's high enough for contact burn."

"Josef will probably spend the next week in the hospital, hoping he doesn't start losing his hair long before his time. Marrow damage, for sure." Athena's scowl deepened. "Damn. This wasn't in the parameters, not even after our probe data additions. Where's the radiation coming from?"

"I told you. Flux. It must be the magnetic flux lines: it's tearing even the stable hydrogen apart. There's lots of energy in that jet, more than we expected. The neutron flux must be nearly off the scale. Hmmm." He keyed up another reading and winced.

"I want better sails on the chevron," Athena demanded.

"You'll get them. Maybe we can add some more magnetics to ward off some of the heavier stuff. How much lead do you have for hull shielding?"

"Water is easier: it'll help shield against the secondary cascades. But I still want more dense metal. I may have to tear down a few interior walls."

"Not too many walls, Helm." He smiled at her and saw her humor flash into view in response, righting her mood into a better balance. Stefania squeaked in times of crisis: Athena took intensity off the scale, with sparks on whoever got in her way.

"You're a mellow companion in a crisis, Sailmaster," Athena said and tipped her head to the side.

"I've just got a simpler perspective. We went into the jet and got out again: I like basic facts. But even the precautions aren't going to eliminate the hazard. We'll just have to keep it quick—and when we run out of skyriders for a roster, we're done, I guess. I hadn't figured that in." He tipped back his head and stared blankly at the ceiling, trying to run the calculations in his head.

"Or go in without skyriders," Athena said, obviously voicing her best preference.

"Robot probes? They aren't sophisticated enough. We put all our best hardware on the skyriders."

"So automate the skyriders."

"That would take a month or more, if only that. Most of the modules would have to be rebuilt inside the brain—assuming we have the parts—and you still won't get full function." He shook his head. "This wasn't a limitation I thought we had. We're too people-dependent."

Athena shrugged. "Well, I just had six skyriders go off roster, with four others already downchecked. Two are down with some kind of sniffling awfuls, another broke his hand larking around, and then Kate, of course."

"She told you, then."

"She'd better. She'd be off roster even on a comet run." Athena scowled. "I'm going to run all the women through the lab, and I might even take them off this roster altogether. We have good treatments for low sperm count from radiation damage, but it's harder to repair damaged ovaries." She sighed. "My ladies will not like that at all."

"Vacuum suits might add some protection. Janina has them to spare from her outhold crews."

"Maybe." Athena took a deep breath. "I wish this was easy. No risk, no danger...."

"No money if it was. Think money, Athena."

"Think staying alive. Sometimes the people are more important than the ship." Athena punched angrily at some keys and flipped quickly through a set of data scans. Pov watched her face until she glanced at him.

"Do we have to use six skyriders?" he asked.

"Programs for full plasma stream are configured for six—you know that."

"Easy to reconfigure. If we put out robot probes to support a single skyrider . . ." He raised a hand as her mouth opened. "And you will *not* volunteer, Helm. Nor can I," he added candidly with a wry shrug. "Andreos wouldn't like it, not that we're irreplaceable—but shifting command midway in a new technique is not ideal." He spoke as if his or Athena's getting personally wasted was nothing but a side datum, and saw Athena's eyes light with amusement. "So who should it be?" he asked.

Athena thought about it, shaking her dark curls. "I'd like to give Stefania the responsibility, but she doesn't know enough about sails. It has to be Second Rank at least—Third doesn't have the expertise or time in rank on either of our staffs." She frowned. "This is when we could have used a few upper-echelon transfers from *Dance*. They have the longer experience."

"Ceverny tried, Athena."

"I know."

"I'd like to send Roja, but you're right. So it's Tully." He looked at the radiation curves, wondering if he'd later regret this calm technical discussion, knowing how much he could regret it if Tully got hurt.

Athena shook her head. "Tully doesn't have the pilot skills, you know that."

"Or maybe I could talk the captain into letting me go, anyway. . . ."

"I'm first in line." Athena thumped his arm hard enough to sting. "Tully's youngest kid is only three, right? Mine are older if matters go sour."

"And I don't have *any* kids," he said stubbornly. "And the focus is the sail monitors, not steering a course."

"I can read sail data as good as you anyday, Mr. Smart-Pants Janusz, and I can outfly any skyrider hands tied, much less a fumble-fingered groundhog like you. No? Even in helm rank, I am still the best pilot on *Net*. I've got the practice runs to prove it." She crossed her arms and glared at him.

"All you have to do is steer a straight line," he said dismissingly, knowing it would irk her—and knowing he was going to lose the argument. In a tight pinch, the skyriding would count. He scowled dauntingly at her, then endured her smug smile. "Pilots," he said, disgusted. "There's more to life than ducking a strut."

"Not much," Athena said. "So, let's go assault Andreos. We can't risk a full chevron, and Josef's already picked up enough rads today. So it's me." She smiled. As she started to get up, Pov caught her arm, then stood himself and pulled her into a tight embrace, half hampered by the chairs. Startled, she looked up at him, then threw her arms around his neck and kissed him hard enough to make his ears ring.

"Ah, Pov, it's really too bad, isn't it?" She sighed.

"Gregori would love to hear that," he said lightly, then hesitated, suddenly conscious of a dozen covert glances from Athena's helm officers through the open door. One of these days his impulses might do him in, he decided, and loosened his hold on Athena. She gave him a little shake, then let him go.

"Oh, he will. I'll see to that, and he'll smile lazily and know like always he's got nothing to worry about. What a shame." Athena smiled up at him. "Thanks for loving me a little like you love Kate, Pov. I treasure it." She thumped his arm again. "Let's go assault Andreos with the Big Idea." And she bounded away, heading for the elevator. As Pov followed her more slowly, he heard the whispering slip around Helm Deck like a cascading wind. He stepped into the elevator beside Athena and saw her eyes dancing with mischief. The doors hissed shut. Looking at her face, Pov realized he'd just given Athena something to tease him about for weeks, just as Kate did, had. He sighed.

"What's the sigh for?" Athena teased. "A plea to fate or regret over kissing a gaje in public?"

"I never think of you as a gaje, Athena." He saw that, for once, he had surprised her. "Strange, but I don't. Maybe you're really a gypsy baby that the Greeks traded on the sly and somewhere a Greek girl is still very confused. That'd explain it."

"I sincerely doubt that scenario, Pov. But believe it if you must." She wrinkled her nose. "And as much as I'd love to tease, I won't—I can see that in your face." She punched the button and stopped the elevator. Their eyes locked for a moment.

"No," he said firmly, "I don't have a crush on you. No, I'm not regretting anything you have with Gregori. I'm happy with what I have as your friend— and I'm damned sorry I got impulsive. I'm sorry I embarrassed you. Sorry."

"What's the matter, Pov?" Athena asked softly. "And stop looking at your boots. Look at me."

"Avi did some research on the Rom. She didn't like what she read." He shrugged fatalistically.

"You mean those awful Russki tapes? The ones by the pinch-brains who got outtalked by every gypsy they ever met and never caught on?"

"Yeah. She said ... Well, she said that ... Oh, hell." He reached for the elevator button, but she caught his hand in a warm grasp.

"And so that's why?"

"No, it's not *why*," he said, glaring at her. "You're just like Kate. You go barging around and someday you're going to get yourself killed, and it's all pilot panache. Let's lift a glass sadly to Athena; she went out with jets flying. But you're still dead, and nothing will change it when it happens. So I care. So I got impulsive. Is that a crime?" He detached his fingers from her grasp, fuming. "I'm sorry," he said a moment later, not looking at her.

"Sometimes I feel glass walls around me," she said, "this image I have to keep up—worrying about my pilots, letting Gregori smile his complacent smiles, tussling with Milo, sparking my pilot's strut. But with you, sometimes, like you with me when you're not looking, there are no walls. It doesn't last: I remember I'm a hot-jet pilot, you remember the Rom, but sometimes we get surprised. Is Tully always gaje to you, too, Pov?"

"Tully thinks of himself as gaje. We never get very much past it—too many dinners of my mother glaring at him. It molds the spirit." He smiled at her a little sadly, then looked away. "And Avi was never anything but, and she obviously wants it to stay that way."

"I'm sorry, Pov." Athena slipped her arm through his. "I promise not to act like a hot jet out there," she said softly. "I promise not to get myself killed for no reason." He looked down into her dark eyes and pressed her arm against his side.

"Thank you, Helm."

"You're graciously welcome, Sail." Athena pushed the elevator button with her other hand, and they rode upward together, arms linked until the doors slipped open again. As their arms dropped apart, they sighed in unison, then laughed at themselves.

"No!" Captain Andreos said. He pointed imperiously at Athena. "And ganging up on me won't work, however you drag Pov back and forth in front of me, dangling him as your threat."

"It's the only choice," Athena said, unperturbed. "Josef has too many rads, Tully is out of practice as a pilot, and Stefania doesn't have the sail experience." She spread her hands. "And Third Rank can't do it. So it's Pov or me—and getting out of trouble fast needs skyriding experience. So it's me." She pointed back at him. "Pov and I already had this argument down in Helm, and he graciously conceded my superior logic."

Andreos scowled. "So we'll take the extra time to armor the skyriders."

"Want to see the radiation data? And I suspect we were in a nice smooth part of the flow."

Andreos shifted his scowl to Pov in a deft dodge. "I'm disappointed in you, Sailmaster. Letting yourself get looped in. Where's your spine?"

Pov put his hands behind his head and rocked himself back and forth in his chair, grinning at Andreos. "She's right, sir."

"Hot jets," Andreos snorted. "Heaven save me from hot jets."

"And she's still right," Pov said. "The radiation's too high and we don't have the drone capacity, not unless we spent a month or two refitting—with several of the parts we need back at Tania's Ring, assuming Bukharin would sell them to us. Doesn't Tania still have a technological-secrets treaty with Aldebaran? Didn't we get the latest probes fully assembled, with service contract attached, no replacement parts?" He shrugged. "We've always considered our drones backup to the skyriders, didn't need the other technology. And so now we're strapped."

"We knew it, sir," Athena said in a syrupy voice, batting her long eyelashes. "We'd find something we really needed and just don't have."

"That related to sail design, and you know it, Helm." He glared at her a moment longer, then drummed his fingers on his desk. "I'm sorry, Athena. I just can't permit it. You're too valuable, and not for the reasons you two are citing about expertise. If I lose you, I lose Pilot Deck, the way your pilots are attached to you personally. And skyriding depends too much on sheer nerve."

"Then me, sir," Pov said, glancing at Athena.

"No. I want you in the interlink on *Net*. Have you considered a simulator?"

"It'll have to be in person, sir," Athena said stubbornly. "We can't count on consistent data stream through plasma to power a simulator. That's what happened to *Dance*, remember?"

Andreos' face darkened with the reminder, and he opened his mouth for a retort. Pov brought down his hands on the desk top with a thud, startling both the captain and Athena.

"May I suggest, sir, that we all run back to zero? We can't send Tully, and Athena would rather not risk two when she need only risk one. So it's Athena." He caught Athena's grateful glance. "She promised me no hot-jet stuff, captain. It's a private promise."

Andreos thought about it grumpily, eyeing both Athena and Pov from under his eyebrows, then harrumphed.

"Shipmaster's decision, sir," Pov prompted.

"Very well," Andreos said at last. "How long to modify the skyrider and drones?"

"A day perhaps," Athena said. "Time for Janina to sort and run some analyses, then store the more radioactive material in exterior pods. Even with a half-run, we'd get a good cargo, I think."

Andreos nodded. "Then do it, Helm. Not that I don't have my reservations." He glared at Athena dauntingly. "Either you're beginning to develop some judgment, Athena, or you've finally subverted my sail-master, and I'm not sure which it is."

"Yes, sir." Athena smiled.

"Then dismissed. Pov, stay behind, will you?"

Athena rose gracefully and then bent toward Pov. "Your turn to get fried," she said playfully. She waved and sashayed out.

"An original," Andreos grunted.

"Cloned by many others, sir, including my sister."

"You sincerely agree with this?"

"Yes, sir. It looks like a good choice, one impelled by conditions we didn't expect. The contortion of the magnetic lines inside the jet is far more pronounced than exterior readings suggested—and that raises the turbulence and radiation levels. Our skyriders aren't designed for that kind of energy impact." He shrugged. "You told me once, sir, that a shipmaster has to be subtle and logic-minded: why do you let Athena warp your trajectory?''

"So who's warped?'' Andreos chuckled and fiddled with some data faxes on his desk.

"Humph,'' Pov said. He smiled at Andreos.

"I will not be cajoled, Mr. Janusz, so give up the attempt.''

"Won't you?'' His smile broadened. "Sounds warped to me.''

Andreos harrumphed, then scowled at Pov. "I will not have that useful word misused. How are you doing?''

"About what, sir?''

"This ship is a sieve. Remember that. In time all things are known—and there are many ears willing to listen, young man. Talk to me when you have need, will you? However *warped* my trajectories, I do have a few more years of living than you do—and I don't want to lose you without a chance to forestall it—for my sake and perhaps yours.''

"Lose me, sir?'' Pov blinked.

"A shipmaster listens to the sieve,'' Andreos said obscurely. "And I've been very much aware of certain rival authorities on my ship, especially involving several of the crewpeople I tend to value. For the ship's sake.''

"My mother?'' Pov finally caught his drift.

"The *puri dai* among us. When Margareta's hold-tech efficiency rating goes down, she's paying attention to something else, in this case enough for Janina to complain unofficially. She might even get docked a fraction of profit share. So what is it?''

"Ask her, sir.'' Pov crossed his arms.

"A gypsy's secrets?''

"Exactly. You know the Rom rules about that kind of stuff. I'm having trouble sorting some things out, but some rules always apply.'' He grimaced. "Where's the line, captain? When do you give so much away you begin losing yourself?" He looked away uncomfortably.

"Is she planning to take the Rom off *Net*?"

"Out here? Not much real estate."

"Stop dodging," Andreos said with asperity, then stopped short as Pov winced despite himself, realizing belatedly his mother might consider exactly that. "But I see your point," Andreos said more quietly, "and I don't mean to conflict you. But think about telling me—I need the warning to set up my countermeasures." He smiled genially, his eyes glinting.

"The famous countermeasures."

"Even a Rom needs those, don't you think?"

Pov wondered how much Andreos guessed: the man seemed to know things Pov wasn't sure he wanted him knowing—yet was glad in a way he did. He opened his mouth, then shut it and shrugged.

"Ah, at least you're tempted to say," Andreos declared. "That's a good sign."

"I don't understand you, sir," Pov said stubbornly.

Andreos stood up and rested his hand on Pov's shoulder for a moment. "Don't worry about it. The last thing I want to do is add to the burdens. Just get us through a successful run here, give us some room in a tight place. Then maybe *Net* can help the Rom with their narrow spaces, open up the road again. It's possible, you know: sometimes the gaje have their uses."

"Thank you, sir." Andreos nodded and Pov got up from his chair, then squared his shoulders. "I'll watch over Athena, sir."

"So shall we all."

Chapter 11

Tully raised an eyebrow when Pov walked onto Sail Deck early the next morning, and Pov thought to comment that he had the right to intrude anytime, but let it go. He sat down with a sigh beside Tully, then watched the main wallscreen. *Net* was holding station next to the jet stream as Janina sorted the first run's product. Though *Net* kept a prudent distance, the gas jet filled the wallscreen, each blazing whorl and eddy convulsed with energy beyond imagining, each minor tendril of the smallest whorl enough to engulf a hundred *Nets*.

"Pov?" Tully said.

"What?"

"Lev could do some modeling on the gas stream. Might sort out the gas fluxes."

"Sounds good."

"Monosyllable time, Pov?" Tully said with some asperity.

"I gave you two syllables," Pov protested.

"Oh? I heard 'sumgud': with proper glissades and the ending grunt, it comes out as one word. That's only two. Read your linguistic tapes."

"Do you want me to leave?"

"Hell, no. I figure you're here for a reason. Can't be to watch me run Sail Deck after all this time."

"Boy, you're insecure."

"So are you." Tully studied his face a moment. "Rom problems?"

"You Greek. How'd you know that?"

"You always have a certain expression when it's your mother—or your Uncle Damek—turning the screws. Kind of mournful but proud, reflective but troubled, Rom to the core but wondering about it. Don't worry, Pov: you'll never stop being gypsy. I know that—why don't you?"

Pov shrugged. "In the old days, the Rom knew it was a mistake to tell gaje anything. Wrong to trust outsiders, dangerous. Wrong to be anything but what you were, a little world inside a bigger world. Sometimes the rules that preserve what we are seem to close doors."

"Don't tell me your mother is after *me*?" Tully pretended to shudder. "I thought she'd gotten used to me."

"Not really. You're a good friend, Tully."

Tully sobered and looked at him carefully. "It's been quite a month for you. First the Powers threaten to take away Sail Deck, now you're worried about something else. Or am I intruding where I ought not?"

"Not really." He shrugged.

"Well, then come eat Greek tonight and return the favor of Irisa's cooking for you. The kids haven't seen you for a while. Bring Avi."

Pov hesitated and saw a shadow cross Tully's honest face. "I'd like that. But maybe we ought to skip inviting Avi. She and I are cooling things off right now."

"What's the matter?" Tully actually sounded indignant—at Pov? Or at Avi? Maybe both.

"What's *always* the matter," he said. "Ah, hell."

Pov got up convulsively and took a step toward the elevator, but Tully caught his arm, stopping him. It caught the attention of nearly everyone on deck, and both men were immediately aware of it. Tully released him, but Pov stopped, looking down unhappily at his friend.

"I'm sorry, Pov," Tully said in a low voice.

"I just feel divisions everywhere." He tried to drag

together a smile. "I'd like to come, but let me sort
out some things first."

"Surely, Pov."

"See you later."

"Right." Pov took a few steps, then turned around
and walked back to his chair. He sat down.

"Welcome back," Tully said ironically.

"Hell."

"Indubitably." Tully wiggled his eyebrows.

"Life used to be easy, friend."

"We could always go to another pilot party."

Pov smiled. "Please, no."

Avi came onto deck and stopped short when she
saw Pov, then gave him a brief smile and retrieved
something from her comm station, talking for a while
with the comm officer on watch. Then she smiled at
Pov again and walked past him and out. Pov stretched
out his legs and folded his hands on his stomach.

"What happened, exactly?" Tully asked as the elevator closed behind her.

"The Omsk gypsy studies."

"Oh, the hedgehog soufflé and idiot intelligence
studies?"

"Why? Have you read them?"

Tully rocked his chair. "Sure. Research is always
useful. Helps maybe figure out a certain friend of
mine, though I admit Russki ideas of uncooperative
Rom weren't very helpful. Open to a suggestion?"

"What?"

"Just a sec." Tully leaned forward and keyed something on his screen, then cross-indexed to something
else Pov couldn't see. Then he sat back. "Take Avi
home for lunch."

"What will that solve? She's been at my apartment
lots of times."

"Not your apartment, the *real* home. You know,
the one on B deck where all those other gypsies live
together? Jog a memory? According to the watch list,

your mother has a hold meeting and won't be in. That should help."

"Are you crazy? They'll chew her up alive."

"I doubt that."

He thought about it, then scowled.

"Aunt Narilla can serve the hedgehog," Tully added helpfully.

"Oh, soar off."

"Pov, Avi's never really had a real family, just a lot of stolid types building the Rodina. You aren't aware of it, but your family is rather special. Why do you think I kept coming around, as much as I love my own folks? All those cousins and the pushing around, the humor and the crazy love: you can't see it because you're inside it, have always had it. Show her what the Rom really are. Let her see for herself."

"Hmmm. You really think so?"

"Try it. It can't hurt. She's still in the polite stage."

"I'll be back."

Pov took a deep breath as he and Avi walked down the corridor to the Janusz common apartment. He chimed the doorlock, and Avi's fingers flexed nervously on his.

"Relax, Avi."

"Sure." Avi tightened her lips and looked tense, her dark eyes rebellious. Noticing her expression, Pov suddenly thought he might get it from both sides. Then Karoly answered the door and smiled broadly, surprised to see him, then saw Avi behind Pov.

"This is Avi Selenko," Pov said determinedly. "I've invited her to lunch."

Karoly hesitated, then nodded to Avi. "Ms. Selenko. Welcome." He stepped back and waved them grandly into the apartment.

The other *Net* Rom shared a common family apartment, a triple-space altered to two big rooms in gypsy style, one a side kitchen for cooking and bathing, the other a much larger common room with mattress bedding in the back, guest seating in the front. His eldest cousin, Karoly, and Karoly's two teenage sons lived there with Karoly's parents and Pov's mother, with Uncle Damek's youngest daughter, Tawnie, keeping house for her parents, widowed brother, and her young husband, a tradition of a multigenerational family that had patterned gypsy life since its beginnings.

As Pov stepped into the main room, he smelled Tawnie's cooking and wrinkled his nose appreciatively. His young cousin was a great cook, determined in her bride year to out-wife every other Janusz female in the tribe with her skills and already succeeding. Tawnie heard the voices in the outer room as he and Avi came in and appeared in the kitchen doorway, balancing her baby boy on one hip.

"Pov!" she cried in delight, her small face lighting up with a big smile. She swept across the room and deftly handed the baby to her brother, then pulled Pov into a fervent hug, laughing up at him. Avi hesitated by the door, then looked startled as Karoly graciously took her elbow and walked her toward the seating cushions. A moment later, Aunt Narilla waddled into view from the other room, her sour old face beaming, followed by Karoly's two boys, sixteen-year-old Lenci and his brother Cam, now thirteen, both handsome copies of their father's lean dark looks. Lenci and Cam swarmed over Pov, wrestling his arms away from Tawnie, dragging him down. He picked up Cam, having to grunt hard to lift him, and flipped him upside down.

"You're getting too big for me, Cam," he said, puffing.

"I was *always* too big for you." Cam squirmed like an eel, and Pov dropped him with a thump, then dodged as the younger boy came swarming up from the floor again, determined on mayhem. Pov danced away, letting Cam chase him until they both fell in a heap on one of the mattresses in the back of the room.

Cam shrieked and Pov stuffed a pillow in his face, then grunted as Lenci piled onto his back.

"Off!" he demanded and tried to grab at Lenci's arms. Together the two boys pinned him flat in seconds, and Cam sat triumphantly on his chest, hooting.

"Got you, coz."

"That you did," Pov conceded humorously. "Ease off, you, so I can breathe."

"That's enough, boys," Aunt Narilla sniffed. "Imagine! Treating your cousin that way in front of a guest!"

Aunt Narilla shot an uneasy glance at Avi, now seated on a cushion. Well, Avi was indubitably a guest, even if his aunt didn't know quite what to think of it. Narilla had acted the same, every time, long after he'd started bringing Tully home. Narilla turned and gave Cam a scowl all of his own.

"Cam! Lenci!" she bellowed.

"He deserves it," Cam declared in a loud voice. Lenci got up obediently to his grandmam's command, letting go his hold on Pov, and Pov promptly flipped Cam off his chest and tossed him away.

"It still takes both of you," he pointed out as Cam sputtered and righted himself off his nose. "It'll be a while until it's one—if ever." Cam snorted his vast opinion of that, then jumped on Pov again, giggling as Pov wrestled with him.

"Cam!" Narilla's voice gained a no-nonsense lash that both Pov and Cam automatically obeyed. Grinning, the boy dashed into the other room to wash up for lunch, with Lenci pelting after him. Pov made a show of creaking bones as he got up, about as much out of breath as he pretended, to his discredit.

"If ever?" Karoly asked meaningfully, bouncing the baby on his knee as Cappi began to fret, then looking around helplessly for Tawnie as the baby howled. "Actually, I think 'ever' might be already here."

"You're a big support."

"Just older and wiser, Pov. Comes with my superior years—and knowing better from bad experience."

"Humph." Pov collapsed on the floor cushion beside Avi and drew up his knees, then held out his arms. "Give Cappi to me, Karoly. I'll hold him while Tawnie's busy."

Tawnie had hurried back into the living room at the first solid shriek from Cappi. As Pov took the baby, intercepting her maternal descent on them both, she smiled with more relief than she'd probably admit to. "Thanks, Pov," she said. "Lunch'll just be a minute." Then she was gone in a swirl of her colored skirts.

Avi looked back and forth, then folded her hands in her lap, sitting uncomfortably and tensely between Pov and his cousin. Pov smiled at her and arranged the baby more comfortably on his lap, then tickled Cappi's feet until he stopped his fretting and began kicking vigorously at Pov's hand, his tiny mouth turned up in a smile. "God, he's growing fast."

"Babies do that," Karoly said. "If you were around more, you'd see for yourself."

"Don't nag, Karoly," Pov said equably, and tickled Cappi some more to make him laugh. "I'm here, aren't I?"

"And welcome, of course. Sorry." Karoly did not sound too regretful about the nagging, and Pov repressed a sigh, expecting a full course of similar comments from his family, dished up with the lunch. *Net*'s Janusz tribe did not disappoint him, but he enjoyed himself throughout the meal, teasing the boys with more tough-guy trade-offs, praising Tawnie for her meal, until she colored prettily, then rolling his eyes, man to man, at Lenci behind Narilla's back as his aunt grumped and complained about whatever it pleased her to notice. As the conversation passed back and forth, Avi gradually relaxed, still not talking much but watching everything with wary eyes.

Halfway through lunch, Tawnie's husband, Del, burst in and endured a tirade about his lateness from Narilla, but managed to kiss Tawnie and the baby, gulp lunch, smile shyly at Pov, and rush out back to work. Uncle Damek strolled in a few minutes later, raised a surprised eyebrow at Avi, then listened stone-faced as Narilla started in on him while he ate his way slowly through his lunch. He finally silenced her with a roar, and Narilla retreated to the kitchen, muttering under her breath and angrily cleaning her pots. Pov smiled happily. It never changed, not a datum—but his enjoyment of his family's antics wasn't enough to persuade him to move back in, whatever Uncle Damek hinted unsubtly, as he always did when Pov moved into range.

Near the end of the meal, Narilla finally shooed Tawnie out of the kitchen, preferring to grump alone in magnificent dignity, and Tawnie collapsed gratefully beside Pov on the cushions. She took Cappi from his knee, cuddling her baby with a happy smile. Though Tawnie and Del had a traditional arranged marriage, settled years ago when both were still children and *Dance* was leaving for Tania's Ring, Tawnie seemed happy. He had watched her grow up from a short clever moppet with dark curls, always into everything, able to cajole even her glum father into smiles with her teasing. Now, at sixteen, Tawnie was a very pretty young woman, married, settled, devoting as much energy to her housewifery and minor duties in biolab as Kate gave to skyriding. We take the family with us, Pov thought, giving her a smile. Tawnie was easy to love, and he had always loved her, unalloyed, unchanging, knowing that his cousin loved him and everyone else in exactly the same way. Tawnie leaned into him and kissed him on the cheek.

"Good to see you, Pov. Glad," she said.

"Cappi's a lot bigger."

"Yes, he is," Tawnie said proudly. "He looks like Del more and more." Tawnie sounded immensely sat-isfied with that last, making Pov smile again. Avi gog-gled at her, then shut her mouth with a snap.

Romni wife meets modern woman, Pov thought, amused by Avi's reaction. Avi gave him an odd look, then started to smile. "Can I hold him?" she asked Tawnie, lifting her arms.

"Of course." Avi took the baby gingerly, apparently not knowing quite how to arrange him on her lap, then let Tawnie show her. She tickled Cappi's feet, watching him laugh, her dark-haired head bent over him. The baby kicked his feet, giving her a wide toothless smile.

"You trying to convert me?" she muttered low enough for only Pov to hear. "To what? I walked away from this, remember."

"This? Since when have you had lunch with a mob of gypsies?" He grunted as Cam pounded on him from above, then pushed the boy firmly away. "Careful of the baby, coz. You get too rough."

"Sorry," Cam muttered, then pretended to duck as Tawnie came after him. She chased him across the room, Cam giggling as he fended her off.

"Cam!" Narilla shouted from the other room.

"This family is *boring*," Cam declared in disgust.

"That's enough, Cam," Karoly said, then arranged his glass on his plate and got to his feet. "Well, back to duty. Nice to meet you, Avi. Come back again." He smiled at her, then pointed at his boys. "And both of you back to school."

"Ah, Papa!"

"No arguments. You can watch T Tauri on the screens tonight. It'll still be there." He nodded again to Avi and left, followed by Damek. Damek hadn't complained about Avi, but he hadn't talked much to her either. Pov scowled, then decided he should be grateful for the lesser favors. The boys dashed out a few minutes later.

Tawnie settled herself on her cushion, craned her head to check on Cappi, then arranged her skirts neatly.

"Why didn't you and Cappi stay behind with *Dance*, Tawnie?" Pov asked. "Bavol had lots of room, and Shuri would've loved to play little mother." Bavol's five-year-old was fascinated by babies, especially Cappi.

"Do you think I should have?" she asked uncertainly. "Marya in Biolab said that . . ."

"Only the truly loyal go with *Net*? It wasn't that kind of choice, Tawnie. Not for you."

"Del wouldn't leave." She shrugged, making her earrings dance. "And I agreed with him, even if it does mean a risk. We're *Net* Rom now. You take the road as you find it." She smiled at Avi. "But I envy Avi her front-row seat on Sail Deck. I get to watch the wallscreen in the aft lounge. As Cam says, *boring*." Then she clucked to herself and checked her wristband. "Ooh, I have to change. I have watch, too." She leaned over and gave Pov a hug that left him short of breath, then took Cappi from Avi and settled him in his low crib by the mattresses. Then she bustled back into the kitchen. Pov helped Avi to her feet.

"End of lunch," he said.

"That I can see," she said.

"I'll walk you back."

As they walked down the corridor toward the central companionway, Avi was frowning a little. "Pov . . ."

"What?"

"Why did you ask me there?"

"Didn't you enjoy it?"

"What? Your cousin totally preoccupied with her 'little mother' act? Those hyperactive sons? The uncle who sits like a lump and roars at intervals?" Pov took a deep breath, hurt, and dropped his hand from her elbow. "Was this supposed to be some kind of test?" she asked acidly.

"Well, run it back to zero, Avi. Sorry to bother you."

"Listen, Pov, I know they're your family . . ."

"Just skip it, Avi. Listen, I'll leave you here and see you later on watch. Okay?"

She stopped short and stared at him. "Pov . . ."

"See you around, Sail." And he walked away from her.

She caught up with him on the companionway, grabbing at his elbow and pulling him half around to face her. Everyone passing in the corridor nearby glanced at them, wondering: most of Pov's arguments lately had turned public, it seemed. "Don't you walk out on me!" Avi said angrily.

"There are lots of ways of walking out, Avi. Look at yourself."

"Listen, I'm sorry, Pov. I shouldn't have spoken so frankly. . . ."

"Forget it." He shrugged. "It's not important." He meant to hurt her, and managed it nicely.

"Don't you say I'm not important." She was furious now, and Pov told himself he didn't care a bit. So much for Tully's great ideas. So much for everything.

"Is that what this is?" he asked coldly. "Just ego? How important you are? Thanks so much, Avi, but I had enough of that with Dina."

Her eyes widened in outrage. "How *dare* you!" They were shouting now.

"Go ahead. Call me a gypsy. That's next, right? Go ahead."

"You're insufferable!"

"Comes with the breed." He turned and started to walk off again, and she grabbed his arm, hauling him back. Pov saw a lab chief, an older man, turn around and head back toward them, intending to interfere; Avi saw him, too. She turned and gave the chief an artificial smile, enough to make the chief hesitate, then manhandled Pov into walking with her down the bridgeway.

"Let go," he muttered, prying at her fingers, all too aware now of the public attention.

"Not yet." She spotted a doorway ahead and pulled him bodily into a side lounge, something pastel with pretty prints on the wall. A female tech looked askance at Pov as she walked out of an inner door and then hurried past them outside.

"Hell, Avi," Pov said disgustedly. "This is the ladies' bathroom. Let me out of here." Another woman walked out of the inner room and stared at him, then escaped just as quickly.

"Sit there!" Avi ordered imperiously, pointing at the couch along one wall.

"Absolutely not." He shook off her grip, and stepped away, but not far. "It's called a purity rule," he said snidely. "No male types in female bathrooms. It doesn't make sense—after all, biology is biology and we're all scientists, right?"

"But there's no place else to argue around here. And don't be ridiculous."

"Argue? I thought we were saying goodbye."

Avi seemed to crumble in on herself, her dark eyes filling with tears. She turned away from him, hiding her face.

"Why did you take me there?" she whispered. "Answer me that. Why?"

He sighed and ran his fingers through his hair, at a loss. "It was Tully's idea. He thought if you could see my family, you might get off some of those lurid ideas in the Omsk tapes, maybe get a balanced view. I guess it wasn't a good idea."

She turned and looked at him, surprised. "That was the reason?"

"What'd you think was my reason?"

"I wasn't sure." She blinked. "I thought, well, maybe you'd decided we wouldn't work out and expected your family to chase me off and solve your problem for you. But it didn't work—they were *nice* to me. Sort of." She paused. "I mean, they *were* nice."

"Ah, Avi. How could you think I'd do something like that?"

"But it was the other?" she asked slowly. She closed her eyes a moment. "I'm sorry, Pov," she said faintly, then smiled a small bitter smile. "Somehow I don't feel you can say 'suits' to this."

"Why not?"

She stared at him. "You are unbelievable."

"And insufferable."

"God, the words I said."

"Words can be fixed, including 'insecure.' Though it helps if you clue me in when you're spinning out again."

"Likewise, when you're set on educating a certain Russki."

"True. Maybe we can post signs."

She snorted with amusement, then took a small step toward him, still hesitant. He gathered her up in his arms and took a deep breath, smelling the clean warmth of her skin, then kissed her. She clung to him desperately, as if nothing could erase certain words and all would be lost once they were spoken. Who had taught her that? he wondered, sad for her. He did his best to reassure her, wondering himself if words erased themselves that easily.

That night Pov slept restlessly, lost in an unending flow of searing gases that curled around his body with hot steam fingers, scorching it clean. He woke in the middle of the night, covered with sweat, and pushed off the covers, then got up carefully, so as not to wake Avi. He prowled his apartment in the semidarkness of *Net*'s many lights. Finally, he sat in his window chair and watched T Tauri's jet in the distance, a glowing maelstrom of whirling gas that reached toward them with a single glowing finger a star-breadth across. *Net* had retreated a million kilometers from the gas jet to reassess its first run, and no one felt satisfied.

For some reason, Milo had immersed himself in that debate, handing out cautions and sage advice to anyone who asked. He's not a science tech, Pov thought, resenting Milo's subterfuge—though what the chaffer's motive might be eluded Pov. Andreos could spin his theory of two sons in contention, but linking *Net*'s fortunes to upmanship by the other son seemed extreme even for Milo. It was Milo's profit share, too, and he doubted Milo had any interest in being second to *Dance*'s Molnar again. Yet Milo did dispute, quietly, persistently, spreading doubt through the ship. A few other voices sounded their discord, afraid of the risks to the ship after the disappointments of the first run.

Maybe we off-shipped the wrong personnel, Pov thought uncharitably as he comfortably rearranged himself in his chair, half inclined to get a drink but too sleepy to bother. He watched the gas jet slowly unwind itself past his window, a nastily lethal collection of gas and energy that *Net* had not conquered. At least not on the first try. There was hope in that: *Net* had survived to try again. God, I'm tired, he thought, and felt irritated at himself for his restlessness. Where were the dauntless nerves, the ineffable calm of a proper sailmaster?

True, sailmasters usually guessed better. Maybe that was the difference, he told himself gloomily. Maybe Milo was right to doubt.

"Pov?" He heard a rustle in the bedroom behind him as Avi got up.

"Go back to sleep, Avi," he called.

He heard her footsteps pad toward him, then the creak of upholstery as she sat down in the other chair. She stretched out her bare legs, then rearranged the tails of her nightdress to cover her thighs, shivering slightly in the cool air conditioning of the room. Her toes wiggled in the gloom, and the smooth cool flesh of her long legs gleamed faintly in T Tauri's light.

"I think you spend a lot of time in that chair," she said. "More than I had thought. Communing with your goddess?" She nodded at the shrine in the far corner, where St. Serena stood again in residence.

"In all her manifestations." He hesitated. She

hadn't sounded sarcastic, only interested. He glanced at her shadowed face. "Nice view, don't you think?"

"A gorgeous view, one suiting a sailmaster in love with this gorgeous ship. We all find our quiet places, I think. I have a place up in the garden by the stream—you know, the black rocks and the small stream and all the tiny flowers peeking out from the moss. I miss the sound of falling water."

"That's the first time I've heard you regret leaving Tania's Ring."

"I miss a few points, I will admit. Is part of being a gypsy watching *Siduri's Net*?"

"For this gypsy, yes. Is part of Russki listening to falling water?"

"Suits. I'm sorry for what I've said—it wasn't fair. Nor good timing. Worrying about me is the last thing you need right now. Sorry."

"Fair depends on your point of view," he said cautiously, wary of some delicate ground. "It's easy to interpret things differently."

"Don't be so generous—or, rather, keep on being what you are, Pov. Did you really go shout at Andreos about Benek's getting tossed off the ship?"

"Not shout at—talk to. It wasn't like that at all." He grunted. "Maybe I should just make public announcements over the all-ship channel. It would save the sieve some work."

"I don't understand why you would do something like that. It's not just sympathy."

"Part of having a sail crew. I'd do the same for you."

Avi stretched her legs comfortably. "Is *that* part of being a gypsy?"

"No, not for gaje. Gaje aren't supposed to get that kind of loyalty."

"Who says 'supposed'?"

"Tradition." He reached over and tentatively took her hand. He hadn't a clue where Avi was going now, but he preferred this milder Avi as she frowned delicately to herself, thinking Avi thoughts. Then his heart turned over as she looked at him, surprising him. Her lips curved upward in a smile.

"Yet you gave the loyalty to Benek, anyway." She squeezed his fingers. "I've been thinking, worrying how I could lose something very special just by being stupid. I've been thinking how easy it is to push people away, to live all alone in all the ways." She turned her head toward him, her dark eyes shadowed, every line of her face softened by the dim light of the window. "I grew up not needing God. The theory was that God is a weakness of frightened men and women, that humanity doesn't need the help. What we see is all there is." She gestured with her other hand at the glowing stream of gas. "The immensity is irrelevant: all that matters is the Rodina and what we build there, what we know in our lives. The Great Rodina, the motherland, the goddess of the Russki soul. And I gave even Her away."

"And found *Net*."

"Another goddess who often eludes me. I envy you what you see when you look at *Net*: I don't think I see all of it yet. I envy what you see in your family, and feel just as blind. I'd like to see—but I *don't* think it's found in sorting laundry and pasting yes-no labels on other people."

"All I can do is show you what I have. Maybe you'll find what you want to see somewhere in the collection."

"Maybe. The other day—what was that name you gave a gaje wife?

"*Gaji romni*. Romni means wife in Romany. A gaje never loses the label."

"Hmmm. Well, at least that's consistent." She smiled. "I told you in the beginning I was plotzed on you. It's getting worse—enough to make me worry about arranging the same malady for you."

"Arranging?" He smiled and felt her hand press his again.

"Of course, arranging. Why do you think they call them 'feminine arts'? Men always *think* they choose. The reality is sadly different."

"Sounds very Rom to me."

"I think I love you, Pov," Avi said abruptly, then laughed softly at herself. "What a crazy thing to let happen. What happened to 'just good times' and 'so long, we'll be friends'? Whatever happened to 'Avi Alone and Liking It'? What happened to independence of woman?"

"Why define independence in those terms?" he asked slowly, thinking of Kate's restraints as a woman in a Rom tribe, how they chafed, how they defined and limited. Hard for Avi.

"I don't hear you saying it back," Avi said, her voice sad, and she gently withdrew her hand. He reached and promptly took it back into his again.

"Are we supposed to be at the same point all the time? And who says I *don't* love you? Come on, Avi: either be a romantic or don't. If you're the arranger, you've got to have clearer goals than this." He tugged her closer and bent to kiss her lightly. "I *do* love you, I'm sure, but I'm still sorting things out. So don't be sad. Who says you can't have everything you want?"

"History." She leaned back in her chair and sighed. "The dark Russki soul again, tempered by loss and blizzard and wolves chasing the sleigh. I already wrecked one marriage."

"A few weeks ago we weren't even sure we were starting a romance." He raised her hand to his lips and kissed gently. "How did we get to marriage so fast?"

"Are we at marriage?"

"You're the arranger," he said carefully, wondering if he was fair to encourage her. Yet this was Avi, precious to him. As *Net* is precious, he thought, looking out at the winking lights of *Net* and the maelstrom beyond her. He blinked in surprise, realizing it *was* the same feeling.

Avi scowled amiably. "Right. Like you really get

pushed around to where you don't want to go? I know you enough already to know how often that happens, whatever you pretend."

"So if I get pushed, it means I'm not resisting, right?"

"Humph. What would your Rom think of me? Would they keep on being nice?"

"Probably. Maybe with an exception or two—like my mother."

"But I have to be this *gaji romni*?"

"And it'd take years before they forgot you're Russki, if they did. It's part of what we are, Avi, that identity, those lines, those labels. It builds a fortress around us that preserves what we are."

"They don't accept Sergei, do they?"

"That's different. There are other things involved, mainly my mother's plans for Kate. It wouldn't be as hard for you, not that it'd be easy." He shrugged. "Tradition: the Rom accept gaje women into the tribe, but not men."

"Why not?"

"I'm not sure. There's probably a reason." He frowned. "Maybe it's because women are more adaptable. Men keep the essence of what they are by birth, can't change it: women can."

"What a theory," Avi snorted.

"Are you really thinking about it?"

Avi sighed and said nothing.

"I'm not pushing," Pov added.

"Women push, men get arranged."

"Another theory, very female."

"Well, I'm female—comes with the territory. This is a comfortable chair." She sighed. "I don't want to play games, 'yes I will, no I won't.' I'm just totally confused, and I don't think you're in better shape, Pov my love. Do you want to just sit for a while?"

"Sure." They sat together, hands clasped, and watched the glowing stream of gas wind by *Net*. The soft light of the gas glinted off every metal surface of the ship, shifting as the gas current moved, brightening suddenly as an eddy flared. The glow flashed across the ship, awakening colors where it bent across angles, then vanishing in an instant. *Net* shimmered, immersed in the light.

"Wonderful," Avi breathed. He leaned over and kissed her.

Chapter 12

He awoke in the chair much later with a stiff neck and groaned as he sat up, every muscle protesting the change of position. He felt logy and blinked, trying to orient himself to wherever he was. Avi had curled herself up on the carpet beside her chair, her legs pulled up to her chest under her nightdress for warmth. He went into the bedroom to get a blanket to cover her. She sighed as he wrapped the soft folds around her, then opened her eyes.

"People will think we're odd," she said. "Sleeping in chairs?"

"Why not?"

"A spirit I like. Help me up, sir." She reached out her hand and he pulled her to her feet, then stooped for the blanket. Avi wrapped it around herself, kissed him soundly, and then stomped off toward the shower.

Twenty minutes later, Avi headed for her own apartment to get fresh clothes. Pov set out shortly afterward, feeling a little ridiculous in his *Net* uniform but deciding he needed all of *Net*'s spells today. Before he left, he slipped St. Serena into his pocket, borrowing some Rom magic, too.

Before going to his sail watch, he decided to check on Josef and yesterday's skyriders in the hospital, where all were taking sickbed ease while undergoing tests, half of Pilot Deck finding a similar excuse to visit, too. He chaffed with Josef and the other skyriders, then smiled at Kate as she walked in to join the horde. He slipped out to a doctor's station and tapped into the medical computer, then scowled at the chart notations. Biochemistry wasn't his strong point—he'd always been more interested in mathematics than cells—but it looked as if Josef and the others were past the worst. Athena breezed in, and even Captain Andreos and Milo showed up a few minutes later. Pov decided all the captains seemed to be circulating today. They all put on a calm face, leaders to the fore, staunch and capable, and showed their nervousness only in the restless movement.

As Andreos began dropping into each sickroom, Pov and Athena left for watch, Pov to Sail Deck, Athena to skydeck as her techs worked onward at the modifications to the drones and a skyrider. On Sail Deck, Pov settled again into his interlink sanctum, using the computer equipment to tap data from all over the ship. He accessed Janina's initial hold reports from the first run and took some encouragement from the quality of the product she had harvested, short as it was. Though *Net* had aborted its first run, the sort had yielded a significantly higher proportion of the heavier isotopes, with the side benefit of unusually high concentrations of lithium. Though *Net* had come for tritium, T Tauri's wealth of the other fusion fuels tempted even better daydreams.

The cloudships had been experimenting with lithium technology for several years, using supercolliders in convenient vacuum to smash up the lithium, then shooting the fragments at other selected pure atoms. The result often cascaded into other atomic transmutations as the cloudships perfected their control of magnetic fields; it was a genuine philosopher's stone in a robot box. Subatomic distillation worked best in open space, and several of the colonies had built small space platforms to copy the cloudship technology, when they could steal it, but were just as limited by the difficulties of the technology, with lithium-6 a little too rare to waste wildly on mistakes. Beyond lithium lay a parallel chemistry for heavier ions and carbon-

60 dust, which Karoly and *Net*'s other chemists sought to develop. If the cloudships developed an efficient technology, with the convenience of vacuum and free-fall they could outmanufacture anything the ground-hogger colonies could produce, and the colonies knew it.

Biters get bit, Pov thought. Suits.

He engaged his sail program and began matching it to the real-time data *Net* had collected on the first run into the eddy, then let the computer spin better parameters for the light sails carried by *Net*'s sky-riders. Tully wandered in and watched for a while, then sat down to offer useful ideas. They modeled new sails for Athena's skyrider four times, but could not get the radiation cascades into a safe range. He called Athena on the intership monitor to skydeck.

"Yeah?" she said rudely, glaring at him from the small screen. She looked frazzled, her hair mussed and a smudge across one cheek. Behind her half a dozen skyriders were working on the innards of the drones.

"You'll have to ride behind the skysail. Can you guide the drones well enough through both the sails and the bow wave?"

"What do you mean, 'behind my skysail'? I most certainly will not."

"Want to glow in the dark? And you promised me, Athena."

"Arghhh!" Athena threw up her hands and stomped away across the deck.

"I assume that's an on," Tully said, grinning.

"Helm is an intense type," Pov agreed. Halfway across the deck, Athena reversed course in a single stride and stomped back toward him.

"You're sure?" she asked.

"Yes. We modeled it four times. The heavy particles are *too* heavy for light sails, period, and inert matter is inert matter, including you, pilot. Sorry."

"You mean I can't be heroic and brave the elements

in my lone skyrider? I have to skulk inside *your* sails while the drones get all the glory?"

"That's about it."

"How about more water? We can pad more of the cabin with the water cases, put up maybe three feet of water shielding—"

"Athena. No. It's not enough."

"Andreos put you up to this," she accused. "You faked the data."

"Don't be rude."

"I have an idea," Tully said. "Maybe Athena could skyride just a bit below the skysail, then dart back up when hell comes our way." He sketched a sail and skyrider with his palm and a fingertip, demonstrating. "You'd still get a good dose of bad rads, Athena, but I doubt you'd get totally fried."

"It would help the reception from the drones." Athena thought about it. "Do you have the feeling that *Net* just crossed into pure improvisation?"

"The idea woke me up last night," Pov admitted. "And I thought my specs were such great stuff, too."

"These aren't typical conditions, Pov, not up close. That star is unwinding itself like a top. I think we're back into wind ship against water, with the storm raging overhead. But I'm not going to give up." She set her jaw and looked utterly formidable. "Tell Andreos that."

"I'm *not* in cahoots with Andreos."

"Tell me another gypsy tale, Pov." She smiled, taking the sting out of it. "I'll be ready in another hour."

"That's on." She nodded and the screen blanked.

When *Net* again approached the edge of the gas jet, Pov started a search for a more hospitable tendril of gas. On his interlink screen, Athena's probe ship came into view as a small triangle within the boxy outline of *Net,* shielding itself just behind the downward edge of the starboard spinnaker. As Athena released her drones, a flow of data began running across one of the interlink subsidiary screens. The tiny chevron of robots plunged toward the gas jet, accelerating quickly.

"Skyrider checking in," Athena said.

"Acknowledged," Pov replied. With the added water shielding inside the cabin, Athena had a tight fit, and had made jokes about sardines and goldfish all through her insertion into the skyrider by her sky-deck crew. She winked at him over the video. "Radiation check, please," Pov said pointedly.

"Radiation rising," Athena said. "I read magnetic flux ahead. Suggest change forty degrees to port."

"No guarantee it'll be any better a thousand klicks down the stream, Athena," Stefania argued over the Helm channel. "It could be worse."

"Whatever it is, directly forward is too hot. Helm. I'm reading radiation from cascade fragments, high-speed neutrons, and a whole range of odd beasties that bit us yesterday." Athena gave a ghost of a chuckle. "That is amazing. I know a professor on Perikles who would give his tenure to see these readings." She paused. "And I just saw a quark, *Net*."

"Nonsense," Andreos said.

"So what's that curlicue over there, right next to the pi meson?" The screen shifted to a radiation display as Athena made her point.

"Quarks don't exist in free state. They can't."

"Maybe T Tauri has a better idea on that, sir. Just because we can't make enough energy to break them out of particles doesn't mean stars, can't, right? Hey, maybe we could catch a quark and take it back to Omsk, then let the Russkis play with it for a hundred thousand credits. The only captive quark in Taurus: they could change viewer fees for all the tourists who'd come to see it. Shall we try?"

"I'd rather have tritium. How far port do you want to go?"

"Until we stop seeing quarks, sir. Casual suggestion."

Pov cleared his throat. "Athena, you're drifting away from the spinnaker."

"Get better readings this way. I'm not getting much radiation exposure."

"You promised me, Athena. Save the fancy stuff for next time."

She sighed. "All right. Drifting back now."

Net cruised for five hundred kilometers beside the jet, receiving steady reports from Athena of high radiation that continued onward without letup, too dangerous to enter, even behind full sails. After another ten minutes of useless touring, Andreos put the interlink on hold and came down to Sail Deck, frowning. "Show me your models for this," he ordered.

"Different phenomena, sir. We haven't seen this before."

"What's powering it? The overall energy level has risen thirty percent."

"We don't have enough close data—or rather not long enough. Do you think the magnetic lines are bleeding energy? That might explain the particle weight."

Andreos raised an eyebrow. "Your best guess? Since our sails are magnetic, we don't dare go in to see, right? I can't imagine what would happen if your sails hit one of those frozen field lines."

"Well, either the sails collapse or they suddenly get very long." Pov rocked his chair. "You said we might not have designs we need. I tracked back into our first run's readings, and we had those quark signatures there, too."

"They aren't quarks, Pov."

"Well, whatever. We didn't expect those heavy particles, either." He pulled up his sail program and began filtering the data they had accumulated in two days, factoring again and again to simpler formulae. As Pov reached for still higher variables, the screen gradually resolved into a faint curving wave.

"Hmmm," Andreos said, his eyes lighting with interest.

"It's a field wave—a million kilometers long, but a field wave. There's your magnetic flux, sir. It's frozen but it cycles." He pointed out the trough in the gross wave on the screen. "It makes sense: the magnetic flux is shedding into the nearby particles, yet keeps them close—and supercharged—by its own standing wave."

"Cycles," Andreos muttered. "Don't you have a model for this?"

"Sir, *that* was not in the data." He waved at the gas jet, which seemed to glow malevolently. "I've never seen a cloud charge like that. Comets just shed ionized ice: this jet is powered by two infant stars trying to shed momentum. It comes out as energy, so much energy it can't radiate it all and so the extra energy packs into the subatomic shells, maybe even imploding into the deeper structures. As you said, quarks don't usually get loose." He smiled. "What it really looks like, sir, is a sail."

Andreos stared at him, unconvinced. "Loose quarks," he muttered, then sighed. "Well, there's still the diffuse nebula."

"No, sir," Pov said firmly. "It would take us three weeks to fill our holds and half the catch to power the runs. The nebula is lithium-rich but not as concentrated as that jet—and inside that jet all that extra energy is making the tritium we need. If we're going to go, let's go downstream and wait until we get past this flux. Look at Athena's scans."

"Tritium doesn't do us any good if we get fried while collecting it."

"The jet is still the best producer of what we want. I say we should risk it. There's a cycle, I'm sure of it. If we can get in, collect, and then get out before the upward flux ..."

"Show me that screen again." Andreos hesitated as the flux curve again plotted itself across Pov's screen, then looked at Pov keenly. "You're sure—or just stubborn?"

Pov closed his fist and lifted it, then spread his fingers. "If you grasp something too tightly, the Rom say, it always eludes you. In the old days, a sailmaster could read the wind and waves. It's not a skill comet-sailing really needs: the phenomena are too predictable. But those ancient sailors used to sail Earth's oceans, sir, without perfect 'parameters' or even a fifty-fifty chance they'd make it to the next port. When does *Net* open its hand, captain? I see a cycle: I think we should risk it."

Andreos paused, then nodded. He leaned over and pressed the toggle for a direct link to Helm. "Helm, accelerate down the gas stream. And tell Athena to stay behind that spinnaker."

"Yes, sir," Stefania replied calmly. *Net* increased speed, and a half hour later the radiation began to fall off—still high, still dangerous, but not impossible. Pov felt his heart beat faster as the data confirmed his hopeful theory, then looked up at Andreos. Andreos grunted noncommittally, then went back up to his interlink office and called all the captains back into the link.

"We'll try it again, captains," he said.

"Yes, sir!" Pov thumped his console hard, then grinned at Athena.

"Port, into the jet," Andreos ordered.

"Yes, sir," Stefania replied, her voice tense. "Port, into the jet."

Net turned directly toward the edge of the jet and Athena sent her probes farther forward, spreading the chevron across a thousand kilometers, just at the edge of their transmission range in the charged cloud. The picture that came back showed a bewildering pattern of fractured and jagged lines shifting in phase with the flowing gas, but downward, downward. Pov leaned forward in his chair as Stefania drifted *Net* close to the edge of the stream. Wisps of charged gas swirled into the sails in odd patterns, reacting as much to the jet's magnetic field as to the curving fields of the sails.

Then they plunged into heavier gas, the bow wave slowly forming itself over the ship, curving backward in a graceful loop far behind the ship's engines. Stefania turned the ship slightly, adjusting the attitude of the ship to steady the flow. Pov sighed to himself, then glanced at Andreos's face after the shipmaster made the same approving sound at almost the same instant.

"Nice entry, Helm," Andreos commented. "That looks better. Radiation's down." He and Pov grinned at each other over the link. "How's the flow, Janina?"

"Starting to come in, sir," Janina said. "A few weird beasties in the gas, but nothing like yesterday. We're sorting okay. If I see a quark, can I catch it?"

"Athena is an infectious disease," Andreos groused.

"This is new?" Janina said drolly, then whistled. "Holy Mother, I just filled an entire tritium bottle in a few seconds. I didn't know it came pure."

"The flux fields must be sorting by weight," Pov suggested. "Imagine that, sir: a cloudship as big as this jet stream."

"Not in our generation, young man. And I wouldn't want to be the one trying to drive that kind of ship. Neither should you." He lowered his eyebrows and gave Pov an intimidating stare.

"Magnetic lines fracturing ahead," Athena reported from her skyrider. "One of my probes just blitzed out. Turn four degrees to starboard, Helm."

"Turning."

"Fracture again, all stop. Another probe just went dark. I think something is coming at us, gentlemen, but I don't know what it is." She paused, her face perplexed. "I've never seen plasma data like this"

"Talk to me, Athena!" Andreos ordered.

"It's coming fast," she said, still frowning. "And accelerating. Definitely electromagnetic. Hell, sir, I think it's attracted by our metal."

"Get behind the hull!"

"No time, sir."

Pov swept his hands across his command boards, taking the sails from Tully on manual, and flipped the starboard sails through a half-circle to shield Athena on the port side. Claxons sounded immediately as he exposed the other half of the ship to the gas flow, but Stefania's helm computers cut in and turned the ship sharply to starboard. The magnetic flux hit them hard seconds later, enough to shudder through the ship, but his reinforced half-sail held. Cautiously he extended the starboard sails again and watched the stream of gas reform in the sails, spiraling downward into the holds.

Andreos opened his mouth, then shut it with a snap. "It *is* useful to practice maneuvers like that in simulation first."

"Yes, Captain—provided you can think up the need for the maneuver in advance. I don't think much radiation got through."

"If that had been a *major* flux . . ."

"Yes, sir."

"You had that all figured out in advance?"

"No, sir. I was protecting Athena—the rest was mere genius." He looked at Andreos, giving him stare for stare. "Sometimes people come first, then the ship." He nodded at the hold monitors. 'She's collecting nicely again."

"I see another one coming up," Athena warned. "This is definitely a wave phenomenon. Are we going to flip our sails again?"

"Well, Sailmaster?" Andreos asked.

"We're still in that flux's down cycle. Your call."

Andreos thought about it, then rubbed his hand over his jaw. Then he smiled and shrugged. "We'll need a label more dignified than 'sail-flip,' I think."

"Sail attitude adjustment, sir—called SAA."

"I'll SAA you. This time clue in Stefania and let her do the turn."

"Yes, sir. Helm, prepare for sail-flip."

"Here it comes," Athena warned.

Net rode through the next flux with another shudder, and Andreos scowled in severe disapproval as several alarms went off. "We'll need to check the rivets after that one, I think."

"Think of it as yacht races," Athena suggested. "After all, we're a sailing ship, right? This is fun." She paused. "Brace yourselves, *Net*," she warned abruptly. *Net* rang like a gong as another wave shuddered through. "Where'd that come from?" Athena asked. "Or does this stuff even have rules?"

"We're probably building up a static charge," Pov suggested. "Or else the flux is fluxing upward with wavelets or something."

"That's a comfort," Andreos snorted. "Janina, how's your sorting?"

"Got a big bunch this time, captain. I'd be happy if we got out to sort a little before Pov takes us over another bump like that."

"Take us out, Helm," Andreos ordered.

"Taking us out," Stefania said. As *Net* turned outward, Pov adjusted the sails smoothly to lie along the upper bow wave, giving the ship more protection. When the cloudship escaped from the wispy edges of the eddy into open space, he heard ragged cheers, a few from his deck outside and more over the open intercom.

"Do it *again!*" Athena shouted, her fist impacting on her console. "Hey, *Net*, this is all right!"

"I'd call that a 'sort of,' pilot," Andreos growled. "Captain Rybak would have fainted by now."

"You're of sterner stuff, sir," Athena told him. "I have a feeling sailing a protostar is something for the young." Athena then gave a long yodeling yell, promptly echoed through the intercom by every throat in Helm Deck and skydeck as her skyriders enthusiastically agreed.

Net accelerated quickly away from the jet, and Pov went down to the skyport to meet Athena. All the skyriders were already there, with more people pouring in from Hold and the other decks. Kate spotted Pov and pounced on him with an enormous hug, then grabbed Sergei and danced him away as the skyriders started a war-dance all over the deck. When Athena's skyrider rolled through the inner hold doors, the skydeck crew quickly opened the exterior hatch and unpacked the water shielding. Then, as Athena climbed out, the entire crowd cheered, followed by enthusiastic applause for *Net*'s shipmaster as Captain Andreos pushed his way through the crowd.

"Seat of the pants," Athena crowed to them all, waving her hands over her head. "Works every time."

"You people get back from the skyrider," Andreos warned. "Let the deck crew run their radiation scans. Who knows what she's shedding right now? And who let you in here, anyway? Where's the skydeck chief?" He put his hands on his hips and glared at the lot until the crowd moved back good-naturedly, then looked up at Athena. "Athena, I want you into decontamination."

"Yes, sir." Athena took off her helmet and waved it at the crowd, then stomped down her ladder and off toward the waiting biolab crew. Andreos chased the crowd off the skydeck with a firm hand, then followed Athena through the far door.

Pov looked at the skyrider sitting on the pad as spacesuited crew started working her over with the radiation washes, craning an ear to hear the readings. High—the crowd shouldn't have come to meet the skyrider, true—but salvageable. He put his hands comfortably in his pockets and rocked on his heels, smiling at the skyrider, then glanced down at Siduri's emblem on his uniform sleeve. It worked: it just took Siduri *and* the uniform to work the charm.

We're fishers in a great sea, he thought, elated by *Net*'s latest run—and knew he wanted to go back for more.

Andreos came back, looking solemn. "Humph," he said noncommittally.

"We did better," Pov suggested.

Net's shipmaster did not look wholly pleased. "True," he acknowledged. "Model it some more, Pov. It's still too rough."

"Sir."

Andreos's face relaxed a little, then he looked at the skyrider and the crew still busy around it. For a moment, the strain showed badly, but then Andreos shook himself a little, nodded absently, and walked off. Pov turned to watch him go, sobered by the worry he had seen in the captain's face.

He turned back to the skyrider. More, he thought.

After watch, Pov walked *Net*'s bridges and corridors for a while, doing errands mostly for the excuse to tour *Net*. To his surprise, he found most of *Net* agreed more with Andreos than with himself and Athena, after the first surge of elation had cooled. The crew was still pleased with the partial success of the latest run, but talked more about risks, of maybe not trying another run, of getting out while *Net* was still whole. It was a more sober mood, with Milo again in the middle of it, talking here and there around the ship, pushing at it. Pov walked longer than he intended, raising a thin stickiness of sweat across his shoulder blades, and reminded himself to get more diligent about workouts in the gym. He keyed open his own door and walked through, tugging his shirt off over his head, then hit the main lights with an elbow and headed for the shower. The sight of his mother in one of the window chairs stopped him short. She gave him a thin smile, then tipped her head, her earrings bobbing.

"I'm taking a shower," he said. "You can wait if you want—or do another disappearing act. Your choice."

That did not please his mother, but he walked past

her into the bedroom and took his time showering off
and dressing in fresh clothes. He was combing his wet
hair when he saw his mother's reflection in the mirror.
She was leaning against the doorjamb, her expression
noncommittal, one foot negligently tucked behind the
other, a graceful stance, as she was always graceful.
Her Hold Deck jumpsuit fitted her well, tailored
neatly around the curve of hip and breast, her rank
badge glittering above her left breast pocket. Only the
gypsy coloring of her hair and face and a distinctive
gypsy glare marked her as Rom, and he expected she
was here as Rom, not as hold tech. Pov went back to
combing his hair, considering strategy.

He and his mother had rarely jousted, part of the
freedom of sons that Kate had mentioned: the careful
guarding against marime, impurity, was mainly the
task of Rom women with their many extra rules,
though male Rom had their own customs, as carefully
followed. He finished his hair-combing and then laced
his boots, then washed his hands again, following the
rituals that divided the body at the waist. He turned
and looked at her directly.

"You're still here?"

"Insolence does not become you, Pov," his mother
replied in Romany. "Nor have I earned such insolence
from my son."

"Haven't you?' he replied in Czech, refusing to
make this talk a Rom affair. She scowled.

She straightened and pointed an imperious finger at
him. "You will speak in our language, the speech we
have kept for over a thousand years. You will remember what you are, my son. Your own reluctance has
not gone unnoted by the elders."

"Is that a threat? Am I going to have a *kris*, too?
And I'll speak Czech anytime I want." He walked
toward her and made her back away into the bedroom, then continued on past her into the living room.
He opened the refrigerator and poured a glass of juice,
then sat down in one of his window chairs, looking

over *Net*. His mother plopped down into the other chair, her expression dangerous. Pov took a swallow from his glass, then put it on the side table. "I'm waiting for you to act like a mother. When you do, I'll be a son."

"I do not like this division between us," she said, persisting in her Romany. "Why haven't you come to see me this last week? Why do you come for meals only when it pleases you? That, too, has been noted."

"I've been busy." Pov propped his foot on the cushion, then crossed his other foot across it comfortably. "And why should I come home for anything, when all I see in my family's faces is pleasure that I lose something dear to me?"

"You don't know that. How can you, when you weren't there?"

"Let's say it was a good guess. Why are you here, Mother?" His mother's timing had a reason—she always had a reason for everything—and he suspected part of it lay in *Net*'s success this day. He looked at her resentfully, irritated that all she saw was her own Rom agenda, how *everything* got bent into that constant issue, everything.

"Why haven't you come to see me?" she demanded. "Are you no longer my son? Am I to be shunned as if I were marime to you, a gaje?"

"Why did you walk out on Kate at that dinner?"

"I would think it was obvious."

"You *hurt* Kate, Mother. I don't like it. Sergei observes our customs and has tried to learn it all: you can't fault him in that. He's fully willing to live as a Rom, and only your opposition has prevented their formal marriage. If I'm not a proper son, let's talk about being a proper mother. You're acting more like a Rom mother-in-law, at war with her son's wife, than the mother you once were. You suffered under that for years with Grandmam until she finally died: it's not the best of our traditions, you'll have to admit. What are you trying to create now with Kate?"

"Kate must be brought to reason, Pov."

"Whose reason?" he demanded. "Is yours the only reason?"

"My reason is Rom, and only Rom is the proper way." Margareta lifted her chin, her mouth firm with her displeasure. "The Rom have never permitted gaje as husband, only as wife—and even a *gaji romni* is never allowed to forget she was born gaje, however she is accepted into our way of life. It is our tradition."

"The Rom have survived through flexibility," Pov countered. "We've gathered and shed customs in every country we've wandered. Maybe once we thought the gaje were a kind of nonpeople there to be fleeced, all those impure outsiders we could trick and cheat and avoid, but now we share a life with the gaje, especially on this ship. It's hard to keep the balance, but we aren't as isolated as we were. We have a greater purpose than mere survival in an unfriendly society. Don't you think that's a step forward?"

His mother's lips tightened. "He is a gaje."

"That he indubitably is, Mother. But he loves Kate. How many gaje would be willing to set aside their own lives to take up ours? It's not easy to join another nation, and ours is a culture very different from his. He wasn't raised to think of rules for upper and lower body, nor touching as possible impurity. It's part of how we Rom maintain what we are, that constant attention to marime that builds the common identity, that draws the boundaries around our family to bind us closer together."

"I've read the same sociological treatises, please."

"But it's gaje science and so can be disdained? Can't science and tradition see the same truths? Our nation has kept Rom law during all its existence. The Machwaya Rom may build their fortunes and the Churara Rom keep their secrets, but Europe's gypsies, our Lowara, we guard the law. It's our reputation among the other Rom nations. But the Lowara Rom have always kept a prudent law, one that binds instead of rends. We've learned to be flexible to keep the people together, to keep what we are."

"Don't tell me our history," his mother sputtered.

"Who will if I don't, Mother? Who can tell you anything now? But I *am* telling you this: if you stay on this course, you'll tear the Janusz apart—to lead us where? Back to Perikles and a nomad life on the edge of society? Is that the only way the Rom can survive? Is sacrificing Kate the only way you can prove to the Rom on Perikles that our family is still true Rom?"

"She will change her mind," his mother said confidently.

"No, she won't."

"She will not give up what she is. She cannot do that."

"Mother, Kate doesn't have to give up what she is, in or out of the Rom. She's skyrider, *romni* wife to Sergei, and my sister: a *kris* can't change that, whatever its decrees. Maybe that's where we're differing. You think a *kris* defines reality, can declare a Rom isn't a Rom. You can break the bonds, expel us from the family—but we will still be Rom."

"*We*?" His mother looked at the threat, then disdained it with a flip of her hand. "Rom *is* the family, Pov."

"Rom is a choice of life. And Kate can choose to be Rom and keep Sergei. You had better understand that." He took a sip from his glass.

"I have a responsibility as *puri dai*—"

"That outweighs your duty to your own child?"

"My duty *is* to my child," his mother said angrily. "To correct and warn, to enforce if necessary."

"And so you will lose her." He looked at her squarely. "And don't be so confident you won't lose me, too, whatever you think. Are you here to persuade me to support you? Do you think I have a special line into Kate's spirit that you can exploit? Don't be so sure. I don't believe Rom means anguish to one's children, nor using tradition as an excuse against a son-in-law you don't want."

"*Excuse*?" Margareta said in outrage, her dark eyes flashing. She stiffened and glared at him even more fiercely.

"Excuse. You're an intelligent woman, Mother, and you get craftier every year. That, too, is tradition, after a lifetime of learning the skills. But this appeal to tradition doesn't sit well: after all the changes you've permitted, it's not consistent to suddenly regret what you've done. It starts small, you know." He waved his hand at the room. "You permit me to choose quarters away from the family section. You permit me to enter sail training instead of settling in a more menial job. You permit me to bring Tully home to meals, to get involved with Dina. And you've tolerated other changes for Karoly and the other cousins. This is a new world, Mother, our cloudships: either we Rom adapt, as we've always adapted, or we don't. You can't wrench us back by making an example of Kate." He grimaced as he saw his mother's stubborn expression. "But you aren't listening, are you? I'm disappointed in you, Mother."

"I would expect you could at least see my position."

"Oh, I can see it. But if you force a choice, my stand is with Kate. Karoly says that there's a middle ground somewhere, and he worries about my attachment to Sail Deck. I agree I love Sail, but I think I can love Sail and the Rom both. Personally, I think my position *is* the middle ground, the right ground. But I'm willing to discuss it: you aren't."

Margareta stood up and looked down at him, her expression very displeased. "You only confirm what I've been saying."

Pov set his jaw and gave her the glare back. "And now she walks out."

"Is that my fault, walking out on that dinner?" she demanded.

"Yes." He saw his mother hesitate, then she did

turn on her heel and walk out, the door hissing shut behind her. Pov sagged in his chair and looked out bleakly over the winking fireflies of *Net*.

Perhaps this will be the time, he thought, the time I remember as the end. But what else is there but anger? Is there anything left but that?

Are you so sure, Pov Janusz?

A minute later the door chimed and he got up to answer it. As the door slid open, he saw his mother standing there, hands on her hips, glaring at him. "I will not give up on you," she announced, not caring if the gaje walking by heard their argument. She was beyond that, obviously. "I will not," she said more loudly.

"Then don't force it now. Not now."

She tightened her lips, her dark eyes flashing with their mutual anger, both stubborn, both willful—and both convinced of the right. Maybe we're both wrong, Pov thought, and doubted his mother ever even entertained the idea. Finally she tossed her head in a gypsy gesture of disdain and pride.

"All right. I won't force it now. But I make *no* promises about later."

Pov's breath gusted, and he saw his mother's lips quirk in reaction, half amused by his relief but still very angry. Well, so was he. They glared at each other again.

"You are a trial to me, my son," she said bitingly, tossing her head.

"It's mutual, believe me, Mother."

"Ah, well. Such is life." She shrugged her vast indifference, then pointed her finger at him. "I will win."

"No, you won't."

"We shall see about that." She whirled and stomped off down the corridor, ignoring the three people who had stopped to stare and listen. Pov nodded casually at his neighbors, then shut his door. Such, indeed, is life, he agreed.

And no, you won't.

Chapter 13

Later that afternoon, Pov took Avi to see Kate. They found his sister bent over some data charts piled high on the living-room table, and she welcomed them with an obvious relief.

"What's all this?" Avi asked, looking at the charts.

"Oh, one of Sergi's pregnant-wife-who-can't-skyride ideas. He said I needed something to do, keep me occupied, so he brought me these reports from the physics lab to sort for him."

"Good idea," Pov said, then grinned as Kate gave him a disgusted look.

"I'm a skyrider, not a physicist. This is *dull*, Pov, nothing but numbers. After a while all those numbers start afflicting my eyeballs like a grunge."

"So tell Sergei that."

"I can't do that. It'd hurt his feelings—quite aside from his maybe thinking up something *worse* for me to do. This stuff is T Tauri, by the way, courtesy of you and your detectors. Next time don't detect so much, Pov."

"I'll remember that." Pov shifted one of the data stacks and sat down. Kate moved more of the stacks to a sidetable, then brought out some wine and small cakes, determinedly playing the fine hostess with a serenity older than her years. This time she and Avi seemed more comfortable with each other as they chatted. Pov eyed his sister, wondering at the difference, then saw Kate's wry look as she caught him watching.

"How's the baby?" he asked.

"Busy assembling itself. I'm only two months along, Pov: I won't feel anything for several weeks yet. I don't even show." She stood up and raised her tunic to give him a profile. "See that great figure: enjoy the nice view while you can. Pretty soon I'll start waddling like a duck." She wrinkled her nose.

Pov took one of her cakes onto his plate, then poured more wine into his glass. "I thought women liked being pregnant," he said, then pretended to flinch as Kate turned on him. Kate snorted and sat down, then sent eye signals to Avi. Eye beams, he just knew it. Avi sent more signals back, probably all of it commentary on the outnumbered male in their midst. He saluted them with his glass.

Kate saluted back, then smiled. "You two look good together. Or is it just that your new sails finally worked, sort of, despite all that worrying that creased your brows?"

"Josef and the other skyriders are still in the hospital because of my sails, and Athena's had to have radiation therapy, too. We need better ideas for next time, improvements on the few that worked. And, yes, we look good together."

"Romance moving along nicely?" Kate winked at Avi.

"Stop meddling, Kate."

"Oh, ho, who's talking? I've already heard about your fight with Mother today. Mother went home and ranted at Damek, who ranted at Narilla, who ranted at the boys and Karoly. Tawnie said she hid out in the kitchen and stopped Cappi's ears. The hooraw stopped only when Mother had to leave for watch. What did you *say* to her, anyway?"

"The gist? 'Butt out.' "

Kate grinned. "A useful suggestion, but don't hold your breath, not when Mother's involved. Tawnie thinks you're wonderful, by the way. So do I. Have you warned Avi about Mother?"

"Not quite, a few hints. I think I've got Avi pretty settled on the main Rom object, me: now I'm amplifying on you." Avi sat back in her chair and crossed her arms, watching them both with wry amusement. "If Sergei comes home for lunch in a timely fashion," Pov added, "we'll try a semi-Rom. Next week, assuming *Net* gets through tomorrow: another lunch at Uncle Damek's, though without Mother. One step at a time."

"When Mother finally gets to be at your lunch, Avi's on the menu," Kate warned. "A Rom mother-in-law is a horror, Avi. I count myself blessed that *my* mother-in-law is a groundhogger on Tania's Ring and safely stored far away from me." Kate pretended to shudder.

"Nice to have some of the rules fix themselves," Pov grunted.

"Ah, Pov," Kate said, "they're still the same rules. Mother does have her consistency; you have to grant her that. But Avi's different stuff from Dina. If Mother understands anybody, it's other women, gaje or otherwise—and she had Dina pegged from the start."

Pov scowled. "Nice of her to warn me."

"You weren't listening, so? But Avi's different. Don't you love being discussed as if you're not even there, Avi?"

"I try to enjoy all experiences," Avi said dryly.

Kate chortled. "The essence of the lady Rom, Avusha, is the scheme, the sleight-of-hand, the maneuvering and subtle joust. It keeps our wits honed in a society that has tried to erase us for centuries, with some genial help from our men from time to time, not that they meant it poorly. Rom women are better at wits, but the men have to know how just to keep up—as much as they can." Her mockery turned suddenly grim. "My mother is *puri dai*, the leader of the Siduri Rom, and she is your enemy, Avi. Don't ever forget that."

"Now, Kate," Pov protested.

"You think not?" Kate gave him a level stare. "You can hope for sweetness and light all you want, but Avi has to live with it if she ends up a *gaji romni*. You always hope for things, Pov, thinking people are reasonable and deserve to be protected no matter what they do. It makes you a good leader, Pov, but sometimes it makes you look a little dumb."

"I need a closet. This is going too far."

Kate smiled, then snickered at Avi's confusion. "That threat does get repeated, I admit. I am a Rom, Avi, and I will stay a Rom—no matter what the Rom do to me. It is what we are, something very precious. My brother taught me that." She smiled widely at Pov. "But that doesn't mean it's easy. I was lucky with Sergei: he loves me enough to put up with anything. Sometimes all he has to go on is that love, and he keeps finding that it's enough."

Avi sighed. "I envy you."

"Rom or gaje, love can bind—and when it's Rom *and* gaje, love is sometimes all there is. I can bounce around and be juvenile, typical pilot panache, but sometimes you have to take the time to prepare for the battle. So I've been thinking a lot lately—and appreciating what I have." She made a face. "I've had lots of time to think. It's only been two weeks and I miss skyriding so much my teeth ache." She waved a hand at the computer on the desk with its litter of lab reports. "I can't believe Sergei enjoys that stuff. Help me out, he says, keep you occupied, he says."

"He probably gave you the stuff he doesn't like," Pov said. "It's called opportunity."

"I've suspected that—and I'm preparing a good revenge. Another key to the Rom, Avi: revenge. Ask Pov about his closet and how much that worked, ho-ho: he'll tell you."

"Closet?" Avi demanded, turning to Pov.

"An old story. Thanks, Kate, for trying to help. Avi's been wondering."

"You two are *that* serious?" Kate pretended to be startled, then examined Avi anew, making an act out of it. Avi lifted her chin and posed, tossing it back, more at ease with Kate than Pov had expected. He looked at the two women, so thoroughly pleased that he sighed involuntarily. Kate raised an eyebrow, her dark eyes dancing.

"You're pushing, *chavali*," Pov said.

"Who's a kid?" Kate declared indignantly. "I'll have you know, big head, that I've got proof I'm *not* a kid." She patted her stomach meaningfully.

"Sergei does have his compensations in bed. So do I." As Kate started around the table, Pov got up and moved around Avi, putting her between them. "Truce, Kate."

"Truce? What a soddering limp you are! I can't believe we're related." She stomped back to her chair.

"Does this go on all the time?" Avi asked, amused.

"Only when Kate's feeling good." Pov circled the table and sat down. "Nice to see, Kate."

"So you two are that serious," Kate said, dodging the comment, and put on her amazed act again. "I'll be damned. Let me tell your fortune, Avi—a little guidance right now might save you from a *big* mistake." She smiled to take the sting out of it, and got up to clear the table and get her cards out of the cabinet drawer.

"Fortune?" Avi glanced at Pov uncertainly.

"As in fortune-telling," he said helpfully. "Kate's pretty good at it."

"Does this go along with ancestors watching over us?" Avi asked, looking very dubious.

"Sort of. It's complicated." Avi scowled at him.

"Cute, Pov."

Kate took a small wooden box from the drawer and set it on the table, then lifted the lids. She brought out the deck of brightly colored cards and set them carefully to one side. A black cloth came next, spread neatly between herself and Avi. Kate sat down and briskly shuffled the cards, then spread them in a fan in her left hand, holding them out to Avi.

"Pick a card, Avi." Avi kept her hands in her lap, eyeing the cards suspiciously. "Come on, Avi," Kate said. "Pick a card. They won't bite."

Avi lifted a hand toward the cards, then looked at Pov, hesitating. Then she put her hand back in her lap. "What if I hear what I don't want to hear?"

"Then you don't have to listen," Kate said, then dropped her voice ominously and shook her head. "And your life will fall apart into shambles, with one disaster after another until you die horribly."

"Kate, stop that," Pov reported. "She's really hesitant about this."

"Hesitant?" Kate looked at Avi as if Avi had sprouted twigs in her ears. "Why?"

"Because she's not Rom and she's never seen a gypsy tell fortunes and because she's Russki. The Russkis learned a long time ago never to trust gypsies, like all the rest of Europe. If you don't want to Avi, you don't have to." Pov gave Kate a genial glare.

Avi hesitated, then took a deep breath and reached out to the cards, choosing one from the middle. "What do I do with it?" she asked Kate.

"Put it on the cloth, face up and facing you." Avi did so, and Kate leaned forward to see the card. "Ah, the Two of Swords. Swords is the suit of intelligence, the spirit of the air and the breath of the inquiring mind: this card speaks of serenity, possibly in a difficult situation. For now, the conflicting choices are kept apart and all is quiet, but the spirit is restless, fearful of upsetting what is held. Eventually the storm must break, for this balance cannot be kept forever. For now, though, and for a time to come, there is balance."

Avi looked down at the card. "That's what it says?"

"That and other things. Is that a good card for your question?"

"I didn't ask a question," Avi pointed out.

"The cards know without being told," Kate said mysteriously, then gave Avi a sweet smile, dropping the mockery. Kate laid out the rest of the cards face-down in the Star design, then turned over the card at the upper corner. Avi leaned forward, biting her lip. Then she caught herself and sat back, delivering a bland look to Pov as he smiled at her knowingly.

"Easy to believe, isn't it?" he asked.

"It's only superstition," Avi said, tossing her chin.

"Not so loud," he warned, pointing at Kate's cards. "You'll annoy the cards, and they have powers unseen it's not wise to tempt."

"It is *still* superstition, Pov Janusz," Avi declared, "and I don't believe cards can get annoyed, not for an instant."

"It's also magic." He caught her hand and brought it to his lips. "Lots of things are magic." Avi thought about that, then turned up the corners of her mouth and let him keep her hand.

"Maybe."

"Russkis are suspicious sorts," Pov told Kate. "Go on, Kate. What does the next card say?"

Kate turned the card around to face Avi. "The Queen of Cups represents water, the power of reception and reflection," she said softly, her face transforming. When Kate read the cards, and wasn't making a game of it, Pov saw a different side of his sister, one she kept wholly for the cards. In those moments, she was truly beautiful.

"Her image holds purity and beauty," Kate said, her voice resonating. "With infinite subtlety, she is robed by endless curves of light, as the water reflects the light of a standing pool. Her truth and true friends are two joys that will bring delight and success, without illusion." Kate raised her hands, framing the card and Avi between them. "The Queen of Cups is the goddess of the heart, the fixed quality of water, the companion of Scorpio and his passionate tenacity, and the holder of the Tui, the Truth of the *I Ching*. With the aid of the Queen of Cups, the questioner can own one's feelings and express them without blame or judgment."

Kate lowered her hands, took a deep breath, and quietly turned over another card. "The Six of Wands is . . ."

"But what does that mean?" Avi interrupted, her eyes intent on Kate's.

"The cards speak to the intuition, Avi: most of the meaning is known by the listener, not by the speaker. You've probably heard that fortune-telling is something different, but this is the Rom way, the way we tell the cards to ourselves. It enlightens the inner mind, reveals intuitive knowledge that we ourselves know." She smiled. "Cups is the suit of the emotions: the Queen is a good card for that area."

"Hmmm." Avi bit her lip and shot another glance at Pov.

"The Six of Wands," Kate continued, her young face solemn, "is the card of victory, of triumph but also the confidence and firm action that can lead to triumph. Wands is the suit of Fire, the active and creative power that inspires, warms, makes anew." Kate stopped and studied the card silently for several moments.

Avi leaned her chin in her hand and watched Kate closely, intrigued now despite herself. Kate turned the card to face Avi.

"In this suit," Kate continued dreamily, her eyes still on the card, "comes the awakening and struggle, and the burning spirit. The Six of Wands is the fire that drives through obstacles, yet warms the heart and mind. The Six of Wands is the desire of the body, the urge to create. The Six of Wands is the intuition that is honored and trusted."

Kate paused and lifted her eyes to look at Avi, her expression luminous. "Another good card. I like the Six of Wands. The Wands hold a skyrider's spirit, I think, more than the other suits—though in my less intuitive moments, I can be as skeptical as you, Avi. Are you enjoying this now?"

Avi smiled. "More as it goes on. This isn't what I expected."

"If you'd like to learn, perhaps I can teach you," Kate said, then slowly turned over the remaining seven cards, entrancing Avi onward with her speaker's talk as she explained each card. Pov watched them both as Kate talked, knowing that Kate could have tormented Avi by mocking her, as she'd started to do at the first, but instead had given Avi a true reading, one that awakened something between speaker and listener, that bound, not divided. It was the *puri dai*'s art, to know the cards this way.

After the last card, Kate sat back and sighed, then smiled at Avi. There was a brief silence.

"I'm still not sure what it means," Avi said slowly.

"Later you'll look back and see how right I was," Kate replied.

"Humph. With that kind of ambiguity, you can cover a lot of different futures."

Kate grinned. "Of course. That's the point."

Pov glanced at his wristband and stood up regretfully, sorry to end this. "We've got to go. Have you spread the cards for yourself, Kate?" he asked, then regretted it as a shadow crossed his sister's face.

"Sometimes the cards lie," Kate said obscurely. She clasped her hands in front of her, her fingers moving restlessly. Pov walked around the table and kissed her. "Avi's right, you know. It's only superstition."

"Yes, I know. Thank you for coming, Pov." She smiled at Avi, more herself again. "Come back, Avi. Next time I'll *scare* you with the cards. It's a treat."

"I can hardly wait," Avi said dryly.

"You'll like it. I promise."

Pov and Avi left Kate there, and Pov hoped Sergei would be home soon so that Kate wouldn't sit alone too long. He wondered what bothered Kate, and knew surely his sister would not tell him even if he asked. Kate took her cards more seriously than she pretended, and he felt annoyed when she let them upset her.

As they reached the main companionway and its busy traffic to and fro, Avi slipped her hand into his. "I enjoyed that. Kate seemed sad at the end."

"Sometimes the scaring goes both ways."

"I'm trying to figure out what I missed again," Avi said. "Enlighten me. Why did you have a fight with your mother? About what?"

"Mother doesn't approve of Sergei, and the baby makes it worse."

"Why?" Avi sounded totally befuddled. "I'd thought she'd be happy."

Pov glanced at her, then squeezed her hand. "I appreciate your different window on things, Avi. I don't have a why, except that Rom women aren't supposed to marry gaje, even handsome compliant sorts like Sergei who agree to become Rom as much as a gaje can. It's been Rom tradition for a long time."

"Sounds like racism to me," Avi said disapprovingly.

"And Tania's Ring doesn't limit its immigration to Great Russians? Who's calling whom racist?"

"I no longer identify with Tania's Ring, and so that zinged right over my head. Besides, how can you build the Great Rodina with Afghanis and Balts and all those other pseudo-Russkis?"

"How can you remain Rom when a child doesn't have both parents born to the blood, who know what Rom is down to their bones by being born to it, raised in it, committed to it?"

"Is that the theory? So how come there are *gaji romni*?"

"There aren't many—and most go back to the gaje eventually, though they have to leave their children behind when they do. It's gypsy law. It's the children that keep them for a while, or I think they'd leave sooner." He looked at her unhappily. "It's hard enough being a daughter-in-law without the other thrown in. That's what cultural barriers are for."

Avi shook her dark hair. "I don't understand this— and yet I do. But I left that kind of closed mentality behind when I joined *Net*—I thought."

"And *Net*'s First-Ship Slavs are open-minded?"

"But why, Pov?"

"Well, when there're lots of them and only a few of you, barriers help. The Japanese knew it; so did the Jews. Where's the line between racism and protecting what's important? Who says we *owe* things to anybody?"

"There speaks the gypsy. A sentiment I hope we can toss at Captain Rybak, as rich as we might be. At least Kate likes me." Avi smiled, as if it surprised her a little. It added a softness to her face that he liked. "At least I think she does."

"She does." It amused him that Avi liked to be liked this much.

They turned off the companionway and had an early drink in the lounge, then ended up in Pov's apartment. Avi watched him fix dinner, daring to ask questions about the procedure, as if it were some kind of arcane surgery. When she ate the food, she had a puzzled frown, as if it ought to taste different—and he teased her about it. She tossed her chin and smiled, not rising to the baiting.

"Trying to acclimate?" he asked.

"Exercising an open mind. It's called the Two of Swords. Something you could try, Sailmaster, sir. Quit mocking me."

"Humph."

"Humph yourself. By the way, I would think that a society with such strong sexual roles would be more conservative in bed. I haven't noticed much difference—we've been pretty straightforward about manners and means." She smiled archly, not quite bringing off the joke if she meant one.

"Why? Do you want to experiment more?" He looked at her over the plates. She had changed into something silky and long, in a pale blue that set off her fair skin nicely. She shook her head, then gave him a lazy smile.

"When I want to, I'll suggest some new things. Do you like going to bed with me?"

"Yes. Of course." He wondered why she would even ask. Avi was obviously off on a new tack about something; he tried to keep up better this time.

"As much as with Dina?" she asked.

"Comparisons aren't fair. I haven't asked you about your ex-husband."

Avi ignored that. "She took you to realms uncharted, as the proverb goes?" A faint line appeared between Avi's brows.

Pov shrugged. "I'd never had sex much before, not steady. It grows on you when it goes on for weeks on end. Why do you want to know?" Avi's pretty face had gone remote, as if she were somewhere else than with him. "Avi?"

Avi shook herself slightly, then blinked. "Ah, never mind."

"I'd rather not 'never mind.' I want to understand you."

"Oh." Avi shrugged, then focused on pushing food around with her fork, not meeting his eyes.

"Avi," he said gently.

Avi looked up, her eyes filled with pain. "So what do I tell you? Stay out? Not your business? It'd be easy."

"You could, if you wanted to. Aren't we beyond that now?"

"It's not fair to keep comparing, yet I do. I see more than maybe you think I do, but I don't trust it. I feel like a little girl staring through a bakery window, wanting everything that she can't have. I feel if I went in, I'd find some rule that says I can't. Life is hard, not easy." She shook her head sadly.

"My mother can make it as hard as you like. Kate was right about that."

"Oh, that." Avi waved her hand. "Believe me, friend, I've been put down by experts. I'm a tough broad."

"Yeah, real tough." A tear slipped down her cheek, and he leaned forward and gently brushed it away. "Just like I'm a sneaky gypsy horse trader who can't manage a single scam. Both you and Kate have laid into me about 'silly trusting Pov' and 'dumb-minded Pov' and 'idiot Pov.' "

Her lips turned up slightly in amusement. "I don't remember those exact adjectives, but I admit the feminine commentary."

"You and Kate outnumber me about four to one: I think it's quite reasonable to just mellow out." Her smile broadened through her tears, then she firmly wiped her eyes and took a deep breath.

"Mellow out. I envy you."

"What did Andreiy do to you?"

"Oh, you mean wife-beating? Nothing like that. If it was physical, I could get my divorce and point at him as the reason. But it was only silence and shrugs and those suffering frowns of disapproval, a constant commentary on my failure as a wife. You know, trivia that sound trivial and stupid and excuses. No matter how hard I tried, he didn't like anything—and I did try."

"Why'd you ever get married?"

"I loved him." She smiled wryly. "He was tall and strong and sexy, had this drawling voice that shivered me down to my boots. And so competent and strong— I felt flattered that he even noticed me, much less decided I'd suit him as wife. I didn't know he was looking for a deferent type, though I admit I fit that bill. I thought he married *me*." She laughed harshly. "After a while, I learned not to care, and I perfected that particular art. I've been not-caring for years and doing quite well."

"Except about *Net* and comm station and Sail Deck?"

"And a few Russki friends. We tended to flock together the first several months. But after a time you find other friends." She poked at her dinner again.

"I followed Dina around like a sex-struck sheep."

"It wasn't that bad, Pov."

"You weren't there most of the time." He grimaced. "Later you wonder how you could have possibly acted so stupidly."

"Yeah." Avi shook her head. "So I keep expecting you to disapprove somehow, start in with the silences and frowns. What do I get? 'Suits, Avi.' Suits this, suits that, suits I'll-brain-you. You go over to see your sister just to let her one-up you, you defend that brain-wipe Benek, you go around being this perfectly wonderful person who takes me home to lunch with your family. You state your ground and keep it. I'm not that kind of person."

"You got out of your marriage, off Tania's Ring and onto *Net*."

"True."

"And when I got soused at the party, you stiff-armed all comers and pounced. I'd say that's a forceful type." He smiled. "So who's a wimp?"

"There you go, doing it again."

"So? Just stop dripping tears, will you? It makes blotches on the table."

"I'll drip tears if I want to."

"Suits." He laughed at her expression. "Listen, Avi. Sometimes you hang on too long, waiting for somebody to get a life. Andreiy never did, and so he lost you—it happens. I don't want you to be a tough broad: tough broads don't need anybody much. I don't want you to try to smile bravely when you see Rom this or Rom that, but you're too damn polite about it. Maybe you're trying too hard."

"And afraid I'll drive you away with it," she said in a low voice. "As I almost did before."

"Being driven requires my cooperation, right? I like what I see, and I'll 'suits' you forever if you want it." He raised his water glass and saluted her. "Especially in that silky dress. Want to go get inventive?"

"I'd like straightforward more." She wrinkled her nose. "Thank you for being patient."

He looked at her, seeing the edge of new tears, wondering why Avi would ever think patience such an unusual gift—and who else had helped convince her of that mind-set. "Afraid of repeating patterns?" he guessed, trying to read her expression.

"Yeah, listen to me: grateful you pay attention to me. Some tough broad." She wiped away more tears.

"Kate hates herself when she cries, too. Calls herself a snively woman."

Avi snuffled dramatically, then tried to patch together a smile. "Suits."

"We'll work it out, Avi."

"You're sure of that?"

"No, but why not assume?"

Avi lifted her chin and tried a ragged smile. "Tough broads don't assume. They always expect the worst."

"So don't be a tough broad." He stood up and spread his arms, wanting somehow to erase that hardness in her glance, that armor she had built—and wasn't at all sure if she'd let him, could let him in. Avi came into his arms and sighed as she laid her head on his shoulder, then wrapped her arms around his waist. He slipped his hands up and down her shoulder, sliding slowly over the silky fabric warmed by her skin. She sighed again and lifted her face to him. The kiss was long and lingering, half regret, half promise, both and none, and neither of them knew yet which applied.

"I'm sorry, Pov," she murmured. "I'm sorry to ..."

He kissed her again, stopping the apology, then sighed himself. "Complicated," he said.

"Maybe." She seemed to shake herself and stepped

back a little, then pulled him imperatively into the bedroom. "Let's ignore all that for a while."

"You're sure?"

"That's the only thing I *am* sure of, I think." She laughed shakily and did her damnedest in bed to show him how sure she was, leaving him very gratified and a little awed. And she seemed happier, curling on her side and nestling back against him.

It's always different, he thought as Avi fell asleep, her back curved into his body, her breath warm on his arm. I thought I loved Dina, was certain of it, as certain as I was of everything else. When does love stop and love begin? He thought about that, totally aware of Avi's lean softness, the gentle pushes on his chest as she breathed slowly and deeply, the warmth of her. And, thinking of losing her, he understood some of what she had been feeling, maybe, afraid of pushing something away as one longed to pull it closer. It was an oddly familiar emotion, linking Sail Deck and Kate and Avi all together in a muddle.

And what would be the future? he wondered. He could talk blithely about remaining Rom without the Rom family, but the family was an essence. Sergei had pleased Kate by trying to adapt to her customs, giving up his own for love of her, though he knew the rituals seemed arbitrary and marked by the other times a millennium ago when the Rom had formed themselves into a people. The sociologists the Rom disdained, by long persistence through the decades, had gathered enough information about the gypsies to draw some parallels, and he knew his own culture more closely resembled the South Asian culture that had birthed it than the Western cultures through which the Rom had long wandered. The Rom had never interested themselves in their own history as the outside society understood personal history: to a Rom one's ancestral descent through bloodlines and the lore of the *puri dai* gave a Rom his identity: he needed nothing more.

He got up restlessly and went out to watch *Net* from

his chair. However she tried, he couldn't see Avi doing what Sergei had done for Kate: certain Rom beliefs were easily labeled sexist, half confusing the form with the reality of practice. He thought about that, wondering if beliefs he had accepted all his life were oppressive. Technically Kate as wife was subservient to Sergei, but the *romni* wives had always ruled equally despite the customs that suggested otherwise—with the promise of full coleadership with male elders after a lifetime of training. The women of the tribe often made the better leaders, the leaders with vision, for they learned the restraint and patience imposed by marime. But Avi might see only the purity rules that feared contamination by women, blind to the impurity a Rom man could pass on if he was imprudent.

I think I love Avi, he thought, and smiled at himself. She's strong and lighthearted and smart, good to me, good to other people, one of the best. I doubt if Mother would object to her as my wife, gaje or not— since that's in the tradition. He twisted his mouth, then guessed his own choices would not deter or console anything. Maybe Avi'll surprise me and it'll lead to a life together—but should it be a Rom life? How could it not? I'm not sure she'll agree, even if I asked. Should I ask? The issue was still hanging between them, unanswered.

He got up and paced the room. It was easier, he thought, when the parents arranged the marriage. You got stuck with a girl you'd hardly seen—but you never had to wonder where your mind had been if it didn't work out. On Perikles most Rom marriages were still arranged, usually between second cousins as still the preferred choice: had he remained there, he'd have been married now for years, with four or five children to support. Even though the Rom now married later than at twelve as in the past, most still married by their mid-teens: maybe seven or eight kids by now, if his wife carried them all to term and they were born whole. He imagined himself with kids, little data copies of himself shrieking and racing around the wagons. He imagined his Rom wife—his mother had had three or four suitable choices on his father's side of the family, one of them he remembered as quite pretty. It would have been a different life, indeed.

If I went back now, gave up *Net*, could I find that life that never was? Or is something forever lost when you wander too far, as Rom must wander?

He did not believe he would be allowed to keep his Rom family. Nor did he believe, even though he had told her, that his mother understood the breach she was creating, thinking it a temporary expulsion from the Rom that other Rom would observe until he and Kate submitted to their mother's choice for their lives—only Kate would never submit.

Why couldn't his mother see reason? What has happened through the years that he and Kate had moved so far onward while she remained behind? His mother didn't particularly enjoy her work aboard *Net*: it was a routine counting job under Janina, little more, without enough interest on his mother's part to prompt Janina into special attention to Margareta's ship career. Yet his mother had never sought more than that, as he and Karoly had done, as Kate had found on skydeck, content with her family doings and her Rom scheming, her position as *puri dai*. She dominated Damek and ignored Narilla, confident of her senior elder's wisdom, her power among the Janusz. But she had been left behind, as assuredly as a grandmam accidentally left behind in town when the wagons moved on. The caravan always came back for the grandmam: how could the Janusz children come back for Margareta?

Are you so sure, Pov Janusz? He thought about that, looking at everything all over again. Do the gaje have your soul?

Maybe they do, he thought slowly, but maybe it's all right that they do. He thought about that, thinking of Tully and Athena and Avi, all the Slavs on his sail staff, all outsiders, gaje, that the Rom had scorned for centuries. He thought of Milo thinking a thing is real once it's written down, neatened up, ordered by clause and phrase, a deft arranging of the universe into a secure certainty, as if a cloudship's fortunes could ever be certain. But in that ordering, Milo had a blindness, of not seeing what he *could* have if only he looked. Are you that different from Milo, Pov, with you and your wishes?

What do I do? He paced again, worried anew about the next ship run, uncertain about Avi, of being fair to Avi.

He finally stopped in front of the shrine and looked on the graceful lady who stood there. The light from the windows gleamed faintly on the curves of Siduri's gown, the grape leaves entwined into her hair, the cool sweetness of her bare arm and the hand upraised in blessing. What do I do, Siduri? he asked her silently. How do I give up half of myself? And which half?

He turned to face the window and the many lights of his ship, life to him, Siduri's ship sailing her dark ocean, the star glitter sparkling on the depths. Life to me, Andreos had said, life to both of us.

Where is the answer?

Chapter 14

The next morning the captains met to decide about a third run. Athena's skyriders blithely assumed the vote would turn out the way they wanted, and so busied themselves adding even more shielding to Athena's pilot ship, a protectiveness that irked Athena—and did not mollify Captain Andreos. The shipmaster's face mirrored the doubts now spreading through the ship, doubts that grew more vocal as the hours passed.

"I am *not*," Andreos said, "putting *Net* on a sine wave, up and down, up and down. Two of our holds vented to space from the metal strain of that flux."

"Not much," Janina said. "I can fix."

"*And*, shielding or not," Andreos said, ignoring her interruption, "I won't expose my people to that kind of radiation damage." He looked at Athena almost resentfully.

Athena tossed her head. "A closed fist never gets much, sir. Pov had the right of that. I'm okay."

"So you say."

"Our holds are half full with good product," Milo said smoothly, twiddling his pen. "We have enough for a decent profit, even with the extra transit cost. I suggest we've risked enough."

Athena scowled at him. "Our purpose is more than a 'decent profit,' Milo. Do we have enough to pay for *Dance*'s repairs?"

"A significant down payment," the chaffer hedged, not meeting her eyes.

"The hell with that. I vote for a third run."

"Pov?" Andreos asked.

"You know how I vote, sir."

"All we need," Athena said, "is a better way to get enough advance warning. Right?"

"How many drones do we have left?" Pov asked.

"We've used most of them. Twenty, I think. I'd have to check. Why?"

"Is there some way we can boost a drone's transmission to send it farther ahead? Say put it on a single frequency and tell it to scream at us?"

Athena thought about it. "An x-ray laser might punch through—if you really want x-rays pointed at us."

"So point it at a remote sensor—another drone, say, that can relay to us. Then when the forward drone blips out, we know there's a flux coming." He looked at Andreos.

"Humph."

"Even if we *did* have better warning," Milo asserted forcefully, "we've still got the conditions inside the eddy. We could get torn apart. I say it's too much of a risk, and a lot of the ship agrees with me."

"Thanks to your talk-talk ever since we left Omsk," Athena said angrily, "along with rougher conditions than we expected. What's the matter, Milo? Didn't have enough to do?"

"I have a right to an opinion—"

"At the right time and place," she interrupted. "You had your chance before we undocked at Omsk. You could have called a vote about T Tauri, cut all this short before we even left. Why didn't you?" She jabbed a finger at him. "Because *you* knew it wouldn't work. *Net* wanted to come to T Tauri. They came because Captain Andreos thought it was a good idea, because it was a challenge, an adventure, a way to win free. But you didn't want that. You like your chaffer's life with another ship to joust words with and show off how clever you are. You like the security of letting *Dance* make the tough decisions, right?"

"I don't have to listen to this."

"We're supposed to listen to you. Why shouldn't you listen to us?"

"If we made a third run," Milo said, "we could get destroyed."

"So?"

Milo threw up his hands. "Pilots! All you do is barge around, taking risks and dying heroically. Go ahead, do it, but don't drag the ship with you."

"Ship? When do *you* talk about the ship? All you're thinking about is Milo Cieslak and his pet dreams about succeeding Molnar on *Dance*. Get to be lead chaffer, get to pal around with Bukharin. Why don't you say what it *really* is?"

Milo stood up, his face red with anger, nearly sputtering in his outrage.

"Who do you think you *are*?" he shouted.

"Sit down, Milo," Andreos said quietly.

"I don't have to listen to this!"

"Yes, you do," Andreos repeated. "Sit down." Milo reseated himself slowly, trembling. Andreos steepled his fingers on the table before him and studied them carefully.

"The decision," he said, "is whether *Net* attempts a third run. Pov and Athena suggest an improvement on procedure, one that seems promising. Milo objects. I have my doubts. Janina? What is your opinion?"

Janina opened her mouth and closed it, then shot a glance at Milo. "What do I think?" she asked blankly.

"Yes. What do you think?"

Janina looked around wildly at the other captains. "What do I think?" she repeated stupidly, then flushed and as quickly turned pale. "Why, nothing at all," she said, then laughed suddenly. Then she met Andreos' eyes and smiled at him sadly. "We all have to choose eventually, don't we, captain? No fence-sitting, no easy rank because you're a Slav, no protections because you think it's easy and it's owed to you."

She took a deep breath and folded her hands. "I

have doubts, too, but I think Athena was right when
she defended Pov for the sake of the ship. I think that
if we turn back, with these divisions among us, we will
always be divided, always think ourselves cowards. I
think you can't live with a closed fist."

"The risks," Milo hissed, his face showing his des-
peration. "You can't."

"Why not? Because I'm a Slav? Because I'm supposed to vote on your side, every time? Don't you get
the point, Milo? Now is the time when everything
counts. Perhaps it's foolish, but I vote for *Net*."

She shuddered and covered her eyes with her hands.
Milo gaped at her, then lunged to his feet and stalked
out. When he had left, Janina dropped her hands.

"You'll have to off-ship him when we get back to
Omsk, captain," Janina said quietly, her plain face
showing its distress. "He'll never accept this."

"But if we succeed . . ." Pov said, surprised.

"Then he'll have been wrong, Pov." She shook her
head. "*That*'s what he won't accept. Take it from a
Slav. I'm an expert." She smiled crookedly, then gave
Andreos a genial glare. "You set me up," she accused.

"No, I didn't."

"Yes, you did. I know you, Leonidas Andreos. I
know you very well. Now, if you captains will excuse
me, I'm going to stalk out, too. I have holds to prepare." She got to her feet and walked out with dignity.

"Did you?" Athena asked Andreos, frowning. "Set
her up?"

"So?" he said pointedly, mimicking her earlier comment at Milo. "I warned you about pushing Milo."

"Yeah, you did. But if you have doubts, why did—"

"I *always* have doubts, Athena. It's part of being
shipmaster. Think about that the next time you spout
off." Andreos got up himself and straightened his
shoulders. "Now I think I will stalk out. Try to have
your drone ready by alpha watch tomorrow. We'll set
the third run for then."

"I'm sorry, Leo," Athena said contritely.

"It's all right." He walked out, leaving Athena and Pov to look at each other.

"But we won the vote," Athena complained. They looked at each other wryly for a long moment.

"Poor Milo," Athena said. "Poor Janina. Ah, it's nice to be a pawn on the board." Athena sighed and leaned her head on her hand.

"You look pale," he said.

"I always look pale, it comes with being Greek, and don't you shift sides on me, Sail."

"And how many rads did you get out there yesterday, double sail or not?"

Athena shrugged and stood up to stretch. "If you close the fist, life passes you by. I heard that somewhere."

"Yeah, so did I."

Athena walked around the table and pressed his shoulder, then bent and brushed his lips with hers. "Here's to ambiguity," she said drolly.

"Games from you, too?" he asked, disappointed in her—and perhaps misunderstanding. He looked down at his hands and rearranged his fingers into a lattice, then rearranged them again. Athena sat down beside him and laid her hand over his.

"We have the same spirit, Pov. You get yours from the Rom; maybe mine comes from those old Greeks who ranged up and down the Aegean, clanging their swords and chasing off after legends. I'm sorry. I wanted to comfort you."

"I'm mixed up, and you aren't helping." She raised an eyebrow, inquiring. "Avi's having trouble adjusting to the whole Rom idea."

"Avi's a good woman."

"Yes, she is, but I've had my fingers burned. I keep believing, just go on believing, and wonder if I'll end up a fool." He looked up into her gray eyes. "Women are a plague in my life right now," he said, reproving her.

She chuckled and flushed slightly. "I agree I'm not helping."

"Athena . . ." he said uncomfortably.

"I'm sorry to stress you. I don't know either." She smoothed back his hair in a caress, then laid her palm briefly on his cheek. "Nobody knows much of anything. But maybe it's only family, Pov, all of us a family. And I can be as fierce as Kate in supporting you." She smiled. "I felt very alone out in that skyrider, but you were there, protecting me. Isn't that what binds people together?"

"Toward what?" he asked cautiously.

"Does it have to lead to sex? Being in love? Aren't you in love with Avi?"

"Probably. I think so—but it takes two to really find out, I think."

"Well, I love Gregori. I love my daughters and this ship. I love skyriding and Helm and a certain Rom sailmaster who has been acting shell-shocked lately, with cause." She laced their fingers together fiercely. "And the binding gives me life. Milo forgets that—he looks for other things, if he even knows what he wants. Janina hasn't found out yet, but maybe she will. But you and I are alike in that, loving this ship and the family she brings us. Greek and Slav and gypsy, a new people, a cloudship's people beholden to no one but bound together."

"Avi thinks I was a fool to defend Benek."

"As I defend Stefania? Did you see how well she adapted to the interlink, even with the curves you threw at her?"

"But Andreos booted Benek off *Net*, like so much excess cargo. He didn't even ask me."

"So get him back when we're back at Omsk. Learn the games, Pov. We'll both have to, it seems, if we're to take *Net* to the Pleiades. Which we must." Her eyes looked levelly into his, fierce and determined. He pressed her fingers and smiled.

"So stop at the kisses, Athena. They confuse some basic synapses I've got, being male."

"That's on, Pov." Athena chuckled. "Sorry." They both hesitated, very conscious of the other's closeness, then both stood up convulsively to move away from each other. Athena laughed and Pov joined her in the laughter a second later as they circled the table, keeping away from each other.

"Life is hard," Athena said, tsking.

"Toughens the spirit, Helm."

"Oh, *sure* it does. Let's go review the last run so I know how to duck those particles a little better."

"You still look pale."

"I'll get more so before this is over." Athena set her jaw and dared him to comment further. He good-humoredly gestured her out the door.

"After you."

Siduri's Net again cruised slowly a thousand kilometers from the glowing star jet that linked T Tauri with its small companion, hunting for another downward gap in the radiation levels. The plasma roiled and shimmered, shedding its coiled energy in a wide spectrum of energetic wavelengths. At Andreos' suggestion, Tully extended the spinnaker sail to a wider extension and kept it prudently between the ship and the jet, wary of the x-ray and UV radiation that peaked too easily to dangerous levels.

Despite its partial success, Pov's sail-flip maneuver on the last run had put several people into the hospital for observation. Pov scowled, watching his interlink screens, and tried to think of better ways to protect *Net*'s people—not that he expected T Tauri to cooperate. This time they would try the suicide drones and a series of dip-and-run courses, testing the ship against the elements. Earlier sailors had the same challenge, he remembered, with the risks just as final if they guessed wrong.

On a telescopic display in a top screen, the dust

core far below them flashed ruddily as the infant star flared. An instant later, an answering flash leaped through the planetary disk like lightning sparking through the clouds, shocking through the disk of dust and gas. Well, it could be worse, he told himself. We could be over there.

As he watched, he saw the flare effect begin climbing the jet toward them, emitting high into the x-ray spectrum. Were x-rays the key? he wondered. The flares were definitely fueling part of the activity in the jet.

"Suggest we start the run now, Helm," he said to Stefania.

"Based on what data?" Stefania's voice was tight with strain.

"That flare is climbing the jet, though I admit it isn't climbing fast. I love the way T Tauri keeps adding new variables, don't you?" Stefania did not respond to the cajoling. "I just don't think it's going to get better, so we should try it while we can. Do you agree?"

"You ask *me*?" Stefania gave a short bark of laughter.

"You're Helm, and you rode us through the last one. Yes, I'm asking."

Stefania hesitated. Athena flashed Pov a smile over their direct video link but said nothing, giving Stefania the lead.

"That's on, Sail," Stefania said, her voice steady. "Beginning course."

Pov watched the data stream across his interlink screens as *Net* turned again towards the star jet and plunged into its outer gases. Athena sent her drones plunging out ahead of them, like a scattering of arrows. *Net* spread her sails wide, snatching at the gases, then steadied on course as a smooth bow wave formed over the ship, the gases spiraling tightly into the forward sails. No one spoke as *Net*'s course stretched out minute after minute, her readings steady, a smooth flow streaming into her holds.

"Flux approaching," Athena said at last. "Number-one drone just winked out."

"Suggest we dodge, Stefania," Pov said.

"That's on, Sail. Turning down and starboard."

Stefania turned the ship neatly and accelerated out of the jet, then made a long looping trajectory as the flux pulsed past them. When the cycle had passed, Athena launched a new array of drones and *Net* plunged again into the star jet, an unlikely dolphin sporting in a cosmic fountain. Another flux brought *Net* roundabout again, dodging back to the safety of open space. Stubbornly, *Net* turned again and plunged back into the jet, sails spread to catch her rich harvest.

"Dip-and-run is right," Andreos said, deciding to grump.

"Holds at ninety percent," Janina said firmly.

"Flux," Athena warned. "Take us out, Stefania."

"That's on, pilot," Stefania said smoothly, her voice only slightly nervous now. "Exiting the jet. Hold, advise when you're at max."

"It's coming in fast," Janina answered. "Counting six to ten minutes at most, Helm."

"One more dodge-and-weave, Stef," Athena crowed from the skyrider. "One more pass and you're the first to finish it, ever. Do it now."

"I can't believe this," Stefania muttered. "Beginning a new pass." *Net* sailed gracefully through a long looping curve, dipping shallowly through the outer edges of the jet, then plunging inward for a short hard turn and racing outward again as another drone disappeared ahead. "Oops. We'll catch the edge of this one. Hold on, everybody."

"Watch it, Tully!" Pov called out to Sail Deck.

"I see it. Bracing sails."

Net shuddered as the flux yanked hard. Tully hastily threw more power into the sails, trying to maintain their integrity. The port spinnaker tore free, then wavered as it reformed, then spun holes again. Pov cursed as Tully struggled with the waveforms of the tattered sail, then they both swore as the flux yanked at the edge of the topsail, threatening to rip it, too. Then the ship's momentum had pulled them free and *Net* accelerated back into open space.

"Athena?" Stefania asked anxiously. "Are you with us?"

"I'm here, you marvel. First-rate!" Pov heard Athena's fist pound her console.

Pov was on the main Sail Deck a moment later. "Close," he said to Tully, bending over him to look at the diagnostic screens on the command console. The sails steadied, then ruffled from portside. Pov sighed feelingly. "Goddammit, it's the *same* generator."

"A sail fault we can handle," Tully said tensely, "though I can't believe I'd ever be happy about a 'mere' sail fault. We nearly lost the whole spinnaker." He blew out a breath and signed to Roja to call up the repair crew.

"New idea for future modeling. Catching the edge isn't smart. I think we're learning a whole new set of rules."

"It took you *this* long to figure that out?" Tully asked ironically.

"Soar off. Let's go down and see what Janina's caught."

"What about duty?" Tully looked around at the staff of beta watch, then raised an eyebrow as Pov tugged at his arm. "Remember duty, Pov? I'm surprised."

"Come on," he said as he bodily dragged Tully to his feet. "Roja can watch." He collected Avi from her apartment on the way, and hauled both of them down to Hold Deck. Halfway there, they passed a lounge as Janina began broadcasting her hold report to the entire ship. Janina's voice sounded awed by the wealth now filling *Net*'s holds, and she had already set her staff to sorting the product, using as many tethered storage units as she could scatter into space, like a mother duck ordering her nestlings into shelter.

"God, what I'm not using!" Janina declared as the three sail officers invaded her Hold Deck. Janina stood in midroom at the main hold console, exulting over her screens. She waved her small hands expressively, her broad face aglow. "Lab has found *twenty* new carbon and oxygen radicals at quantum levels we've never seen in open space. Now if only we could keep those beasties at that kind of energy—it could revolutionize our power systems and materials engineering. Look at this!" She called up display after display on her screens, clucking with amazement.

Avi grinned at Pov and dutifully looked, then moved aside for Pov and Tully to look over Janina's shoulder at the screen displays. "Is that deuterium reading accurate?" Pov asked, abruptly as awed as Janina.

"Deuterium, tritium, helium-3: you name it and we've got it. I never knew it could be this rich! Hot damn!" Janina pounded her hand on the top of the console in jubilation. "Oh, God, aren't we rich! And all of it high-energy. I'll take the storage problems for those blessed little active electrons." She grinned at Pov. "Dip-and-run was the ticket, you called it, Pov. We filled the holds in just one tiny course, less then an hour's time. I can't believe it."

"You'll have to trail cartons behind us all the way back to Tania," Tully warned. "All those little electrons are emitting particles like a New Year's Day."

"Suits. What the hell?" Janina waved her hands again, and Tully had to dodge as her enthusiasm nearly clouted his ear. Then Janina did a little shuffling dance, before she remembered her dignity and stopped short, though the grin stayed. "We are truly and utterly rich, sirs."

"Any need for another run?" Pov asked.

"Why? And where would we put it? I'm venting

only ten percent of this stuff instead of half. I say let's keep in one piece, now that we've got the loot. Let's go home and tell Rybak where to stuff his clauses."

Janina did another little dance, making everyone on her staff look around in wonder—well, nearly all. His mother stood at her side station across the room, carefully ignoring Pov as much as he ignored her—though they were exquisitely aware of each other. Out of the corner of his eye, he saw his mother give Avi a raking glance from head to toe, to which Avi was thankfully oblivious. Pov took Avi's elbow possessively, reacting automatically to his mother's threat, then made a smart and graceful retreat.

Not so hard, he had told Avi, counting on his mother to tolerate Avi as much as she had tolerated Dina. But Dina had never really threatened as wife, whatever Pov thought at the time, and the blood wars between mother-in-law and wife were a Rom tradition that still persisted. He felt glum as he and Avi walked back to the main companionway, and she picked up his mood deftly. "What's the matter?"

"Well, uh ... I ought to get back to watch."

"Quit dodging. What's the matter? You ought to be dancing like Janina—it worked. Your sail plans worked, and everything worked." Avi spread her hands and copied Janina's shuffling dance, then grinned and slipped her arm comfortably inside his elbow.

"Well, uh ..."

"Pov."

"It can wait—let me do my own sorting first."

He smiled, got a wide grin back. Avi spread her hands and did Janina's dance again, then laughed as two people walking past on the bridge promptly mimicked her, thumping their feet and clapping their hands enthusiastically, rotating in place with as much jubilation as Janina had. Janina's little dance on Hold Deck must have gone over the all-ship interlink channel, a fact that would chagrin *Net*'s holdmaster.

He saw Janina appear in the far doorway and stop short, her face horrified as she saw what was happening on the companionway. He laughed and waved her over, then danced her around in a little circle. It was not an idea Janina approved of; her face was bright pink with embarrassment.

"Come on, Janina! Dance!" the crowd called out to her, laughing as she sputtered in Pov's grasp.

"Stop that!" she said finally, pushing him away. Tully came over and pounced on her, then danced her away helplessly into the crowd, passing her from one group to the next, each dancing with her and laughing as she protested.

As more people poured onto the central bridge, Janina's dance elaborated into a dozen folk dances, each a noisy vigorous pounding of the feet and a wild waving of arms, as the Poles, the Greeks, the Hungarians, and the Czechs tried to outshine one another, with the skyriders egging it on as they war-danced up and down the companionway. Pov prudently retreated to the nearby windows as Kate swerved suddenly toward him, sheering her off with a quick gypsy spell, then stood with his arm around Avi, watching happily as *Net*'s celebrations went a little crazy.

Then a man standing by the opposite window began singing aloud, his voice lifting above the noise of the crowd.

"After summer's heat through the day.
As the sun falls to the west:
Comes the evening ..."

It was an old Czech harvest song, a song sung often on *Ishtar's Fan* in the early years, one people's memory of a beloved homeland that had been passed down to *Fan*'s new generations, to *Dance* and to *Net*. The sound of the man's voice lofted over the noise of the dancing, clear and piercing, and suddenly he was drowned out by a hundred voices chanting the old song together.

"*. . . Cool and welcome,*"

the crowd sang, their voices rising strongly as they picked up the refrain, linking their arms together and turning to face the windows, their many faces suffused by the glow of T Tauri's brilliant jet.

"*To heal the fevered day:*
Pray God give us peace in the night."

Avi and Pov joined in, linking their arms with others nearby, then made room for Tully and Janina between them. There on the companionway, the people of *Siduri's Net* sang the Czechs' old song of the fields, of tilling the soil, of harvesting the peasant's wealth of cascades of golden grain, remembering the old, celebrating the new.

"*As we make our way home from the fields*
To our lighted homes, family within,
Comes the evening, sky with diamonds,
to light our weary way:
Pray God give us peace in the night.

For all good things come from the Lord,
Even summer's heat to ripen our grain
And comes the evening, God's blessing
To all his harvestmen.
Pray God give us peace throughout the good night."

The song faded out, and a hush swept down the companionway as everyone stood together for a long moment, arms linked, one people united in the golden light of T Tauri, one people at last. Pov looked at Avi.

"Family," he said softly.

"So I see," she said, then laughed happily.

Net had triumphed today. With the wealth in her holds, *Net* might choose any destiny, any star course to wherever she chose, even to the Pleiades. *Net* could join *Arrow* and Gray's choice of a destiny, could wander even farther, even to the nearly unending seas of the Orion Nebula, where a people might forge even greater dreams.

Could a Rom, a true Rom, refuse that kind of journey? In his heart, he knew he could not.

And with *Net* would go all her people, Slavs and Greeks and at least two Rom, taking with them music and the dance, the family, the wife: all a man needed to be happy. He might not keep the whole of both his worlds, *Net* and Rom, but he would travel with *Net* wherever her goddess took her.

You had the right of it, Siduri, he thought. Gilgamesh never listened to you, foolish in his dreams. But you knew. You always knew, as women sometimes know the essentials when men do not. But sometimes a man can listen, can see what you see.

He smiled at the people crowding the central bridge as the celebrations broke out all over again, egged on by the skyriders and their war-dancing, then looked down into Avi's dark eyes.

Life to me.

The perils of the
Cloudship of Orion
continue in this
suspense-filled
teaser chapter from
<u>Maia's Veil,</u>
coming from ROC
in May 1995.

The ship cleared the walls of the bay and fell slowly away from the station, descending toward the planetary atmosphere far below them. As the sails caught the upper wisps of stratospheric ozone, *Net* slowed still more and descended faster, falling around the curve of the planet toward nightside. Pov tracked *Net*'s sail pressure on a subsidiary interlink screen, watching the data steadily fed to him by Tully from Sail Deck's main computer. On the green, he thought.

Sneaking a cloudship away from Omsk Station wouldn't be easy, but *Net* had timed her departure carefully. By leaving far into Omsk's night shift, *Net* might gain useful time while tentative subordinates awakened grouchy chiefs. Captain Andreos hoped to put some useful distance between *Net* and Omsk's laser defenses, then slip around Tania's Ring before either Omsk or *Dance* thought to ask *Net* for reasons.

"Tracking into planetary shadow," Athena said on screen from her own interlink room on Helm Deck. Behind her through an open door, Pov could see Helm Deck's huge screen track *Net*'s trajectory, slowly shifting its course line as *Net* plunged into the planet's thin upper atmosphere, molecules screaming into her sails. "Beginning ascent out of orbit."

"Sit tight, people," Andreos said over the interlink, his long face tense. "They'll be asking why in a minute or so. Sailmaster?"

"We have the touring sails rigged, sir," Pov said, adding a sail display to the bank of monitor screens on his panel for the others to see. "You can have full acceleration whenever you want it. *Dance* will notice our sails, if they look fast enough, but Bukharin doesn't know enough about our configurations to recognize the out-system set."

"Good," Andreos grunted. "Bukharin's the one with

lasers and guard ships. Maybe he'll argue with *Dance* about our sail set instead of where we're going."

Net fell more rapidly through the planet's shadow, accelerating into a hyperbolic curve that would carry her away from the planet's gravity pull. Behind them Omsk dwindled to a distant speck, then slipped out of view behind the darkening curve of Tania's Ring. They all relaxed slightly as *Net* put more of the planet between them and Omsk's lasers. Though intended for meteoroid defense, a laser capable of pulverizing a significant rock had enough power to cripple *Net* if Omsk shot them in the right places. Andreos blew out a breath, then raised an eyebrow at them all, getting weak grins back. *Net* increased speed still more, lifting away from atmosphere into open space, counting off the minutes to safety.

"Contact signal, Captain," a voice said over the audio channel. "*Dance* to *Net*."

"*Dance*?" Andreos asked, sounding a little surprised. "Not from Omsk?"

"No, sir. It's Captain Rybak, via a circumpolar satellite."

Andreos drummed his fingers on his desk, thinking about it a moment, then scowled worriedly. "Put him on the interlink," he said, "but feed him the return signal only from my screen."

"Yes, sir." One of the upper interlink screens promptly lighted with the sour patrician face of Captain Rybak.

Half the time I've seen him the last year, Pov thought, *he looks like that, furious and unreasonable.* He sat back and tried to get more comfortable in his chair, half his attention on *Net*'s steady course away from Omsk Station, putting precious distance between his ship and a Russki colony that coveted the tritium fortune *Net* now carried away in her holds. Andreos had hoped for Omsk to call first, and worried that it hadn't.

"Captain Rybak," Andreos said courteously, then waited the few seconds for the radio beam to bounce around the circumpolar comsat back to Omsk. Already *Net* had moved far enough to create a slight delay in unassisted radio. The signal wavered as *Net* slipped through the solar wind eddies that trailed behind Tania's Ring, then steadied as the comm chief compensated for the particle interference.

"Why aren't you at Omsk Station?" Rybak demanded angrily. "I didn't get any request for *Net* to undock."

"We're leaving," Andreos said. "And you know why, Sandor. Take your 'non-value production clause' and 'uncertain market glut' and stuff it."

Rybak blinked in shock, then looked genuinely surprised, for once jarred out of his usual display of contemptuous pride. "Ceverny told you?" he asked incredulously. "Is that where he is? On *Net*?" He sputtered a moment, then glared at Andreos as he realized exactly what Ceverny might have told *Net*, that *Net* knew everything now. "You told me that he wasn't on ... Bukharin's been combing half the planet trying to find him!"

"Helpful Nikolay," Andreos said unsympathetically.

Ceverny had appeared in the doorway of Pov's interlink room, leaning on the doorjamb to listen. He and Pov exchanged an ironic look.

"He's surprised," Pov commented.

"I can't imagine why," Ceverny said tartly. "I told him I was taking my vacation, the hell with him."

"You sort of left out *where,* sir," Pov reminded him. "The Pleiades *is* a bit far away from Omsk."

Ceverny shrugged elaborately, an unconcern that he didn't quite carry off. Whatever the good reasons for his decision, Sailmaster Ceverny still saw himself as a traitor to *Dance*. Many on *Dance* would agree with him, and that grief showed in the old sailmaster's shadowed eyes. Pov looked back uncomfortably at the interlink screen.

"I'll deal with Ceverny in due time," Rybak said ominously. "As shipmaster of *Dance,* I am ordering *Net* to return to Omsk Station."

"Sorry, *Dance,* I can't do that," Andreos said cheerfully. "*Net*'s crew has voted, and as shipmaster of *Net* I am obeying that vote. I think you can guess what the vote was." Then he grinned deliberately, provoking Rybak.

Rybak flushed darkly red, then visibly tried to control himself, not too successfully. "We have a legal duty to Tania's Ring," he began lecturing at Andreos, his tone as harsh and proud as ever, as if *Net*'s senior captain were a halfwit.

Pov curled his fingers in his palms and looked down,

his stomach churning with an all too familiar response to that particular voice. How many times had he heard Rybak speak like this, whatever the other's rank, whatever the need, the stern parent to a disobedient child? He had never changed, never would—and now his inflexibility was costing him *Net* and risking *Dance* to Bukharin's greed, yet still he could not change, could not moderate that hectoring tone. Did *Fan* lose *Ishtar's Jewel* this way? Pov wondered. By a mere tone of voice, by a prideful unreasonableness?

"*Your* duty, Captain Andreos," Rybak continued, his voice heavy with his displeasure, "is to negotiate any dispute you might have with us or with Tania's Ring. This precipitate action is . . ."

"He's stalling," Ceverny said and closed his eyes in pain, knowing what it meant that *Dance* would stall for Omsk's advantage. Pov looked up at him, not knowing what to say to *Dance*'s sailmaster, who still loved *Dance* more than life itself. "How's our distance?"

Pov glanced at the small screen showing Tania's Ring and a schematic of Athena's helm map. "Out of range of the weapon sats now. Haven't seen a guard ship yet."

"Wait a bit," Ceverny said. "You didn't see the green in Bukharin's eyes at the meeting with *Dance* when Rybak agreed to sell *Net*." He shrugged tiredly. "I'm going elsewhere. I don't want to watch this."

"Of course, sir," Pov said. Ceverny straightened his lanky frame, shot a quick, bitter look at Rybak's face in the monitor, and left.

"We're *not* going to sell you to Bukharin," Rybak was saying to Andreos, his hold on his temper growing ragged again. "That is not reasonable!"

"Bullshit," Andreos said, not smiling now.

The two shipmasters glared at each other for a long moment, and Rybak abruptly changed to open menace. "*Net,* you're risking breach of contract," he said coldly. "I could demand penalties for this." Stalling, Pov agreed. He quickly scanned the telescopic shots of Tania's Ring, looking for the first flicker of ship metal as Bukharin sent his ships after *Net.*

"Assess away, Captain," Andreos said, waving his hand. "We'll pay them. For your information, *Net* plans to offload half our tritium cargo as we leave—if Bukharin allows us to. Tell him he'd better allow it, or you're dusted for sure, *Dance*. That tritium is intended to buy out our contract and pay for *Dance*'s repairs, *plus* your penalties if you want. I suggest you detach a skyrider to get the tritium before Bukharin steals it."

"You can't do this, Leonidas!" Rybak shouted, his fist hammering on his console. "I will not accept—"

"Oh, no? Watch me."

"Two guard ships just came out of planet shadow," Athena reported over the interlink. "They're accelerating toward us."

"Good-bye, Sandor," Andreos said, his face saddened. "We wish *Dance* good fortune, whether you believe it or not." He gestured to his off-screen aide and Rybak's screen abruptly blanked in mid-word. "Increase speed, Helm," he ordered.

Janina blinked, startled. "But, sir," she protested, "we have to offship *Dance*'s—"

"Look again, Janina," Andreos said heavily. "Those aren't just guard ships with a few hot lasers to shear off our antennae. They're Bukharin's orbital *warcraft*, the ships Tania's Ring used to put down that grain revolt a few years ago. You may remember what they used on one of the villages."

"Fusion bombs?" Janina said, her eyes widening. "On us?"

"As long as they aim for the prow, the hold canisters should survive just fine for pickup. I accordingly suggest we continue accelerating and put them well behind us." Andreos looked at Janina with quiet sympathy, knowing how this decision would impact *Net*'s Slavs. First Ship families had crewed the Slav cloudships for two generations, and such ties would linger even through a quarrel as bad as theirs with *Dance*. "Janina," Andreos said softly, "if we drop *Dance*'s tritium here, one of those ships will break off and confiscate it as 'abandoned salvage.' You can guess what luck *Dance* would have in Bukharin's court trying to get it back."

Janina's plain face showed her obvious distress. "Maybe we could orbit the tritium around an outer gas giant as we leave," she said. "Then tell *Dance* to hire a retrieval ship to go—" She stopped, thinking about it, then slowly shook her head as she found her own answer. "And what if *Dance* does pick it up and decides to lie, saying we still owe them the buyout? You've thought this out, haven't you?"

"I considered the possibilities," Andreos acknowledged, "especially the chance Bukharin might use his warships. We need an impartial witness to the transfer, Janina, someone to document that we did pay—not Bukharin and not *Dance*. Not if we want to be free without question, without entanglements in courts up and down the chain for years. So we'll sell the tritium in the Pleiades and send back the credits to *Dance*." He spread his hands. "It's the only way."

"And what if Bukharin declares *Dance* bankrupt," Janina said, "and nationalizes her as Omsk property? Before we can send our credits back?" They looked at each other bleakly.

"I didn't ask for this, Janina," Andreos said softly. "You know *Net* did not ask for this—all we wanted was our freedom."

"I know, sir," she said heavily. "I know."

"Sir, the warships are gaining on us," Athena said, her voice high with surprise, then leaned back in her chair to look out onto Helm Deck, rechecking her screen data against the visual track on the Helm map. "They're angling to intercept, too," she added, sounding even more startled, "trying to cut us off. They must think they have speed to spare."

"*What*?" Andreos said. "*Net* should be able to outrun any planet-bound craft."

Athena shook her head and straightened her chair with a thump of her feet. "I think our friend Nikolay is a lot smarter than we thought—and we weren't fools in guessing about him." She quickly tapped her computer bank to display a screen of data on one of the interlink screens. "See? My monitors say their engine emissions are star-drive frequency: Bukharin must have cannibalized one of the Tania's Ring freighters, then put the jump engines on the warships. They can indeed outrun us, sirs. We have more tonnage than they do, and they aren't using sails for shielding, just slag armor on their prows." She glanced at Pov. "Our sails are slowing us down, Pov."

"We can't drop them, Athena," Pov said, alarmed. "Not running through in-system dust."

"I know, I know. I was trying to be amusing." She winced. "Sorry. Even if Janina dumps tritium at full steam into the engines, I'm not sure we can outrun them. *Net* has too much mass to compete with the kind of stripped-down speed they're getting."

"So let's use some different atoms," Janina suggested. "I've got lots of superheavy pets from T Tauri to play with."

"We haven't run spec analyses on that material," Andreos warned. "Most of it's already degraded into lighter isotopes."

"Not all, sir," Pov said, jumping on Janina's suggestion. "I'd rather risk *Net* than let Bukharin enslave a cloudship, however much he thinks we deserve it." He waved at the monitor screen, where two lean, fast ships hurtled after them. "Omsk hasn't tried to contact us: they obviously intend force, sending ships like that after us. We aren't going to turn back meekly with a shot across our bow—you know that and I know that. Even if they aren't planning the worst, it'll escalate to hull shots the moment we won't slow down."

"And once they close on us, sir," Athena said, "we won't get away again."

Andreos scowled, his eyes flicking from face to face. "Does anyone have a better idea?" he asked. "Please take time to consider, for *Net*'s sake."

They all thought furiously, watching the warships steadily advance on *Net*, visibly faster and on course intercept. One had already shifted slightly to strike across *Net*'s bow ahead of its companion, a pincer movement that would box *Net* neatly between them. Athena was right: *Net* was not a warship, and hadn't the weaponry or maneuverability to fight those twin combat craft at close range.

"What if we call Omsk?" Janina suggested. "Try to reason with Bukharin."

"And say *what*?" Athena asked, waving her hand. "Leave us alone? We already did that. *Dance* talked to us through Bukharin's comsat relays, and I can't see Nikolay not tapping in to listen." She shook her head ruefully. "We didn't think about that engine overhaul, sirs, and now we're stuck. I say it's T Tauri all over again. Ride the wild wave or get fried. God, what a choice."

"I can't think of anything, either," Andreos said, then closed his eyes a long moment, took a deep breath. "We'll dump your atomic pets into the engines, Janina," he said then. "How long until they're in effective laser range, Helm?"

On her screen, Athena leaned back and conferred with Stefania through the door for a brief wait, then straightened back up and raised her hand, still looking over her shoulder into Helm Deck. "Helm Map is computing it now, sir. Six minutes, forty seconds ... mark." Her hand dropped sharply.

"We dump at two-minute that tick," Andreos said. "Put the interlink on all-ship. Let *Net* see this."

"Yes, sir." Athena complied briskly. "Sir, we just had a ranging laser splash on our starboard wing. No damage, not at this distance." Athena set her jaw. "And I confirm launch of two torpedoes, aimed to intercept our forward track. Sir, they have *fired* on us."

"Burn out the torpedo sensors, Pov," Andreos said. "Use your skysail laser."

"Yes, sir." Pov took the function from Tully's main console and slowly rotated the skysail laser toward the pursuing ships while Tully laid Athena's course data into the sail computers, overriding the automatic programs that watched ahead for dust, not behind for pursuing torpedoes. The two torpedoes crawled steadily toward them, their own engines adding more speed to the momentum of the ships that had launched them.

"How long to impact?" he asked Athena.

"Our engines are now at full exhaust, and we're overhauling some of the torpedo speed. It'll moderate their climb. Say eight minutes, maybe nine. Time enough, Pov."

Pov watched the sail-laser data change on his interlink screen, shifting its columns of numbers into new patterns as the skysail laser began to track on its different target. Tully boosted the laser's power and let it cycle upward.

"Tracking now," Tully called from the outer room. "Power climbing ... Ready!"

"Fire!"

A ruby red beam lanced backward from *Net*, hitting

squarely on the nose of the forward torpedo, blinding its sensors into a melted slag.

"Recycling . . . Ready!" Tully called out again.

"Fire!"

A second bolt lanced out, splashing hard on the other fusion torpedo. An instant later, the torpedo exploded, shattering itself into a cloud of scintillating gas and sending a lethal rain of invisible particles in all directions. One of the pursuing ships hastily changed course, dodging before it plowed straight through the deadly remains of its torpedo. Pov heard a cheer go up on Sail Deck outside his interlink room, echoed on the audio channel from other decks.

"Radiation count!" Andreos shouted.

"Not much hard stuff, sir," Janina answered. "Within safety limits." She smiled tightly. "The Russkis got it worse than we did, I'd say. I hope Bukharin has good hospitals for those crews." She shot a meaningful glance at Athena, who smiled wanly.

"I glow less in the dark now, thank you so much. And not enough to care that they're going to." She gestured contemptuously at the Russki warships.

"Veer course ten degrees," Andreos said. "Get the other torpedo out of our wake. I don't want it following us to jump point, blind or not."

"Yes, sir," Athena said.

One of the warships returned *Net*'s laser bolt, badly aimed and out of range. The attenuated bolt splashed through *Net*'s engine emissions, creating a cascade of sparkling ions in its wake, a ripple quickly gone. A second bolt, better aimed as *Net* finished shifting her course, hit *Net* amidships, damaging a minor sensor. *Net* had sensors to spare, but it was not damage they needed, not when the Russkis promised heavier shots as they closed the range. Andreos scowled, his fingers drumming a slow beat on his console.

"Prepare for dump, Janina," Andreos said.

"Now?" Janina looked at him wide-eyed.

"Now."

Janina turned her hand and gave quick orders to her Hold crew. Then she turned back to the interlink and smiled almost gaily. "Hold onto your seats, *Net*. We're about to ride the wave."

"Or maybe get fried," Athena said, shaking her curls, then glanced at one of her lower interlink screens. "No, I take that back. Sirs, they have just launched two more goddamn torpedoes. Dump it fast, Janina."

"Dumping now."

Janina spilled a canister of the superheavy atoms from T Tauri into the roar of tritium falling into *Net*'s fusion engines. As the heavy fuel exploded in the plasma stream, *Net* surged forward suddenly, overriding *Net*'s internal gravity field and swatting hard at Pov's chair, tipping it over and backward. He fell in a crash on his back, and heard the squawks on the deck outside as Janina's "pets" upended others on Sail Deck. Cursing, Pov tried to untangle himself and get up, then lost his balance as *Net* surged again, then fell a third time as the last of the heavy atoms exploded in the engine exhaust. By the time he dragged himself up on the console and looked at the interlink, Bukharin's warships had vanished from his screen and Tania's Ring was only a tiny white speck far behind them.

He whistled, awed. "And that was *one* canister? Pretty hot stuff."

Then he looked at *Net*'s acceleration curve and whistled again. In only minutes, the heavy fuel had boosted *Net* up to one-quarter of lightspeed, acceleration that usually took a whole day at full power. Hot stuff, indeed, he thought elatedly, realizing that *Net* had done it. *Net* was free.